THE UNCOMMON LIFE OF ALFRED WARNER IN SIX DAYS

THE UNCOMMON LIFE OF ALFRED WARNER IN SIX DAYS

Juliet Conlin

BLACK & WHITE PUBLISHING

First published 2017
by Black & White Publishing Ltd
29 Ocean Drive, Edinburgh EH6 6JL

1 3 5 7 9 10 8 6 4 2   17 18 19 20

ISBN: 978 1 78530 082 0

A CIP catalogue record for this book is available from the British
Library.

Typeset by Iolaire, Newtonmore
Printed and bound by CPI Group (UK) Ltd, Croydon, CR0 4YY

'Twas night in the dwelling,
and Norns there came,
Who shaped the life of the lofty one;
They bade him most famed
of fighters all
And best of princes ever to be.

– Helgakviða Hundingsbana I
Poetic Edda

But if I were in a state of sin, do you think the Voice would come to me?

– Joan of Arc

What I don't get, like . . . is when I tell someone about them [the voices] *. . . everyone assumes they're coming from inside my head, and not outside, you know?*

– Tommy H., 23, voice-hearer

DAY ONE

The day I met Alfred Warner, *né* Werner, he had travelled over seven hundred miles eastwards and was sitting, hungry and exhausted, on a regional train heading from the airport towards Berlin's central train station, Hauptbahnhof. He had been so intent on keeping an eye on his suitcase, which sat in the train's luggage rack, wedged between a bright pink hardshell wheely thing and a filthy beige rucksack (it worried him to think that his case might be jammed in too tight for him to remove it, unless the owners of the other bags took theirs out first) that he had completely lost track of the stations. He had written down the entire train route, stops and all, on a sheet of paper the night before, after his granddaughter Brynja had rung to tell him that she was so sorry, but she wouldn't be able to make it to the airport to pick him up, and that she would meet him at Hauptbahnhof at around two o'clock.

Alfred reached inside his jacket pocket and pulled out the piece of paper, knowing even as he did so that he had packed his reading glasses in his suitcase.

Blind as a bat bat bat!

But he unfolded it anyway and rested it on his thigh.

'It's easy to find, Grandad,' Brynja had said on the phone. 'Just take the regional train all the way from the airport. You can't get lost.' And then she had laughed. As if it were that easy. A loose, unselfconscious laugh that curled off in all directions. Alfred was beginning to dislike her before he'd even met her.

A whoosh of hot air came out of the radiator grille underneath his seat, almost burning his calves. He jerked his legs out in front of him, causing his feet to collide with the shins of the man sitting directly opposite.

'Oh, sorry,' he said, and then corrected himself: *'Entschuldigen Sie bitte.'*

The words coming out of his mouth were behaving badly, foreign words in his native language that made him sound slow, or worse, senile.

It's those NHS dentures. They're not used to the lingo.

But the man opposite just shifted in his seat and waved the apology away with a scowl. The heat emanating from beneath Alfred smelled slightly foul, and he was suddenly worried that the smell might be coming from him. He pulled his jumper away from his neck, tugged once or twice, and sniffed as furtively as possible, but all he could detect was a faint mixture of sweat and the lavender shower gel he'd used in this morning's bath.

Kssss, you're not the stinker, then.

The train began to slow and several passengers got up, rearranging coats, jackets, scarves, and blocking Alfred's view of his suitcase. He got to his feet, keeping his balance with some effort, and tried to make out the name of the station through the opposite window. The train was at a mere hissing, shrieking crawl now, but Alfred's eyes still couldn't quite focus on the passing station signs long enough to read them. He sighed and turned his head back to the luggage rack. A young woman dressed in black was blocking his view of the suitcase, but he could see her tugging at the pink wheely case. A moment later, she had jerked it out of the rack. And Alfred's suitcase was gone.

He shuffled past the woman in the seat next to him, *entschuldigung, entschuldigung,* down the aisle towards the luggage rack, breathing heavily as he tried to avoid stepping on the handbags, coats, and toddlers that were blocking his path, and reached the luggage rack just as a pony-tailed youth was heaving his beige rucksack from the shelf. Alfred lifted a hand to tap the young man on the shoulder, noticed the tremor, and dropped it again.

'*Entschuldigung.*'

The young man turned and smiled.

'Sorry, no German,' he said.

Alfred thought he recognised a Scottish accent.

'That's all right,' he replied.

Where's he from? Go on, ask him!

'Can I help ye?' the young man said, negotiating the rucksack onto his back and bumping it into several people in the process.

'My suitcase. I can't seem to find it,' Alfred said, embarrassed at the trace of desperation that had crept into his voice. The train had come to a full stop now and Alfred was becoming very anxious that if this was indeed his station, he would need to get his suitcase and disembark.

3

'It was just here – ' He gestured towards the pile of luggage still on the rack, then turned back to the man and suddenly spotted his case standing in the aisle a couple of feet away. The young woman must have put it there when she was getting her own case out. 'Oh,' he said, his voice small. 'There it is.'

'Need any help getting it off the train?' the young man asked.

'Are we there?' Alfred asked.

Are we there? Are we there? How's he *supposed to know where you want to get off?*

The man began to move slowly towards the door along with the other passengers wanting to disembark. 'We're at Hauptbahnhof, if that's where you need to be,' he said over his shoulder.

Alfred felt his head tremble on his neck. The young man took this as affirmation and picked up Alfred's suitcase.

'I'll just pop it on the platform for you mate, all right?' Then without waiting for an answer, he headed for the door.

Alfred stepped slowly and carefully off the train, concentrating on keeping his balance while being jostled and bumped by those in more of a hurry to get on and off.

Impatient lot.

He hadn't had a proper piss since that morning at home; he had tried to go on the aeroplane, but the door to the small and smelly cubicle had stubbornly refused to lock, and the fear of the door swinging suddenly open and his being exposed to a plane full of passengers with his flies undone and his shrivelled, seventy-nine-year-old sex poking out for all to see had made peeing all but impossible. He had only managed to squeeze out a few hot, painful drops of urine. Then, on the train, the pressure on his bladder had taken centre stage again, but he hadn't dared to seek out the toilet, in case a) someone stole his suitcase, and b) he missed his stop.

And so now he was sitting on the platform, not managing to think beyond a visit to the toilet and wondering how he might politely put his need to Brynja when – if – she finally turned up. The cold blew along the platform through the station, from one tunnel opening to the next. Alfred could barely remember what she looked like. She had sent him a photograph with her third letter, the one containing the aeroplane ticket, and in which she had said she was thrilled that he was coming, but he had forgotten to take the photograph with him. He'd laid it on the low walnut side table, one of the few items of furniture he had been allowed to take from his home in Barton Road to Gladstone Court Care Home, but the nurse had rushed him out of the door that morning – bad-tempered that he wouldn't be there over Christmas even though he'd said he would be, and now there would be three left-over Christmas dinners, what with Eleanor Dougan passing away unexpectedly the night before and Frank Martins deciding to spend the holidays with his daughter after all – and he'd been in the taxi speeding towards Birmingham Airport before he knew it.

'And make sure to tell her about your diabetes,' the nurse had shouted at him, confusing his (good) right ear with his (bad) left. 'We don't want to have to start you on jabs when you get back, just because you couldn't say no to the Christmas pud.'

And although Alfred knew he wouldn't be back, he nodded and smiled.

Indeed, six days after I met him, Alfred Warner died of heart failure.

Two Thousand and Five

They're coming. They're coming now. You can feel them coming before you even hear them. It's always the way. Every time. It's one fifteen and you have to leave the house soon if you want to be there on time. But there's no way you can leave the house if they are there. There's no way you're taking them with you. No way.

You feel them coming before you even hear them, a slight shift in air pressure just before a thunderstorm. And even as you start humming, a counter-stimulation one of your doctors suggested, you know that humming to prevent the voices from coming is as effective as raising a fist to the heavens to prevent that thunderstorm. And sure enough, they arrive, in a low-level crackling, peppered with the occasional cough and grunt.

The little girl's voice arrives first through the static, sharp and clear: *We know, don't we. Don't we. We know. We have too much gravity. Too much, tooooo much gravity. We know about the gravity, don't we. We are heavy, heavy in the gravity.*

You stop humming as you realise you are rocking backwards and forwards on the soles of your feet. You are still standing in the hallway, keys in your left hand, jacket in your right, ready to walk out the door.

Ooooh, so heavy. Bryn, *Bryn,* Brynja, the voice says, mocking you by rolling the r, revving it like a motorcycle.

It's too late to take your meds now. You stopped taking them after Erich left, when you needed to feel the pain to feel alive. Because otherwise, what's the point? It's too crazy Brynja, he said, after the fire. I can't live like this, he said. This is not going to work.

If you're lucky, it'll only be the little girl. The others might not follow. There's no way of telling.

The voice drops away, leaving behind a decreasing hush of white noise. You look up and down, from side to side, listening with your eyes. For one sweet moment, all is still. But just as you lift your arm to slide it through the jacket sleeve

SHAME ON YOU! You slut, you dirty, filthy SLUT!

The two women. Twins, you imagine, speaking in unison, giving their harsh, brittle voices a surreal, artificial quality. Or maybe just one voice spoken twice, one superimposed on the other like a sound technician's recording.

You will be punished, you will not escape your FINAL JUDGEMENT. Look at you, your jeans so tight, so tight up against your crotch. Your dirty, disgusting, bulging camel toe...

Without wanting to, you look down at your crotch.

Yes, you see! They will all be looking at you, watching you, you and your disgusting pussy-bulge.

You let keys and jacket drop to the floor and run into the living room, to the IKEA desk over in the corner, plough through piles of paper, books, sweeping them to the floor, you don't care, looking for your iPod, your precious music, music, but nothing's here, so you run across the room and flip open the laptop that sits on the coffee table and switch it on. The screen lights up and you stare at the green processor light blinking furiously, trying to ignore the

FAT! FAT and UGLY and SLUTTY! Ooh, you want them to touch you, touch you down there . . .

until the laptop is up and running and you click open YouTube and type in Coleman and open another tab and type in Takayanagi, concentrating hard to find the correct spelling through the shouting, and you turn the volume to its highest and are hit by sound from EVERY-WHERE – skewed saxophone and violent guitar, the fierce jazz fighting the voices and causing pain like glass inside your head.

You crash down onto the couch and close your eyes.

At some point during the screaming sax-guitar cacophony, the abuse trails off, the twins unwilling, perhaps, to fight against the noise. And several minutes later, the tracks have also ended, leaving you in silence on the couch with ringing ears and racing heart, sweating profusely and knowing you should concentrate on remembering something that was important to remember, although the inside of your head is raw like freshly peeled flesh. Needing to stay still, just for a short while, just until the nerve-endings have stopped shrieking and the nausea has passed. Lying on your back, counting breaths.

The silence is exquisite.

Brynja.

Your eyes fly open.

Brynja. Sit up.

You sit up and immediately vomit onto the carpet. Then you start crying. Softly.

You are being very silly.

It is the voice you fear most of all.

You know, I'm losing patience with you, I really am.

Loud, powerful, voluminous. Inside and outside of your head at once.

For a start, sit up straight when I'm talking to you. Wipe your chin. And look at that disgusting mess you've made. I should make you lick that up.

You continue to sob and wipe your chin with your sleeve. You drop to your knees and lower your face to the floor. The sour-sharp smell makes you gag.

What are you doing? Get up, you stupid girl! It's soaked into the carpet by now, anyway. Right, let's take a little walk to the kitchen.

You sit back on your heels, weeping loudly now. Don't, you say. Don't make me hurt myself. Please.

'Don't make me hurt myself. Pleeeease.' We've been through this, Brynja. I don't know how many times. You give me what I want and I will leave you alone. It's as simple as that.

But I don't know what... You don't bother to finish your sentence. She is right. You've been through this countless times. Cigarette burns. Rope burns. Cuts: knives, razors, needles dragged across the skin, shards of glass. But you still don't know what she wants. After all these years. For years she's been coming at you; sometimes she gives you riddles, but they never make sense.

(What is the point of an any-angled mirror?

10

If I took away your eyes, what would you see?
How far is a breath thrown in the rain?)

Or you are just too dumb to solve them. But you try – oh god, you try so hard!

She is the one you are most frightened of, because she is the one who owns your thoughts. Hers aren't random bursts of abuse, like that of the twins; or kaleidoscopic, nonsensical ramblings like the little girl. But she knows what makes you tick. She knows what makes you sick. Haunting you, taunting you, flaunting her power over you. She knows how to get under your skin and make you bleeeeeed. And she is most cruel when you come off your meds. That's when she really takes her revenge. She isn't stupid; she knows you have ways of silencing her – Chlorpromazine, Largactil, Stelazine. But sooner or later, you stop taking your pills because of what they do to your mind, to your body – a thick hot blanket smothering your thoughts, your tongue swollen, breasts and ankles too, poisoning you in a way you can't put into words to explain to the doctor. Can't think straight, can hardly get out of bed, fall asleep on buses and trains. Wrecked when you're on your meds. Wrecked when you're off them.

Get to your feet! Come on, right now! You're worthless, d'you know that? I don't even know why I bother.

You stand up. Hum the first bars of 'Twinkle, Twinkle, Little Star' – the first tune that comes into your head – but this is so pathetically lame you stop almost immediately. Scared of angering her. Best just to do what she says. But it's too late. She's heard it.

Baby songs? Are you serious? Well that's it, Brynja. I've had just about enough of this. I was going to give you another chance today, a chance to give me what I want – and you know what I want, so don't even bother pretending you don't – but no, you don't want to play along. She sighs. So it's time now. I think it's time.

You start walking towards the kitchen.

Nope, Brynja. Not the kitchen. Not this time. Oh, I know how much you like playing with the sharps and pointies. But not today. To the balcony! Come on, you know it's time.

You turn and head back through the living room to the balcony door. Still crying.

You're making me do this. You know that. We've got to a point where this is just not working anymore.

You touch the handle. Cold metal, makes you shiver. Shiver so hard you can't turn it.

No, please, don't make me. You're terrified and the words don't come out properly.

What's that, Brynja?

Don't make me. Please.

Come on, you can do it. Deep breath now.

You breathe in and out and the shaking subsides. You turn the handle.

Good girl. You see? It's not that difficult, is it?

You open the door and step out onto the balcony. The air is freezing but you don't feel it. The balcony is enclosed by a wrought-iron railing you painted black last summer.

One step, two step, three step, four. Go on, just keep moving, stop thinking. We've been through a lot together, you and me, girl. And now it's time. You understand that, right? It's time.

You nod. The sobbing is making you shake again, or maybe it's the cold.

It'll be over before you know it. A couple of seconds, tops. Milliseconds.

You begin to climb over the railing. Your left foot gets caught on one of the decorative iron swirls and for a moment, you almost lose your balance and fall. Your stomach drops to your groin.

Whoa! Steady there! We want to do this right, don't we?

Your heart is pumping hard now, as you manoeuvre yourself so that you're perched uncomfortably on the outside of the railing with both buttocks, your feet pressed against a small protruding row of bricks.

Do it. Do it. It's not worth holding on. Do it. Now.

You let yourself fall forward. Your body slices silently through the freezing air. You are still conscious when you hit the concrete, hear the sound of your skull cracking, feel the pain, spectacular pain. And then silence.

DAY ONE

Here is how I met Alfred:

I arrived at Hauptbahnhof – on the same day as Alfred – from a weekend trip, on the Eurocity 378 from Prague. The heating system on the train had been broken for the final hour of my journey, and so I was frozen through by the time we arrived in Berlin. It was only a couple of days before Christmas and the train station was teeming with people. I had every intention of quickly squeezing through the crowds and out, when I thought I heard someone calling my name. I turned around and scanned the crowd, straining to pick out a familiar face. But nobody was looking in my direction, and mine is a common enough name, so I turned back and headed towards the escalator. As I did so, the heel on my left boot got caught in a metal grating and snapped clean off. I cursed under my breath, and then remembered that I'd packed a second pair of shoes in my case – a pair of bright orange Nike trainers that would look atrocious with my burgundy jeans, but were better than limping about with

a broken heel – so I looked around for somewhere suitable to sit and change my shoes. I spotted a bench at the
middle of the platform holding four grey moulded plastic
seats; an elderly man sat at one end and a young couple
occupied the two seats at the other. I hobbled towards
the bench and sat down between the young woman and
the old man. As I began to rifle through my suitcase,
which I'd placed on the floor between my legs, the old
man spoke. Because there was no one else in the vicinity,
I assumed he was talking to me. I sat up.

'Wie bitte?' I asked, as he had spoken quite softly and I
hadn't quite heard what he'd said.

He turned to me and frowned; he had a kind of vacant
look, as though he were just emerging from a daydream.

'Haben Sie etwas gesagt?' I asked. Did you say
anything?

He shook his head and looked away again. I bent
down and continued to grapple with my bag: I'd packed
my trainers at the bottom of the case – as one does – and
was now fighting my way through hairbrush, toiletries,
dirty knickers and a blouse or two to the bottom.

'Utter nonsense!'

It was the old man again. Rather than sit up straight, I
looked up over my right shoulder at him.

He continued. 'No, no. She hasn't forgotten. You wait
and see.'

I realised he was speaking English, although his voice
was barely above a whisper. He was staring straight ahead,
or rather, he was facing straight ahead, but it didn't look
as though he were staring at anything at all.

I straightened up. 'Can I help you?' I asked.

Again, he looked at me, moving his lips soundlessly

at first. Then finally he said, 'I am dreadfully sorry to impose on you, but the person who is supposed to pick me up hasn't arrived yet, and I would very much like to ... to make use of the lavatory facilities, but I am unfamiliar with this train station and don't know where they are and my suitcase is far too heavy for me to be carrying it around looking for the public toilets. Assuming there are any. So I was wondering if you might be kind enough to keep an eye on my case while I pop off and ... '

It came out in such a rush and with such urgency that I couldn't help but say, 'Of course.'

'Thank you,' he said. 'I was afraid that if I left the platform for a moment, my granddaughter might think I had never arrived.' His face seemed to melt a fraction. 'She was supposed to pick me up at two o'clock,' he added.

'Well, I'm sure she just got held up,' I said. 'Just take the lift down two floors, I think it's best to avoid the escalators or you might get lost, and then keep to your left. There should be a sign, anyway. I'll keep an eye on your case and look out for your granddaughter. What does she look like?'

'Well,' he said, frowning. 'I'm not quite sure. Never actually met her. I had a photograph, but ... Blonde, I think. Yes, quite sure about that. Blonde hair. Rather short. Has a pretty smile. Though I can't say I much like the way she laughs. Oh dear. Now ... if I may?'

'Of course, off you go,' I said. 'I'll be right here when you get back.'

The man hurried off toward the lift. I sat down again and changed into my trainers. I shivered and hoped he would be back soon. Keeping my eye out for a petite young woman, who may or may not have blonde hair, my mind wandered forward to the next couple of hours, where I had mentally unpacked my suitcase, taken a hot shower and eaten whatever was left in the fridge.

But as it happened, things turned out very differently.

Some ten minutes or so after the old man had left in search of the public toilets, I spotted him ascending in the glass lift, looking very worn and old and helpless, and for a fleeting moment this uninvited responsibility overwhelmed me, and I imagined taking my trainers at the advertised promise of their manufacturer and to *just do it* – to just grab my case and run. But I didn't. And my reward was Alfred's story.

1932

Alfred climbed down the steep narrow staircase – backwards, as he had been taught – looking for his mother. For days now, there had been a general sense of unease and excitement at home; a thundercloud of a feeling, crackling and heavy, that seeped into the cracks of conversation, scooped out the silences, blossomed darkly on his father's face when he put Alfred and his siblings to bed at night with a kiss. Alfred had been too young to experience this feeling consciously in the days before his younger sister Martha was born, but now, at the age of six, he was old enough to understand that his mother might give birth at any moment. So when she failed to appear at lunch, Alfred had taken his father's request to find her as seriously as if he'd been asked to ensure that the cowshed was properly locked.

The cottage was so tiny that it was impossible to remain undetected there for any length of time, forcing games of hide-and-seek to the outdoors. So Alfred began his search outside. At first, he ran around the

18

farm randomly, checking the barn, the henhouse, the cowshed, before – quite anxiously now – backtracking to the small outhouse that stored the winter wood. The outhouse, though primitive in structure, had a small cellar. This was the only underground construction on the estate – with the exception of the expansive wine cellar beneath the von Markstein manor house – and was perhaps the best aspect of Karl Werner's job on the estate, as it enabled the family to store food for far longer than would otherwise have been possible. They stored whatever the season had produced in excess, or whatever their small self-cultivated vegetable patch yielded, and usually had a reliable stock of onions, carrots, cabbages and potatoes.

Since the unexplained disappearance of several jars of crab-apple marmalade a few months ago, the cellar had become strictly out-of-bounds for all the Werner children, which is why Alfred hadn't considered looking for his mother here first. When he got to the bottom of the staircase, which was more of a ladder than a staircase, really, he wiped his hands on his short trousers. It was pleasantly cool down here, a refreshing relief from the heavy August heat that had sucked every ounce of moisture from the soil, scorching the crops and leaving the cows' udders hanging slack and withered beneath their bellies. A few narrow sunbeams, made visible only by the motes of dust they carried, pierced the joints of several wooden slats that blocked off the high-set window. Alfred turned around and saw his mother. At first, he thought she was praying, which confused him, because he had never witnessed her doing so before and, even at his age, possessed a sensitivity acute enough to recognise – even if not to comprehend fully – that his mother's lack of religiosity was one of the few sources of discord in his parents' otherwise harmonious marriage.

To be fair, to any casual observer ignorant of Freyja's particular brand of spirituality, it would appear obvious that she was, indeed, praying. She was kneeling close to the centre of the room, head slightly raised, hands folded and resting atop her very large, very round belly. Her eyes were closed and the light from several thick, smelly candles beside her fell onto her hair and made the blonde appear golden-white.

And she was speaking, or rather mumbling, to herself. As if in supplication. But no, something about the way she spoke – pauses where you wouldn't expect them, not in a prayer anyway, the way she moved her face, frowning, then smiling, the tiniest shake of her head – appeared to Alfred that she was, in fact, in conversation. With whom, he couldn't tell. He looked around, made a full turn to see if perhaps someone was standing or sitting in one of the many dark recesses of the cellar. A low scratching sound behind the vegetable rack, but that was most likely to be mice. Other than himself and his mother, there was no one there. He stood stock-still; his mother had her eyes tightly shut, but even in the gloom he could see her eyelids quivering as her lips formed words he could barely hear. He stood in silence and watched her, taking pleasure in this rarest of moments in which it was just the two of them: no father, brother or sisters clamouring for and receiving her attention, her words, her thoughts, her smiles and – occasionally – her fury. Yet then he realised that if she didn't know he was there, then it wasn't really the two of them, just him here and her there. He took a small step forward.

'Mama?' he whispered (for this seemed appropriate to him under the circumstances).

She nodded, her eyes still closed, as though she had known all along that he was there. She muttered a final series of hushed words and then opened her eyes and turned to him. His heart seemed to expand as her mouth formed a smile, a perfect upward curve of bruised pink, directed at him. Then her smile faded.

'How is Martha?' she asked.

'She's still coughing,' said Alfred and let out a little cough before he could stop himself. Martha was his younger sister, who had been ill for several weeks now.

'But no blood?'

Alfred shook his head.

'Come here, *mein Täubchen*,' Freyja said, unclasping her hands and stretching an arm out towards him.

He walked forward and kneeled down on the ground beside her, ignoring the hardness of the floor against his knees. Freyja put her arm around him and drew him in close. He pressed his face against her body, his nose and mouth against her soft ripe breast, smelled her sweat and a vague odour of onions, and listened to her heartbeat. It was a slow gentle throb, regular as clockwork, but nothing so mechanical; no, it was organic, and to Alfred, contained all of life itself. Listening to the thump-thump of his mother's heart, he suddenly became infected by his father's anxiety, as though it had managed to creep out of the cottage and into the outhouse. It was so strong, it made his lungs feel tight. He let out a quiet gasp.

'You're not afraid, are you?' his mother asked.

Alfred shook his head without removing his face, then nodded, then shook his head again. Freyja laughed softly, making her breast tremble.

'Don't be afraid, *mein Täubchen*,' she said. 'There's nothing to be afraid of.'

She took his hand and placed it on her belly. It was firm but soft. Alfred turned his head to look at her hand on his, keeping his head close to her chest. Her heart was drumming now.

'She'll be with us in a few days,' Freyja continued. 'Sweet and small and lovely, you'll see.'

Her belly hardened suddenly, he could feel it, hard as steel. He suppressed the urge to squeeze it, to see if it would soften again beneath his hand.

'She's getting ready to come. A few more days, that's all.'

They sat like that for a while, Freyja's belly contracting and softening painlessly every so often. One of the candles beside them spluttered noisily; the flame expired briefly, and then came back to life for a short, glorious farewell before dying completely. Alfred shifted his position so that he could look at his mother's face more clearly.

'Mama?' he said. 'Who were you talking to?'

Freyja smiled and stroked his hand, still resting on her belly. 'Friends,' she said, and nothing more. Alfred placed his head back on her breast and closed his eyes. He was tired; Martha's coughing had kept him awake for most of the night. That, and the fact that since she had become ill several weeks ago, he no longer shared a bed with her – tip to toe – and his sleeping self missed the warmth and plumpness of her three-year-old body next to his. Now, she slept alone in the bed and he slept, or tried to sleep, on a mattress of blankets in the corner of the bedroom.

He felt his mother changing position. 'Come on, help me up,' she said, rising to her knees. 'I'll be glad when I'm only myself again.'

Alfred got up, far more lightly than his mother, and held out a hand. She smiled at him and heaved to her feet. Alfred took a step towards the ladder, but Freyja didn't move.

'Alfred,' she said, and in the dim light she suddenly looked very troubled. 'You must – '

'Yes?'

But before she continued, she gave out a low moan and bent forward, squeezing her eyes shut.

'Mama?'

She breathed in deeply, once, twice, through her nose and then straightened up. 'Just a few more days, *mein Täubchen*, just a few more days.'

And Alfred wasn't sure whether she was addressing him or the baby in her belly.

Four days later, on Sunday, Alfred's sister Marie was born in less than an hour. The following Tuesday, Alfred's sister Martha died of tuberculosis. It took her many hours to die. And that was the day the voices came to Alfred for the first time.

It had been the longest day any member of the Werner family could recall; each minute of Martha's dying was experienced by Karl and Freyja, as well as their children Emil, Johanna and Alfred, acutely and consciously – each minute as inflamed and painfully swollen as Martha's joints, from that moment at seven in the morning when it had become clear she was dying, until she exhaled her final, wispy breath just before sunset, some fourteen hours later. These long hours of anticipatory grief affected the family most profoundly, invoking a synchronicity of feeling, as though these weren't five individual people at entirely different stages of emotional development, but instead a unit of desperation, anxiety, pre-grief, in which there was no room for Karl and Freyja's parental authority, or Alfred's infant solipsism, or Emil's recklessness, or Johanna's bossiness. Although every one of them, from the oldest to the youngest, had witnessed the harshness of nature – lambs asphyxiated by umbilical cords, chickens decapitated by foxes – the impending death of one so close was impossible to bear alone.

However, when Martha finally died that evening, the spell broke, and the unit fractured back into the sum of its parts: Freyja retreated to grieve in bed with baby Marie latched – permanently, it seemed – to her breast; Karl wailed openly and relentlessly, pacing the tiny cottage, which had always felt too small for the large man at the best of times and had now shrunk even smaller faced by the enormity of the man's grief; Emil took his slingshot and sat in the front yard on the dusty ground for hours, firing pebbles at dandelion clocks that burst into a thousand spores when he hit his target; and Johanna held a doll on her knees and sang lullabies until her throat grew hoarse.

And Alfred did what he always did when overpowered by feelings his childish spirit couldn't comprehend. He hid. He ran into the forest that began just behind the cowshed, picked his way through bushes and brambles and thousand-year-old tree roots, until he was so far inside the forest that the fading sunlight came through in dapples of emerald and gold. He found a huge ash tree, whose trunk had split into two just a metre above the ground, and climbed into the age-old nook carved out in the fork of the trunk. He pulled his dirty knees to his chest and rested his chin there. He stayed as still as he could, fearing that if he moved, this feeling of dread inside him would intensify. It was the kind of feeling he experienced when he accidentally bashed his bare toes against a rock: for a split second, there is no pain, just that frightening anticipation of pain, which is just as bad as the pain itself, if not worse.

The forest air was warm and drowsy and smelt of dusk and moss. Alfred knew that later on, after sunset, the forest would lose its sluggishness and be transformed into a wondrous strange and busy place, alive with crisp rustles and sporadic skirls: quick sharp movements as prey evaded predator, or else succumbed to claw and beak and tooth. But for now, at the end of a long, hot summer's day, the forest was listless and quiet. Alfred began to feel sleepy and he closed his eyes.

Then he heard a voice. It was a whisper – *hissskkss, shhhhts, psstss* – coming from somewhere above him to the left. Alfred had spent enough of his young life in the forest to know that this was no bird or other creature, or any other sound the windless forest could produce. It was a human voice, a woman's voice. It was too low for him to make out the words, but something in the inflection made him recognise it was a question. A moment later, another voice, slightly to the right. And although this too was a whisper, or perhaps more of a sigh, he could tell that this was a different voice and that it was answering the first. He opened his eyes and lifted his head to the boughs above him. He did this out of curiosity, not because he was afraid, being, developmentally, on the cusp of leaving a world in which hearing voices could still quite easily be reconciled with the stark objective realities of life.

However, with his eyes open, the voices seemed to dim. He shut his eyes again, opening his hearing to its most sensitive, and then:

OF COURSE HE'S NOT AFRAID, ARE YOU, ALFRED?

Alfred fell from his nook and hit the ground hard. He fell, not just because of the loudness and suddenness of the voice, but because he realised at once that the voice had not come from outside, but from inside his head. He sat up and covered his ears with his palms of his hands.

OH, GOODNESS, HE FELL OFF THE TREE!

Clear as day, the voice ricocheted inside his head, the shout bouncing from ear to ear.

The poor boy, he heard. *I hope he isn't hurt.*

Perhaps he should stand up to make sure there are no broken bones, he heard.

Dutifully, Alfred stood up and slapped the damp earth from his backside. He wriggled his limbs. All was well. Besides, he'd fallen from greater heights before without coming to any real harm.

KSSSS, IT WAS FUNNY THOUGH, HOW HE JUST – PLOP! – FELL ON HIS BOTTOM!

I think you can stop shouting now. He can hear us perfectly well.

Now, Alfred was a fairly shy and quiet boy. He was not prone to the extroversion and gaiety of his older siblings, ten-year-old Johanna and eleven-year-old Emil, although he enjoyed their exuberance by proxy, delighting in Johanna's cartwheels across meadows of poppies and cornflowers, admiring Emil's shows of courage when he climbed to the top of a pine tree and hung there, swaying dangerously as the wind made the tip dance from side to side. On occasion, Alfred's father would chide his son's exaggerated prudence and apparent lack of spunk, but Alfred was mostly quite content to sit among the wild-flowers, grinning at each forbidden flash of his sister's underpants, wondering how heavy Emil would have to be for the tip of the pine to snap during one of its dances. Much later in life, Alfred would come to learn that these qualities – a reserved demeanour and a keen mind – were of great benefit when it came to coping with life.

But right now, he was a six-year-old boy in a darkening forest, listening to a conversation between three women, or wood nymphs, or faeries – he knew not which – none of whom he could see. And although this intrigued him somewhat, his reticence got the better of his curiosity. So instead of answering back, or engaging in conversation, he turned to face the tree and waited. He didn't quite know what he was waiting for, but his silence appeared to have silenced them, because there was nothing more to be heard.

Dusk had washed out the last of the light from the forest. The shriek of a nearby owl officially proclaimed nightfall, and suddenly recalling his father's tales of wolves, Alfred decided it was time to go home. He circled the ash tree once, just to make sure there really was no one there, and headed back. He knew the woods well, every gnarled tree root, every cluster of fruit-bejewelled brambles, the surreptitious streams that gurgled through the forest like life-blood, all imprinted as an elaborate mental map in his brain. Thus, even in the increasing gloom, he was able to stride confidently and unerringly back through the forest to the cottage. It was completely dark by the time he got back, and as he headed down the sandy path that led from the cowshed to the cottage, he spotted his father sitting on the doorstep with his head in his hands. For a moment, Alfred felt a swell of guilt. Firstly, he realised at the sight of his father that he had, for a short while, forgotten all about Martha. Secondly, it occurred to him that perhaps his father had been sitting there for goodness knows how long, waiting for him to return.

As he approached the cottage, however, it appeared that his absence had gone unnoticed. His father looked up, his face still contorted in grief. He opened his mouth as though to speak, but then wordlessly let his head fall back into his hands. Alfred climbed the steps past him and entered the cottage. The windows had been flung open to let some of the cool of the evening into the room, and the whitewashed walls were already pricked with an array of gnats and mosquitoes, lured in by the light of two petroleum lamps that stood on the mantelpiece.

'I'm hungry,' Alfred said to Emil and Johanna, who were sitting on a rug playing cards. Despite the open windows, the air in the cottage was still heavy from the day's heat.

'I'm hungry,' Alfred repeated, his voice rising to a whine. Emil slapped a card on the rug between himself and Johanna with a triumphant 'Ha!'

Johanna got to her feet and tossed her cards onto

the floor. 'I'm not playing with you anymore,' she said crossly. 'You're cheating.'

Emil shrugged and began to gather the cards together. 'You're just a bad loser,' he said.

Johanna paused, as if trying to think of a suitable rejoinder. Then she placed her hands firmly on her hips and said, 'Right, I don't think we should wait for Papa to put us to bed tonight.'

'I don't need anyone to put me to bed,' Emil said, getting up off the floor. He had a smudge of dirt on his right cheek.

Johanna bent over to pick up the cards. 'Well then,' she said, still addressing Emil, 'you can put yourself to bed whenever you like.' She looked up and spotted Alfred. 'You. Upstairs. It's time for bed.'

At these words, hunger and tiredness undertook a brief battle in Alfred. Tiredness won.

'You're not in charge here,' Emil repeated, but this time in a lower voice.

'That's not – ' Johanna began, but stopped as they all heard a loud wail coming from upstairs. She and Emil exchanged a glance.

'What's wrong?' demanded Alfred, made anxious by the exclusion from their understanding. The sound from upstairs had suddenly taken the edge off his tiredness, but had simultaneously reminded him of his hunger.

'That's Mama,' said Johanna quietly. 'She's – ' she hesitated. 'She's doing all of her crying today so she'll be better tomorrow.' And then she nodded her head as if to affirm this statement for her own benefit and turned and began to climb the stairs. Emil hesitated for a moment and then followed her. Alfred watched them walk upstairs, wondering if he should go to the kitchen to fetch an apple, when a disoriented bat suddenly flew in through an open window, drew a couple of bewildered circles around the room and then flew out again as abruptly as it had entered. Spooked by this, and the thought of other creatures that might be lurking in the dark outside waiting to come in, Alfred dashed up the stairs behind his siblings.

Two Thousand and Four

Fuck, Brynja!

Erich is pissed off, really pissed off, but there's nothing you can do about it now. Your stomach is growling.

Brynja!

Yeah, I heard you. You push past him into the kitchen, feel the vibration of his rage. Ignore it. I'm fucking starving, you say.

You open the fridge, yank it open too forcefully – can't judge your own strength when you're on meds – making the milk bottle in the door clatter against the beer bottles. A few drops of milk splash out and onto the floor.

Shit.

Erich comes up behind you, clutching the letter. He is barefoot, you can hear the soles of his feet on the kitchen tiles. Why didn't you show me this, Bryn? It's dated June thirteenth. That's – he pauses, counting in his head – like nine weeks ago.

Eggs, hard lump of cheese, wilted coriander (from Erich cooking Thai), a jar of olives. And bread. Erich has a habit of keeping bread in the fridge. Makes it stay fresh for longer, he claims, although you hate cold bread. Always have to pop it in the toaster for ten seconds just to warm it up to room temperature. You grab two slices, straighten up and turn. Collide with Erich. He is not just barefooted, but also bare-chested. Wiry black curls sprouting around his nipples. There's a heat wave. He looks at you and tries to establish eye contact, but you evade him. Move your head from side to side. Eye contact makes you uncomfortable. So instead, Erich puts his hand on your shoulder. His hand is hot and heavy.

Brynja, he says, moving his head in synch with yours – a snake charmer with his snake – still trying to catch your eye. Brynja, look at me.

You surrender for a moment, meet his gaze and then quickly look away again. You wipe a trickle of drool from the corner of your mouth. The skin on your shoulder beneath his hand is starting to sweat.

I need to eat, you say and dip and step away from his touch.

Erich follows you to the kitchen table. On the table, cereal bowls from breakfast, small shards of cornflake encrusted on the inside rims. You'll have to soak them in the sink. Also covering the surface of the table: papers, sketchbook, pencils, a bowl of fruit rotting in the heat. Your laptop. You sit and take a bite of cold bread. Chew.

They'll evict us, Erich says.

It's your name on the rent contract, he moved in with *you*, not vice versa. He reads your thoughts.

Okay, they'll evict *you*, he says. He likes to get his facts straight. That's what attracted you to him when you met. His straight facts.

You chew and swallow. You say, I'm sorry.

Yeah, well sorry doesn't do it. You owe two months plus the fine for it being overdue.

We, you say. Your mind is suddenly sharp.

What?

We owe. You live here too.

I live here too, but I pay you my half of the rent every month. By standing order. Which means you have my money but didn't pay the rent with it.

Not as sharp as you think, obviously. You can't tell, here, under the blanket. Been on Stelazine for over two months now.

I'll sort it out, you say.

Yeah, I hope so, he says.

He grabs a bright white t-shirt that's hanging on the back of a chair. How does he get it so white? He uses the same detergent, same machine. Your whites always turn grubby-grey. Always. Inevitably.

Right. I've got to get to work, he says and leaves the room.

You wait. Eat your bread. Five minutes later, the front door clicks shut, quietly, politely, passive-aggressively. You take your bread and a bottle of water into the living room, switch your music on and light a cigarette. Let yourself fall onto the couch. It's hot. You should've opened a window. Inhale. Berlin is famous for its summers. Exhale through pursed lips. Outdoor karaoke. Everyone loose-limbed and tanned, giving even less of a fuck than usual. Or more fucks than usual. You smile. Like you and Erich, last summer, fucking all day, everywhere, you didn't care. Once, sitting next to him on the bus, you pretended to drop an earring and gave him a blowjob.

In the bedroom, Erich likes you best when you're off your meds. Like when you met last summer. He wouldn't say it, but you know it's true. Sometimes the twins' voices arrive when you're having sex, and you use them to turn you on. You come in no time when they're screaming *FILTHY BITCH! COCK-LOVING SLUT!* in your ear as you ride Erich. But you don't tell him this. Don't tell anyone. A secret between you and your madness.

But like this, on meds, nothing. You're drooling again. You wipe your mouth on the back of your hand, roll onto your side and tap your cigarette ash onto the floor. You'll sweep up later, before Erich gets home from work. You haven't got much else to do. Then you roll onto your back and slide your other hand down the waistband of your shorts and then your underpants, feel the springy hair and cushiony skin, shove your fingers a little lower, rub, pinch. Nothing. Zero. Zilch. Not a tingle, not a tickle, not a prickle; instead, a void of feeling, a black hole of arousal. You sit up slowly, somnambulant, reach for an ashtray on the coffee table and stub out your cigarette. Tongue thick in your mouth. Take a sip of water and light another cigarette.

Erich is the schizophrenic one. He likes you when you're off your meds. You're fun. You party. You're wild in bed. He hates you when you're off your meds. You cry all the time. You misbehave in restaurants. You act like a crazy person in public and in private. He wants to buy a flat, wants to tame your illness with a mortgage, a wedding ring, babies, move to a part of town where you're fucked if you haven't got a car because public transport is for cleaners and school children and the nearest bus stop is a good twenty-minute walk away. And you love him for that, because he's sweet and naïve enough to think it would be that easy.

Your eyes are stinging. The room is full of cigarette smoke. Lying here, looking across the room, the TV is veiled behind layers of grey and white. A smoke screen. You realise you need to open a window. The hot air is heavy on your body. High air pressure, that means lots of air molecules squashed together in one place, right? That's what makes the air feel heavy, doesn't it? You force yourself off the couch, although you're tired, really tired, push your body through the squashed-up air molecules to the other side of the room and go out onto the balcony. Lean on your forearms on the railing and look down, wondering when Erich will be back. He'll come home and cook something nice. You smile.

Erich's GOT. IT. TOGETHER. You love him because he broke the pattern of loser boyfriends. You go and lie back down on the couch. Light another cigarette although your tongue is furry. Your mother would have approved of Erich. She would've liked his get-up-and-go. She wouldn't have approved of his atheism, but you wouldn't have told her. You could've pretended to go to church every Sunday. Or to synagogue every Saturday. Or to mosque every Friday. Or to temple whenever. Whatever. You turn to your side, let your eyelids slide shut. Maybe you'll take Erich to the cemetery some time. You want this to work.

A sharp pain between your index and middle finger. Your cigarette has burned all the way down to the filter. You flick it away, not far enough, it lands near your feet on the couch between the seat cushions. Shit. Shit shit shit shit. You jump up – try to jump up, but can't get your body to work that quickly. Wisps of smoke already curling up from between the cushions. The smell is disgusting, like when moths fly into the halogen uplighter. You pull a face. What to do? Your mind stalls. It's fucking hot; you feel sweat gathering beneath your breasts.

Water. You say it out loud, to the room, to no one. An orange flame darts up from between the cushions, disappears again. So quickly, you're not sure if you really saw it. But then. Again, another flame, two this time, and three. Until they all become one big flame and the smoke is black, and – I'm not my mother! – and you look around for your bottle of water, and

Get out the way!

and Erich is coming up behind you, pushes past you, throws a wet towel onto the flames. You look at him, grateful, embarrassed – your saviour and judge.

He looks at you, shakes his head.

This isn't going to work.

1932

Several days after Martha's funeral, Alfred woke abruptly in the middle of the night to a voice in his ear.

Ooohh, she can't breathe, she can't breathe!

It was one of the voices he'd heard in the forest. He opened his eyes. It was pitch black in the bedroom.

Quickly Alfred, quickly! he heard (a different voice this time, richer, fuller than the first), and he sat up, waiting for his eyes to become accustomed to the dark. When they had, he looked across to the grey shapes of Emil and Johanna, who lay in their beds, not stirring.

Now Alfred, I need you to listen to me. You must go to Karl and Freyja's bedroom. Now. Go on, get up. Hurry.

Alfred stood up. He padded barefoot across the room and into the hall, his eyelids heavy and his mouth slightly open. The door to his parents' bedroom was closed, and he stopped. There he stood, a small figure in white flannel, still half asleep, if truth were to be told. And all of a sudden he feared he might be dreaming, and then what would his mother and father say if he woke them up? Their average working day was rarely under sixteen hours, and they needed their sleep.

What are you waiting for – a written invitation? Go on! NOW!

It was the same voice that had woken him, and he knew now that he wasn't dreaming.

Please, Alfred, the second voice said, *don't be scared. But you must hurry. There isn't much time. Please.*

Alfred pressed his lips together and turned the handle. He pushed the door open slightly and peered in, but the room was as dark as the one he shared with his siblings.

The baby   **Wake her up!**

Alfred, Alfred!

Go, go ...   *HURRY...*

OVER THERE ...

Before it's too late!

They were all speaking – or rather shouting – at the same time. Alfred mustered all his courage and opened the door wide. The moonlight from the hall provided some dim illumination, enough to see across the room to his mother's side of the bed, next to which Marie slept in a wooden cradle.

Yes, over there. Good boy, Alfred. Quickly now. She isn't breathing. Go and pick her up.

Alfred was frightened now, but he headed quickly to where his baby sister was sleeping. There she lay, on her stomach, face pressed into the mattress, the silken blonde hair covering her scalp like down. He reached into the cradle and scooped her out, unsure how to hold her yet marvelling at her lightness. And just as the voices had said, she wasn't breathing.

Wake your parents. NOW!

Wake the baby! The baby!

Alfred glanced across at his mother. She lay on her side, facing the cradle, and even in her sleep, the traces of her sorrow were apparent on her face. A deep crease between her eyebrows suggested that grief had followed her into sleep and her breathing was ragged and uneven, as though her lungs were too sad, too exhausted to inflate and deflate properly. Without thinking, Alfred reached forward to stroke his mother's face in a gesture that denied his youth – but in doing so, he caught his nightgown on the cradle, stumbled forward and almost dropped the baby onto his parents' bed. Freyja stirred, Karl grunted and Marie broke forth with a sudden wail that seemed to reach into the darkest corners of the room. It was a quivering, existential howl that woke both Freyja and Karl immediately.

'It's me, Mama,' Alfred said to the dark figures of his parents who were now sitting upright in bed. 'I have Marie.' He couldn't think of what else to say. He held out the baby – whose whole body now seemed engaged in the effort of filling her lungs with oxygen: hands pumping furiously, legs stretched out stiffly, her face the gaping hole of her open mouth – towards his mother as though handing her a gift. Freyja looked confused for a second but then took the baby off him and began shushing her.

'What are you doing in here?' Karl said, his voice hoarse with sleep. He reached over and lit the petroleum lamp that stood on his bedside table. A warm buttery light spread through the small room, and Karl, Freyja and

Alfred all looked down at screaming Marie. Although Alfred had saved his baby sister from asphyxiation, its traces were still evident in the baby's purplish lips and tinge of blue on her skin. But it appeared as though Freyja's shushing was managing to calm her, and Marie's screams gradually turned into choppy, shuddering breaths. Karl looked up at Alfred.

'What are you doing in here?' he repeated.

'Marie,' Alfred said. He felt blood rushing to his face.

'Alfred, it's the middle of the night,' Freyja said, looking up at him. On the front of her nightgown, Alfred could see two large damp circles of yellowish breast milk that had leaked out despite the layers of gauze she wore inside her brassiere. 'What are you doing here, *mein Schatz?*'

'She wasn't breathing,' Alfred said and nodded at Marie. She had been calmed back to sleep by her mother. Like this, her lips in a pout and her tongue sucking at an imaginary nipple inside her closed mouth, it was hard to believe she was capable of producing such an assaulting sound.

'How did you know she wasn't breathing?' Freyja asked. She carefully handed the baby to Karl and patted the blanket next to her to invite Alfred onto the bed. He climbed up gratefully and Freyja began to stroke his hair.

'The women told me.'

Freyja stopped stroking abruptly. 'What women?'

'I don't know. They said – '

'There's someone in the house?' Karl said, his voice slightly raised now. He swung his legs out of bed and got up, baby Marie in his arms, and looked around for his slippers.

'No,' Alfred began. 'I mean – '

Karl, having found his slippers, crossed the room towards the door, but stopped when he realised he was holding the baby. He glanced around quickly as if trying to find a suitable place to lay her down, but then he turned back to Alfred. 'Were they in your room? Come on, boy, out with it.'

Alfred frowned. He felt annoyed that the voice-women had got him into this mess but now had no advice to give him on how to proceed. It wasn't *his* fault he was here in the middle of the night. He hadn't woken his parents on purpose. He'd only been doing as he'd been told – but where were the voices now? Why couldn't they tell him what to do now?

'They woke me up,' he said, shrugging. 'They told me to come in here because Marie couldn't breathe.'

'Karl,' Freyja said, brushing a strand of Alfred's hair behind his ear, 'come back to bed. Alfred was probably having a bad dream, weren't you, Alfred?'

Karl walked over to the cradle and placed the sleeping Marie inside. He stared down at her for a long time. 'But she might have – ' he said quietly, but didn't finish his sentence.

'Then let's be grateful to Alfred, *liebling.*' Freyja held out her hand towards her husband. 'He probably had a bad dream and came here for comfort. He must have noticed how quiet Marie was. That's what happened, isn't it Alfred?'

Alfred nodded, although he wasn't sure anymore what had happened. He was very, very tired now. Perhaps his mother was right, perhaps it had just been a bad dream. He rubbed his eyes with the balls of his hands. He couldn't be sure.

Karl straightened up and breathed in sharply. 'I'll go and check on the children,' he said. 'To make sure.'

And without clarifying exactly what it was he was making sure of, he left the bedroom.

Freyja leaned back against the wall and pulled Alfred's head onto her chest. 'Do you wish to sleep here with us tonight?' she asked.

Alfred's heart skipped a beat. This was unusual indeed, given that none of Karl and Freyja's children had spent a night in their parents' bedroom past the age of three months, so hoping most sincerely that he hadn't misheard the question, Alfred gave a small nod, his cheek rubbing up and down against the cotton of his mother's nightgown. Freyja began making the same shushing sound she'd made earlier to calm Marie, and then placed her index finger gently but firmly against his forehead, just between his eyebrows. Her fingertip felt as hot as ice and within moments, Alfred was asleep.

DAY ONE

Half an hour after Alfred had returned from the Gents,
I persuaded him to give me the address of his granddaughter, as unfortunately she hadn't thought of giving
him her telephone number. It was by now evident that
she wasn't going to show up. She lived in the Kreuzberg
district, which was just a slight detour en route to my
home in Schöneberg, so I offered Alfred the share of a
taxi.

'Oh. I'm afraid I have no European money on me,' he
said. 'But if you point me in the right direction . . . I don't
mind a walk.'

'It's more of a walk than you think,' I said. 'You're
welcome to join me. It won't cost me any more than if I
travelled alone,' I added, not quite truthfully.

Alfred hesitated, but then nodded. He looked
exhausted.

'Oh, and by the way.' I held out my hand. 'I'm Julia.
Julia Krüger.'

'Very nice to meet you,' he said, taking my hand in

both of his. They were pleasantly warm and dry, the skin slightly papery. 'I'm Alfred Warner.'

'Well, come on then Alfred,' I said, and together we headed for the exit.

Throughout the drive, for just under twenty minutes, Alfred sat staring out of the window, although by now the sun had set and there wasn't really much to see. A few perpetual building sites, the black canal, and – inserted among crumbling late-nineteenth century apartment buildings that hadn't been modernised since the end of the war – those unimaginative post-war tenement blocks with tiny windows and uniform façades. Alfred kept staring out of the window, motionless. Once or twice I heard him mumble something, but it was fairly clear that he wasn't conversing with me, so I just sat back and closed my eyes, wondering if I had enough eggs in my fridge to make an omelette, and if so, whether they would still be fresh.

By the time the taxi stopped in front of Alfred's granddaughter's building on Schönleinstraße, I was close to falling asleep. The taxi driver gave a grunt to let us know we'd reached our first destination, and Alfred opened the door. He turned to face me for the first time since we'd set off from the train station.

'Thank you so much for your kind help,' he said. 'Perhaps if you'd like to wait, I'll see if Brynja can give me some money to cover my share?'

I shook my head and smiled. 'No, that's okay. As I said, I would have had to pay the same fare if I'd been on my own.'

'Well, thank you again,' Alfred said, and proceeded to climb out of the taxi. It was then that I noticed that his head was trembling in a most worrying manner. Of course, he was an old man, some thirty years or so older than myself, and an occasional minor tremor of head or hands is to be expected, but this appeared far beyond normal.

'Alfred,' I called.

He turned and bent down to look into the car. 'Yes?' His breath clouded in the freezing air.

'Um, perhaps I'd better help you up the stairs.'

'Oh no.' Alfred shook his head, which multiplied the effect of the tremor, so that it looked as though his head were about to bob off his neck. 'That won't be necessary. You've been more than helpful. Besides, she lives on the fourth floor.'

Well, this made my mind up for me. I leant forward towards the driver and instructed him to wait for me while I accompanied the gentleman upstairs. The driver shrugged and picked up a newspaper from the passenger seat.

'Alfred,' I said, getting out of my side of the taxi and making a show of scrambling through my handbag. 'I'm afraid I shall have to come with you. This is most embarrassing, but I, um, I don't think I have enough money for the extra fare after all.'

Alfred straightened up and smiled, which seemed to lay the tremor to rest, at least for the time being. 'Yes, all right. Well,' he turned and tipped his head back to look up at the balconies adorning the front of the building, 'let's go then.'

It seems odd in hindsight, but I can swear that neither of us noticed the police tape that sectioned off a few square metres to the left of the building, let alone the bloodstain it enclosed.

1932 – 1934

The summer of 1932 drew to a close languidly, almost as though it were offering an apology for its earlier severity. The temperature dropped gradually, one degree every couple of days, making the Werners' outdoor chores on the estate – splitting firewood in preparation for the winter, digging out the last of the potatoes, repairing fences – less disagreeable than at any other time during the year. It rained gently and silently during the night, nourishing flora and fauna, turning the morning air clean and fresh, and bringing the heady, musty fragrance of mushrooms to the forest.

The heat-bleached landscape began to recover its colour, and although there was occasional news of political rumblings in the nearby capital, for the Werner family, it was a mellow, peaceful, healing time. Day by day, they became better at coping with the painful loss of Martha; although still mourners by day, Freyja and Karl were once again lovers by night and the children dared to laugh loudly and uninhibitedly without fear of upsetting their parents. If truth were told, there was a wretched hole in Freyja's heart that would never quite heal; Karl still had vivid and distressing dreams about Martha and the older children felt at times a stab of guilt when they noticed they had forgotten about their sister for a moment or two while playing – but these were little secrets they each chose to guard from one another.

Only Alfred was somewhat at odds with the world. Ever since the voices had woken him that night and he had saved baby Marie's life, he felt a coolness coming from his mother, or at least some alien feeling he couldn't put into words. As the weeks passed, Alfred might well have come to the conclusion that she was somehow angry or disappointed with him, for whenever they happened to be alone in a room together, she would suddenly think of a reason to leave, or when she washed him in the tub, she would avoid looking him in the eye. On occasion, Alfred had caught her staring at him, just like that, across the kitchen table, or from the window when he was in the yard. And she had a sad, melancholic look in her eyes when she stared at him that way. Yes, he might well have come to the conclusion that she had even stopped loving him, had it not been for the fact that he had grown a good three inches over the summer and needed clothes that fit him before he began school in several weeks' time.

Thus, early one morning, instead of being sent out to feed the chickens, Alfred was told by his mother to stay behind in the kitchen after breakfast so that she could adjust two pairs of Emil's shorts he had grown out of several years ago. He was surprised when she told him to stay, and at first hovered around the back door, thinking she might change her mind at any moment and tell him to go outside after all. But Freyja just smiled a distant smile and went to tuck the blankets firmly around Marie, who was lying fast asleep in a bassinet next to the hearth. Then she picked up a pair of grey shorts from the sideboard.

'Here, try these on,' she said, holding out the shorts.

Alfred took off the too-small shorts he was wearing and stepped into the ones his mother had handed him. The fabric was scratchy and coarse, stiffer than what he was used to, and it smelled funny too, a bit like shoe polish. Alfred knew what shoe polish smelled like because his mother occasionally had to clean the riding boots of their landlord, Fritz von Markstein, when his housemaid Gretl was sick or busy.

'A bit loose around the waist,' Freyja said, slipping two fingers between the waistband and Alfred's stomach and sliding them back and forth. 'But they'll have to do. Now, step onto the chair so I can pin them up.'

Alfred climbed onto the kitchen chair and stood facing his mother. This way, he was almost the same height as her. Her hair was braided and pinned up into a crown at the back of her head, and the pale morning light picked out a few blonde wisps that had come loose. For a moment, she looked directly at him, and her face held a look so serious that Alfred felt a twinge of panic. He dropped his gaze down to the grey woollen shorts that came to just below his knees, and was wondering if he might mention to his mother that they were very itchy, when without warning, she cupped his face in her hands and kissed him gently on the mouth.

'*Sérstakt*,' she whispered in her native tongue, and she tilted her face forwards, resting her forehead against his so that he could feel her warm breath on his face.

'Mama?' Alfred felt frightened and thrilled all at once. The heat from her forehead spread across his face and down and through his small body. Although he had often experienced such physical closeness to his mother, what he was feeling now went beyond the normal corporeal affection of such a gesture. What he was feeling now was symbiotic – it was as though her brain were sending signals to his, his heartbeat drumming to her pulse, her skin stretching to meld with his.

Then a clear voice: *Careful, Freyja. Don't you think he's a little young?*

It was one of Alfred's women-voices, but she wasn't addressing him. His heart and her pulse began drumming a little faster.

Freyja shook her head very slightly. 'No,' she whispered, 'it's good. Now is good.'

'Mama?' Alfred asked again, but this time his lips just formed the words soundlessly.

'You hear them, *mein Täubchen*, don't you?'

Alfred wanted to nod, but was afraid he might disrupt the connection between them if he moved. He remained stock-still.

'I know you can hear them,' Freyja continued. Her voice was so soft and breathless that anyone standing more than a yard or two away wouldn't have heard a thing. 'They woke you that night, didn't they? The night you saved Marie.'

'Yes.' He breathed the word.

A noise escaped Freyja's throat – a sound between a sigh and a moan.

'I'm sorry,' Alfred said. He wasn't sure why, but he thought he had disappointed his mother, and this made him feel profoundly sad.

'Oh!' Freyja threw her arms around him and hugged him so tight he could hardly breathe. 'Oh, Alfred, don't be sorry!'

He hears us very well. Don't you Alfred? A different voice, but definitely one of the three he had heard before. *It is most unusual, Freyja. For one so young.*

'Yes, I know,' Freyja said, loosening her embrace but keeping Alfred close. 'I wasn't sure, but now …'

'You're not cross?' Alfred asked. He wanted to be sure.

Nobody's cross, Alfred.

'No, little one, nobody's cross,' Freyja echoed. 'But please – ' She looked up and around in the space just above Alfred's head, and he realised that she was addressing the voices. 'Please be quiet while I explain things to him. He might get confused, and it's important that he understands things clearly.'

And then – as the sun inched up ever higher in the sky, slowly turning the pale light into autumn gold; as Karl stood in the yard with Emil, teaching him how to split a piece of wood with a maul; as Johanna finished sweeping out the cow shed and went to feed the last of the corn to the chickens; as baby Marie kicked against her blankets in her sleep in the basket beside the hearth – Freyja began pinning up Emil's old shorts and telling her son Alfred about the voices.

She told him that he was one of a long line of voice-hearers in her family, reaching back many hundreds of years, to a time of perpetual volcanic eruptions and the Age of the Sturlungs, when her mother's home country of Iceland was under the rule of violent and bloodthirsty chieftains.

'During this time, there lived three sisters who managed to avoid capture by the chieftain's men by luring them into the mists, where the men got hopelessly lost and died of hunger and thirst. When the chieftain learned of the women's act, he sent out a hundred men to find them and bring them to him. After a year-long hunt, the sisters were finally caught and killed by the chieftain himself, who pierced each of their hearts with his spear and watched them bleed to death.' Her pitch was melodious; the inflection the same as the one she used when telling her children bedtime stories. 'Years later, the three sisters were brought to life again, but only as voices and not in body, by magic words spoken by one of the sisters' sons, a renegade prince, to help him in battle against the chieftain. Since that time, the women – to whom you are related by blood – continued to appear to each generation as both agents and witnesses. And Alfred – ' She paused for a moment and looked at him intently. When she next spoke, her voice was dark and cautionary. 'They are very powerful. They spin the threads of life.'

This meant nothing to Alfred, but he stayed silent, while his mother pushed a pin in here, and a pin in there, and told him how one hundred years ago, the island began to grow increasingly cold, and when there had been three hard winters in succession, so hard that no plants could grow and no animals reproduce, Valdís Jónsdóttir, Alfred's grandmother, had travelled to Germany. It was here, thirty-six years ago, that Freyja was born.

Freyja had been Emil's age when she first heard the voices. 'I was frightened, of course. My mother hadn't told me of them, because nobody knows beforehand who will be chosen. But one day, she heard me talking to them,

51

and she explained to me what I am now telling you.' She paused to restock the pincushion she wore strapped to her wrist. 'One of the sisters, the youngest, can be a bit silly,' she continued. 'Excitable. But I think you will like her. The eldest, well, she's never silly. But if you treat her with respect, she will guide you. You can – and you should, Alfred – rely on the advice she gives you. She knows much about the future, and what is owed to the past.'

She stopped talking for a moment and stepped back to align the legs of Alfred's shorts.

'And the middle sister. Hmm. Clever, I'd say. A little impatient. She's never wrong. But she may get quite angry if – '

Only ever for good reason, Freyja.

Freyja put hands on her hips. Her eyes darted to the left. 'Yes, if you would please let me finish.' Then she looked back at Alfred. 'You may find them distracting or inconvenient at times, but you must never resist them or be afraid of them. They will protect you, if you let them. If not . . . ' she lowered her voice, 'well, let's just say I've heard stories. That the spirits of those killed in the mists rise up, angry and vengeful.' She paused and shook her head slightly. 'But those are just stories.'

Alfred ignored the worried undertone in her voice. Although there was much he didn't understand, her stories were like a fairy tale in which he himself was a prince of sorts. He imagined riding across the country on one of von Markstein's fine horses, the reins in his left hand and a raised sword in his right, fighting chieftains and their savage warriors.

'There,' Freyja said as she slid the final pin into place. 'You can take them off now.'

Alfred climbed off the chair reluctantly. He would have liked to listen to his mother's stories all day. But instead, she took the shorts off him and sat down.

'Alfred,' she said, taking his hand in hers. 'Listen to me now. Carefully. You are so very, very young to be hearing them. It is best not to tell anyone else about the voices, do you hear? Many people will not understand; they will think you are mad, or bad, or both. Tell only those you know you can trust.'

'Like Papa?'

'Yes. But – ' Freyja shot a glance towards the door. 'Papa knows that I can hear the voices, and he understands. But perhaps it's best if you don't tell him that you can hear them too.' She tried to smile, but Alfred could tell it was an effort. 'So he doesn't have to worry.'

She got up, smoothed her apron down and went over to check on Marie, who was now making kitten-like mewing noises. She turned to Alfred who was still standing next to the chair: 'Go on, outside. Maybe you can help Johanna beat the rugs. They're absolutely filthy, you know.'

Alfred crossed the kitchen, but paused as he reached the back door.

'Mama?' he asked.

'Yes?'

'Can I tell God?'

Freyja sighed; it was a weary, heavy sigh. 'By all means,' she said, lifting Marie out of the cradle. 'Tell your god. If you ever meet him.'

Alfred went through the rest of the day as though he were hovering several inches off the ground. His head was filled with a stream of excited chatter – the youngest of the voice-sisters, Alfred surmised – and because his daily chores inevitably involved being around one or other of his family members, he had to take some care not to answer back or tell her to be quiet. But as he wasn't a particularly loquacious boy at the best of times, this he managed fairly well. In fact, the hovering feeling lasted well into his first weeks and months at the village school, where he – in contrast to Johanna and Emil – very much enjoyed going every day. It was perhaps Alfred's good fortune that the previous schoolteacher – a man with a lust for humiliating and beating his pupils – had suffered a minor stroke during the summer holidays, and had now reduced his workload to teaching (and torturing) only the older children. Unfortunately for Emil and Johanna, they were now in grades four and five, and thus among the older pupils at the school. They were to suffer another two years of Herr Münzenstätter's cruelty.

But Alfred's teacher, Fräulein Walter, was kind and warm-hearted, and readily quenched her pupils' thirst for knowledge, including Alfred's. He loved school, loved the sound of chalk on blackboard, the smell of Fräulein Walter's soap when she leaned over to check his homework, the praise he garnered almost daily as a result of his good, quiet behaviour. And when the voices came to him every now and again, their sound was by now so familiar to Alfred that he no longer responded with a surprised 'What?' when one of them called his name. He had incorporated their existence into his life quite comfortably, and even came to rely on their advice when it came to choosing the best nooks and crannies in the schoolyard when he played hide-and-seek, or waiting until exactly the right moment for Fräulein Walter to turn her back so that he could perform addition using his fingers, rather than mentally. Occasionally, the voice-women used words or phrases he didn't understand, but these he merely ignored with a shrug, intuitively aware that he would grow into understanding more and more.

Sadly, this life that Alfred would gladly have lived forever wasn't to last. Over the course of the next two years, many things happened very quickly: the people elected a new leader, this leader declared himself omnipotent and proceeded to lead his people on a course of action so heinous as to shame them for many decades to come. Fritz von Markstein, Karl Werner's employer and landlord, had for a long time deplored the impotence that had characterised his country for the past fifteen years – a weakness that, in von Markstein's opinion, resulted directly and unequivocally from the forces of democracy and socialism. Naturally, he adored and applauded this new, strong, ruthless leader who promised to create the empire to end all empires, and readily signed up – like a million other Germans – for membership of the National Socialist Party. He quickly rose to *Ortsgruppenleiter*, giving him a range of powers that included the assessment of the racial and political reliability of the citizens living within his municipality.

Although she had held German citizenship since her marriage to Karl, Freyja Werner had foreign roots and was thus subject to such an assessment. One day in October 1934, she received a letter summoning her to attend a formal interview and physician's examination to ascertain her racial purity.

'This is preposterous,' Karl said, stamping his mud-caked boots at the kitchen door before entering. The children were already assembled at the table, waiting for their father to sit down to supper. 'Von Markstein knows very well who you are.'

Freyja spooned a ladleful of vegetable stew onto each child's plate and then wiped her hands on her apron. Her belly was ever so slightly swollen; none of the children had guessed yet, and Freyja and Karl had planned to tell them at Christmas. 'He's just a big bully, that's all,' she said, and winked at the children. 'There's nothing to worry about.'

But her cheerfulness was obviously a pretence. Alfred could tell from the crease between her eyebrows, and he sat there, spoon in hand, waiting for his voice-women to speak some words of comfort, as they so often did when he was feeling anxious or confused. However, unusually, none came.

'He's more than a bully,' Karl said darkly and took his seat at the head of the table. 'It's just not right. I've never liked the man, that's true, but I've always shown him respect and courtesy. So how dare he – '

'Shush now, Karl. I do not wish to discuss this at the dinner table.' Freyja sat down with Marie on her lap and turned to her oldest daughter. 'Johanna,' she said, passing her a loaf of bread, 'please cut the bread. And make sure your father's is a big slice; he's been mending fences all day. On his own. He'll have quite an appetite.'

Karl took a slice from Johanna and dipped it into his stew. 'And you know why I'm working alone, don't you?' he said. 'Because he made me get rid of Friedberg and Kaminski. Without notice, just like that. It's a disgrace.'

He ripped a chunk of bread off with his teeth, chewed noisily and swallowed. 'I don't like it, Freyja.'

'But they're Jews,' Emil said brightly, as though in sudden possession of a unique insight. 'They were probably stealing. Fritz says his mother caught their maid Elli stealing bread from the pantry. And she's a Jew. Herr Münzenstätter says you can't trust them further than you can – '

Before he could finish, Karl stood up, reached across the table and struck his son across the face. Fortunately for Emil, the table was fairly wide, which reduced the strength of Karl's blow.

'Karl!' Freyja exclaimed.

Karl had never struck any of his children before. He stood white and shaking, gripping the edge of the table. Emil held his hand to his cheek where his father had hit him. His lips were tightly pressed together, and from the way his mouth curved downwards, it was clear that he was trying very hard not to cry.

When Karl spoke, his voice was trembling. 'You will not speak that way ever again in this house, do you hear me?'

Emil nodded, but held his father's eye.

Karl looked around the table. 'None of you will ever speak that way.'

Alfred and Johanna immediately shook their heads.

'No, Papa,' Johanna said.

Alfred looked at his mother. She was staring at the left hand corner of the ceiling. From her unfocused gaze, though, Alfred realised that she was, in fact, listening. He then also opened his hearing, but there was nothing. After a few moments, Freyja looked back down at her plate and shook her head. It appeared to Alfred as though she too had waited in vain to hear the voices.

They ate the rest of the meal in silence.

A week later, early in the morning, Freyja – uncharacteristically melancholic, hugging her children every few minutes and releasing a waterfall of pet names – wrapped bread and butter sandwiches for Alfred and Emil and sent them off to school. Johanna was to remain at home to look after two-year-old Marie, while Freyja and Karl cycled to the nearby town of Löwenberg, where the interview was to take place. The route from the estate to the town was arduous: their trip took them through the forest, across fields and along ditches. It was hard cycling, but they had travelled this way many times before, dismounting to cross streams and stiles, pushing bicycles up muddy inclines, until they reached the main road. Here they were able to pick up some speed, Karl ahead of Freyja, and the strong headwind they were cycling into was also clearing the sky of clouds, so that after a few minutes of reaching the road, a plump yolk of a sun was warming their faces. Karl slowed down a little to let Freyja catch up and held out his hand.

'D'you remember?' he called out as she reached out and grabbed his hand.

'How could I forget?' she answered. It was the way they had cycled, hand-in-hand, thirteen years ago to inform Freyja's parents that Karl had proposed marriage and she had accepted.

They cycled on in silence. It was the first time they had been out alone since Marie was born two years ago, and Freyja was almost grateful for this opportunity, imposed by von Markstein, for her and Karl to feel like young lovers again. Just this once more, before the end. As they reached a curve in the road, Karl squeezed her hand to indicate that they should decelerate. They both softly engaged their pedal brakes, still holding hands. Freyja smiled at Karl, and at that very moment heard a chorus of wails inside her head so despairing it made her skin crawl, at that moment looked ahead and saw a truck coming around the bend at high speed towards them, at that moment felt the love for her children and her husband rise up to cover her like a blanket, and she died on impact with the truck, feeling blissfully happy and profoundly sad at once. Karl survived, unconscious, until his arrival at hospital, where he was pronounced dead on the grounds of severe internal bleeding and a fractured skull.

DAY ONE

It was early evening when we arrived at the hospital, some three hours after I'd first met Alfred at the train station. After a very agitated neighbour had informed us, three flights up on the way to Brynja's flat, that there had been a terrible, tragic accident and that the 'poor, poor young woman had been scraped off the pavement and taken to the nearby Vivantes Clinic', it suddenly hit me that I was momentarily responsible for a helpless, possibly confused elderly gentleman.

The taxi was still warm and waiting downstairs. We reached the hospital less than five minutes later; it was indeed just a few streets away. There was a brief moment of awkwardness between Alfred and me when I handed the driver a fifty euro note – more than enough to get me home and back – exposing my earlier statement about a lack of funds for the lie it was, but neither of us dwelled on it.

We entered the accident and emergency department though a set of sliding glass doors and were immediately beset by the visual and auditory (not to mention olfactory) disarray that is typical of any urban A&E at this time of year. But I quickly focused on the task in hand and looked around to see if there was someone who might be able to provide some information as to Brynja's whereabouts. A few hospital staff were buzzing around the place, but they were stubbornly avoiding eye contact with anyone.

Then Alfred spoke. 'I know. I heard you the first time.'

'Pardon me?' I said.

'Yes, that's quite obvious, even to an aged fool like me,' he continued.

I looked at Alfred; there were people milling about either side of him, but he didn't seem to be addressing any of them, nor me. Instead, he was gazing, slightly unfocused, into the middle distance.

'Are you all right, Alfred?' I asked.

He blinked rapidly. 'What? Yes, quite.' Then he seemed to notice my expression. 'Oh goodness, have I been talking out loud?'

I laid a hand on his arm. The place seemed to be getting noisier by the minute. 'Listen, would you like to sit down for a moment? I can try and find out about your granddaughter's whereabouts and then come and fetch you.'

Alfred placed his hand on top of mine, gave it a gentle squeeze and shook his head. 'No, I am perfectly fine,' he said. 'But this is not where we will find Brynja. She is on the second floor, in the intensive care unit.'

I paused, trying to recall the conversation with Brynja's neighbour, thinking I had perhaps missed this piece of information, but drew a blank. The neighbour had only mentioned the hospital, not any specific department.

'Well, perhaps I should ask someone anyway,' I said and set off towards the long queue at the admissions desk. But Alfred didn't follow me.

'No, no. She's upstairs,' he said, and then turned and walked off towards the lifts. I had no choice but to go after him. The lift door opened onto a corridor leading to the ICU. A nurse was sitting on guard behind a counter, stapling small piles of paper together in a very self-important manner.

'Yes?' she asked without looking up from her stapling as Alfred and I approached.

'We're looking for a young woman,' I said. 'She was brought here after an accident. Brynja ... ' I looked to Alfred, realising that I didn't know her last name.

'Warner,' Alfred said. 'Same as mine.'

The nurse looked up at me. 'And are you a relative?'

I shot a glance at Alfred. 'No. I ... I'm a friend of the family.'

'Yes, Julia is a friend of the family,' Alfred repeated. 'I'm Brynja's grandfather, Alfred Warner. We would like to see Brynja, please.'

It was the first time I'd heard Alfred speaking more than a single word in German (the conversation with Brynja's neighbour had been pretty much a one-sided outburst on her part), and I was surprised by his fluency. It hadn't occurred to me that he might be German.

'Very well,' the nurse said, 'please wait here. I'll have to call ahead. They can't just be letting random people into ICU.'

She typed something into her computer and then picked up the telephone.

'Come on, Alfred,' I said as she began a muted conversation, which I wasn't sure was actually related to Alfred and me wanting to visit a patient on the ICU. 'Let's take a seat over there.'

I pointed to a row of chairs lined up against a wall. The old man looked exhausted. I checked my watch. It was quarter to seven.

'Shall I get us something to eat?' I asked. 'Perhaps a snack from the vending machine?'

Alfred sat down and seemed to collapse into himself; his head sunk into his neck and his upper body appeared to shrink. He looked very young and very old all at once. With his head down, he glanced from side to side as though scanning the floor for an answer.

'Wait here,' I said, before he had found one. 'I'll be back in no time.'

It took me less than ten minutes to find the canteen, buy us a couple of sandwiches and two bottles of water and get back to the ICU waiting area. Alfred was sitting as I had left him, staring down at the linoleum. It struck me that perhaps he hadn't even noticed my absence.

I took a seat next to him. 'Here,' I said, handing him a sandwich.

Alfred took it from me and unwrapped it silently. He held it in his lap for a minute or two and then said, 'I've never even met her.'

His voice was soft and apologetic, and he looked sorely in need of a hug. But suddenly, the guardian of the ICU was upon us to admonish us for eating in an area that was labelled 'NO FOOD OR DRINK. NO SMOKING. NO USE OF MOBILE PHONES' somewhere at the far end of the corridor, and also to tell us that we may enter ICU once we had disposed of said food and drink.

It was an effort for Alfred to keep up with the swift pace of the nurse who led us to Brynja's cubicle. She left us with a few curt, clipped instructions not to touch anything, including the patient, until the doctor had been in to see us. Brynja looked dreadful. She was lying on the bed, which was angled up to prop her up slightly on her back in order to facilitate breathing – so the ICU doctor later told us – should her lungs decide to start working again without the help of the ventilator. The tube coming out of her mouth was pulling the corners of her mouth downwards, so that she looked as though she were on the verge of crying. There was a whitish bandage wrapped around her head and her eyes were large, purplish bruises.

So there we were, standing in the cubicle, not daring to sit down or even lean up against the wall. For a long while, Alfred just stood there, gazing down at Brynja. Then, disobeying the nurse's instructions, he took Brynja's limp hand in his, and placed a trembling index finger on her forehead, ever so gently, just below the bandage.

'I hear them too,' he said softly.

Two Thousand and Three

Yeah, no. You know what I mean. He's a real – You're interrupted, laugh into the phone. A full laugh, the kind your mom likes. When you were little, you'd make her laugh by mimicking the newsreaders on TV, you had a real talent for caricature, your mother said. The voice on the other end of the line is clear, human, real. Ayla. Your new best friend from work. You're holding a conversation like it's the easiest thing in the world. Which it is.

$$C_{17}H_{19}C_1N_2S$$

You've looked it up – in your bloodstream, blocking dopamine receptors, making you feel . . . just *grand*, thank you very much! Eight years of trying and now they think they've found the right medication. The one to kill the voices without killing you. You must be fucking kidding me, Ayla, you say. Your friend is in hysterics.

On your way to see your mother for a coffee before your shift starts at the community centre. Never thought you'd manage to hold a job down, especially not teaching art, but it's been four months now, and everyone seems pleased with you. You don't care that it's only misfits working there, people like you, who are too damaged to do much else. But that's what qualifies them, says Gregor, the team leader. That's what qualifies the alkies, the junkies, the schizos, the wife beaters and beaten wives. Ayla's a victim of child abuse. No, scrap that. She's a *survivor* of child abuse. Big difference.

You turn the corner onto Karl-Marx-Straße. Last night's rain has washed the street clean. The cobblestones are dark grey and shiny, reminding you of the dolphins you saw when you went to SeaWorld with your mother, Sabine. How many years ago? At least ten. Sabine moaning and bitching about animal rights the whole way through the show, embarrassing you beyond belief. Waving her tanned arms around, bangles jingling, dreadlocks (white woman dreadlocks!!! You still feel a stab of shame in your gut thinking about it now, ten years later) swinging around her angry face. Cut it out, Mom!

On Karl-Marx-Straße at eight in the morning. Poor but sexy. A couple of punks sit on a bench, waiting to scrounge a cigarette from the next smoker passing by. The Turkish greengrocer on the corner sloshes a bucket of water across the pavement to clear away the dog shit. Two children with enormous satchels on their backs scurry past like white rabbits, late late late for school. A Roma woman, kneeling with a cardboard begging sign. A *Späti*, a tattoo parlour, both unlit, still too early in the day. Maybe you'll get a tattoo? Hey, Ayla, d'you think I should get a tattoo? Step: springy. Heart rate: normal. Life: good. Better than it's been in a long while. But what's this? You stall. Something wrong with the scene in front of you. Can't place it immediately. Bye, Ayla, see you later. You say it or think you say it, and switch off your phone and pick up your pace. Yeah, the new meds are good, but there's still that split-second reaction delay before everything

—slides

—into

—place.

Before all senses are aligned to make sense of the pungent smell, the bright red truck, the bell ringing, people shouting. Blue lights flashing noiselessly. Take a deep breath.

Sorry, you can't come past here. One of the fire-fighters puts his arm out, holds up his gloved hand, palm facing you. Stay behind the cordon, he says. You look up. The blackest smoke pours from a small window on the second floor. So dense it pours out like liquid. The kitchen window; your mom's kitchen, where right now, your mom should be sitting with a hangover and a roll-up and a cup of coffee, #1 MOM!, chipped but cherished, a gift for Mother's Day nineteen eighty-nine. Let me through, you yell, my mother lives there! There! You point to the window.

Wait here, the firefighter says and turns to talk to one of his colleagues. And then one appears from inside the building, appears from a cloud of smoke like some magician, wearing full protective gear and breathing apparatus – no, not a magician, a Martian disembarking from the mother ship. You suddenly want to cry, but the meds have dried you up. The Martian is carrying a body. Covered in a blanket or sheet, drawn up to the face. Unambiguous gesture. One arm hangs loose. The skin is red-raw and black.

1934

Up until the day his parents were killed, Alfred had had
very little contact with Fritz von Markstein. This was
primarily due to von Markstein's open dislike of children, and accordingly, Karl and Freyja Werner had kept
theirs well out of sight on the rare occasions whenever
von Markstein visited their cottage. When he came, it
was usually to show off to Karl some new agricultural
technology he'd purchased or read about – the wonders
of commercial fertiliser, or the fanciful idea of artificially
inseminating dairy cows – and was more often drunk
than not. The few times Alfred had seen him, he had
reminded him uncomfortably of the tailor in Emil's
favourite storybook, *Struwwelpeter*. However, when he
came to visit the cottage on the evening of Karl and
Freyja's death, von Markstein was perfectly sober.

Emil and Alfred had been brought home earlier that
afternoon – mute and uncomprehending – by the local
police constable. They were greeted at the cottage by a
local villager, Frau Kühnel, who had been called on to

look after Johanna and Marie until the youth welfare authorities had been informed of the children's sudden status as orphans. Childless herself, Frau Kühnel had only the vaguest of ideas of how to handle the children, especially under such exceptional circumstances, and so she clucked and fussed around them, insisting they eat the stodgy porridge she cooked for them, although not one of them – not even Marie, who refused to leave Johanna's lap – had the stomach for it. They sat pale and wordless around the kitchen table, while Frau Kühnel circled the table behind them, wringing her hands.

'You poor children. Oh goodness, look at you. Oh little Alfred,' she stopped behind the boy and awkwardly ruffled his hair, 'and Marie! Poor little Marie!'

Alfred stared down at his bowl of cold porridge. He felt numb. And frightened, the way he used to feel when he was younger and woke in the night-time to a bad dream, awake in the dark and yet still trapped inside the nightmare, before he had the voice-women to comfort and soothe him. Since they arrived, he'd never feared the dark because they were always there with him. But now, years before he learned to call them, it seemed as though they'd deserted him, and he felt unbearably lonely.

Suddenly, Frau Kühnel made a grab for Marie, who was grizzling quietly on Johanna's lap. 'Let me have the poor baby,' she said. 'She's cold – look, she has goose bumps on her legs.'

Johanna twisted the child out of Frau Kühnel's reach. 'No! Leave her alone. She belongs with me.'

Frau Kühnel looked at first shocked, and then indignant. She wasn't used to dealing with children, and certainly not with disobedient ones. 'Give the child to me at once! She does not belong with you, you silly girl.'

Johanna jumped to her feet, struggling to keep her balance with Marie in her arms. 'Leave us alone, you horrible woman!'

Frau Kühnel pulled her arm back to strike Johanna, but Emil was quicker. He was almost as tall as his father, though with the gangliness of a thirteen-year-old, and he caught Frau Kühnel's arm by the sleeve.

'Please,' he said, 'she didn't mean it.'

Frau Kühnel pulled her sleeve from his grip and shook her head, and then Emil took Marie from his sister's arms and handed her to Frau Kühnel. Johanna let herself fall back onto her chair, weeping loudly. Through the commotion, Alfred heard a voice.

Alfred, you must eat something. You must keep up your strength.

It was barely above a whisper, but he heard it clearly. His heart began thumping in his chest and he had to suppress the urge to respond aloud. He waited, hardly daring to breathe, terrified he would hear nothing more, but then

Oh little one. So sad and lonely. Please don't despair, the pain will pass, I promise.

This was more than Alfred could take. He started to cry, setting off Marie in the process. Indeed, the room was so full of sniffles and weeping, as well as an angry and overwhelmed Frau Kühnel, that nobody heard the car pull up outside the cottage.

Von Markstein entered without knocking.

'Heil Hitler!' he said, and the room fell silent. He took

a few steps forward and removed his cap. 'My condolences.'

Frau Kühnel placed Marie on the floor and put her hands to her hair, pinning back a few strands that had come loose in the commotion. 'Herr von Markstein,' she said, in a slightly breathless voice. 'It's good of you to ...'

Von Markstein held up a hand and she fell silent. He glanced quickly around the room, while everyone waited for him to speak. Alfred had never seen him up close in his uniform. He recognised the boots; the ones his mother had cleaned, leaving her fingers stained with black shoe polish.

Von Markstein pointed at Emil. 'You, what's your name?'

'Emil.' His voice was strained but polite.

'Age?'

'I'll be fourteen in March.'

Von Markstein gave a clipped nod. Then he turned to Frau Kühnel. 'And the girl?' he asked.

'Which one?' Frau Kühnel asked nervously.

Von Markstein tipped his head in Johanna's direction without taking his eyes off Frau Kühnel.

'Do you mean me?' Johanna asked, an unmistakeable note of defiance in her voice. 'My name is Johanna.'

Von Markstein turned his head slowly to look at her. At twelve years of age, Johanna Werner was already quite beautiful, despite her red and puffy eyes. She had her mother's fair skin and her father's dark hair and straight back, and was assumed by many to be older by three or four years.

'The girl's apron is filthy,' von Markstein said. 'Make sure she's cleaned up before she comes to the house.'

Then he clicked his heels together and raised his right forearm. 'Heil Hitler.' He strode across the room and out of the front door.

'Heil Hitler,' Frau Kühnel echoed, and then turned to the children and shrugged. 'Then I suppose we'd better get all of you washed if you're to go up to the house. Not that I should be responsible. I'm not his skivvy,' she added, quietly.

Nevertheless, she heated a large pan of water in the kitchen, got Emil to carry the tin bath to the living room, and began washing the children, youngest first, in front of the fire. When they were all sufficiently clean (Johanna and Emil insisted on washing themselves), Frau Kühnel lit the petroleum lamps and cooked some fresh porridge. She ordered the children back to the table. None of their appetites had increased much, but Alfred did as the voice had earlier instructed and managed to eat a few spoonfuls. It was thick and lumpy, and very sweet. It was an effort to swallow. Just then, a pair of car headlights swept the room, and a minute later, there was a loud knock at the door.

'Oh look,' Frau Kühnel said. 'He's come to fetch you in the car. You are a lucky lot.' She attempted a smile and then went to the front door and opened it. But it wasn't von Markstein. Instead, a young man, well over six feet tall and with huge square shoulders, stepped in.

'Anno Schmidt,' he said. 'Youth welfare. I've come for the children.'

Frau Kühnel frowned, looked at the children and then back at the man. 'But Herr von Markstein is ... '

The man cut her off. 'He's taking the older two. A boy – ' he took a sheet of folded paper out of his jacket pocket,

'Emil Werner, and a girl, Johanna. The young ones are coming with me. I'm to take them to the orphanage in Tempelhof.'

'But . . . ' Frau Kühnel was shaking her head. 'But that's in Berlin.'

The man nodded.

'But Herr von Markstein said . . . ' she trailed off.

Johanna and Emil got to their feet and went to stand behind Frau Kühnel.

'What's going on?' Johanna asked.

The man shrugged. 'All I know is that a call was made to the youth welfare office, putting in an adoption application for Emil and Johanna Werner.'

'But von Markstein has no wife!' Frau Kühnel's voice was raised.

'I reckon *Ortsgruppenleiter* von Markstein doesn't need a wife in order to adopt. Also, without children, he has no heir.' He rubbed his chin. 'That's what I reckon, anyway.'

Frau Kühnel narrowed her eyes. 'Do you have any identification?'

The man reached inside his jacket and presented his papers. Then he handed her another document. 'My orders,' he said.

Frau Kühnel inspected all the papers and sighed. She turned to the children.

'Well,' she said. 'I don't know what to say. But if the man says he is to take you, then you must go.'

Johanna folded her arms across her chest. 'If the little ones go, we all go,' she said. Then she rushed to the table and took Marie from her chair, holding her tight and away from Frau Kühnel. 'She's not going anywhere without me.'

'Don't be silly, girl,' the man said, moving forwards. Johanna took several steps backwards until she was standing with her back to the wall.

The man shook his head. 'Talk some sense into her, will you?' he said, addressing Frau Kühnel. 'I don't want to have to use force.'

'Emil, help me,' Johanna cried. 'They can't do this. They can't!'

Emil remained where he was standing, white-faced. 'It's no use, Johanna,' he said, his voice cracking. 'Just do as they say.'

But Johanna pressed her lips together and held Marie even tighter, so tight that the child began to cry. 'Mama!' she wailed, over and over again. 'Mama! Mama!'

'Right,' the man said, 'I'm sorry, but orders are orders. Take it up with von Markstein if you want.' He walked over to Johanna, his boots thumping loudly on the wooden floor, and began to wrestle the child from her arms. After a moment's hesitation, Frau Kühnel joined him, and between them they managed to get hold of Marie, who by now was screaming at the top of her lungs. The man took her and pressed her head gently to his chest.

'Shhh, baby girl,' he said, with a tenderness that seemed at odds with his huge physique. 'It's all right, shhh.'

Marie's screams turned into a quiet whimpering.

'Now, Alfred,' Frau Kühnel said, turning to the boy. 'You go with Herr Schmidt. It's no use protesting. The man has official orders.'

Alfred sat motionless at the table, still clutching his spoon, willing with all his might that this be nothing but a bad dream. Then the voice-women came back.

Don't worry, little one.

Go with the man. He will take care of you.

'But I don't want to!' Alfred said out loud.

Johanna walked over to him and cupped his face with her hands. 'Don't worry, Alfred,' she said. Her voice was shaking. 'I'll speak with von Markstein. I'll make him let us join you. Just you wait. We'll be together in a couple of days.'

The man opened the front door. 'You can send any of their belongings to the orphanage,' he told Frau Kühnel, before ushering Alfred out of the cottage and into the waiting car.

The journey to Berlin led them through the dark countryside. There was a fine rain falling from the sky, and the wipers squeaked noisily across the windshield. Alfred sat huddled with Marie on the back seat of the car, dizzy with shock, while Anno Schmidt drove silently. Only once, shortly after they had set off, did he turn to them and speak.

'I'm sorry for your loss,' he said quietly. Then he took a small parcel from the passenger seat and handed it to Alfred.

'Here. Eat something. And make sure the little girl eats, too.'

Alfred mumbled his thanks and unwrapped the parcel. It contained two meat sandwiches. He gave one to Marie and realised only when he brought the bread to his lips how ravenous he was. Marie gnawed on the hard crust for a while, but then became overwhelmed by tiredness and put her head on Alfred's lap, falling asleep in an instant. Alfred took the remains of her sandwich and ate this as well. Then he lay his head back on his seat and closed his eyes. Before long, the sound and vibration of the engine mingled with the sound of singing coming from his left, close by and hushed, as though she were singing directly into his ear:

> *Sofðu unga ástin mín,*
> *Úti regnið grætur.*
> *Mamma geymir gullin þín,*
> *gamla leggi og völuskrín.*
> *Við skulum ekki vaka um dimmar nætur.*

It was a lullaby he recognised from his mother. He felt the tears gather behind his eyes and let them come silently, let them roll down his face, to hang quivering on his chin for a moment before they landed on his coat. Soon enough, he was asleep, too.

He woke with a start when the engine was switched off. He rubbed his eyes and felt the heavy warmth from Marie's head on his lap. Anno Schmidt opened the car door on the opposite side and, pressing his fingers to his lips, gently slid Marie out and into his arms. The little girl stirred but didn't wake. Then he gestured for Alfred to get out.

The night was sharp and cold. The first thing Alfred noticed was the smell of smoke that hung in the air all around. He had never been to the city before. The street was quiet and dark, save for the yellow light given off by the hissing gas lamps that lined the pavements. Several of the buildings were adorned with awnings of red-and-white flags, like party decorations, rising and falling in the chilly breeze.

Anno Schmidt, carrying Marie in his arms, began to walk towards the huge red-brick building they had parked in front of. It was four storeys tall and wider than any building Alfred had ever seen. There were no lights on. Schmidt climbed the stone steps to the front door and rang the bell. After a few moments, the door opened and a woman appeared. She nodded at Schmidt and guided them inside, closing the door before switching on a small lamp that stood on a table near the door. Alfred could detect a strong odour of urine and disinfectant.

'I've been waiting an hour,' the woman said. Her eyes twitched as she spoke, and she sounded angry. Her black hair was scraped back into a bun, revealing a very white section of scalp. Alfred took a step closer to Schmidt. Then the woman turned to the wall, where Alfred saw three rows of wooden handles attached to brown cords. She tugged on one and turned back to Schmidt.

'The nurse will have to check them first,' she said.

'Can't that wait until morning?' Schmidt said, keeping his voice low. 'They're exhausted.'

'I'm not having them sleeping in my nice clean beds if they're full of lice,' she said. 'They will be checked first.'

Alfred heard footsteps coming from a dark hallway that led off the entrance area. A stout woman dressed in a white uniform appeared. She ruffled Alfred's hair and winked at him.

'The girl first,' the woman said to her. 'Then she can be put straight to bed.'

'Very well,' the nurse said and held her arms out for Marie. Marie let out a soft murmur when Schmidt handed her over, but remained asleep. The nurse retreated to where she had come from with the little girl slumped against her plump breast. It was the last time Alfred was ever to see Marie.

The woman turned to him. 'You sit over there and wait,' she said, pointing to a chair in the corner. Alfred obeyed wordlessly. He was dreadfully tired. The woman and Schmidt disappeared into a side room, leaving the door slightly ajar. He could hear them talking, but couldn't make out any words. His lids slid over his eyes.

Don't fall asleep just yet, my dear.

The voice was hushed.

Alfred. Open your eyes.

Alfred didn't want to open his eyes. They seemed glued shut, too heavy to open.

Come on, Alfred. Wake up.

The voice was joined by another: *Yes, wakey-wakey. Not the time to sleep now. Wake up.*

'Leave me alone,' Alfred mumbled.

Come on, wake up!

Keep your wits about you, boy!

'No. I'm tired. Leave me alone.' He screwed his eyes tighter shut. 'I want to sleep.'

Alfred, you –

'No! I want to sleep!' Alfred opened his eyes and immediately felt his heart jump into his throat. The woman and Schmidt had come out of the room without making a sound and were now standing in front of him.

'Who are you talking to?' the woman demanded.

Alfred shook his head. He felt sick. 'No one,' he whispered.

'You were talking to someone,' she said. 'We heard you. I repeat: who were you talking to?'

Schmidt turned to the woman. 'Leave him be,' he said.

'That's where we're going now. I have no idea if they'll take you. You don't exactly look … well, I don't suppose that matters. But it's all I can think of to do. And he's a good man, Heinz. You can't believe what you hear about the Jews. My Magda's a fine girl. And so are her parents.'

He lapsed into silence, while Alfred recalled what Emil had said about Jews that day at the dinner table. About not being able to throw them very far, or something. He yawned. All he wanted to do now was sleep. And tomorrow – tomorrow Johanna would come and find him and Marie and take them home.

A short while later, Schmidt slowed the car and they came to a halt.

'We're here,' he said, although it sounded more like a question than a statement.

Alfred climbed out of his side of the car. The building in front of him was separated from the pavement by a wrought-iron gate. Alfred looked up at the building, which was the largest on the street as far as he could tell. To the left of the entrance, a leafless poplar tree reached up to the second-storey windows, which were all framed by Juliet balconies with boxes of geraniums. At the very top, just beneath a curved section of roof, he read the inscription:

II. Waisenhaus
Der Jüdischen Gemeinde
✸✸✸ In Berlin ✸✸✸
Erbaut im Jahre 1912-13.

Schmidt rang the bell beside the gate.

'I hope someone is awake,' he said, rubbing the side

of his face. They waited for a long while, Schmidt shifting his weight from one foot to the other to keep them warm, or perhaps with nerves. Finally, a light came on in a downstairs window. A minute later, the door opened and a man peered out.

'Who's there?' he called.

'We're in luck,' Schmidt said to Alfred, and then called back, 'Heinz. It's me. Anno.'

The door opened more widely and the man stepped out. He hesitated momentarily, squinting in Alfred and Schmidt's direction, and then hurried down a set of stone steps and unlocked the gate.

'Come in, come in,' he said, and added, 'you can't be too careful these days.'

The men embraced briefly.

'I've brought you something,' Schmidt said and nodded in Alfred's direction. Nadel glanced at Alfred, frowning, and then led them inside.

'It's very late,' he said to Schmidt, once they'd taken off their coats.

'I'm sorry,' Schmidt said, 'it's a bit of an emergency.' And he explained the situation to Nadel, while Alfred looked around. In front of him, a large stone stairwell curved up and to the left; to his right, a spacious corridor was dimly lit by four lamps that hung on chains from a high vaulted ceiling. There were two double doors; one marked SPEISESAAL, the other marked BIBLIOTHEK. Apart from Schmidt and Nadel's hushed conversation, the place was eerily silent.

'I can't say that I like it,' Nadel said finally. 'The situation is fragile enough already. As you well know, Anno.'

'I know, Heinz.' Schmidt sighed. 'But what should I

do with him? I can't take the poor lad to the asylum. If he's not an idiot, that would certainly make him one.'

Nadel looked down at Alfred. Then he took off his round glasses and rubbed the top of his nose. 'Very well, Anno,' he said in a tired voice, 'I suppose there's no harm in giving him a bed for the night. He looks exhausted. But in the morning, I'll have to take it up with the director. This is not my decision to make.'

Schmidt smiled and took Nadel's hand in his, shaking it warmly. 'Thank you Heinz.' Then he put his coat back on and turned to Alfred. 'All right, little man. I'll be off now. You're in good hands. Just make sure to do as you're told. Wash your hands before dinner and go to bed without a fuss.' Then he took Alfred into his arms and hugged him. 'Be a good boy, Alfred, and no harm will come to you.'

The front door closed softly behind him, and moments later, Alfred heard the metallic clunk of the front gate opening and closing outside. Nadel stretched out his hand.

'Heinz Nadel,' he said.

Alfred took his hand and shook it. 'Alfred Werner.'

'Well, Alfred Werner, I suppose we'd better find you a bed.'

DAY TWO

That night, I lay in bed unable to sleep. Although I had closed my bedroom door, I could hear Alfred's snoring coming from the living room. I wasn't used to such close company, and it made me feel oddly claustrophobic. I'd only been living on my own for two months, since my father died, but I had got used to it surprisingly quickly.

Just the thought of an extra body emanating warmth inside the small flat made me uncomfortably hot. I kicked the sheets off me and felt chilly instantly. So I slipped back underneath the sheets and turned onto my other side. I felt hot again. Finally, I sat up and checked the time. Five thirty. It was still completely dark outside, but I had to accept that the chances of me getting any sleep were approaching zero, and so I decided to call it a night and get up. Very quietly, I slipped into the living room, not wanting to wake Alfred until I'd had a chance to look through his belongings. I wasn't being nosey, but given the circumstances, I thought it might be a good idea to try and find somebody to get in contact with, some family member or something. In the light coming in from the hallway, I could make out Alfred's sleeping shape on the couch. He was wearing a pair of blue flannel pyjamas.

I looked around and spotted his jacket hanging on the back of a chair. I tiptoed over and patted down the pockets. The right pocket was empty. There was something soft in the left pocket, but assuming this was most likely a handkerchief – not a disposable tissue, but rather one of those elderly gentleman's fabric handkerchiefs, the kind my dad insisted on using despite my hygiene objections – I restrained from putting my hand inside the pocket to find out. The only pocket remaining was on the inside left, and indeed, here I struck lucky: a letter from Brynja addressed to Alfred.

I went straight back to the bedroom, where I switched on my laptop, accessed the Internet and, trying not to feel too guilty about prying into his private affairs, typed in: Gladstone Court Residential Care Home, Franklin Road, Stoke-on-Trent. Listening out for the rhythmic asthmatic rasp of Alfred's snoring, I dialled the number shown on the screen. Ring-ring, ring-ring, ring-ring. I was about to give up, remembering only then that England was an hour behind, making it shortly before five there and thus unlikely that anyone would be awake to answer the phone, when I heard a very sleepy, 'Mmm? Hello?'

'Oh, hello. Good morning. Sorry if I've woken you,' I said. 'Is this the Gladstone Court Care Home in Stoke-on-Trent?'

'Yes. Is this an emergency?'

'Um, no. Not really.'

'In that case, do you realise what time it is?'

'Yes,' I said. 'I'm very sorry if I've woken you. It's just

that I'm calling from outside the UK and I'd forgotten about the time difference.'

'You haven't woken me, madam,' the woman replied. 'At Gladstone we provide round-the-clock quality care for our residents, which means that there is a member of staff on duty at all times.'

'That's good to know,' I said, keeping my voice friendly, although her tone reminded me of why I hadn't put my own father into a nursing home. 'And actually, I am calling about one of your residents. Alfred Warner.'

There was a short pause on the other end.

Then: 'Are you German?'

'Yes.'

'Mm. I thought I detected an accent. Then you must be Alfred's granddaughter. To be honest, I was never entirely sure he would actually manage to find you. He seems a little ... confused at times.'

'Oh, that's ...'

She interrupted me. 'Yes. Well, you know, we don't like to use the word "demented", although between you and me, what's wrong with calling a spade a spade? It's not as if it makes any difference. Certainly not to them.' She sighed. 'But nobody ever asks me.'

'Excuse me, Ms ...'

'Clarke. Jocelyn Clarke. And to be honest, Ms Warner, although Alfred isn't the worst I've seen, well, he does upset the other ones, sometimes. Now I know this is something that should be discussed in person, face to face as it were, but seeing as you're the only relative he's ever mentioned, and you're not exactly a frequent visitor, are you?'

'Ms Clarke ...'

'Yes, well, as I was saying. When Alfred gets back – and when is that exactly, anyway? He was in such a rush to get off, he didn't fill in the away schedule properly. And that's *precisely* what I mean, he just refuses to do as he's told sometimes.'

'Ms Clarke, I just . . .'

'I mean, a lot of them talk to themselves, that's quite normal, but Alfred . . . he just refuses to stop, you know? And it's not just a quiet mumble, he's having whole conversations – in his room, in the common room, at dinner – and it's upsetting people. To put it bluntly, Ms Warner, your grandfather's going to have to leave if he continues with this non-compliant behaviour. It's all written down in our General Terms and Conditions, if you care to look. We have a three-strikes-and-you're-out policy, and I'm sorry to have to say this, but Alfred's coming close to his third.'

The next words that came out of my mouth took me by surprise: 'Well in that case, you stupid woman, consider *this* his third!' And I cut her off, at the same time horrified at what I'd just done. I could feel my pulse racing; in fact, I was close to tears. Then I heard a voice behind me.

'I'm not going back, you know.'

My heart bounced up into my throat and down again. I almost dropped the phone with the fright, and turned around to see Alfred standing at the door, still wearing his blue flannel pyjamas.

'Jesus!' I blurted out. 'You nearly gave me a heart attack!'

'Sorry,' he said, and then added, 'I don't mean what I said in a petulant way. I'm not being difficult. It's just . . . I'm not going back, that's all.'

I put the phone down on the table and walked over to him.

'Listen Alfred.' I placed a hand on his arm. The flannel was very soft to the touch. 'I'm sorry. I – I thought . . . oh, I don't know what I was thinking.' And I felt suddenly awful; he probably didn't have enough money for a hotel, and even then, there was no way of knowing how long his granddaughter would be in a coma. He nodded, or perhaps his head was wobbling involuntarily.

Then he said, 'Yes, I know. I was just about to mention it. You treat me like a child sometimes. It's quite infuriating.'

'Pardon?' I dropped my hand from his arm, irritated by his remark and the sulky tone with which he'd said it. But he immediately took my hand in his warm, papery hand and squeezed it.

'Oh no,' he said. 'I didn't mean you. I was . . . ' He let my hand go and shook his head. 'Never mind. I was going to say that I understand. Your hospitality and care have been remarkable. Thank you indeed. And Christmas is here, and you will surely have other things, other people . . . ' He trailed off.

We stood in awkward silence. Finally, I said, 'Well, perhaps we can sort out a hotel? I'm not sure it'll be easy to find something, but . . . ' I stopped when I saw his expression. He looked utterly forlorn.

'I'm such an old fool,' he said. 'What was I thinking? It didn't occur to me for a moment that Brynja . . . well, I should have anticipated something like this.'

I let out a long sigh. I'll confess that I wasn't ready for this yet, not by a long shot, not so soon after my father. But what choice did I have? I put my hand on his arm again.

'It's all right, Alfred. You're welcome to stay here for another day or two. I'm sure the hospital will have some more concrete information about your granddaughter soon, and then we'll work something out. In the meantime, is there anyone else I should contact, any other family members?'

'No,' he said. 'I've nobody else.'

1934 – 1938

Alfred never did find out what was discussed by Nadel and the director on the morning after he arrived at the orphanage. He was never to discover whether Nadel argued emphatically that the asylum was no alternative (Nadel was, Alfred learned later, an emphatic kind of man with a busy, energetic mind and the strongest courage in his convictions), or whether both men decided quickly to adopt Alfred as one of their own, or whether there had been a protracted debate regarding the dangers of taking an eight-year-old German boy into a Jewish orphanage. But whatever the contents of their discussion, the outcome was that Alfred was to spend the next four years there, in a place so very different from the life he'd known so far.

He was roused the next morning by the clanging of a hand bell, and the sound of twelve boys yawning and clambering out of their beds. The dormitory he had been assigned to the night before was more spacious than it had looked in the dark, when he had climbed into bed with limbs and soul aching from grief and exhaustion. When he woke, he lay quietly in his bed, watching the other boys getting dressed and making their beds, hoping they wouldn't notice him. He felt suddenly overwhelmed and out of place, but it didn't take long before he was spotted. A small group of boys formed in the centre of the room, staring and whispering. Alfred sat up, half expecting them to start pointing and shouting, feeling acutely vulnerable in nothing but his underwear and wondering where Nadel had put his clothes the night before. But then his empty stomach let out a growl so loud and ferocious that the boys started laughing. One of them, a lanky boy several years older than Alfred, stepped out of the group.

'Fritz Rosenberg,' he said. 'I'm head of the dormitory.'

Alfred sat up straighter. 'Alfred Werner.'

'Breakfast is at seven,' Fritz said. 'Did you get here last night?'

Alfred nodded.

'Half or full?'

'What?'

'Are both your parents dead or just one?'

Alfred swallowed. 'Both,' he said quietly.

'Like Salomon over there,' Fritz said, nodding his head in the direction of a boy still in the process of smoothing his blanket down.

'Hello,' Salomon called.

'And this is Walter,' Fritz continued, nudging a boy on his left with his elbow. 'Him, Robert, Simon, Hans, little David and big David and me – all still got their fathers. Bert, Horst, Siegfried, Aaron and Günter, well, they're the mummies' boys.' He laughed, but not unkindly.

Alfred got out of bed and looked around for his clothes.

'They'll have taken them to the laundry room,' Fritz said, noticing. 'Just in case. To boil the lice out. Hey Salomon, you're about the same size. Let him have some clothes.'

Alfred gratefully accepted a shirt and a pair of shorts from Salomon, quickly dressed and then followed the boys downstairs to the breakfast hall. Nobody spoke to him at breakfast, which suited him perfectly, because he was hungrier than he had ever felt before and ate until he thought his stomach would burst. He had, of course, heard many tales about the Jews, and he glanced around surreptitiously, looking for some sign or mark of difference among the other children there, but they all looked perfectly normal to him. Then, just as he lifted a third glass of milk to his lips, a hand tapped him on the shoulder. It was Nadel.

'Finish eating, Alfred, and then come with me,' he said softly.

Alfred swallowed hurriedly and got to his feet.

'This way.' Nadel led the way out of the dinner hall, through the hallway Alfred recognised from his arrival, and into a small room at the back of the building. A young woman sitting behind a desk rose as they entered.

'Is this the boy, Heinz?' She smiled at Alfred.

'The very one,' Nadel answered.

'Hello, Alfred,' she said, coming around the desk and holding out her hand. She had raven-black hair and strikingly blue eyes. 'I'm Fräulein Merz. I'm the girls' housemother and also resident nurse. I just want to examine you quickly to make sure you're healthy.'

Alfred shook her hand. Her skin was warm and smooth.

'Please sit down,' she said and gestured towards a chair. Nadel remained standing near the door.

'So, Alfred,' she said. 'How do you feel?'

Alfred glanced at Nadel, who nodded. 'Fine, thank you,' Alfred said.

'Good.' She picked up a stethoscope from the desk. 'Now, I'll have a quick listen to your heart and lungs, make sure everything's as it should be. Lift your shirt for me, please.' She smiled. 'Might be a bit cold.'

Alfred sat perfectly still as she gently placed the stethoscope first on his chest, then on his back, and then looked in his ears and mouth. Finally, she straightened up. 'Would you mind undressing for me, Alfred? Just a quick look and then I'll let you go.'

Alfred did as he was told. But when he dropped his pants, Fräulein Merz let out a small gasp of astonishment. 'But the boy . . . ' she said, turning to Nadel, 'the boy has no foreskin!'

Nadel took a step forward for a closer look. Alfred felt himself blushing and had to fight the temptation to place both hands over his genitals.

'I thought you said he was *goyim*,' she continued.

'He is,' Nadel said frowning.

Alfred felt a small twinge of panic, as if he had been caught out, though he had no idea for what.

Phimosis.

He didn't understand. 'What?' he asked out loud.

'Anno Schmidt told me that you weren't Jewish,' Nadel said, adding to Alfred's confusion.

Phimosis. Go on, just say it.

94

You were only three at the time, Alfred. You couldn't possibly remember. But just say the word.

'Phimosis?' Alfred said hesitantly, adding in a small voice, 'I was only three.'

'Ah,' Fräulein Merz said. 'Well, that would explain it.' Turning to Nadel, she said, 'A too-tight foreskin. He must have had it removed.'

Nadel shrugged. 'It's good, I suppose. He won't stand out from the others. And . . . ' he added after a slight pause, 'if he ever does decide to become a Jew, he has a head start.' He chuckled.

Fräulein Merz blew out a thin stream of air. 'It's still an awful risk, Heinz.'

'I know. But it's been decided.'

He waited for Alfred to get dressed again. When they were back in the hallway, he turned to Alfred. 'We have decided that you may stay with us. At least for the time being.' He paused as a group of girls skipped past, laughing and chattering when they spotted Alfred. 'But your stay here is subject to certain conditions.'

Alfred looked down at his shoes. He urgently wanted to tell Nadel about Emil and Johanna, about the fact that some sort of mistake had been made and that his brother and sister were bound to be searching for him.

'Look at me, boy.' He cupped Alfred's chin and raised his head. 'These are dangerous times. I can't assume that you fully understand what it means to be . . . ' he paused and let his hand drop. 'But perhaps you can. The main thing is that for the duration of your stay here, you will be as one of us. That is the condition. You must do what is asked of you and not question instructions. If you break the rules, you will put us all at risk. Do you understand?'

You understand, don't you Alfred? This is a kind man, you can trust him.

Alfred nodded.

Nadel stood and gazed at Alfred for a few silent moments. Then he gestured for Alfred to follow him down the hall.

'I've put you in Fritz Rosenberg's dormitory. They're good boys, there. High-spirited, a couple of them. Best watch Robert and Simon, if you want to stay out of trouble. Caught the two of them mooning a *Hitlerjugend* procession from the second floor window last week.' He shook his head. 'Silly, silly boys.'

'Herr Nadel?' Alfred said.

'Yes?'

Alfred stopped walking and took a deep breath. It was now or never. 'About my brother and sister. You see, Herr Nadel, I think there's been a mistake, and my sister, her name is Johanna and she's twelve, she says she'll come for me, but if I'm here she won't know where to look. So I was thinking, perhaps we could send her a letter.'

Nadel stopped and placed his hand on Alfred's shoulder. 'I understand,' he said. 'Anno Schmidt explained what happened to your family. But Alfred ... ' he closed his eyes briefly. 'Alfred. I'm afraid there's nothing we can do but wait. If ... if the situation changes, I'm sure we will be able to send news to your sister. But in the meantime, we must wait and see. You must give me your word that you will not try to contact her.'

Alfred felt like crying.

*Give him your word, little one. You owe him that. The risk
he is taking for you is enormous.
And we will surely find Johanna. Be patient.*

Alfred blinked back his tears. 'I give you my word,' he
whispered.

During his first week, Alfred took every opportunity to
search out a spot at the window facing the main street,
spending hours with his face pressed up against the glass,
hoping with every fibre of his being that the next car to
stop in front of the building, the next person to turn into
the street, would be Johanna. But she never came.

Then, as first weeks, then months passed, he found it
increasingly difficult to remember the details of his earlier
life; he grappled in vain to recollect the ripe, fetid odour
of freshly spread manure, the majesty of the horizon at
sunset, the fragrant verdancy of the forest. But also the
bitter cold draughts that shrieked through the cottage in
winter, the gnawing hunger in his belly when there had
been nothing but turnip to eat for three days in a row,
the perpetual fatigue written on his parents' faces. His
world had shrunk and expanded all at the same time. His
homesickness was to fade almost completely, appearing
only in occasional dreams, from which he would wake
with a tear-wet face and an aching heart. In this, he
discovered, he was no different than other orphans here.
As cheerful and raucous as the boys were during the day,
he could hear many of them crying themselves to sleep
at night.

The only constant, the only thing that linked his
previous and his current life, were the voices. And they,
too, settled into the rhythm of Alfred's new life, were at

times admonishing (when Alfred was invited by Simon to an illegitimate excursion over the back wall), at times comforting (when his grief-ripe heart threatened to shatter), and at times mischievous (giving him ideas for pranks to play on the girls). He discovered, too, that he was a skilled football player, making him very popular among the boys; and that his singing voice was as sweet as his mother's had been, making him very popular among the female members of staff. He had a good memory, for both words and melodies, and was even called upon to sing a stanza of the *Ma'oz Tzur* during his first Chanukah at the orphanage.

There was, as Fritz had indicated, only a small number of 'full-orphans' at the *Waisenhaus* – those who were both motherless and fatherless; these children were the subject of special attention, both from the staff and the home's generous patrons. At Alfred's first Chanukah, a few months after his arrival, he and the other full-orphans each received, in addition to sweets and cake, some wooden toys and a shiny silver Reichsmark from the orphanage's most generous benefactor, neighbouring cigarette manufacturer Josef Gabárty-Rosenthal. Alfred kept this coin, and those he received each subsequent Chanukah, safely hidden in a pair of socks in his dresser. It was several years before he came to need them.

It was a liberal, not an orthodox religion Alfred encountered here, with days marked by school lessons and physical exercise, music and theatre. There were many chores at the orphanage that the children were responsible for, including peeling potatoes, mopping out the dinner hall, cleaning out the large bird cage situated outside the teachers' staff room, carrying out minor repairs to broken chairs and wobbly desks, and tending the school garden. Some, although not many, of the children had little knowledge of the Jewish religion, either because their parents had converted to Christianity, or because they were atheists. Thus, Alfred's ignorance of the existing rites and rituals wasn't called into question. One of the few aspects of the *Waisenhaus* that characterised it as Jewish was the imposing prayer hall on the second floor of the building – a breath-taking room with huge candelabras dangling from a coffered ceiling, and on the eastern wall, a Holy Ark crowned by a large Star of David – in which a service took place every Friday evening. To Alfred, the hall appeared more like a theatre – full of unfamiliar rituals and exotic-sounding prayers – than a place of worship. At first, he chose to remain close to the back of the hall during services, holding silent conversations with his voice-women, to ease the feeling of foreignness the place gave him. One day after worship, not long after Alfred had arrived, Nadel approached him. 'A word please, Alfred?'

After a moment's hesitation, during which Alfred was afraid he might have broken some rule he was unaware of, Nadel said, 'I noticed you were praying. If you ever feel the need to talk to God, please tell me and I'll see what I can arrange.'

Alfred shook his head. 'Oh, but I haven't met him yet,' he answered brightly.

Alfred's best friend was Salomon Bronstein, a fellow full-orphan, whose parents had died of pneumonia, within a week of one another, when he was three years old. His grandparents, a wealthy shoe manufacturer and his wife, had cared for him at home for as long as they could, but had given him over to the care of the orphanage when he turned school age. They visited him regularly, often bringing gifts for Salomon and the other children. Salomon was a shy, stocky boy, one of the few to wear a *kippah* at all times, at the insistence of his grandparents. He complained that the skullcap impeded his movements, preventing him from climbing and swinging off the trees like the other boys, for fear of it falling off, and he indignantly declined Fräulein Merz' suggestion that he use kirby grips to fix it in place. Secretly, though – as he confessed to Alfred when the bonds of their friendship had taken hold – he was rather glad of this excuse, because he, like Alfred, was rather cautious when it came to such foolhardy displays of physical exuberance. Thus, the two boys soon became friends – Salomon instructing Alfred on the dos and don'ts of Jewish observance, Alfred in turn teaching Salomon how to fashion a bow and arrow from twigs and twine (he had studied his brother Emil carefully). Most often, however, they were to be found tending the vegetable patch in the school garden, where Alfred would find scraps of memories popping into his head – rhubarb protects beans against black fly, don't plant potatoes next to cucumber – and year after year, they would harvest the largest pumpkins, the juiciest carrots and the plumpest tomatoes.

One night, Alfred was woken by Salomon tapping him on the shoulder.

'Can I come in?' Salomon whispered.

'What?'

'My bed's ... wet.'

Alfred pulled his blanket back and let Salomon slide

in beside him. Alfred closed his eyes and felt Salomon's warm breath on his face.

'It's not my fault,' Salomon said quietly. 'I can't help it. Please don't tell.'

Alfred opened his eyes. 'I won't,' he said, and felt the warm weight of his promise, like a blanket that had been wrapped around the two of them.

'I have a secret, too,' he whispered into the dark, but when there was no response, he opened his eyes and saw that Salomon had fallen asleep. He heard a soft cluck of disapproval in his ear. It was an uncomfortable night's sleep, for the bed was narrow, but Alfred didn't mind. It reminded him of sharing his bed with Martha. At dawn, Salomon woke him again, and they crept across the dormitory and quietly changed Salomon's sheets before the others woke. This was the closest Alfred ever came during his years there to spilling his own secret.

Alfred's tenth birthday coincided with the Olympic Games that the city was hosting, and to mark the event – despite the fact that, or perhaps *because* of the fact that Jewish athletes were barred from taking part – the orphanage director, Kurt Crohn, organised a *Waisenhaus* 'Olympics'. There was a fifty-metre dash across the schoolyard, a football match (Alfred's favourite – his team won 6–2 on penalties) and an obstacle course involving buckets of water, women's clothing and copious amounts of *Wackelpudding*, leaving the children and teachers in hysterics. For the three-legged race, the boys lined up in pairs at one end of the schoolyard, Alfred's left leg tied with a strip of cloth to Salomon's right.

'*Auf die Plätze … fertig … los!*' Crohn shouted, and

the boys began running and limping and stumbling across the yard. Salomon, one of the least athletic of the boys, was a dead weight for his partner Alfred, and they manoeuvred forward in a clumsy, awkward three-legged gambol before landing on the dusty ground in a tangled heap, several metres short of the finishing line. Salomon began to giggle as he and Alfred extracted their limbs from one another, and soon, Alfred was laughing too – in great whoops of excited, breathless hilarity, before oddly, he found himself crying. And then he couldn't stop, couldn't calm his shuddering diaphragm no matter how many gulps of air he took, couldn't prevent the streams of tears that were running down his face, couldn't interrupt the spasms of grief that shook his small body – even as he heard calls of 'Is he hurt?', 'Quick, someone fetch Fräulein Merz!', 'Does he need a doctor?' – and only managed to calm down a long while later after Heinz Nadel had picked him up off the ground and taken him in a tight, warm embrace.

'It's all right, son,' he whispered, 'it's all right.'

Given the tragic events that had put him there, Alfred's time at the *Waisenhaus* was as untroubled and happy as it could have been, though if he had paid more attention, he would have spotted the portents of what was to come: an unspoken anxiety that seemed to weigh more and more heavily on the adults with every newspaper article they read silently over breakfast, every wireless broadcast they prohibited the children from listening to, every unanticipated knock on the large front door after nightfall, and the furtive, late-night discussions among the older boys and girls that seemed to revolve around the terms 'Nuremberg Laws', 'Palestine' and 'youth Aliya', terms that meant nothing to Alfred at the time.

Then, in Alfred's fourth year there (he had turned twelve in the summer), several events occurred in quick succession that would upset this fragile tranquillity of his life for good. One day in late October 1938, he came down with a stomach ache and diarrhoea. Fräulein Merz was summoned, who diagnosed a mild case of gastroenteritis, administered a dose of milk of magnesia and prescribed a day of bed rest. Alfred was distraught. His entire class, all twenty-three boys as well as three members of staff, were preparing for an excursion across the city to the synagogue in Münchener Straße to attend Salomon's bar mitzvah. Such outings had become increasingly rare – indeed, during Alfred's final year there, a siege mentality had begun to develop at the *Waisenhaus*. None of those living at the orphanage ever quite became accustomed to the shouts of 'Death to the Jews!' and 'Kill the dirty pigs!' that were hurled regularly over the school walls, growing in frequency and vehemence, and the insults and abuse targeted towards the children when they were out in public had long since threatened to tip over into real violence. But an exception had been made at the request of Salomon's grandparents, Gustav and Margarete Bronstein, to hold the bar mitzvah at their local synagogue in the district of Schöneberg. The children's excitement at the prospect of this special outing was palpable, and the staff were faced with the difficult task of conveying to a group of giggling, restless children the real dangers they might encounter beyond the secure *Waisenhaus* gates.

Alfred lay alone in his dormitory, listening to the excitement swell and pulse in the corridor outside, feeling utterly sorry for himself. The medicine had helped settle his stomach, and although he felt somewhat weak from a night spent on the toilet, he was sorely disappointed to be left out. He was just resigning himself to a day in bed, bored and miserable, when he heard

Alfred. Get out of bed and get dressed.

'I can't,' he answered silently. 'I have to stay here.'

Nonsense. Now get up. Go and tell Fräulein Merz that you are feeling better.

'But it's useless. She won't let me go.'

Not if you keep that sorry look on your face, she won't. Just do as we say and tell her your stomach ache has gone. Salomon is your best friend, isn't he? Do you really think she'll prevent you from joining him on this special day if you're feeling better?

Alfred thought hard for a moment. Then, realising he had nothing to lose by asking, he jumped out of bed and got dressed. Fräulein Merz demurred for all of two minutes, infected perhaps by the general excitement as well as Alfred's enthusiasm, took his temperature for good measure and declared him fit for the outing.

It took them a good hour to reach Münchener Straße. One tram driver refused to let them board, forcing them to take a twenty-minute walk to the nearest bus stop that would take them anywhere near the synagogue. When they finally arrived, frozen through, Alfred was beginning to regret not having stayed at home in his nice warm bed. But the ceremony, though solemn, was exciting and enjoyable for all, Salomon stumbling more or less smoothly through his *haftarah* reading, and the event culminated in an exuberant celebration, during which the boys were permitted a small cup of wine each and as many jam doughnuts as they could stomach. As a result, the mood of the entire group was markedly more jovial when returning home than on the journey there. Unhappily, this wasn't to last.

Waiting at the tram stop, two of the boys who had surreptitiously snuck a few more cups of wine than allowed, began to sing. It was a popular song, a pleasant upbeat melody that Alfred was familiar with, a song that invited dancing and foot-tapping. And it was in Yiddish. Several of the people waiting at the tram stop looked over at them, some of them shaking their heads.

Nadel rushed over to the boys. 'Be quiet!' he hissed. 'You're drawing attention to us.'

The two boys fell silent immediately, blushing and mumbling apologies. But across a green square of lawn, a group of six or so young men in *Hitlerjugend* uniforms had also heard. They began walking towards the group just as a loud bell announced the tram's arrival.

'Boys, get in line,' Nadel said, unable to hide the anxious tremble in his voice. 'Youngest first. And get on quickly as soon as the doors open. No dawdling.'

Alfred, close to the back of the line, saw Nadel and the other two teachers looking over their shoulders nervously. It seemed to take an age for the tram to finally come to a halt and open its doors.

'Quickly now,' Nadel instructed. The boys at the front of the line began boarding the tram, one of them tripping on the step in his hurry to get on. The group of youths was only some ten metres away.

'Hey, *Judenschweine!*' one of them called out. 'Who let you out?'

Another picked up a stone and threw it at the boys. It hit Alfred on the shoulder, but hadn't been thrown with enough force to hurt him. He turned back around to board the tram, and it was then that he caught sight of a girl on the opposite side of the street. She was wearing a woollen coat and her hair was covered with a scarf that was tied beneath her chin – but from the swing in her step, the way she held her shoulders proud and her back straight, Alfred recognised her immediately. It was Johanna. His heart started beating so fast he thought he might faint. He cried out, 'Johanna!', but his shout was lost in the commotion. The tram driver had left his seat and was now herding the boys on board.

'Come on, pick up your feet,' he said, ignoring the hissed whispers from several of the passengers. Alfred remained motionless, staring across the road. But the girl had disappeared around a corner.

'Alfred! Come on!' Nadel shouted. 'For goodness' sake, move!' And he grabbed Alfred's coat and dragged him onto the tram. The doors closed before Alfred could offer any resistance. Releasing himself from Nadel's grip, he rushed over to the other side of the moving tram and pressed his face up against the window. As the tram moved forwards and past the corner of the building opposite, Alfred spotted the figure of the girl again, walking away. He wanted to call out to her, shout her name, scream and pummel the glass, but he knew it would be futile. And so instead, he imprinted the street names on his mind, knowing that before long, he would somehow find his way back here, to the corner of Münchener Straße and Grunewaldstraße, to look for her.

Day Two

After the disastrous phone conversation with the nurse at Alfred's (former) care home, I took him through to the kitchen to make a cup of tea. Alfred stood with his back to me, looking out of the window.

'This is the *Bayerisches Viertel*, isn't it?' he asked after a few minutes. 'The Bavarian Quarter.'

'Yes. Münchener Straße. Why, do you know the area?' I asked.

Alfred frowned. 'It was a long time ago. Very long time. I didn't recognise it at first.'

I left him standing there and went to pour the tea.

'Yes, the synagogue, of course I remember.'

It was Alfred, whispering to himself.

'Yes, yes, that's where . . . Johanna. I know! What?' A pause. 'I'm not sure. Sounds a bit rude, if you ask me.' Head bobbing around, nodding, shaking, it was hard to tell the difference. Then, 'OH FOR CRYING OUT LOUD, JUST ASK HER YOURSELF THEN!'

Although I may well have written off the first few

comments as an old man's mumblings, which are to be politely ignored, this last sentence came out with such force that I couldn't possibly pretend I hadn't heard it.

'Alfred, is everything all right?' I asked.

He was clutching the windowsill, knuckles white, head still atremble.

'Julia, I would like you to do me a favour.' He didn't look up as he spoke.

'Sure. What is it?'

He didn't respond at first. Instead, he sat down, very slowly, at the kitchen table, and gestured for me to do the same. I passed him a cup of tea and sat down. His head had stopped trembling, thankfully.

'You are a very kind lady, Julia,' he began. 'And I cannot begin to tell you how grateful I am for all your help. It's incredible, really. Just think about it!' He let out an unexpected chuckle. 'Picking up some doddering old fool you'd never laid eyes on before, giving him a bed for the night, driving him around town, taking him to the hospital to see his . . . ' He faltered at this point and took a sip of tea. 'Yes, you are a very special lady,' he continued. 'A great generosity of spirit. But I must ask you to do me yet one more favour. I am very concerned for Brynja. I don't mean her . . . her injuries; I have every confidence that she will recover fully. But – *Damn*, it's so difficult to explain!'

Then he did something quite peculiar: he shifted his gaze slightly to the left of my head and, as though I were not there at all, began a one-sided conversation. It was most bizarre to witness; it wasn't as though he was talking to himself. No – he spoke, then paused, sometimes nodding or shaking his head. His body language was also in on the act: shrugs, frowns, raised palms.

'I know, but what?'

'That's easy for you to say ... '

'You know as well as I do ... '

'Again?'

'But she can't take it back.'

'Take, not make! With a T!'

But then the conversation appeared to turn into an argument, with Alfred raising his voice, seemingly being interrupted in mid-speech, and turning rather red in the face. Apart from the plain weirdness of him holding this unilateral conversation in the middle of my kitchen, it soon began to concern me that he was becoming very upset.

'Alfred. Stop it!' I spoke louder than I had intended, but it proved effective. Alfred blinked and looked straight at me. He was quiet.

'Who are you talking to?' I said.

He let out a heavy sigh. The colour of his face slowly returned to normal. 'I ... ' he began.

'Alfred, what's the matter?'

'Very well,' he said. 'I will try to explain it to you, but you must let me finish. I – I can hear voices.'

'Oh – '

He raised his hand to interrupt me. 'Please, Julia. It's not important now for me to explain why or how. But it is important that you know firstly, that I am neither mad nor dangerous. Secondly, you must know that my granddaughter Brynja also hears voices. But she is much tormented by them. Very much so. She hasn't been ... she doesn't ... ' He struggled to find the right words. 'Brynja doesn't understand,' he said finally. 'It should be a gift, but to her it is a curse. I need to let her know that.'

'Hmm,' I interjected, not knowing if it was my turn to speak yet, and if so, what exactly I should say.

'The problem,' he continued, 'is that I will not have the opportunity to tell her. My days, as they say, are numbered. And I'm afraid those days and her regaining consciousness will not overlap.'

He paused and took a sip of tea. 'Well, Julia? Do you think you might do me this favour?'

'What favour?'

'Tell her my story, of course.'

'Oh. Well, Alfred, I ... '

'I will tell you, and you will tell her. When she recovers.'

1938 – 1939

A week after Salomon's bar mitzvah and Alfred's sighting of Johanna, the hitherto safe perimeters of the *Waisenhaus* were finally breached. One afternoon, a group of men broke down a side door – having tried unsuccessfully to storm the building through the front entrance – and entered the building, shouting threats and abuse. Alfred was sitting in a classroom on the first floor when he heard shouting and the sound of breaking glass.

'Get under your desks,' the teacher said, and left the room to see what was happening. Ignoring the teacher's instructions to hide, Alfred, Salomon and David crept out after him, to the large stairwell that led down to the entrance hall. Below them, they saw a mob of around fifty young men, some in uniform, some in work clothes, armed with sticks and pipes, knocking over furniture and smashing mirrors and pictures. The noise was deafening.

Nadel was standing at the top of the stairs, a small boy in his arms.

'Ingrid,' he called to Fräulein Merz, who came running out of one of the girls' classrooms. 'Call the police.'

She rushed back down the corridor, and was back a few minutes later. 'They said they're busy. That I should call back later. I tried to explain, but – '

She was interrupted by an enormous crashing noise and the sound of wood splintering.

'Make sure the children are safe,' Nadel said and began walking down the steps, the child still in his arms. 'These are just children!' he shouted at the mob. The young boy he was holding began to cry. The men looked up. 'Are you not ashamed of yourselves?' Nadel continued, pulling his shoulders back.

'Heinz!' Fräulein Merz whispered. 'Come back!'

But Nadel took another step down. The air seemed to quiver, as Alfred and the others held their breath, not daring to move.

'I would like you to leave at once,' Nadel said. His voice was loud and eerily calm. The tumult downstairs ceased, and then, like a balloon deflating, the group of men stopped what they were doing, turned and left. If he hadn't witnessed it himself, Alfred would not have believed it. When the men were gone, and the doors had been shut and bolted, Nadel sat down on the stairs and wept.

After this incident, things moved very quickly. The following day, Nadel and Direktor Crohn came into the classroom during a geography lesson and called out a list of names, among them, Alfred's. The children, twelve boys and fifteen girls, were to pack a small case with clothing, toiletries and one or two small personal items, and report to Crohn's office that afternoon. When the children later assembled there with their belongings, Alfred realised that he was standing among most of the full-orphans living at the *Waisenhaus*. Without giving the children the opportunity to ask any questions, Crohn told them that in light of yesterday's attack, he had decided to do everything in his power to bring the children to safety, and that they been selected for the *Kindertransport* to take them to England.

'But I can't go!' Alfred blurted out.

'It's all right,' Crohn told him gently. 'We have room for you, too.'

Alarmed, Alfred called his voice-women in his head. 'I can't go to England. Not now. I need to find Johanna!'

They responded immediately.

Be calm, Alfred. Do as you're told. This is no time for disobedience.

'But *you* took me to see her!' he continued silently.

Ksss! We did no such thing.

'Yes! Yes you did!'

But the voices didn't respond to this, and Alfred had no choice but to take his place among the children that were now lining up at the front door, suitcases in hand. Some of them were weeping quietly, others seemed stunned. Robert and Salomon were giggling nervously and kept nudging each other with their elbows. Fräulein Merz appeared and gave each of them a kiss on the cheek, holding back tears herself. She cleared her throat.

'Right. If any of you needs to visit the lavatory before you leave, do it now.'

Alfred's arm shot up. Fräulein Merz nodded and he sped off down the hall. Nobody seemed to notice that he had taken his suitcase with him. When he got to the end of the corridor, instead of turning left to the boys' toilets, he took a right, treading as lightly as he could, and opened a door that led into the enclosed yard. From here, he moved silently to the back wall, his heart pounding, not daring to look over his shoulder, and before he knew it, he had climbed up and over. He was now on the grounds of the cigarette factory. Up ahead, close to the road, was a small shed. Alfred tried the door – it was unlocked – so he crept in and sat down on his case.

Oh Alfred. What are you doing? They are waiting for you.

'I'm not going. I need to find Johanna.'

Get up and go back immediately!

'No!'

Do as you are told, Alfred! This is your final warning.

It was a tone he'd never heard them use before, cold and harsh. But he was desperate. 'I said: NO!'

Then the sound hit him, a sound so loud it made him nauseous, made his ears ring and his head spin.

A L F R E E E E E E E D ! ! ! ALFREEEEEEED!!!

One of the voices sounded as though it had split down the middle, making his eardrums vibrate so badly he feared they might start bleeding. It was as though his head were being squeezed through a mangle. But he covered his ears (which didn't help), screwed his eyes tightly shut and curled up into a ball, waiting for it to end. Which it did, eventually, leaving him feeling sick and exhausted. But the silence that followed was almost as painful as the noise.

When the gloom inside the shed had turned into blackness, Alfred dared to open the door. Night had fallen. He snapped open his suitcase and retrieved the

Reichsmarks he'd received on Chanukah for the past four years from a rolled-up pair of socks, slipped them into his pocket, and then crossed quickly to the edge of the site, where he managed to squeeze himself and his suitcase through a hole in the fence. The street was empty. Without glancing back at the orphanage, he set off down the road.

He used one of the coins to buy a tram fare heading south. The conductor eyed him suspiciously – it was a lot of money for a young boy to have – but Alfred kept his eyes down and waited, hand outstretched, for the conductor to count out the change onto his open palm. He didn't want to go too far on the tram, in case he got lost in a part of town he'd never been to before, so he disembarked a few stops early and began to walk. It had snowed briefly earlier in the day, but the ground was still too warm for the frost to take hold. Nevertheless, the wind was icy and stung his face and neck as he walked and walked and walked, one hand gripping his coat tightly shut, in the direction of the place he'd seen Johanna the week before. When he arrived at a crossroads that looked completely unfamiliar, he began to panic and called on his voice-women to help him, but they remained silent. Perhaps they were punishing him for his disobedience; he wasn't sure, but it was too late now, anyway. Salomon, Robert, Simon – his friends for the past four years were on their way to the train station to be shipped to England, a safe place, safer than here. His heart thumped in his chest and he felt a sudden stab of regret, but then dug his fingernails into his palms. Johanna was here somewhere, and all he had to do was find her. Then he would be safe, too.

When he finally reached Grunewaldstraße, he almost

wept with relief, before realising that this was just the beginning of his search. For a long while, he stood on the corner of the street, close to the tram stop, just waiting. He remained there, shivering, until a man with an angry dog passed by him and he had to step aside. He could really feel the cold now. Tired and freezing and not knowing what else to do, he crept into some bushes that lined a small square of grass set back from the street, and lay down.

The first thing he heard on waking was a hissing sound, like air being let out of a tire.

Ssssssssssssss.

Then: *Pssssst. Alfred.*

He tried to sit up, but he was suddenly beset by a series of spasms that seemed to shake up all the bones in his body.

Try rubbing your legs together. There. Now your hands. See? Get some of that cold out of your body.

Alfred did as he was told, and soon he was able to move his limbs again, albeit stiffly. 'I'm sorry,' he whispered.

Well it's too late for that now. But you need to stand up and move about before you freeze to death.

Alfred got to his feet and scrambled out of the bushes. A group of early-morning commuters were standing at the tram stop. A man, wearing a hat at an angle, so that only one of his eyes was visible, kept looking suspiciously in Alfred's direction. So Alfred kept his distance and crossed the road, to the side where he had seen Johanna. He was hungry and thirsty, and worst of all, he had no idea where to start looking. He was shivering; the cold seemed to have penetrated his body through to the bone, and he thought he would never be warm again. From a distance, he heard police whistles; instinctively, he dodged into a house entrance that led into a series of back yards. The sun had climbed high enough to light up a small corner of the first yard, and here he went and sat to warm up until he was chased off by a red-faced woman wielding a carpet beater.

Have faith, little one. Be patient.

Alfred stalked the street for almost two hours until he began to feel faint from the cold and lack of food. His small suitcase, though containing only a few items of clothing, his toothbrush, a pad and pencil, and a penknife he'd received on his last birthday, seemed to weigh a ton. He walked to the top of the street, switching the suitcase from one side to the other to alleviate the pain in his shoulders. Situated here was a small square, enclosed by some eight shops, an apothecary shop and a bakery, the latter emitting a smell so heavenly that Alfred stood open-mouthed in front of the glass, hoping that the fragrance of freshly baked bread alone might assuage his hunger. But when the saleswoman behind the glass looked up sharply and caught him staring, he quickly moved on.

Back down to the tram stop, back up to the square. Finally, when his legs threatened to buckle beneath him, he laid his suitcase down flat on the pavement outside the apothecary shop, sat down and wept. He didn't care about the passers-by, didn't bother to cover his face in his hands, and when one of the voice-women called his name, he ignored her. A hand touched his shoulder.

'Alfred. I can't believe it. Is that you?'

Alfred shrugged the hand away.

'Alfred! It's me! Johanna!'

And suddenly the hand became an arm, a body, an

embrace that lifted him almost off his feet. He pressed his face into her hair and breathed in, sobbing loudly now. They remained in this position for a long time, until Johanna took a step back, still clutching his shoulders with both hands.

'You're so tall!' she exclaimed, her face as wet as his. 'And filthy,' she added, attempting a laugh that turned into weeping momentarily.

'I'm so hungry,' Alfred said before he could stop himself.

Johanna nodded furiously. 'Yes. Stay here. I'll be right back.' And she hurried off towards the bakery, coming out a short while later with a paper bag full of pastries. She handed him the bag and stooped to pick up his case. 'Come on, Alfred darling. Let's go home.'

'Home' turned out to be an enormous, turn-of-the-century apartment on the *bel étage* of a nearby building on Barbarossastraße. Johanna unlocked the front door and led Alfred inside, turning to stroke his face again and again, as though to make sure he was no illusion. She helped him out of his coat and hung it up.

'Johanna, is that you?'

A thin, high-pitched voice rang through the apartment.

'Yes, Franziska. It's me,' Johanna answered and then smiled at Alfred.

'Did you get everything?' the voice asked.

'Of course.'

Johanna pulled a white paper bag out of her coat pocket. 'Just wait here,' she said to Alfred, and left him standing in the hall, torn between wanting to burst into song and yet paralysed with fear that he might be lost in some dream, or that he might have died of cold in the bushes during the night. He didn't dare move in case he broke the spell. From the depths of the apartment, he heard the mumblings of a conversation. Shortly afterwards, Johanna returned.

'Come with me,' she said purposefully. 'Remember to speak only when spoken to. And just follow my lead.'

She grabbed his hand and took him through a large room with a parquet floor in a herringbone design, full of dark, heavy furniture and ornate wall hangings, the stucco on the ceiling as pretty as cake icing, to another narrow hallway, from which he could count at least four further rooms leading off. Johanna stopped in front of a set of double doors, knocked lightly and stepped in.

'Franziska, this is the boy.' She tugged at Alfred's hand and he followed her in. It was a south-facing room, but the light was drowsy. The curtains were drawn, with only a smudge of light coming from a small table lamp in the corner. When his eyes had adjusted to the gloom, he could make out a large room, with pristine stucco on the ceilings, the walls almost entirely covered in paintings, large and small, and an old woman sitting in a high-backed chair, her eyes closed and her head leaning against the backrest. Her very white hair was pinned up in an elaborate hairdo, atop of which sat a large peacock feather that quivered as she breathed. There was a sharp pungency in the air, a smell Alfred couldn't identify.

'What?' the woman said hoarsely, her eyelids flickering. She wore an old-fashioned-looking velvet dress with a full-length skirt and a high lace collar.

'The boy, Franziska,' Johanna said. 'The one I told you about.'

'Oh. The boy. Of course.'

'And Emil?' Alfred said, dying to hear news of his brother.

Johanna let out a bitter laugh. 'Emil has turned into a fine young man,' she said. 'A fine, upstanding member of the Reich. Group leader of his *Hitlerjugend* division, no less. Three shoulder pips at the last count.' She spat into the fire.

Alfred waited for her to sit down again. 'What about Marie?' he asked hesitantly.

Johanna closed her eyes for a moment. 'Oh, Mariechen,' she said. 'It was her sixth birthday last week, wasn't it?'

Alfred nodded and hoped his face wouldn't betray his shame. His baby sister's birthday had never crossed his mind.

'When I arrived here, I contacted the orphanage straight away,' Johanna said. 'I was so full of hope that I'd find you both there, safe and sound.' She wrung her hands. 'But there was no record of you – Alfred, where have you been? – and Marie had been adopted almost immediately. That's no surprise really – she was such a sweet and pretty little girl. They wouldn't give me any information on her whereabouts. But I'm sure ... ' her voice faltered slightly. 'I'm sure we'll find her one day. Just like we found each other.' She leaned forward and kissed Alfred on the forehead, just like his mother used to do.

In return, Alfred told his sister, in as much detail as he could recall, about his time at the *Waisenhaus*: his friends, his football skills, the experience of sharing a bedroom with twelve others, the kindness of the staff and exoticness of sabbath worship.

'I'm glad they were so good to you,' Johanna remarked tenderly. The only thing he concealed from her, something far more than a mere detail, was the voices.

When a grandfather clock somewhere in the apartment struck four, Johanna got to her feet. 'Come on,' she said. 'I'll show you around.'

She led him out of the kitchen, which was at the far end of the apartment, and back through the long corridor, stopping to look in the rooms. Closest to the kitchen was a very small, narrow room that appeared to be used as a store room. Then a larger room, with a bed, table and chair, a dark wooden wardrobe and very expensive-looking rugs and curtains. This was Johanna's room. The front of the apartment contained two enormous reception rooms, whose ceilings were even higher than those in the rest of the apartment and also decorated with elaborate stucco. In each of these rooms, a chandelier hung, dripping with crystals. Overall, Alfred counted a total of six rooms, plus the kitchen and a small bathroom. When they passed by Frau von Markstein's room, on tiptoe, Alfred remembered how Johanna had introduced him.

'What did you mean when you said to her "It's the boy"?' he asked, when they were back in the kitchen.

Johanna shrugged. 'I made it up, on the spur of the moment. The old woman is ... confused. If I tell her we'd talked about hiring a boy, then she believes me.'

Although the flat was impossibly large for two – and now three – people, Alfred spent the first months sharing a bed with Johanna. They slept soundly, limbs entwined, desperate for the warmth and tenderness they'd had to forgo over the years. It was only when Alfred woke one morning to find the sheet beneath him damp and shamefully sticky, that Johanna wordlessly made up a bed for him in the adjoining room.

Late one night in November, Johanna woke him in the dark and took him up to the attic. The roof slanted at a steep angle and they had to crouch to get to the small round window at the front of the house. Before Alfred could ask her what they were doing up there, as it was cold and he was shaking in his thin nightgown, she opened the window. They watched as great curls of smoke rose from buildings all over the city, saw groups of men with stones and torches yelling and cheering. They watched in silence until they were too tired to keep their eyes open, so they clambered back downstairs and into bed. The following morning, the pavements of the city were covered in a million shards of glass.

The weeks rushed by, past Christmas (Alfred's first Christmas in four years; he and Johanna celebrated quietly with a meal of jellied carp and potato salad, but no gifts to speak of – Franziska von Markstein rarely left her room and made no exception on this occasion), past New Year, past Johanna's seventeenth birthday, until Alfred finally felt at ease wandering through the large apartment, emptying the tiled coal ovens of ash, relighting fires, fixing broken chairs and whacking the dust out of carpets on a metal bar installed on the large front-facing balcony. He almost felt at home.

Spring arrived, meteorologically speaking, but the winter retained a severe grip on the city. The Reich had recently expanded to the south with great fanfare, and Berlin seemed to be carried on a tide of vicious, almost hysterical, optimism. One morning in early April, Alfred set out with Johanna on one of her outings to shop for groceries and meat, order a delivery of coal, and post some letters. On their way back, they stopped outside the apothecary shop, the very one Alfred had sat outside when Johanna found him.

'Wait here,' she instructed, and entered the shop. Alfred stood outside, stamping his feet against the cold. Several metres away, he saw a yellow-painted park bench with the inscription *'Nur für Juden'* – for Jews only – and felt a sudden stab of longing. He thought of his friends at the *Waisenhaus*, of Heinz Nadel and Fräulein Merz, but somehow couldn't quite get his mind to imagine anything dreadful happening to them. Two policemen walked past him. One of them stopped and turned.

'Everything all right?' he asked sternly.

'Yes,' Alfred answered. 'I'm waiting for my sister.' He pointed to the shop.

'Come on, Klaus, the boy's doing no harm,' the other policeman said. 'It's bloody freezing out here.'

The first policeman hesitated.

Smile, Alfred. Don't let them think you're up to no good.

Alfred attempted a polite smile. The policeman barked a 'Heil Hitler' and re-joined his colleague.

A moment later, Johanna hurried out of the shop. 'What did they want?' she asked breathlessly.

'Nothing. Just asked if everything was all right.'

'Nothing else?'

'No.'

'Then let's get home,' she said, looking back over her shoulder briefly.

'Are you in trouble?' Alfred asked with a grin.

'Don't be smart!' she said, her voice raised.

She said nothing more about the matter until later that

night, when she was placing a hot stone under his blanket to warm his bed.

'I'm sorry for snapping at you earlier,' she said, as he crawled into bed, relishing the warmth of the stone against his toes. 'I suppose you're old enough to know.'

Alfred yawned. 'Know what?' he asked.

Johanna looked down at her hands; her skin was red and coarse, and she had bitten her nails down to the quick. 'Frau von Markstein needs to take a special kind of medicine.'

'Is she sick?'

'Yes, I suppose so. Or rather, she would get very sick if she didn't take her medicine. Oh, Alfred, I don't know how to explain!' She got up, walked to the window, and then came and sat back down on his bed. 'Franziska is a morphine addict. Do you know what that means?'

Alfred nodded slowly, although he only half understood.

'But morphine is illegal, so it's very difficult to come by. I – ' she squeezed her hands together, 'I get it from the apothecary at Bayerischer Platz. That's what I was doing today, and why I was so worried about the policemen.'

'But if you can buy it from an apothecary, why is it difficult to come by?'

'She makes him sell it to her. She knows things about him. She knows that his wife – ' she whispered the next part, 'is a Jew. She converted years ago when they married, but she can't change her family tree.'

'Oh,' Alfred said, and added, 'So she doesn't want his wife to get into trouble?'

Johanna shook her head derisively. 'She doesn't care about that. As long as it serves her purposes. Besides, she *hates* Hitler. She wants the k. & k. back.'

Alfred frowned.

'Kaiser & König. If she had her way, she'd reinstate the king.'

Alfred lay down and put his head on the pillow.

'But,' Johanna continued, 'I've been thinking about something else all day. We really need to get you some papers, Alfred. If you get stopped by the police, you have to have some identification. And besides, you need to go to school. I'm just not sure how to go about it.'

And with this, she kissed him goodnight and left.

NINETEEN NINETY-NINE

You tumble from the party into the bathroom. Giddy. Horny. Forget to put the light on. He locks the door.

Here. He takes your hand and guides it to the front of his pants. A long, hard bulge, hot beneath your fingers. Yeah, he says in a thick voice and then leans his head forward and kisses you, hard, like he's trying to suck your tongue out of your mouth. It's dark; the tiles are cold on the back of your legs as he pushes you against the wall. There will be a line forming outside, but you don't care. You're not at the party now. You're in here, with Michel, who wants you, who finds you sexy and wild, who says you look a bit like Mena Suvari from *American Beauty*. A slice of light at the bottom of the door.

You've kissed before – a guy at a school dance six months ago – but never like this. You work your tongue around his mouth while your right hand rubs and squeezes the bulge in his jeans. The music pulses through the closed door. Not your kind of music. Too hard and thumpy. You're into jazz, now. Found a vinyl copy of

Blue Train at the flea market in the Mauerpark. Play it to death on your mom's old record player. You've had three beers. You shouldn't drink, really. Not when you're taking meds. But you don't care as his hand slips up your skirt and over and into your underpants. For a fraction of a second you're embarrassed because they're damp, and you hope he doesn't think you've wet yourself, but –

Aaah. It escapes your throat. You're fizzing, zinging down there now. The sensation ripples up to your stomach. Down to your toes. So different from when you touch yourself. So – better.

Yeah, he groans again, releasing his mouth from yours and breathing hotly into your ear. Yeah.

What is she doing? What are you doing?

A woman's voice.

You jump. Shit, who's there?

What? He unzips his jeans. Unhooks your bra. Expertly. One-handedly. The other hand rubs and pinches. But. The zing is gone. You try to push him away.

There's someone here, you whisper.

No, shit. Come on, Bryn. There's no one in here. He pulls you close, puts your hand back onto his cock. Yeah, good, like that.

Then the voice splits into two. Talking at the same time.

What are you doing, you dirty slut? You whore!

You stop rubbing, look around. It's dark, but there's no one. Just the voices.

I don't –

Shame on you!

You panic, try again to push him away, but he holds you.

No! I'm nearly done. Come on! His voice is urgent, angry. Then beseeching. Brynja, sweet Brynja. Don't do this to a guy. Kisses you. Grabs your hand and makes you wrap it around his cock. Yeah. Sweet Brynja. Breathes quickly, through his mouth. Then – holds his breath.

Take your hands off his meat! You whore! You slut! You will be punished!

A heavy groan. Hot stickiness on your hand, your skirt. A kiss.

1939 – 1944

Despite her open disdain of Adolf Hitler ('that vulgar little Austrian'), Franziska von Markstein was surprisingly well-respected by the Nazi authorities. Alfred surmised that this had as much to do with her nephew's standing and reputation in the party as with her immense wealth, which she distributed freely and generously to anyone willing to remove 'unnecessary' bureaucratic hurdles. But Johanna had taught him not to question such things too closely. He also concluded that Johanna played an irreplaceable role in Frau von Markstein's life, because after a brief correspondence between Frau von Markstein and the registration authorities, Alfred was in possession of bona fide papers: a folded manila card containing his name (Alfred Franz Werner), place and date of birth (Löwenberg, Neubrandenburg, 18th August 1926), profession (school pupil), height (1.60 metres), colour of eyes (grey) and unchanging marks (- - -). A small photograph was attached on the right-hand side and beneath that, his signature.

Two weeks after receiving his papers, Johanna took him to be enrolled in the nearby grammar school. It was very different here than at the *Waisenhaus*; boys and girls were taught together in one classroom – albeit strictly separated by the aisle – corporal punishment was a daily occurrence and anti-Semitism was ubiquitous, embedded into subjects ranging from mathematics ('The Jews are taking up xxx m2 of living space in Berlin. How many German families, with an average of four family members, could be accommodated in this space?)' to physical education ('The Jew has weak legs. Thus he will always be inferior to the German sprinter'). But overall, Alfred wasn't unhappy at school. He remained quiet and thus exempt from beatings, and excelled in most subjects, not least due to the high quality of education he'd received during the previous four years. Johanna beamed whenever he returned home with his school reports, clucking like a proud mother.

'When this is over, you will go to law school,' she would say. 'Or medical school. You're so good with your hands.'

However, as he passed from grade to grade, becoming increasingly taller and outgrowing his clothes at a rate that frustrated his sister, the external events that had so far overshadowed their lives finally overtook them. Although the country was now at war with almost all of Europe, most of the city's inhabitants attempted to live normal lives. Each of them had dug out their own narrow psychological tunnel, through which they would live out their daily routines: travel to and from work or school; gossip with colleagues, friends and neighbours; celebrate marriages; lament the breakup of relationships; cherish the birth of babies; and mourn the loss of elderly parents. Alfred and Johanna were no exception. They each hoped – silently, secretly, as though to share their hopes would render them invalid – for some kind of happy ending.

But things were shifting around them. Notices appeared outside tobacconists ('*Juden sind Zigaretten oder Zigarren nicht mehr erlaubt*'); posters on advertising pillars announced that Jews were to surrender their radios and telephones to the Reich Ministry of Public Enlightenment and Propaganda; rations for Jews no longer included bread and eggs; and rations for the general German population were tightened further to include marmalade and coffee. One day, Alfred came home after school to find Johanna standing at the door to the flat. Her face looked grey in the unlit stairwell.

'Frau Lindenbaum's gone,' she said.

'Is she?' he replied. Frau Lindenbaum was their sour-faced neighbour, who only ever spoke to them to complain that they were making too much noise.

Johanna pointed across the hall to Frau Lindenbaum's front door. A newspaper was hanging out of the letter slot; several more papers and letters lay scattered on the mat below. 'I knocked,' she said, 'but there was no answer.'

Alfred brushed past her into the flat. He was hungry (he was almost always hungry, these days), and could detect the smell of bacon bean soup coming from the kitchen. Johanna followed him in.

'Don't you understand?' she said, pulling his arm back. 'She's gone. She's been *taken*.' This last word came out in a whisper, as though she was afraid of being overheard.

He shook his arm free. 'I haven't eaten since breakfast, Johanna. Taken where?'

'I don't know.' She raised her arms, and dropped them again. 'I don't know *where*. But she's gone.'

Alfred could sense her distress, but couldn't think of how to comfort her. Ignoring the growling in his stomach, he said, 'Shall we call the police?'

She let out an ugly laugh and looked away. But presently, her face softened and she reached out to brush some fluff off his shoulder. 'No, Alfred. We shan't call the police. I really don't think there's much we *can* do.'

A month after Alfred's fourteenth birthday, the first bombs hit Berlin. Although the damage was slight, and Alfred only experienced it as a distant thumping – barely strong enough to make the chandelier crystals shiver – it frightened him profoundly. His voice-women, who had recently become little more than a gentle, hushed backdrop to his life, began chatting incessantly, offering running commentaries on his daily activities, waking him in the night with well-meant but ill-timed advice (*Comb your hair while still wet to avoid it curling; Alfred, offer Gretl your rice pudding at lunch, then she'll know you like her; a bar of soap in your gym bag will make it smell freshly washed*). It troubled him greatly. Then, as the war drew on, and rumours of Nazi atrocities seeped through to the Allied forces, the bombing became vehement, relentless and seemingly indiscriminate. A normal life now meant a hurried, anxious journey to school. At mealtimes, Alfred and Johanna sat in silence with an ear open to the sound of sirens and more and more often, sleep was cut painfully short, to be spent in the cellar of their building, huddled up next to their neighbours in a state of terror. They continued living this way for a long time. Christmas and birthdays came and went, with celebrations conducted hastily and muted.

Johanna became an expert in obtaining extras to their rations, eavesdropping on people on trams and buses for where bargains were to be had, visiting market halls all over the city to hunt out information on expected shipments of fabrics, soap, buttons, knives. Their rations weren't bad, but it was difficult to acquire more than was expressly allocated, and Johanna had ceased to believe in a quick end to the war – despite Goebbels' boastful speeches on the *Volksempfänger* – so she began carefully, secretly, hoarding everything she could get her hands on.

One dark November evening in 1941, Alfred was waiting for his sister at the Arminius market hall in Moabit. The fish vendors there were under strict orders to destroy any unsold goods at the end of the day, to avoid mass food poisoning of those desperate enough to eat rotten fish. Johanna, however, who had learned from their Icelandic mother ingenious ways of curing and fermenting fish, had spent weeks becoming acquainted with one of the vendors – she never told Alfred exactly how – and had arranged to collect several kilos of herring, mackerel and anchovies (which would shortly begin to give off a heady, eye-watering stench).

Alfred had come straight from school and stood waiting outside the market hall. He looked around impatiently; he had been given several pages of Latin and history homework, and failure to produce it the next day would result in smarting knuckles. There was a dusting of snow on the ground and the air was freezing.

Heads up Alfred!

Instinctively, he took this as a warning and backed into

a doorway, pressing his body against the cold brickwork. He peered out onto the street, looking left and right as inconspicuously as possible. But all he saw were market hall shoppers busily and hastily streaming in and out of the entrance gate. No Johanna in sight. He remained where he was for a moment, then relaxed and stepped back onto the pavement. He was about to ask the voice-women what was going on, when he spotted a woman on the opposite side of the street. She wore a long thread-bare coat and a felt hat, and had a large bag slung over her right shoulder. It was Fräulein Merz.

Without thinking twice, Alfred bolted across the street and called out her name. A look of dread crossed her face and she picked up her pace, almost slipping on the icy pavement.

'Fräulein Merz,' he called again, catching up with her and laying a hand on her shoulder. 'It's Alfred. Don't you recognise me?'

At this, she turned and scanned him from top to bottom. Then she laid a gloved hand across her mouth and shook her head very slowly. 'Alfred,' she said finally. 'Look at you! You've grown so tall.' And she gave out a small laugh.

It was three years since Alfred had last seen her, in the lobby of the *Waisenhaus*. The sudden memory of his surreptitious escape – without a good-bye or excuse – flared up inside him, and with it, a feeling of tremendous shame.

'Fräulein Merz, I . . . ' he began, but his words got stuck before he could articulate them.

She reached out and stroked his cheek. 'It's good to see you,' she said. 'We were so worried when you ran away.'

Alfred swallowed and looked down. It was then that he caught sight of a yellow star-shaped patch sewn onto the left side of her coat, just above her heart. 'You're wearing one of these,' he said.

Fräulein Merz followed his glance down to the patch. 'Of course, Alfred. Why are you surprised? I'm a Jew.'

Alfred mumbled, 'Yes, yes, I know,' because everyone knew about the decree that had come into force two months previously. But it was another thing entirely to see it on someone he knew personally.

Fräulein Merz gave him a bitter smile. 'They even issued instructions on how to sew it on neatly.'

'The others,' Alfred said, 'the *Waisenhaus*.'

She took the bag from her right shoulder and switched it to the left. It looked heavy. 'They closed us down ten months ago. We've moved to Schönhauser Allee. It's small, but there aren't that many children left, anyway.'

'Where have they . . . ' Alfred began, but was interrupted by the sound of his sister's voice.

'Alfred! There you are. I've been waiting over – ' She stopped as she noticed Fräulein Merz. Her eyes flicked briefly across the *Judenstern* and back to Alfred. 'Where have you been?'

But before Alfred could introduce the two women, Fräulein Merz said quickly, 'It was nice to see you, Alfred. I'm sorry, but I have to finish my errands before the curfew. Look after yourself.' Then she rushed off and disappeared into the crowd of shoppers.

A month later, on the first day of his Christmas holidays, Alfred travelled across the city to Schönhauser Allee, where he spent several freezing cold hours walking up

'No!' he shouted, and as he made another attempt to grab her arm, the world turned silent for a second. And then the bomb fell.

For several minutes, Alfred felt as if he'd been thrown out of his body. At the moment the bomb hit the adjacent building, the floor heaved and shook and the windows shattered inwards, as though they had been sucked in by an almighty breath. Alfred could see neither dark nor light as he lay on the floor, ears ringing, and it was only when his sight returned after a long few minutes that he realised he'd been thrown several feet across the room. The air was full of smoke, and the sound of Franziska wailing.

'Johanna!' Alfred called, crawling under the smoke, oblivious to the shards of glass that were bloodying his hands and knees. He finally spotted her in the furthest corner of the room, lying perfectly still, her face the same colour as the plaster that speckled her hair. 'Johanna,' he called and lifted her head onto his lap. A thin stream of blood trickled down the side of her face. For the longest time, her eyelids remained closed, as Alfred bent over her and kissed her face, again and again. Finally, she opened her eyes.

'Franziska,' she said weakly.

'Never mind her,' Alfred answered. 'Are you all right? Can you move your legs?'

Johanna ignored his questions. 'Make sure she's alive. We need her.'

Alfred turned around. Frau von Markstein was not only alive, but had already heaved herself back onto her bed and was tucking her feet under her blankets.

'She's fine,' Alfred said to Johanna. He helped her get

up off the floor – she didn't appear to be seriously hurt – and into her bedroom. 'I'll go and see what happened,' he told her after she'd lay down in bed.

It was only when he walked through the hall to the front of the apartment that he realised how much damage had been done, and how lucky the three of them had been. The entire front wall of the building was missing, so that the living room was now on display to the entire street. He took a few steps forward. It was like standing on some surreal stage. Beyond the apartment door, he soon discovered that the main stairwell was blocked with bricks and rubble, so he quickly walked back through the apartment and down the servants' stairwell. Here, in the yard, he would have expected to find the entrance to the cellar, which served as a makeshift bomb shelter, but instead, there was a huge hole in the ground. The detonation had sliced off the neighbouring section of the building, burying the bomb shelter in the process. Even before he heard the moans and screams coming from beneath and all around him, before he saw the stray bloodied leg that had been severed from its body, before he smelled the stench of burning flesh, he doubled over and vomited.

Seven months later, a week after his eighteenth birthday, Alfred returned from his final day at school before the summer holidays to find Johanna waiting for him on the street outside the building. It was a hot day, and Alfred had been looking forward to spending his afternoon at the Strandbad Wannsee, the largest open-air lido in the city, and a place that had so far been spared any attacks from the air. Alfred had been there a few times this year already, mainly to catch a glimpse of his classmate Gretl in her swimming costume. A large sign outside the entrance notified visitors that entry was prohibited for Jews, a reminder of a reality that made Alfred sting with shame and anger, but the promise of clean sand and cool water had won every time. So when he spotted Johanna waiting for him, he was mildly irritated. His irritation vanished, however, when he noticed how white her face was.

'You've been conscripted,' she said, before he could ask what was wrong. She held up a letter. 'You're to report for your medical examination next week.'

Alfred didn't respond. Instead, he pushed his way past her, up the stairs to the apartment and flopped down onto his bed. Johanna followed him.

'Alfred!' she said crossly. 'Stop behaving like a baby. You must have known this would happen, sooner or later.'

Alfred sat up. 'Of course I knew,' he said. The dispensations hitherto granted to grammar school boys, postponing conscription to the Wehrmacht until they had finished their education, had recently been revoked in the War Ministry's panic over the massive losses in the east, and the Normandy landing in the west. Many of Alfred's classmates had already left for the front. He added miserably, 'I just hoped it wouldn't.'

He passed his physical examination with flying colours; indeed, all the young men lined up in the gymnasium in vests and underpants passed with flying colours. The Wehrmacht needed every soldier they could get their hands on. His orders came through very shortly afterwards. He was to join the 325th Infantry Division, along with three hundred other men, to support the reinstallation of the Siegfried Line near Alsace.

Johanna laughed out loud when she saw him in his uniform for the first time, but it was a nervous laugh, tinged on the edges with a slight hysteria.

'What will do you while I'm away?' Alfred asked, leaning down slightly to take her hands in his. He was by now a good few inches taller than she was.

Johanna attempted a smile. 'Don't worry about me. I'm sure some handsome rich stranger will appear soon to sweep me off my feet.'

'Perhaps,' he said, and added quietly, 'Frau von Markstein's not going to last forever.'

Johanna's face became serious, and she glanced up with an expression he couldn't read. 'Don't worry about me, Alfred. Besides, I know where she keeps her money.' She embraced him, held him for a long time and then released him. 'At least you're going west,' she said finally. 'And it can't go on forever, can it?'

The following day, Alfred and hundreds of other soldiers boarded a train at Anhalterbahnhof, which took them first to Hanover, then in a second train through Frankfurt and finally arriving just outside Strasbourg some eighteen hours later. The journey was long and hot, and the heat of the other men in the overcrowded coach caused Alfred to sweat and itch in his bulky uniform. Upon arrival, the men swore an oath to the Reich and were given three days of basic combat training, where they were taught little more than how to clean, load and fire a rifle.

On his first night, Alfred was assigned a bunk bed to share with Hans Bachmann, a young man from Oldenburg. Hans was a slender boy, about the same age as Alfred, with very dark hair and eyes and a curved, elegant nose, which, Alfred soon gathered, made him a prime target for some of his more malevolent comrades. One of the kinder nicknames they gave him was 'Jew boy'. Unfortunately for Hans, he also had a clumsy and rather effeminate manner, which only compounded the boy's suffering. So although Alfred didn't set out to act as Hans' protector, it took only a few kind words on the first night, when Alfred asked whether he'd prefer the top or bottom bunk, for Hans to adopt him as his new best friend.

A day after basic training had ended, the unit set out on a march towards Hürtgenwald – sixteen kilometres in the baking sun. The men marched largely in silence, the experienced and battle-weary soldiers perhaps saving their strength for what was to come, the younger ones, like Alfred, imagining what exactly that might be. A small pebble inside his boot had been grinding into his heel for hours, and he was now trying to focus away from the pain. But then he was beset by an involuntary mental image of meeting an enemy soldier, perhaps a boy like himself, and then raising his rifle, placing a finger on the trigger as he looked this other boy, this stranger, in the face and then . . .

'I'm not, you know,' Hans said beside him, forcing him out of his thoughts.

'What?' Alfred asked.

'A Jew,' Hans said. 'I'm not a Jew. I can trace my family back to the seventeenth century. I can *prove* it,' he added forcefully.

Alfred shrugged.

'It's just that – ' Hans suddenly stumbled and almost fell, but caught himself and rushed forward to get back in line. He continued a little breathlessly. 'It's just that everyone in my family is dark-haired, my mother, my father, my brothers – '

Alfred cut him off. 'I don't care,' he said, and then noticing the wounded look on Hans' face, added, 'I think you're fine just as you are.'

A smile spread over Hans' face. He pulled his shoulders back and marched on. After just over an hour's march, Alfred's throat felt swollen with thirst. He was just about to ask Hans if he could unfasten his canteen from his pack, when he heard the crack of a shot and the man in front of him dropped to the ground. More shots followed, presumably from a sniper's rifle; then a grenade landed in the midst of the unit, exploding seconds later and blasting several men into the air. Alfred was thrown sideways and must have blacked out for a moment, for when he came to his senses, he was lying face down on the dusty track. Hans was beside him, bleeding from a cut above the eyebrow.

'Quickly!' Hans shouted. 'Get up.' There was shouting all around them and the sound of more shots being fired. The unit was scrambling about wildly, men dropping everywhere. The air was full of smoke and dust, and groans and calls of '*Hilfe!*'

Alfred got to his feet but couldn't quite find his balance. Hans pulled him off the track, into the woods, and they ran, Alfred staggering like a drunk man, through the trees, until the noise fell away into the distance. When they had walked in silence for some twenty minutes through the increasingly dense woods, they sat down on the dry forest floor. Alfred looked over at Hans, who had fished some tobacco out of his pocket and was now attempting to roll a cigarette. But his hands were trembling violently, and Alfred realised he was still in shock from the ambush.

'Here, I'll do that,' he said, taking the paper and the few strands of tobacco from Hans. He was no expert, but he had dextrous hands, and quickly rolled a matchstick-thin cigarette, which he handed back to Hans.

'I – ' Hans started, looking at Alfred from his dark, hooded eyes, but Alfred shook his head.

'You smoke that,' he said quietly, 'and then we'll eat something. Just make sure to put it out properly. We don't want to start a forest fire.'

Although he had no idea when they would next find food, it seemed sensible to keep their strength up for as long as they could and use their rations. He also feared that without any sustenance, Hans might fall seriously into shock, and he didn't relish the thought of carrying the man, however slim he looked, through the forest. So he took his food box – a cream-coloured cardboard box with the words *Nur für Frontkämpfer im Infanterieverband* stamped on it – from his kitbag and opened it. This *eiserne portion* – iron ration – consisted of canned Cervelat meat, some dry, crumbly zwieback crackers and a small bag of coffee powder. They had heard wondrous tales of the rations found on captured American soldiers – items such as chocolate, fruit bars, peanut paste, chewing gum and biscuits, most of which Alfred had never tasted, even before the war. If the tales were true, how would they stand a chance of winning this war? But for now, he was content with what he had, so he opened the can of meat, cut a slice off with his knife and offered it to Hans. Then he cut some for himself. It was salty on his tongue, but tasted good. Soon, they had finished the first can, so they set about the crackers, eating silently but urgently. Then, when Alfred's ration box was empty, they opened Hans' and finished that, too.

Feeling more satiated than he had for a long while, Alfred leaned back on his kitbag and felt the exhaustion tug at his body, felt himself sinking into the moss and dead dried leaves that made a mattress of the forest floor, creating a soft, fragrant bed more comfortable than any bunk. But as it got darker and darker, it soon became clear that without a map, or a radio to contact the rest of the unit, they would have to find shelter for the night.

'Let's sleep here,' Hans suggested. 'Maybe they'll come looking for us.'

Alfred thought for a moment. The night air was certainly warm enough to sleep outside.

No. You're too exposed here.

You must find somewhere safe to sleep.

Alfred knew they were right. Although it felt as if they were miles inside the forest, he couldn't be sure that they weren't camped at its very edge and thus vulnerable to discovery and capture, or worse, to be mistaken for deserters.

He turned to Hans. 'No. We should move on.'

He helped Hans to his feet and they continued through the forest, Alfred bringing up the rear to allow Hans to set the pace. Hans was thus the first to spot the barn. It stood in a clearing, just beyond the fringes of the woods, varnished by the full moon with a white glaze. It reminded Alfred painfully and suddenly of his childhood home.

'Shall we?' Hans asked, looking to Alfred for a decision.

'I'll go and check,' Alfred said. 'You watch the rear.' He crept out of the cover of the trees and headed towards the barn, silently. Hans followed him, treading equally softly, with his rifle at the ready. Alfred opened the barn door and peered inside. It was dark and warm. Apart from a handful of irritable chickens that clucked away furiously around Alfred's feet, it appeared to be empty.

It's all right. You'll be safe here.

'All clear,' Alfred said quietly, lowering his rifle. Hans stepped in behind him and shut the door. It couldn't be bolted from the inside, so Alfred slipped out of his coat and jacket, removed his braces and attached one end to the handle and the other to a large iron ring that protruded from the wall.

'Just to make sure,' he said. 'We'll hear if anyone tries to come in.'

The two of them then climbed the ladder leading up to the hayloft.

'It'll do for the night,' Alfred said, spreading his coat out on the hay, making sure his rifle was within arm's reach.

'Better than some beds I've slept in,' Hans said.

Alfred lay down on his coat. As he shifted about to make himself comfortable, he was hit by the fragrance of hay that brought back a flood of disremembered fragments – playing in the hayloft on the farm, watching Emil and Johanna take turns to jump from increasingly taller stacks of hay, their only worry that they might get caught by their father and receive a stern telling off.

Hans also lay down and turned to face Alfred. 'What'll we do now?' he asked.

148

Alfred unbuttoned his jacket. 'We'd best get some sleep,' he said, 'and decide tomorrow.'

But he couldn't sleep. Despite his weary mind and aching limbs, he tossed and turned on the hay, at the mercy of the thoughts he had managed to suppress since they had been separated from the unit. He relived the blast of the explosion, the desperate cries of the men whose limbs had been ripped so violently and unexpectedly from their bodies; the acute, dizzying fear that he himself might so easily have been one of those lying on a dirty track with shrapnel embedded in his eye socket or a bloodied stump where an arm should be. He forced himself to lie still, and opened his eyes. Through a small round window above him, he could see the sky; it was a sumptuous dark blue, almost purple, with stars larger than he'd ever seen in Berlin. They seemed to wink at him. He turned to look at Hans, who lay fast asleep, two hands tucked beneath his face, like a child. He reminded Alfred a little of Salomon, and not for the first time, wondered what had become of his best friend. Hans' eyelashes were impossibly dark and long, even more so now, with his eyes closed. His mouth, blush-pink and soft, was ever so slightly open, though he slept so silently Alfred wondered if he were breathing at all. Then suddenly, Hans opened his eyes and looked directly at him.

'I – ' Alfred began, but Hans lifted his arm and placed his hand gently on the nape of Alfred's neck, drawing him close. His kiss was hot and dry, but it soon grew wet and thirsty as he parted Alfred's lips with his tongue. He shuffled closer and undid Alfred's trousers nimbly with his smooth slender fingers. Alfred moaned as Hans slipped his hands in and touched him, then he reached across to unbutton Hans. He had to suppress a nervous laugh when he saw Hans' swollen penis; its hooded tip made it look as though it were wearing a little bonnet.

'What?' Hans breathed anxiously, but Alfred shook his head and placed his mouth back on Hans' lips. They stroked each other, first gently, then more urgently, until after only a short minute or two they both came. Afterwards, they embraced quickly, shyly, and lay down facing each other, close enough to feel each other's warm breath on their faces. Alfred closed his eyes and fell into a deep sleep immediately.

He woke before Hans. Daylight had already crept through the small window, shooting a ray of light across the barn. The sky outside was an unbroken, extravagant blue. Carefully, not wanting to wake Hans, Alfred got up and pulled his uniform on. Then he heard the sound of feet scuffing the dirt outside, and a muted conversation in a language – English? – he couldn't understand. He dropped down, out of sight.

'Hans,' he whispered, shaking the boy's shoulder. 'Wake up. There's someone outside.'

Hans groaned and opened his eyes slowly. 'What?'

'Shhh, quiet. There's someone, some people outside.'

Alfred grabbed his rifle and looked around helplessly. He had no idea what to do next. Hans sat up sleepily. He was wearing only his vest and underpants.

More voices outside. It was definitely English. Then Alfred had an idea.

'Hans, listen to me. This is our chance. I'm going to go outside, without my weapon. Here, give me your vest.' He put his hand out, but Hans pushed it away.

'What are you going to do?' he asked. He sounded very frightened.

'Use it as a white flag,' Alfred answered. 'I'll tie it around – ' he looked down from the hayloft and spotted a pitchfork leaning up against the wall. 'I'll tie it around the pitchfork. Then they'll know we want to surrender and they won't shoot us.'

Hans looked panic-stricken. 'I can't surrender.'

'It's our only chance. In fact, it's our best chance.'

Hans' face hardened for a moment. 'I'm not letting them take me prisoner. You know what they do to people like me?' His chin was trembling. 'People like you?'

'Don't be stupid, Hans. You don't know what you're saying.'

'I'm not going to surrender.'

You know what you have to do, don't you, Alfred?

The voice caught Alfred off-guard. 'No, I don't,' he answered out loud, not caring now what Hans thought.

Take your rifle.

Alfred gripped his rifle tighter.

He's panicking. Kssss. He will have you both killed. Use the butt of your rifle to knock him unconscious.

Alfred shook his head violently. 'No.'

Hans was struggling to get dressed. 'We'll just wait in here until they leave,' he said, fumbling with his buttons. His hands were shaking uncontrollably.

You must, Alfred. Do not defy us.

As Hans got to his feet, there was a voice just outside the barn door: 'Check inside.' They looked at each other for a second, and then both dived towards the ladder, Hans beating Alfred to it. He began to climb down, rifle dangling from his shoulder and hitting every second rung.

151

Alfred took a deep breath and then jumped straight from the hayloft, rousing the chickens that began squawking hysterically.

Now's your chance! Knock him out, or you'll be sorry!

Alfred raised the butt of his rifle as Hans came towards him.

'I can't do it,' he whispered.

Now! Hit him, now!

Hans looked Alfred straight in the eye. A look flashed between them, a look both intimate and despairing. Then Hans calmly removed the braces from the iron ring, turned to Alfred and nodded, and burst through the barn door.

Alfred felt the shots as though he'd been hit himself. Sobbing silently, feeling great shudders of wretchedness heave through his body, he tore a strip of cloth from his own vest and tied it around the pitchfork. Then he got to the floor onto his stomach, shuffled forwards, and poked his white flag through the door.

DAY THREE

It was already light outside when I woke up on Christmas Eve; in fact, the winter sun must have been out in force, because I could make out a slice of very blue sky between the curtains. I rolled onto my side and yawned. My bedside clock told me that it was already half past nine and I sat up quickly. I don't usually sleep this late. My inner clock is so attuned to a six a.m. start that even during school holidays I can't help but wake up early. Alfred's presence was obviously affecting my bio-rhythm. Or perhaps my subconscious had needed the extra sleep to process the stories he had told me the day before. Either way, I didn't feel much refreshed, even after ten hours of sleep.

I swung my legs out of bed and got up. Two piles of my pupils' exam papers lay on the desk. I had hoped to have finished grading them before the New Year, but it was three days into the holidays and I hadn't even started. I opened the bedroom door quietly, thinking Alfred was still asleep, but when I got to the living room it was empty, except for the sheet and blankets he'd slept with, in a pile on the sofa. My heart gave a little lurch as I scanned the room for his suitcase.

'Alfred?' I called, trying to sound casual. But nothing. His suitcase was nowhere in sight. I had a sudden image of him wandering the icy Berlin streets, vulnerable and desperate, not knowing where to go. God, why had I mentioned a hotel yesterday? Of course he felt unwelcome. And now he might be lying on some empty street with a broken hip . . . I told myself to calm down and think. Where would he have gone? The hospital. Of course. I rushed over to pick up the phone. But before I could dial, I heard the sound of keys in the lock.

I put the phone down and called, 'Alfred? Is that you?'

His bobbing little head appeared in the doorway. 'Sorry, Julia. I didn't mean to alarm you. You were sleeping, so I thought I'd go out for a short walk. I took your keys. I hope you don't mind?'

'No,' I said, pulling my dressing gown tighter. 'That's fine. I was just . . . worried you might have – '

'I got us some breakfast.' He grinned and held up a paper bag from the bakery on the corner. Then his face dropped. 'You look pale. Did you have a bad sleep?'

I shook my head. 'Just promise me you won't disappear like that again.'

We arrived at the hospital just after lunchtime. The nurse on guard at the ICU let us in without a word. Brynja was still lying in the same position we'd last seen her in yesterday; the machines were bleeping with the same monotonous tone; and the respirator, which sounded awfully Darth-Vader-like, was still on. Alfred walked over to the bed and gently stroked her arm.

Someone at the door cleared their throat in an 'excuse me, may I have your attention please' sort of way. Alfred and I both started slightly and turned to see a youngish woman, mid-thirties or so, clasping a clipboard across her chest.

'Hello,' she said, coming towards me swiftly with an outstretched hand and an air of confidence that verged on the aggressive. I stretched out my own hand to meet hers, having got the distinct impression that if I hadn't, she would have run her hand right into me. 'I'm Dr Baal. Resident psychiatrist.'

Her handshake was cool and tight. She didn't offer Alfred her hand, but perhaps she might not have spotted him; he was standing in the shadow of some enormous life-sustaining piece of equipment.

'Are you Brynja's mother?' she continued.

'Um, no,' I replied quickly.

'Frau Krüger is a friend of the family,' Alfred said, taking a step forward out of the shadow. 'A close friend.'

Dr Baal displayed no evident surprise at his presence, but then again, perhaps she was one of those people who had trained herself never to appear nonplussed.

'Mmhmm. I see,' she said. She stared down at her clipboard for a long while. 'It's a terrible time of year for this sort of thing,' she said finally. 'So. Are either of you in a position to offer an explanation for her suicide attempt?'

I looked to Alfred. He opened his mouth as though to speak, but then shut it again. I was relieved. I wasn't sure this woman would understand.

In the absence of a response from either of us, she continued. 'It's a minor miracle that she survived at all. That was quite a drop. And I'm afraid some degree of brain damage is to be expected when – *if* – she recovers.'

'Oh, I'm not worried about that,' Alfred said.

The woman let out a brief snort. 'Well I'm glad you're taking this with such equanimity,' she said. 'But a skull fracture is a very serious matter, whatever you may think.'

Her beeper must have vibrated or something, because she took the device from a clip on her belt and looked at it.

'I'm sorry, you'll have to excuse me, I'm needed elsewhere. But please don't rush off. Herr Doktor Schmidt will want to speak with you about the possibility of organ donation. You know, just in case.' She paused when she got to the door. 'Oh, and please contact Administration on the second floor as soon as you can. They've been asking about the patient's health insurance documentation. And they can be pretty – ' she smiled curtly, '*insistent* about these things, you know?'

As soon as she had left, Alfred turned back to Brynja, taking her hand in his. He spoke softly. 'I won't let her anywhere near you, I promise.'

1946 – 1947

'Make the hole a wee bit bigger. Aye, that's it.'

Alfred dug away at the moist dark earth until the hole was about twelve inches in diameter. Then he took a handful of bone meal from a small bucket next to him and sprinkled it into the bottom of the hole. Finally, he placed the root of the sapling gently into the hole and filled in the gaps with the earth he'd dug up, pressing it down firmly with his palms. As he straightened up, Harding clapped him on the back.

'Aye, that's it,' he said. He smiled at Alfred, squinting slightly in the sun. 'You've quite the green fingers, haven't you son?'

Alfred smiled back. He liked being called son, although Harding was hardly old enough to be his father. He was perhaps ten years older than Alfred, at the most. But the man's gentle, patient manner, the way he clucked his tongue quietly when Alfred made a mistake, but praised him openly when he got things right, reminded him of his own father. Physically, though, the difference couldn't have been greater: Harding was a small, dark man with caterpillar eyebrows and crooked, nicotine-stained teeth. He had a harsh, frequent laugh, which was never far away from a cough. Alfred had been working with him for two months now, dispatched from Kingencleugh POW camp just outside Mauchline village, as a garden labourer. It was a pleasant change from the back-breaking farm work he had been assigned to since his arrival in Scotland as a prisoner of war eighteen months earlier.

Harding turned to survey the line of trees they'd planted. 'Looking good, aye. Not a crooked one in sight, eh Alfred?'

Alfred nodded. His English was by now good enough to understand most of what people said, and his active vocabulary wasn't bad either, but he couldn't seem to shake off his self-consciousness for long enough to engage in meaningful conversation, fearful of stumbling over his own tongue or forgetting a carefully rehearsed phrase. Harding, however, didn't seem to mind. He liked talking, Alfred had gathered, and evidently appreciated Alfred's listening skills. He hawked noisily and spat a glob of saliva onto the ground, as large as a small slug. Then he reached into his shirt pocket and brought out his cigarettes. He tapped one out and offered it to Alfred, who shook his head.

'Ach, I keep forgetting,' he said, taking the cigarette himself and lighting it with a match.

Alfred wiped his dirty hands on the front of his uniform.

'Be careful, there,' Harding said through a cloud of smoke. 'Dinnae want to dirty your patch, or else they'll nae ken you're one of the good ones.'

Alfred hastily tried to rub his white patch clean with his sleeve but succeeded in making it even dirtier than before. He looked up and saw Harding grinning.

'Don't mind me,' he said and winked. 'I'm just having ye on.'

It took Alfred a good few seconds to understand that that meant he was joking.

'Well, that's the last of them for today.' Harding checked his watch. 'D'you fancy a beer before I get you back? Or a wee dram?' He grinned at Alfred, almost impishly. 'You've an hour until curfew.'

But Alfred was tired. They'd been planting trees since lunchtime and his legs and back were aching. 'No,' he said, speaking slowly and deliberately. 'No thank you.'

'Right.' Harding pinched his cigarette out with two calloused fingers and bent down to pick up the bucket of bone meal. 'Home it is then.'

Alfred lived in a small hostel on Mansfield Road in the village of Mauchline – a former coaching inn that had been requisitioned as accommodation for prisoners of war living and working in the village. It was draughty and damp, but still far more comfortable than the dark and cramped Nissen hut Alfred had lived in for the past year and a half. His room on the top floor was not much larger than a broom cupboard. There was a narrow bed with a worn mattress, a wooden chair, a rag rug on the floor and a wash-basin in the corner. It was very basic, and there was only a tiny gas heater that had no hope of facing up to a Scottish winter despite its insatiable appetite for shillings, but at least he didn't have to share the room. It was his alone. Best of all, the hostel had the luxury of an indoor toilet. It was run by a stout and perpetually jolly woman named Mrs McAllister, whose cheerfulness made up for the blistering wallpaper and shabby furniture.

When he got to the hostel, Alfred mumbled a good-bye to Harding and stepped inside, where the sharp, eye-watering smell of bleach hit him immediately. Mrs McAllister's preferred cleaning technique was to slosh bleach onto everything – floors, furniture, bathroom ceramics, even plates and cups – making it difficult to breathe sometimes and rendering the skin on her hands a worryingly red colour. While Alfred was not exactly an expert on cleaning techniques (although he had done his fair share of slopping out latrines back at the camp), he did sometimes wonder whether this might have lasting effects on his health. Trying not to inhale too deeply, he poked his head into the front room and was greeted by Schulz and Holzdorff, two other POWs who had also been classified as anti-Nazi and thus suitable for relocation from the camp to the village.

'Hey, there's our third man,' Schulz cried when he spotted Alfred.

'We were just thinking of getting a game of *Skat* in before dinner,' Holzdorff added.

'Fritz not back yet?' Alfred asked. Fritz Masowski was the fourth POW in the group living at the hostel, and was working on the construction of a warehouse on the village outskirts.

Holzdorff shook his head. 'No, they'll have him working till curfew tonight. There's a storm forecast for tomorrow and they'll want to get as much done today as they can. So, how about it?' He held up the pack of cards.

But Alfred declined. He was on lesson nine of his

'Beginner's English' textbook – Present Perfect Progressive – and wanted to finish it before dinner. He shook his head apologetically and headed upstairs to his room. He kicked his boots off and lay down on the bed, feeling the heaviness of his body on the lumpy mattress. He closed his eyes for a moment, but fought off sleep and dragged himself up into a sitting position. The room was tucked just beneath the roof, and the air had become stuffy, so Alfred reached up and opened the small skylight that was set into the slanted ceiling.

Chapter 9. Present Past Progressive. I have been planting trees all day.

'All right, all right,' Alfred said quietly. It was unlikely anyone would be able to hear him from downstairs, but he kept his voice low just in case. He picked up the textbook from a small wobbly bedside table and flicked it open.

Has Jane been waiting long?

'No, Jane has been waiting only for ten minutes.'

Incorrect. It should be: No, Jane has only been waiting for ten minutes.

Alfred sighed.

Go on, repeat after me: No, Jane has only been waiting for ten minutes.

'No, Jane has only been waiting for ten minutes.'

Another voice chimed in: *Ksss, I would consider it quite rude if someone made* me *wait for ten minutes.*

That's completely irrelevant. Now, Alfred, how long has Peter had his car?

'Peter has been having his car for two years.'

Incorrect! Trick question, ha ha! It should be: Peter has had his car for two years.

Alfred screwed up his face. His voice-women had proven useful in learning English; he would certainly not have got as far as he had if they weren't at him constantly to practise. But on occasion, like today, they appeared to think it a great joke.

'I'm hungry,' he said and snapped the book shut. The smell of frying was drifting upstairs. 'And I can't concentrate on an empty stomach.'

Tut tut. There's always some excuse . . .

And the voice faded away. Alfred shoved his feet into his slippers (a gift from Mrs McAllister – she didn't like the men thumping about the house in their boots) and headed back downstairs for his dinner. The men received soldiers' rations, which, Alfred soon discovered after arriving at the hostel, were greater than those of the civilians, including Mrs McAllister, so one evening the men had decided, on a vote of three to one, to pool their weekly rations of meat, bacon, bread, margarine, cheese, tea and vegetables, and divide them equally with their landlady. Also, because Alfred was not a smoker (he had of course tried it, but found the experience wholly unpleasant), he happily gave her his ration of cigarettes. In her gratitude, Mrs McAllister had taken on the chore of preparing two meals a day for the men; a hearty breakfast and an even heartier dinner. Unlike his German comrades, Alfred quite enjoyed the stodgy and greasy food. It certainly filled his stomach, and he had even put on a little weight.

The following morning at eight sharp, Alfred stood outside the hostel waiting for Harding. He was not permitted to walk around the village unaccompanied, so he stood leaning against the brickwork, enjoying the April sun, which over the past few weeks had already begun to tan his face and arms. Despite Holzdorff's prediction, it didn't look as though a storm was on its way, but he had learned that here, the weather could turn within minutes. A young couple walked past and nodded a greeting. The man, though limping badly with his left leg, held his sweetheart proudly around the waist.

The war in Europe had been over for nearly a year, but despite his best efforts, Alfred hadn't yet managed to trace Johanna. He had written several letters to the Red Cross, but had received no response so far. Perhaps she had indeed been swept off her feet by that handsome stranger and was too busy planning her wedding, or knitting for babies. It was certainly easier to believe this than to ruminate on the rumours of barbarities committed by the Russian forces in Berlin – especially towards women.

In the distance, he spotted Harding hurrying towards him.

'Sorry I'm late,' he said, wheezing audibly. 'Dinnae mean to keep you waiting, but the wife burned my breakfast, and then one of the bairns hid my keys.'

'I have only been waiting for ten minutes,' Alfred said, grinning at his own audacity and the sudden look of surprise on Harding's face.

'Aye, that's the most I've heard you say in the past two months!' he said, clapping Alfred on the back. 'Was beginning to think ye might be simple.'

Alfred blushed. 'No, I . . . ' But he couldn't think of what else to say.

'Well, I've got a wee treat for you,' Harding said, filling the gap. 'The flower show is coming up in June – a big event round these parts – and I've volunteered you to help.' He nodded towards Alfred's hands. 'Put them green fingers to the test. Now, come on, we dinnae want to keep the minister waiting.'

It was a short walk through the village to the parish church. Alfred had been here several times before to attend Sunday worship along with Schulz, Holzdorff and Masowski. None of the men were especially religious, but they had been welcomed so warmly by the community that it had become a comforting ritual to sit among the villagers, absorbing the songs and words spoken in that soft, gentle language. The war, the bombings, the fear – it all seemed so far away to Alfred now, almost as if it had been some prolonged night terror that now, on a fine, sunny April morning, was nothing but an unpleasant memory. But at the same time, he knew he was one of the lucky ones, not like the young man with the limp he'd seen just a few moments ago. After his capture, when Alfred had heard stories of the atrocities – the word seemed too mild – he hadn't wanted to believe them. The thought of Salomon and his grandparents, Nadel, Fräulein Merz wearing that yellow patch . . . it was too much to bear. At his initial interrogation at the Command Cage in Kempton Park when he arrived in Britain, Alfred had been graded as anti-Nazi, which of course he was. But still, hadn't he put on a Wehrmacht uniform and taken up a rifle, ready to fire it at the enemy? Yet he had met with such kindness and warmth since he arrived here. It was almost impossible, this capacity for forgiveness. He desperately hoped the victors in Berlin had shown Johanna the same clemency.

Harding seemed to read his thoughts. 'Any news from your sister?' he asked.

Alfred shook his head.

'I'm sure she'll be fine,' Harding said. 'It's still chaos over there, from what I hear. Saw the damage on the newsreel, nae a building left standing, from the looks of it.' He paused and a smile crept on his face. 'Mebbe she's still running around looking for a post office.' He mimed a girl running, pretending to toss his hair back and flapping his hands. Alfred attempted a feeble smile, and they walked the rest of the way in silence.

The minister, Reverend John Drummond, was waiting for them outside the vicarage. The front garden was beautifully laid out, with two strips of very green lawn bordered by a sea of lavender. Drummond, a large, portly man with white receding hair and a red nose, appeared out of place in its midst.

'Ah, Mr Harding,' he called as Alfred and Harding approached. 'And this is our young gardener?' He stepped forward and shook Alfred's hand.

'How do you do?' Alfred said.

'Mr Harding speaks well of you,' Drummond continued. 'Said you might perhaps be our secret weapon.' He narrowed his eyes briefly, then opened them wide again and laughed as he saw Alfred's confused expression. 'Just a joke, laddie, just a joke. But we do take the flower show seriously. Cannae be having them Cumnock folk gloating again.'

'Next village south of here,' Harding explained to Alfred. 'They won the competition last time, in '38.'

'Oh,' Alfred said, feeling slightly bewildered. He hadn't a clue what they were talking about.

'Now, let me introduce you to your partner in crime,' Drummond continued. He smiled mischievously at

Alfred and boomed, 'Isobel! Come out here now, lass, and meet Alfred.'

They all turned as a petite young woman came out of the house. She wore a wide-brimmed straw hat and a pair of cotton dungarees.

'This is my daughter, Isobel,' Drummond said to Alfred. 'Isobel, this is the young man who'll be helping you with the planting.'

Isobel gave Alfred a nod. Alfred couldn't think of what to say, not in this foreign language, anyway.

'He's a wee bit shy, is Alfred,' Harding said with a laugh.

'Alfred Werner. How do you do?' Alfred said, forcing out the words and feeling his face redden as he held his hand out to the girl. He recognised her from Sunday service, but had never seen her up close. She had fair hair – 'strawberry blond', his English textbook had taught him – and round hazel eyes that gave her a slight look of astonishment. Alfred thought her absolutely beautiful. He swallowed, acutely conscious of how he must appear in his coarse, ill-fitting uniform, which was marked on one trouser leg with a large white 'P'. But Isobel just shook his hand primly and gave him a smile that could have been interpreted as either shy or aloof, he wasn't sure.

'How do you do, Alfie?' she answered.

This caused Harding to let out a spurt of laughter. 'Alfie!' he said. 'Now that's a fine one!'

Now Isobel turned a deep shade of red. 'Oh, I'm sorry. Isn't that your name?'

'Yes, yes,' Alfred answered, anxious to cover her embarrassment. 'Please call me Alfie.'

She gave him a strained smile and her colour gradually

receded. There was a short tight silence. Drummond came to the rescue.

'Well, it'll nae do standing around and chatting. There's work to be done!' He pointed to the side of the vicarage, where Alfred saw a wheelbarrow filled with dozens of plant pots. 'Those are the primroses,' he said. 'You'll need to plant those before they die of thirst. And then you can perhaps decide on other flowers that might match. Colours, shapes, that sort of thing.' He winked at Isobel. 'But I'll leave it to the experts.'

Isobel took a couple of steps towards the side of the house. Alfred, unsure of whether he should follow her, remained where he was. Then she turned and smiled, the brim of her hat shading the upper part of her face, emphasising her full pink lips and her very white teeth. 'Um, do ye want to come round here? Perhaps start by fertilising the roses?'

Drummond patted Alfred on the back. 'Well, I'll just leave you to it, then,' he said, and turning to Harding, added, 'Mr Harding, may I offer you something to drink?'

Harding nodded. 'Aye, sounds grand.'

And the two men left Alfred and Isobel standing in the garden and went inside. Isobel led the way around the house to the back, while Alfred picked up the handles of the wheelbarrow and followed.

'The compost,' she said, pointing to a small wooden frame close to the fence that separated the vicarage garden from the church grounds. 'And there, a shovel,' she continued. 'I'll make a start over here.' She knelt down on the grass and began unloading the primroses from the wheelbarrow. Alfred stood and watched her for a moment. Her skin was pale and creamy, and her

167

forearms had already begun to pinken in the sun. She must have noticed him staring, because without looking up, she said, 'And just in case you're wondering, he'll be keeping an eye on you.'

She turned to the house and waved in the direction of a small window. Sure enough, Drummond was standing there, looking out. He waved back at Isobel, then at Alfred. Alfred gave him a small smile and picked up the shovel.

They worked side by side for a couple of hours, while the sun gained strength and made the sweat pour off Alfred. Occasionally, he heard one of his voice-women mocking him gently, *Alfie, Alfie*, but he closed his mind to it as best he could. He was surprised at Isobel's strength and stamina, given her slight frame, but he knew how strong the war had made Johanna, how hardship could bring out hidden strengths in people. He wondered briefly how the war had been here, in Ayrshire; he couldn't imagine the place being anything other than perfectly tranquil.

After a while, Drummond called out of the window that they should stop for a breather, so Isobel fetched some cool lemonade from the house and they sat down in the shade of the porch to drink it. For a long while, they sat wordlessly, surveying their morning's work.

Isobel broke the silence. 'Do you miss home, Alfie?' she asked suddenly.

Alfred put his glass down. 'Yes,' he answered slowly. 'Sometimes.'

'I bet you cannae wait to get home to your family.'

Alfred shrugged. Johanna was all that was really left of his family, and in the absence of any response to his letters, he wasn't sure if she was still alive. In fact, he wasn't even sure where home was, anymore. But he didn't know how to put this into words, so he said, 'Your father is a nice man.'

Isobel smiled. 'He can be. Very protective, as you've seen. I shan't think he will ever let me get married.'

'And your mother?'

'Oh, she died when I was a bairn. That's why my dad is the way he is, I reckon.' She twisted her mouth slightly and sighed. 'Cannae even remember what she looked like. But he says I take after her, so I suppose I see her every time I look in the mirror.'

Alfred was dying to say something suave and charming along the lines of *Then she must have been very beautiful*, but he couldn't trust his tongue not to trip him up and make him look as stupid and embarrassed as he felt. So instead, he let out a sort of consenting grunt, more frustrated than ever at his language handicap. He made a firm promise to himself to use every spare moment he had with his English textbooks.

Isobel spotted something on the ground between them. 'Ooh, look,' she said. 'A ladybird.'

They both bent down to have a closer look and their heads almost touched. Isobel sat up quickly, appearing a little flushed, and took a long sip from her glass. 'Best get back to work,' she said.

Presently, Harding and Drummond emerged from the cottage together, smelling deftly of ale.

'Well, looks like they've done a fine job here,' Harding said, taking out a cigarette and lighting it. He quickly succumbed to a coughing fit.

'Indeed,' Drummond agreed, when Harding had caught his breath back. 'Now, Isobel, would you get your friend here a couple of ham sandwiches? He must be hungry.'

Alfred watched her disappear into the house.

'D'you think you can spare him again, say, on Tuesday?' Drummond asked Harding.

'Aye, we can sort something out, I'm sure. What d'you say, Alfred? Fancy helping out here a couple of mornings a week till June?'

Alfred half-shrugged, half-nodded, trying to contain his delight at the thought of seeing Isobel again. 'Yes, I would,' he said, as casually as possible.

Presently, Isobel returned with his sandwich. When she handed it to him, her finger brushed against his hand lightly, causing them both to blush. Alfred glanced over to Drummond, but he hadn't seemed to notice.

Over the next two months leading up to the flower show, Alfred spent three glorious mornings a week in the company of Isobel (though chaperoned at all times by Miss Preston, an elderly member of the flower show committee), helping her prepare the ground and plant the flowers according to the designs of the parish committee.

After a few weeks, Alfred confessed to Isobel that he wanted to improve his English, so she helped him practise unfamiliar words and phrases, laughing a lot when he got things wrong but never making fun of him. He learned that she loved horse-riding and had a crush on Gary Cooper, that her best friend's name was Janice and that she'd love nothing more than to see Will Fyffe in pantomime at the King's Theatre in Glasgow. 'In fact,' she said, 'I'd go to anything in Glasgow, just to go there.'

In return, despite his lack of fluency in English, Alfred told her about growing up on von Markstein's estate, about his parents' death, about the orphanage and wartime Berlin. Once, blushing slightly, Isobel told him about a lad she'd been quite fond of, Robert, but who hadn't returned from the war. She had seemed wistful for a moment, but then smiled and asked if it were true that all German *Fräuleins* looked like Marlene Dietrich.

Alfred borrowed a pile of books on gardening and horticulture from Harding, grateful for the first time that he'd had to endure so many hours of Latin at school. He also worked his way steadily through *Beginner's English I and II*, and by early June was already halfway through *Further English Grammar*, and regularly perused a dictionary of English idioms just before going to sleep every night. (The only book of little use was *Everyman's English Pronunciation Dictionary*, which he consulted often but couldn't quite match up what was written there to the language he heard spoken around him.)

Although he thoroughly enjoyed the work, noticing with some pride his increasing expertise, he was dreading the flower show. Not because he was concerned about winning or losing the Ayrshire in Bloom competition, the first such event to take place since the outbreak of war, but because it would mean the end of his time spent with Isobel. Under any other circumstances, they would have been considered a courting couple – having long since shed their initial shyness. They appraised each other's habits and preferences as though sizing up a possible future together, flirting gently and seeking out occasions when their hands or arms might touch surreptitiously, if only to feel the other's skin against their own. But as things stood, neither of them would have dared call it that. It was, of course, strictly prohibited to fraternise with the enemy.

Then the fourteenth of June arrived in a rush, and with it,

the official opening of the flower show. Despite all the hard work, the town of Irvine eventually claimed first prize, much to Drummond's annoyance and disappointment. But as far as Alfred was concerned, it didn't matter who won. Without the flower show, he would never have met Isobel.

But soon enough, his regular work resumed. There was plenty of it: planting trees, cutting hedgerows, clearing the cemetery of weeds and wilted flowers, mowing great expanses of lawns. Now, he only saw Isobel once a week, at Sunday service, but apart from a few rare instances when she managed to hang behind and chat with him briefly at the church door, they saw very little of one another. Alfred longed for her, with his heart and his body, and his dreams were fuelled by strange dreams that left him both exhausted and even fuller of desire for her.

Then, in September, he was assigned back to working in the fields to assist with the autumn harvest. By the time December arrived, he felt miserable and deflated. Masowski and Schulz received their repatriation orders just in time for Christmas, and suddenly, the prospect of Alfred returning home became real again. He had heard rumours of POWs in the south putting in requests to stay, but these were all skilled workers, men whose professional expertise was considered valuable and necessary to rebuild the parts of the country the *Luftwaffe* had devastated. He lay on his bed one evening, listening to Mrs McAllister humming Christmas carols downstairs.

Cheer up, Alfie.

'Don't call me that,' he answered sullenly.

Ooh, a bit touchy, are we?

Leave him alone. Let him wallow in his self-pity for a bit. It'll do him good to get it out of his system.

'That's easy for you to say. So bloody easy.' He turned onto his side.

Don't be like that, Alfred, I was just trying to –

A knock on the door interrupted her.

Alfred sat up quickly, worried that he might have spoken aloud. 'Come in,' he called.

The door opened hesitantly. 'Alfred, dear, I was wondering if you'd like to come and join us.' It was Mrs McAllister. 'I've made some mince pies. Ever had one?'

When Alfred didn't answer straight away, she came in and sat down beside him on the bed. 'It's hard, I know, to be away from home at this time of year.' She put a plump, chemical-reddened hand on his thigh and squeezed gently.

'It's not that,' he said miserably.

Mrs McAllister clucked softly. 'Ah. I see.'

Alfred raised his eyebrows. 'Do you?'

She smiled, and opened her mouth and, to Alfred's surprise, began to sing.

> *My heart is sair – I dare na tell*
> *My heart is sair for Somebody*
> *I could wake a winter night*
> *For the sake of Somebody.*
> *O-hon for Somebody! for Somebody!*
> *could range the world aroun'*
> *For the sake o' Somebody.*

She had a sweet, youthful voice, and Alfred would have liked her to keep on singing. But she stopped and said, 'That's our very own Mr Burns, you know. Lived right opposite here, many hundreds of years ago. And he knew how to write a love song.'

'Mrs McAllister, I . . . ' The words remained lodged in his throat.

'It's the lass, isn't it? Isobel,' she said gently. Then she chuckled. 'D'you nae think we know all about it? Oh, Alfred, we were all young once, and,' she patted his leg, 'the heart's desire does nae care about this uniform. There but for the grace of God, I always say.'

'I love her,' he said, his voice barely above a whisper.

'I know, of course ye do. But listen now. I'm nae to tell you this, really; Mr Harding wanted to let ye know, but they've lifted the ban and Reverend Drummond has kindly invited you to spend Christmas with him and Isobel.' She clapped his thigh again as she rose to her feet. 'Which just goes to show, ye cannae always see what's coming round the corner.'

Disappointingly though, what was coming around the corner was not a Christmas spent with Isobel and her father, and Alfred's heart remained indeed 'sair'. The day before Christmas Eve, Drummond received a telegram informing him that his younger sister Fay, a war widow living in Aberdeen, had fallen and broken her leg, so he packed himself and Isobel off onto the train, and Alfred was left behind to spend Christmas with Mrs McAllister and Klaus Holzdorff. To compound his misery, Alfred received a letter from the Red Cross on New Year's Eve.

Dear Mr Werner,
In response to your enquiry dated 7th of July, 1946, we regret to inform you that the International Tracing Service has been unable to locate the whereabouts of Miss Johanna

von Markstein (a.k.a. Johanna Werner). The building at the given address (Barbarossastraße no. 39 in Berlin-Schoeneberg, Germany) was destroyed by Allied bombs in March 1945. Should the aforementioned person register on any ITC or Red Cross list, we shall inform you immediately.

Sincerely . . .

Alfred didn't show the letter to either Harding or Mrs McAllister. He kept it with his personal belongings – still hopeful that Johanna had, against all odds, somehow managed to survive – until it was destroyed in a fire two years later.

Winter came and went; Alfred's body became strong and muscular – and lean, despite Mrs McAllister's best efforts to fatten him up. Come spring, and Isobel's twenty-first birthday, he had still not openly declared his love for her. He felt close to bursting with his feelings for her, but each time an opportunity arose that seemed the perfect moment – a shared moment after Sunday service, a chance meeting in the village square – his nerve faltered. He just wouldn't know what to do if she didn't reciprocate his feelings. He finally submitted an official request to the Immigration Office in London for permission to stay, and waited all summer for an answer, but none came. For three weeks during July, Isobel and her father took a holiday in the Highlands, and during this time it rained almost every day. It was as though the weather was venting his feelings, Alfred thought miserably.

But in early August, the grey skies suddenly cracked open to reveal a hot white sun. Alfred and Harding had been tending the local school's playing fields all day in time for the start of the new school year. They walked through the village, exchanging stories about school days. The restrictions on the free movement of prisoners of war had long since been lifted – although Alfred was still officially barred from public houses and the local cinema in his POW uniform – but Harding seemed to enjoy accompanying Alfred home each night, and so they had kept up the habit. On Kilmarnock Road, Harding stopped outside a newsagent's.

'Need to get some ciggies,' he said. 'I'll be just a wee minute.'

He stepped into the shop, and Alfred leaned up against the wall and took out a handkerchief to wipe the sweat off his forehead. He felt his appetite growing in the pit of his stomach and wondered what Mrs McAllister was planning to serve for dinner.

Then: *Alfred. Go inside and buy a newspaper.*

'What? Why?' he asked silently.

Go and buy a newspaper. There's something you might like to see.

Alfred wasn't in the mood for arguing, although he felt hot and cross at what he presumed was yet another of the voice-women's language learning exercises. His English was almost fluent by now. He pushed open the door to the shop. The little bell above the door tinkled brightly and Harding and the newsagent looked over at him.

'Be just a minute,' Harding said, fishing in his pocket for change.

'I . . . ' Alfred began, but then he spotted the rack of newspapers, and realised why he had been sent in. The headline was the same on all of the front pages, in a number of verbose or vulgar variations. It announced the wedding between German prisoner of war Heinz Fellbrich and his English sweetheart, June. It was the first such marriage to take place. Below the headline, most papers carried the same photograph: a couple, separated by a white fence, leaning forward to kiss, and behind them a large sign reading '402 P.W. Camp'.

Harding followed Alfred's gaze and grinned. 'Aye, dinnae let that be giving you any ideas, son.'

Alfred, flustered and feeling the heat rise to his face, shook his head. 'No, I – '

Harding paid for his cigarettes and came to stand next to Alfred. 'Good luck to them,' he said, looking at the couple in the photograph. 'It's about time they let love grow where the seed's been planted. Better than a war, any day. And who knows how long this peace will last?' He nudged Alfred with his elbow. 'Come on, lad, let's get you home.'

As soon as he arrived at the hostel, Alfred bounded up the stairs to his room, washed his face and hands hastily in the basin, and changed into a fresh shirt. He met Mrs McAllister on the stairs on the way down.

'Tea's ready in ten minutes,' she said, but he just grinned at her and rushed to the front door.

'I have something to do,' he blurted out. 'I will hurry.'

'Oh, and there's a letter for you,' he caught her saying. He stopped, one foot already on the pavement, and turned around. 'Here,' she said, handing him the envelope.

He tore it open, and could hardly contain his excitement. His request to stay in the country had been granted. He took Mrs McAllister in his arms and kissed her square on the mouth. Then he rushed out. He ran

177

all the way to the vicarage, side-stepping dog-walkers and women pushing prams, scooting through bicycle traffic, not caring what any of the passers-by thought. When he got to the cottage, he stood on the doorstep for a moment, rehearsing his words breathlessly and trying to compose himself as best he could. His hand was shaking as he rang the doorbell, and after a long few moments, Drummond answered.

'Alfred!' he said, a broad smile on his face. Then his face darkened. 'What's the matter? Has there been an accident? You'd better come in.' He opened the door wider and let Alfred step in.

'Reverend Drummond,' Alfred said, still somewhat out of breath but not stopping in case his nerve left him at the last minute, 'I would like . . . no, I wish . . . no, *verdammt!* Please, Reverend Drummond, may I marry your daughter?' It came out in a rush, not at all like Alfred had planned it, but at least he'd said it. He stood, hardly daring to blink, waiting for a response.

Drummond breathed in and out heavily. 'I cannae say I wasn't expecting this,' he said finally. 'But – ' he stopped and his gaze went to a point past Alfred's shoulder. Alfred turned, and saw Isobel standing at the door to the kitchen. She was holding a plate in one hand and a dish cloth in the other, and from the slight tremble in her hands Alfred guessed she had heard everything.

Drummond continued, 'In that case, I suppose you'd better ask the lass yourself.'

DAY THREE

Alfred sat at the kitchen table while I cleared our dinner plates away. Twice, I banged myself – my elbow and then my hip – against one of the kitchen cabinets. I was beginning to get worried. I could hardly keep Alfred here indefinitely. Somebody would have to be informed sooner or later.

He read my thoughts. 'Don't worry, Julia. I won't be on your hands for much longer.'

I turned away. This particular phrase stung me unexpectedly. 'When I'm dead . . . ', 'I won't be around much longer . . . ', 'You'll soon be rid of me . . . ' I hated it when my dad said these things. In fact, I hated a lot of the things he did and said towards the end, and I hated myself for it.

'I mean it,' Alfred said. 'Listen. I'm well aware how this sounds, but . . . '

'It's all right. We don't have to discuss it.'

'No. I mean, yes. We do have to discuss it.' He sounded urgent. 'Please, Julia. Sit down.'

I put the final plate into the dishwasher and sat down. 'You're welcome to stay for a while longer, Alfred,' I said, 'but we do have to sort out . . . '

'Three days,' he said.

'As long as you like – '

'No. I have three days left.' He spoke slowly but resolutely.

'Alfred, I . . . '

'Please, Julia. Let me explain.' He glanced around the kitchen as though looking for the right words. Finally, he said, 'I have three more days.'

I shook my head. 'Stop it, Alfred. Please. We'll wait until the holidays are over, and then . . . '

'Julia.' He reached over and held my hands. 'I understand how ludicrous this must sound. But I need you to trust me. I have three days to live and this is why I need you to listen to my story. So you can tell Brynja. I need you to trust me,' he repeated more urgently.

I didn't speak.

'My voices – ' He paused and rubbed his face with his hands. When he next spoke, his voice was unsteady. 'My voices have told me. Three more days. Please, Julia. I know it sounds extraordinary.' He reached over again and squeezed my hands.

'Okay,' I said with a sigh, pulling my hands away from his. 'Whatever you say.'

We sat silently for a moment. 'Then may I continue with my story?' he asked.

'Of course,' I said quietly.

Hours later, the bells from the Apostel Paulus church on Klixstraße began ringing out, calling to midnight mass. Alfred had finished talking and was sitting on the armchair with his head resting against the back. He looked exhausted. I was about to suggest turning in for the night, when he spoke.

'May I ask you something?'

'Sure.'

'And please tell me if it's none of my business.' He leaned forward. 'I was wondering why you're alone at Christmas.'

My stomach fluttered but I forced a smile. 'Well,' I said, nodding in his direction, 'I'm not alone, am I?'

'Of course.' His hands began trembling, and he clamped them between his thighs. 'I'm sorry. I didn't mean to . . . '

'It's all right, Alfred. It's no big secret. I'm single – well, divorced – and I've spent the last year and a half caring for my father. He died two months ago.'

'I'm sorry.'

I shook my head. 'Don't be. He was very old, and very sick, so . . . Anyway, I took some time off work to look after him, and I suppose I lost touch with . . . well, it's hard to cultivate friendships when you're . . . busy like that. When he died, I felt exhausted. But more than that, I felt relieved. I just needed a break, you know? And for the first few weeks I kept thinking that when I'd recovered my strength, I could go back to caring for him. But of course . . . ' I shrugged, and when I looked over at Alfred, I realised I was talking to myself. He had fallen asleep, and he breathed in and out slowly with a gentle snore. I covered him with a blanket and went to bed.

1948

Alfred woke to a sound he couldn't quite identify. He opened his eyes, and although the bedroom was still dark, he felt rested and realised that it was almost morning. He turned over, but Isobel's side of the bed was empty. He checked the bedside clock. It was quarter past six, half an hour before he usually got up. He heard the noise again coming from downstairs; it was an intermittent splattering sound, as though someone were slopping water into a pail every few minutes.

'Isobel!' he called, getting out of bed and slipping into his dressing gown. He had to switch on the light to find his slippers; they hadn't yet put down carpeting in the bedroom and the floor was icy cold. 'Is that you? Why are you up so early?'

He made his way downstairs quickly, towards the sound, which was coming from the kitchen.

'Alfie, I . . . '

'Isobel? What's the matter?' he said, coming into the kitchen and seeing her, on her knees, retching into a bucket on the floor. She looked up as he came in and gave him a tight smile, but turned again immediately to vomit into the bucket.

Alfred rushed forward. 'Isobel. Are you sick?' He went to gather her hair with his hands, to stop it falling into her face, but she pushed his hand away. Her face was ashen and a few strands of wet hair stuck to her cheeks. 'You're freezing,' he continued, feeling her cold skin through the thin fabric of her nightie. He ran into the living room and grabbed a blanket. He draped it around her shoulders, as she shivered slightly and vomited yet again. The contents of the bucket were a watery, brownish mess.

'Shall I call a doctor?' he asked, but she shook her head. 'Then let me make you a cup of tea,' he insisted, in his helplessness, and when he thought he saw her nod began to fill the kettle. As the tap spluttered and then gushed freely, the helplessness gave way to anxiety, rising in him swiftly and inexorably and making his hands tremble. Isobel coughed and groaned. Alfred set the kettle on the gas stove and waited for the water to boil. She was sick. If he'd paid more attention, he would have spotted the signs earlier. For it was true: over the past few weeks, Isobel had been going to bed earlier and earlier, and even when Alfred joined her only minutes later, was already fast asleep. She'd complained of headaches and tiredness, and the seemingly inexhaustible capacity for lovemaking they'd experienced for almost an entire year after the wedding had given way to the barest of touches. He poured out the tea while his imagination went on a wild rampage of illnesses she might have acquired – pneumonia, diphtheria, tuberculosis, fatal food poisoning . . . Then suddenly, incredibly, he heard laughter. It came at first from a distance somewhere to his left, but then grew louder and louder, until it was right between his ears, blocking out the sound of Isobel retching.

Tee hee, hee hee! Ha ha, ha ha ha! HA HA HA!

He wanted to shout out 'Shut up! How dare you laugh?', but then the laughter faded and he crouched down beside Isobel, placing the steaming cup of tea on the floor next to her. Finally, it appeared that her stomach had settled, and she sat back on her knees and gestured for him to pass her a tea towel. After she'd wiped her mouth she looked up at him, her face pale and blotchy. She swallowed painfully, but then gave him a wide smile. 'Oh Alfie,' she said, her voice cracking. 'I wanted to save the news till tomorrow, as your Christmas present. But ... Alfie, we're going to have a baby!'

Alfred leaned forward and kissed her sour-smelling lips and then began to laugh, loudly, filling up the tiny kitchen with the sound of his joy.

The terrace house they lived in was small and cramped, with a bedroom and box room upstairs, and a living room giving way to a kitchen downstairs, but it was the best Alfred could afford on his wages. It was a world away from the spacious grandeur of Franziska von Markstein's apartment, but Alfred was more than content. Since becoming officially released from his prisoner-of-war status in the summer of '48, he was now earning £ 4/6s. a week, doing much the same work as before, but now, he was an employee of the East Ayrshire council outdoor amenities services and Harding was his colleague, rather than his guard.

With Isobel now expecting, her rations were increased

to include an extra half pint of milk and cod liver oil, and the local greengrocer, Mr Whitlaw, was known to reserve oranges for expectant mothers. However, more often than not, Alfred was the beneficiary of these additional nutrients. The morning sickness, which in Isobel's case may just as well have been termed 'morning, afternoon and evening sickness', took its toll. Rather than putting on weight, she grew alarmingly thin, her eyes appearing even rounder and larger in her increasingly gaunt face.

'Promise me you will eat something,' Alfred said every morning before he left for work, and she would nod tiredly, but when he returned home, he would often find her lying on the couch, a damp cloth on her forehead, and when he checked the larder, could see that she hadn't eaten a thing. The physician, Dr Cummings, told them that this extent of sickness was not terribly common, but nothing to be worried about. Yet Alfred worried nonetheless. It didn't seem right, a pregnant woman losing weight like that. He tried to picture the baby inside her – how was it to grow if the mother didn't eat?

Then, one morning, he woke to the smell of bacon and eggs. He dressed quickly and went downstairs to the kitchen. Isobel was standing at the stove, taking four rashers of bacon from under the grill and putting them on a plate.

'Morning, Alfie,' she said brightly, and went over to kiss him. Her cheeks were flushed. 'Sit down, breakfast's almost done.'

'Are you feeling better?' he asked, taking a seat at the table. The smell in the kitchen was delicious.

Isobel let out a small giggle. 'Aye, I'm feeling much better. In fact,' she said, placing a plate of bacon, eggs and toast on the table, 'you'd better eat that quickly, or I might just have it.'

Overnight, her debilitating nausea had passed, and during the next few months, her waist began to fill out and her skin turned soft and rosy. Even their lovemaking, which had been suspended for over three months, resumed, though tentatively and in the main restricted to stroking and petting – neither of them felt quite comfortable at the thought of penetrating what they considered the baby's home.

'What do you think we should call it?' Alfred asked one night, as they lay in bed. Isobel was lying with her back to him, curled up against his chest and thighs. His arm was wrapped around her, his hand on her belly.

'Oh no, that's bad luck,' she said.

'What is?'

'To name the baby before it's born.'

'All right, then, but what do you think it's going to be? What does it *feel* like to you?'

She breathed out a gentle laugh. 'Amy says it's a wee lass.' Amy Fraser, a war widow with a lively three-year-old, was their next-door neighbour. She was only a few years older than Isobel. 'She dangled her wedding ring over it, on a string, like this see?' She raised her hand and mimed a pendulum. 'When it goes from side to side, that means it's a girl.'

Alfred smiled. 'Does it work even if it's not your ring?'

Isobel shrugged. 'Cannae get mine off. The fingers are too fat.'

They both laughed. 'Just the fingers?' Alfred said and moved his hand down to her thigh, pinching it playfully.

'Oi, you rascal!' she said, knocking his hand away.

He waited a moment, then slid his hand back onto her stomach. They lay like this for a while, and he had almost slipped into sleep when her belly moved beneath his fingers. At first, he thought Isobel had shifted her position slightly, but then he detected it again, a slight flutter and then felt a small lump moving just beneath her skin.

'Isobel,' he whispered, not daring to speak too loudly in case the moving stopped, but from her slow regular breathing he could tell that she was asleep.

The lump moved again; he could picture the baby squirming against the confines of its soft, dark cave. Was it a foot, or perhaps an elbow? He was feeling childishly excited now. He spread his fingers wider to see if he could catch any other movement, but presently, the lump receded and all he could feel was the warm skin of Isobel's belly.

'Is it really a girl?' he asked silently.

The response was so low, as though coming from a great distance, that he had to strain to hear it: *Wait and see, Alfred, wait and see...*

In September, Alfred took a series of examinations at the encouragement of Harding, which he passed effortlessly. He returned home with the first formal qualification he had ever held in a large envelope clasped under his arm – a diploma confirming that he had achieved Level I of the Principles and Practices of Horticulture. He turned the key in the lock excitedly. He would take Isobel out to celebrate; a fish supper – a rare treat to eat out – and then to the pub, where she could have that glass of stout the doctor was always going on about. He called her name as he entered, but there was no response. Thinking she might be upstairs, napping, he ran up the stairs, taking two steps at a time, but she wasn't there, either. He finally found her sitting in the kitchen in the gloom, in front of her on the table a cup of tea that must have turned cold hours before.

'I called you,' he said, at that moment picking up on the eerie atmosphere in the room, as though the air were filled with a thousand tiny malevolent charges. 'Isobel?'

She looked up and he could see that she'd been crying.

'She's nae moving,' she whispered.

'What?'

'The wee one. She's nae moving.' She began to cry again, very quietly, covering her face with both hands.

Alfred crouched down beside her and put his hand on her knee. 'Perhaps she's just sleeping. She can't move about all day, can she? Aye, she's just sleeping, getting ready for the big day, that's all.' He spoke to comfort himself as much as her.

Isobel dropped her hands into her lap. 'I even tried a hot bath,' she said, gesturing towards the bath that stood in a corner of the room. 'Took me ages to get the water warm enough. Usually that wakes her right up, it does. But . . . ' She began crying again, her face all screwed up and blotchy. 'Nothing.'

Alfred fought against the panic rising in his gut. He said, trying to keep his voice steady to hide his anxiety, 'I'll fetch Amy, how about that. She's been through it. She'll put your mind to rest.'

Isobel nodded without looking up. Alfred hurried out of the house, glad to be doing something, and rang Amy's doorbell. He waited one minute, two, three, then began banging loudly on the door.

'What the hell – ' he heard and the door opened. Amy had her hair tied up in a scarf, and her son, James, was standing behind her, holding onto her leg. 'I'm right in the middle of – ' she said, and then stopped. 'Alfred, what is it?'

Alfred explained breathlessly, expecting her to wave his concerns away with a gesture or a laugh. But instead, her face turned grave. 'How long?'

'What?' he asked, as she picked up James and hoisted him onto her hip.

'When's the last time she felt it move?'

'I – I don't know,' he said, feeling more nervous with every moment. They rushed next door. Isobel was still sitting where he'd left her; the expression on her face was distant, as though she weren't quite there. Amy flicked on the light switch.

'Isobel,' she said, putting James down on the floor and crouching down beside Isobel, much like Alfred had done minutes earlier. 'It'll be fine. Don't get yourself upset, that won't be doing anyone any good. Least of all your little lass here.' She stroked Isobel's belly. 'Now, when's the last time you felt her move?'

'I cannae be sure,' Isobel said, her voice no longer tearful, instead, Alfred thought, rather cold. It frightened him. 'A few days. Mebbe a week. I just thought – '

Amy straightened up. 'Right. I'll pop over to Angela's and make a call to the doctor. Alfred, you . . . make Isobel a cup of tea or something.'

She picked up her son and swept out of the kitchen.

A few minutes later, she returned. 'Dr Cummings is on his way. He said to lie down and not to panic.' She tried a smile. 'Here,' she reached into her apron pocket, fished out a packet of cigarettes and shook one out. 'Have one of these, to calm your nerves.'

But Isobel declined. 'I think that'd make me sick,' she said.

It was a mere ten minutes before Dr Cummings arrived at the front door, but to Alfred it seemed an age. The doctor, a tall, well-spoken Englishman with horn-rimmed glasses, shook Alfred's hand briefly and asked for Isobel.

'In the living room,' Alfred said. 'She's lying down, like you said.'

Dr Cummings placed a hand on his shoulder and squeezed it. 'Lead the way then.'

Isobel was lying on her side on the couch; Amy sat on the armchair opposite with James on her knee, smoking a cigarette. Without wasting any time, Dr Cummings unbuttoned his jacket and went over to Isobel, kneeled in front of her on the floor and snapped open his black case.

'Lift your dress for me please,' he said, adding, 'I would normally ask you to leave the room, Mr Werner, but under the circumstances . . . '

Isobel lifted her dress up to expose a large pair of cotton underpants with an elasticated waist, which she had made herself from a spare bed sheet. She wore long woollen socks pulled up over her knees; her suspender belt hadn't fit around her waist for a while now. She pushed the waistband of her underpants down so that the doctor could see her stomach and lifted her forearm to cover her eyes. A faint dark line ran along the curve of her belly from her navel to her pubic hair. Alfred hadn't seen her undressed for many months, and felt uncomfortable and slightly embarrassed on her behalf.

Dr Cummings took a wooden Pinard horn and warned, 'This might be a bit cold,' before placing the wide end of the horn on Isobel's exposed stomach and leaning forward to listen through the other end. He listened for a moment, and then placed the horn slightly to the left and listened again. He continued to reposition the horn across her belly, eyes closed, his face giving nothing away. Once, James started grizzling on his mother's lap, and Dr Cummings held his hand up and flashed a fierce stare in the boy's direction. Amy shushed him and he quietened.

The *tick-tock* of the clock on the mantelpiece was maddening, louder than it had ever been, it seemed to Alfred, and he wondered briefly whether he should move it to the kitchen, but was afraid even the slightest of movements might prevent the doctor from detecting the baby's heartbeat. Finally, with the horn positioned just beneath Isobel's left breast, the doctor nodded.

'Yes, got it,' he said, and Alfred could hear the relief in his voice. Dr Cummings straightened up and removed his glasses, pinching the bridge of his nose. He looked at Isobel. 'It's there, but it's very weak, I'm afraid. You've two, three weeks to go?'

Isobel pulled her dress back down and cleared her throat. 'Two weeks,' she said hoarsely.

Alfred took a step forward. 'But you heard it, didn't you? The heartbeat? So the baby's all right?'

Dr Cummings put the Pinard horn back in the case. 'I don't want to worry you unduly, but if the baby hasn't moved in several days, and the heartbeat is indeed as weak as it sounded, I think one should consider taking measures. Also, I'm not an obstetrician, but the location of the heartbeat leads me to believe that it hasn't turned yet.' He took Isobel's hand and gave it a squeeze. 'And you don't want it coming out feet first, believe me.'

He stood up and buttoned up his jacket. Then he pulled a packet of cigarettes out of his pocket and offered it around, but Amy was the only one to take one. He lit his own.

'My advice would be to go to hospital immediately,' he said, exhaling a cloud of smoke. 'They can examine you properly and make a decision then. If you like, I can take you in my car.'

Alfred ran upstairs and hurriedly packed a small case: Isobel's nightie, a bar of soap, flannel, talcum powder, hairbrush and toothbrush. Then he helped Isobel into the back of Dr Cummings' car and took a seat next to her. The nearest hospital was in Cumnock, some seven miles away, and they arrived there just fifteen minutes later. Dr Cummings went ahead to inform the resident physician of Isobel's condition, while Alfred helped her out of the car. She followed his instructions wordlessly, as if in a daze, keeping one hand clamped around the lower part of her stomach. When they reached the entrance door, Isobel suddenly grabbed him and dug her nails into his arm.

'I'm so frightened, Alfie,' she said in a whisper. Then she began to cry.

Alfred placed his arm around her shoulder. 'I know.'

Once inside the hospital, things went very quickly: a nurse whisked Isobel away in a wheelchair, the consultant obstetrician explained in a few sentences that he would examine Isobel, but that if Dr Cummings' diagnosis were accurate, they would have no time to lose. They would fetch the baby immediately.

Alfred was left standing in the reception area, still clutching Isobel's small case in his hand. He was too stunned to cry; instead, a sticky nauseous feeling stole through his body, and he was afraid that if he moved, even an inch, he would be sick right there on the hospital floor.

He must have stood there for a good twenty minutes, before he became aware of a sudden bustle and commotion around him. He was almost hit by a stretcher, 'Get out of the way!', 'Quick, down there, theatre one', then saw another two stretchers being unloaded from an ambulance just outside the glass door.

He heard a voice on his right, 'Sir, please step out of the way. You need to make room for the ambulance men.'

Alfred turned. It was the reception nurse. 'Come along please, sir. You can wait just here.' She took his arm and he let her guide him to a row of wooden benches that reminded him of church pews. 'You can wait here,' she repeated softly.

'My wife . . . ' Alfred began, but his voice cracked. He cleared his throat and tried again. 'How long will it be?'

'I couldn't say,' she said. 'Mr Werner, isn't it? I'm sure she'll be just fine. Fretting won't help, will it? Now you just wait here and I'll see about getting you a cup of tea.'

She walked off.

The waiting area was draughty and smelled sharply of disinfectant. An elderly woman was sitting a few yards away, crying quietly and occasionally blowing her nose on a handkerchief. Alfred shifted the case from his lap to the floor.

'Where are you?' he called silently, but there was no

response. 'Please. Tell me if she will be all right.' He thought he heard a soft moan, or a whimper, and he closed his eyes and held his breath, reaching out with his hearing, but then the old woman blew her nose again and the sound was lost.

The nurse didn't return with his cup of tea; either she'd forgotten, or she was too busy. Alfred gathered from the commotion coming from the reception that there had been a serious car accident with several casualties on Muirkirk Road. He sat on his hard bench, numb and abandoned by his voice-women, trying to quash a growing feeling of self-pity and instead attempting to picture Isobel, sitting in a hospital bed with a smile on her face, tired, but holding their small pink baby in her arms. He lifted his hands to his face and rubbed it vigorously, until the skin tingled almost painfully. Finally, the noise outside died down, and the nurse returned.

'Mr Werner? Your wife is out of surgery. If you'd follow me, please.'

Alfred tried to read her face, but she turned away briskly. He followed her to a small room leading off a long corridor. A sign above the door read: Recovery Room. The smell in here was, if anything, even more pungent than outside, and Alfred felt his eyes watering as it hit his nostrils. The light was dull; someone had drawn the curtains. Isobel was lying on a bed, pale and still on her back, her hair matted with sweat. The anaesthetic mask had left a red mark around her mouth and nose. A large machine stood in the corner of the room, fitted with two bottles of gas.

'She'll be awake any moment,' the nurse said. 'But she'll be feeling a little groggy. And sore, from the stitches. Call me if you need anything.' She went to leave.

'And the baby?' Alfred asked, not taking his eyes off Isobel.

'It's a girl,' the nurse told him quietly, 'but perhaps you should put off giving her a name just yet.'

She left the room on hushed soles, leaving Alfred to ponder for several moments what she had meant by her comment. The understanding, when it came, was crushing. He turned to look at Isobel, who had yet to wake from the anaesthetic. She was blissfully unaware of what was happening and he almost envied her. Swallowing repeatedly to keep back his tears, he decided that no child should go unnamed, so he chose – in secret – the name he wished his daughter to have. It was his mother's middle name: Brynja.

Brynja hadn't, in fact, survived being pulled from her mother's womb, but it was only the following morning during the doctor's rounds that Alfred and Isobel were informed of this. At first, Isobel just shook her head briskly, as though shaking water from her ears. From a distance, Alfred heard sobbing, and *Oh, she's gone, the poor babe. She's gone!* And then silence. His heart began to throb painfully until he thought it might explode.

'Where is she?' Isobel asked suddenly. Her voice was unnaturally bright. 'Can I see her?'

The doctor looked at her blankly. Then he said, not unkindly, 'But the body has already been disposed of. I'm sorry.'

Isobel let out a queer, strangled noise and broke into tears. Alfred, for the moment, had no tears. He sat down on the bed and took Isobel in his arms, holding her fast as her body began to shake uncontrollably. After a long while, exhaustion overcame her, and she lay limp, slumped against his chest.

'I love you,' Alfred said. 'I was so frightened you might – ' He stopped. He couldn't finish his sentence. He lowered his face to her hair and breathed in her almondy smell. 'And we'll always have each other,' he said. He heard the limpness of his own words.

She looked up at him for a moment, her eyes dull with grief, and then lowered her head again, pressing her face against his shoulder. 'But Alfie.' Her voice was tight. 'It's just nae enough, is it?'

NINETEEN NINETY-SIX
(PART II)

On the plane. Sabine is sleeping beside you, her face slack with three miniature gins and the jowls of a woman the wrong side of forty. You close your eyes. Breathing in one, one, one, breathing out two, two, two. The woman in the seat on your left moves her arm and bumps your elbow off the shared armrest. Disrupts the breathing exercise. The woman reaches up and presses the call button and within seconds, the flight attendant appears. The woman asks for water and you close your eyes again. The little girl's voice in your ear, singing, off key *la, lala, la, la laaaa*

Breathing in one, one, one, breathing out two, two, the singing fades, drowned out by the sound of the engines. The flight attendant reappears, places a plastic cup with iced water on the woman's tray, retreats back to behind her curtain.

Lufthansa stewardesses are the tallest in the industry, you once read. Five feet seven and a half inches, on average. You are tall for fourteen, taller than your girl-friends back home. Tall is good, your mom said when you stood in front of the mirror a couple of weeks ago, complaining. I wish *I* were taller, your mom said. Besides, you'll fit right in when we get to Germany.

You hope so.

Six weeks earlier, you returned home from school to find your mom happy-drunk, light on her feet but swaying only slightly, clearing out kitchen cupboards, the table piled high with plates, cups, silverware, incense stick holders, linen napkins yellowed along their creases.

Sit down, Bryn, she said, rushing over and taking your bag from your shoulder and flinging it to the floor. I've got some news. Great news.

She took a bottle of Zinfandel from the refrigerator and filled – refilled – a glass. What would you say if I told you we're moving to the greatest city in Europe? Huh? Bryn? She took a large sip of wine.

You remained standing. I, um . . .

I've got a job, Bryn! In a birthing house, well, it's an interview, but I'm through to the second stage and they're desperate for midwives over there. And with my qualifi-cations and experience – she waved the hand holding the wine glass, golden drops sloshed over the rim – they'll take me. I'm sure. And besides, we're going nowhere here, are we? Hmm? This fucking place, this fucking, motherfucking country.

She was no longer happy-drunk.

You felt numb. Numb and dizzy. It wasn't just the pills, the pills that gave you smelly discharge and swelled up your breasts, making phys ed humiliating and painful. You rubbed at the fresh scars on your arm. Your mom noticed, put her glass down and came over.

Hey, *liebling*. Shush. Don't do that. Pulling your hand away from your arm. Wine fumes on her breath. She put her arms around you, her body heat mingling with your body heat. We'll be good, I promise. We've talked about this, right?

You'd talked about it. Sabine had talked about it for years. Since you'd first moved here from San Francisco, shortly after your father had left for New York. That's what he'd told Sabine, anyway. And that's where you and your mom had followed him to, ten years ago. Sabine never found him, although she spent that first year sober and searching. And since then, since you were four years old, your mother had never stopped planning your escape – to Bali, India, Venezuela, Toronto. As though it would be that easy just to leave all the shit behind. But maybe it was. What did you know?

But what about school? you asked.

What about it? You'll go to school there. In fact, you can take some time off, huh? A couple of weeks. She smiled conspiratorially. Give you a chance to get your tongue round the language first. But it'll come quickly, you're such a clever girl. It's all good, Sabine said smiling, her mood tipping back instantaneously. She started busying herself again with the cupboards. She paused and looked up at you. Her t-shirt clung to the sweat on her back. And it might be nice to come home, what do you think?

You are bumped awake as the aircraft touches the runway in Berlin. Your mouth is dry, your limbs stiff.

Morning. Sabine is looking at you through dry, puffy eyes. Sleep well?

I guess.

Okay. The first thing we do is go for coffee. Then we find the hotel – no, shit. First I gotta sort out the paperwork at customs. But maybe I'll come back and do that later. All that stuff. Hey, maybe we'll just buy all new! As soon as I get my first pay check. What do you think? Look, the sun's shining! Specially for us.

But you aren't listening. No, that's not true. You are listening, but not to your mother. You are listening *out*, to be precise. You want to be prepared. It's difficult to tell so far, because the cabin is full of voices, passengers chatting, coughing, groaning, yawning. Sit down we all have to wait in line at passport control anyway don't forget your book all over the place I'm dying for a cigarette watch where you're stepping I'm trying it's stuck taxi or bus take care thank you for flying Lufthansa. But none of them are your voices, and you dare, timidly, to think of your dream, the one where you wake up and they're gone. Vanished. And you're free, and normal, and not crazy, and you can think and talk and sleep and read without the voices cutting into your brain. And then you hear the little girl singing and you gasp because you almost had it, you were almost free but stupid, *stupid* to think it would be that easy and you gasp again, out loud, because you realise that the singing is coming from a REAL GIRL two rows behind you, and you realise that maybe maybe your mom was right and you just left all the shit behind.

Sabine is struggling with a small rucksack beside you.

Hey mom. Your mother turns. You give her a smile.

1948 – 1949

After her release from hospital a week later, Isobel was still stiff and sore from the operation. She found it difficult and painful to take the stairs, so Alfred made up a bed for her on the sofa. Three weeks later, when she was moving about more freely again, she began to complain that Alfred tossed too much in his sleep, causing her scar to hurt. So he moved to the sofa instead. When he came home and greeted her with a kiss, she would turn away, claiming a headache or the onset of a cold. When he sat beside her in church and his arm touched her shoulder, she would shrink back as though stung.

Her words, increasingly cold, always reprimanding ('Must you always leave your dirty clothes on the floor?', 'Wash your hands, they're filthy!', 'Don't chew your food so loudly!'), showed a side to her he wouldn't have imagined existed, and they cut him deeply. Although Alfred and Isobel never spoke of their daughter – and wouldn't, for many years to come – her death had caused a fissure to appear between them, and the more Alfred tried to prevent it from tearing further, the stronger Isobel pulled away, making the fissure grow into a crack, a fracture, an insuperable chasm. *She blames me*, he thought, and although he knew, rationally, that Brynja's death had been a tragic misfortune, he was stricken with, not guilt exactly, but a feeling of desperate regret. He took her to see Dr Cummings, who – after a brief examination – told Alfred that his wife's behaviour was perfectly normal under the circumstances, and prescribed her some tranquillisers to help her sleep.

In the face of his wife's coolness, Alfred became energetic. Perhaps it was the unspent energies arising from his desire for her (for he still, despite her frigidity towards him, desired her greatly), or perhaps by keeping his hands and body busy, he hoped to distract himself from the ruminations on the death of his daughter, or – almost equally painful – Isobel's words to him: 'It's just nae enough.' He was no longer a child; he could no longer seek out some hiding place in which to wait for things to wash over him and settle, so instead, he immersed himself in his work. He began to work sixteen-hour days, although the council couldn't afford to pay him for the extra hours, but unless he had drained his body of every ounce of energy by the time he crept onto the sofa at night, he would sleep only fitfully, leaving him exhausted and red-eyed the next morning. His misery was compounded by the absence of the voice-women, whom he'd last heard at Isobel's hospital bedside. He couldn't help but feel as though he were being punished, by his wife, by his voices, and as the months went by, he had little choice but to accept that they might have vanished forever.

His state of unhappiness wasn't lost on Harding,

who confided to Alfred, in a quiet, almost embarrassed manner, that his own wife had suffered a miscarriage before the two healthy children had been born.

'But as soon as she was, ye know . . . *well* again, we just put it behind us and tried for another. There's no good in holding on to the bad.'

It was something that had, of course, occurred to Alfred, but Isobel wouldn't let him so much as touch her arm, never mind her body. As close as his friendship with Harding had become, this wasn't something he wanted to share.

After some weeks, Drummond also approached him after church one Sunday. 'You are both so young,' he said as they stood on the church steps. 'You and Isobel must put this behind you. Have some faith, Alfred.' He put his hand on Alfred's shoulder.

Alfred didn't respond. Despite his regular attendance at church, any notion of faith, of God, still eluded him; since Brynja's death, the world seemed more godless than ever.

'And please,' Drummond continued after a moment's pause, 'please take care of Isobel. She refuses to talk to me about . . . about how she feels. I'm concerned it might be eating her up, on the inside. It's at times like this that a woman needs her husband, Alfred. And vice versa. I certainly miss Margaret . . . ' His voice was low and weary, and Alfred could only guess how much Drummond missed his wife. Then Drummond patted him on the shoulder, as if to cheer himself up. 'But she has you, and that's my consolation,' he said.

Alfred looked over to where Isobel was standing, several yards away beneath a large elm tree that towered leafless, almost menacingly, above her. She stood, in her Sunday clothes and hat, her hair hanging limply onto her shoulders; it had been many weeks since she had last curled it and pinned it up. She worked her gloved fingers, restlessly, staring with an unfocussed gaze across the neighbouring cemetery. Quite close to her, a group of children was playing noisily, expending the energies they'd had to suppress while cooped up in church, but Isobel didn't seem to be aware of them. Alfred was suddenly struck by how lonely she must be, motherless, childless, with a husband too afraid to knock down the wall she'd built up around herself for fear of causing greater damage. His impotence shamed him.

'There's one more thing,' Drummond said, as they began to walk down the stone steps that led down from the church. 'I haven't mentioned this to Isobel, because I'm not sure how she'd take it.'

'What is it?' Alfred asked, afraid of yet another blow to an already desperate situation.

'It isn't as though this will come as much of a surprise,' he said, 'considering my age.'

A sickening thought struck Alfred. 'You . . . you're not ill, are you?'

Drummond looked confused, and then let out a short fat laugh. 'No! Or at least, I hope not. No, I have received confirmation of my request to retire this autumn,' he said. 'And I shall be moving up to Aberdeenshire, to live with Fay. Isobel's aunt,' he added, as though that needed explanation. 'There'll be a nice young lad to replace me, I should think.' He laughed again, but it was a little forced. They reached the gravelly path at the bottom of the steps, and Drummond became serious again. He expelled a tired sigh and said, 'It weighs heavily on me, the loss you've both suffered. And I dinnae want to intrude, but have you thought of . . . well, trying again? It would be nice to have some good news before I leave.'

Alfred shuffled his feet on the gravel. The same advice he'd been given by Harding. As if a child were that easy to replace. His father-in-law meant well, he knew that, but he didn't understand what it felt like to lose something so precious, something that deserved to live, not to die.

'I'll best be taking Isobel home,' he said as politely as he could, and left Drummond standing on the path.

Many months passed by, during which Alfred's body became muscular and sinewy from his work; the soil became embedded in the creases of skin in his palm, refusing to yield even with the most vigorous of scrubbing. His heart, however, felt fragile and bruised, and if it hadn't been for the reappearance of the voices one night, he might have imagined the vital organ just wasting away. It happened in early May 1949. The winter had finally broken and although the weather hadn't turned warm, it was certainly milder, making Alfred and Harding's work almost pleasant. Over the winter, the council had expanded Alfred's work duties to include planting small gardens for a new housing estate in Mauchline. The houses – hardly grand in size, but cosy enough and with indoor bathrooms – were planned to house the workers of some newly erected factories on the outskirts of the village. The houses were in great demand, and became occupied as soon as they had passed inspection, occasionally at a rate so speedy there was local rumour of bribes and corruption among the council. To increase his chances of acquiring one of the new houses, Alfred – with a surprisingly light heart, he noticed – applied for and was granted British citizenship.

When spring arrived, Alfred was back with Harding, tending a large vegetable garden they had begun planting in early spring in a bid by the council to supplement the villagers' rations. The long hard frost and deep snow the country had seen that winter had destroyed huge stocks of stored potatoes, leading the government to introduce yet another spate of rationing.

At the end of a long day, Harding announced that he was going to the pub and, as usual, invited Alfred to join him. But as usual, Alfred declined. He didn't intend to go home straight away. The thought of spending yet another evening in Isobel's miserable and frigid company was depressing, but he wasn't prepared just yet to become one of those hardened middle-aged men who substituted an unhappy marriage for public houses and beer. So instead, he stayed outdoors until the sun set, earthing up rows and rows of seed potatoes that had broken through, making sure the runner beans were firmly attached to their stakes, weeding between the cabbages and lettuces. He worked until his arms and legs and muscular back were aching and sore, until he felt sufficiently consumed, physically and mentally, to ward off the despair that would otherwise beset him when he lay down at night on his makeshift bed, and then set off on his short journey home.

Indeed, he was drained when he got to the house. Isobel had already retreated upstairs – to listen to the small portable wireless or to read a magazine, or perhaps to sleep, he could only guess – so he ate his cold supper of meat and potatoes on his own, drank a small glass of beer to wash it down and undressed for bed. He fell asleep almost immediately, waking several minutes later as his aching muscles twitched suddenly, like a dog dreaming of chasing a rabbit, but then drifted back into a soft, exhausted slumber.

He woke to a noise, a voice, and was immediately rushed back to the dark bedroom of his childhood, when he had been roused by the voices to go and save Marie.

Alfred, wake up.

Quickly, Alfred, there's no time to lose.

Momentarily disoriented, and still sleep-drunk, it took him a minute to remember where he was. There was enough moonlight shining through a gap in the living-room curtains to make out the patchy armchair, the hearth, the small sideboard that contained the plates and cups that had no space in the cramped kitchen, and, of course, the worn sofa he was lying on.

Quickly, Alfred, he heard again, and then: *Duck! Oh my goodness, get behind the sofa! NOW!*

Without another thought, Alfred hoisted himself over the back of the sofa and landed with a thump on the floor. Seconds later, he heard a huge crash as a brick came through the window. He was about to poke his head over the back of the sofa to see what had made that awful noise, but a voice urged him:

Not now! Stay where you are!

And just then, Alfred caught a glimpse of a quick flash of light as the brick was followed by a bottle; it smashed upon impact with the floor and suddenly, a circle of flames engulfed the small rug in the centre of the room. Alfred jumped up as another bottle, containing petrol, he assumed from the smell, and a rag for a fuse stuck in its neck, flew through the smashed window and landed near the sideboard. And then another. He yelled in fright as the burning fuel spread across the floor, blue liquid flames lapping at the curtains, the wallpaper, the carpets. Before he could react, it seemed as though he were surrounded by fire, the flames hungrily catching at anything they touched. The voice-women were howling in his head. He heard the sound of glass breaking, then the smash of another bottle, but this time not on the ground floor where he was, but above him.

Isobel.

Alfred rushed across the room, coughing wildly now, for the room had become engulfed by a thick, viscous smoke, but hardly feeling the heat that singed the hair on his arms. As he mounted the stairs, he heard a shout from beyond the broken window, 'Nazi whore!', then laughter and more shouting, but he couldn't make out the words, because he was coughing more than ever, the smoke rising up through the small house. He ran into the bedroom and saw Isobel lying on the bed, stirring but not fully awake. He saw at once that there was no fire here, no broken glass, the window behind the curtain quite undamaged. But he didn't stop to dwell on it.

'Isobel!' he called. 'Wake up! There's a fire!'

'What?' Her left side of her face was creased with sleep. She was still befuddled by the tranquillisers, and it took her a moment to wake fully. She sat up and sniffed. 'Alfie, there's smoke!'

'Come now, quickly,' he said, and when she hesitated, he pulled the blankets right off her.

Isobel started but then got out of bed and looked

around, confused. 'Where are my slippers?' she said, 'I left them just here . . . '

'No time for that. Come now!' He put his arm around her shoulders and guided her, almost pushed her, to the staircase. The hot, terrifying orange glow of the fire downstairs was visible from the landing. Isobel shrank back.

'No, we cannae go down there,' she said, clawing Alfred's arm like a frightened animal.

'There's no other way out,' Alfred said. 'But you're right, just . . . just wait here.' And he ran back into the bedroom to grab the blankets and sheets off the bed, took them to the wash-stand in the corner and wetted them as thoroughly as he could. He took the dripping bundle back onto the landing. 'Here.' He wrapped the sodden blanket around Isobel's shoulders and the sheet around his own. 'Come on, we have to hurry.'

The stairs seemed to groan as he led Isobel down; he could feel the heat of the wood beneath the soles of his feet and his only thought now was to get out before the staircase gave way beneath them. Isobel was whimpering hysterically behind him, clutching his hand with hers like a person drowning. The space between the bottom of the landing and the front door was now a wall of fire.

'Oh God!' Isobel screamed. 'There's no way out!'

Alfred shook his hand free. Without stopping to think, he jumped through the flames, felt them brush across his skin, but not painfully, more like warm feathers, and reached out for the door handle. The pain of the red-hot metal on his palm was spectacular. He shrunk back and looked down at his hand; the burn was immediate, leaving behind a throbbing red mark. Behind him, beyond the flames, Isobel was coughing and wheezing. Alfred swiftly wrapped his other hand in the wet sheet and carefully turned the handle, then kicked the door open with his bare foot. The whole room was now dancing with fire – the curtains, the rugs, the sofa, where he'd lain just a short while earlier. From inside the sideboard, he could hear the sound of china cracking, and the wallpaper blistered and hissed as it began to peel away from the wall. Isobel had begun shrieking now, interrupted only by coughing fits that brought her to her knees, so he jumped back through the fire, feeling its heat now, the flames licking at his skin and hair like so many little tongues, and picked her up off the floor. Her face was ghostly white, eyes bloodshot from the smoke. Alfred paused to kiss her cheek before clearing the flames for a last time and through the open door to the cold night air.

Standing on the pavement outside, they both struggled for breath, doubled over and wheezing. Presently, though, Alfred had enough clean air in his lungs to straighten up. What he saw set off a fresh panic. For the bottle he'd heard earlier smashing above him had missed its mark, and instead broken through the window of the house next door. Amy's house.

'Stay here,' he commanded to Isobel, peeling the damp sooty blanket off her shoulders. She was shivering violently, and he wanted nothing more than to take her in his arms and hold her, but looked up again to see the smoke spilling from the top window of Amy's house, the curtains alive with fire.

'What are you doing?' Isobel asked, her voice cracking, as he wrapped her sheet around his shoulders and rushed towards Amy's front door. 'Alfie, no!'

Alfred ignored her and tried the door. It was, of course, locked, and so he took a couple of steps back and threw himself against it. It jarred painfully on his shoulder, but he tried again, and again, until finally the wood around the lock splintered. Alfred stumbled and almost fell to the floor as the door flew open. It was cool and quiet inside – almost grotesquely so. He ran up the stairs clutching the blanket and sheet up against his chin and ran into a curtain of smoke. He took a step back, gasping and choking. The smoke and heat stung his eyes. He wiped them with his hand and opened the door leading to the front bedroom. The sudden backdraft caused a huge lick of flame to flare towards him, and he was momentarily stunned. From outside, he caught the sound of his name being called, 'Alfie! Alfie!' He pushed forward into the blaze and through the smoke saw Amy lying prostrate on the bed. Not daring to go further into the room than necessary, he crouched down and dragged the bedsheet off her, then grabbed her bare ankles and began to draw her off the bed towards him. He caught her just before she hit the floor. She was unconscious. Alfred pulled her out of the room onto the small landing and slapped her gently, then more roughly, across the cheek.

'Amy! Amy, wake up! Where's James?' But he got no response, so he heaved her onto his shoulder and carried her down the stairs, treading carefully to prevent himself stumbling.

'Isobel!' he called when he reached the front door. 'Isobel, I – '

He raised his head and saw that a small group of people had formed on the street. They had all been dragged away from their beds, in dressing gowns and slippers. Isobel was sitting on the kerb with a thick blanket wrapped around her and two of their women neighbours, one of them with her hair in curlers, sat either side of her. A man who lived across the road, Frank McKay, rushed forward and helped Alfred lower Amy to the ground.

'James,' Alfred said, coughing again. His lungs were almost painfully tight, as though a large hand were squeezing them, preventing the clean air from entering. 'He must be – '

'Fire brigade's on its way,' McKay said. He looked up at the two adjoining houses. 'Spread quick, didn't it?'

Alfred didn't have time to explain the petrol bombs. 'She's breathing,' he said, pointing at Amy, 'but she'll need a doctor. I have to get James.'

He took a step back towards the open front door, but McKay grabbed his arm and spun him around. 'Ye cannae go back in there, man!' he said. 'Ye need to wait for the firemen. They'll get him out.'

Alfred tore himself free from the man's grip and, once more, entered the house. Smoke had now begun to creep down the stairs, rolling down slowly, as if testing the steps one at a time. It was an eerie sight. He took a deep breath and ran upstairs as quickly as he could, although he could feel the lack of oxygen in his bloodstream slowing down his movements. Opposite Amy's bedroom was the box room. The door stood slightly ajar. James must be in here, he thought, and gently swung the door open. This room, too, was full of black smoke, and Alfred's first thought was that no one could have survived more than ten minutes in here. He couldn't see a thing, but just beyond the sound of the fire eating its way through Amy's bedroom opposite, he thought he heard a slight scratching. Blindly, with arms outstretched, he made his way through the room. The space was, of course, tiny, but he stumbled badly over some toys lying on the floor and was once again overcome by a coughing fit. He tried to call the boy's name, but his throat was by now too dry and swollen. He swallowed painfully, trying to unstick his tongue from his palate. Then:

Under the bed! Look under the bed! See, you just need to get on all fours. Do it now!

Alfred dropped from his bent over position to his knees and using his right arm, swept the floor in front of him. His hand came into contact with something hard; the leg of James' bed.

'James,' he whispered hoarsely. 'James, are you there?'

Something touched his hand. He stretched his arm out as far as it would go and then felt James' smooth, cool fingers. 'Come on, wee man. We need to get out of here.'

A little fluttering cough came from somewhere in front of him. *He's alive*, Alfred thought, and at that moment all his strength left his body in one swift rush.

'Mr Werner?' he heard. James' voice was thick with tears. But Alfred couldn't move. He rested his cheek on the wooden floor and for one sweet moment, contemplated how nice it would be just to remain lying here, forever, listening to the gentle chiming of the clock downstairs rising up through the floorboards, striking out three o'clock, *ding, ding, ding*, overcome by the delicious calm induced by the carbon monoxide, which was now flowing through his bloodstream. His swollen eyelids slid shut.

He's going, he's going . . . no, Alfred, no!

Don't panic, we haven't lost him. He's still breathing. And it isn't his time yet.

ALFRED! ALFRED! ALFRED!!!

A movement on the back of his hand pulled him back up into consciousness. A stroke, or a scratch, then a pinch. It was the boy. Breathing shallowly, although he longed to take a deep, deep breath and succumb to the sleep that was beckoning him, Alfred forced himself to stretch out his other arm, until he had clasped the small hand between his own. Then he pulled, and James appeared, pale and shaking, from beneath the bed. It took all Alfred's strength to get to his feet, but he managed somehow, and hoisted the child under his arm, carrying him down the stairs on legs that threatened to collapse at any moment. Which they did, as soon as he reached the front door. He felt the world around him spin and a second later, fell to the pavement and cracked his head on the stone.

When he came to, he was lying on a couch whose dusty floral pattern was familiar, but he couldn't place it at once. His right hand was heavily bandaged, and when he put his other hand to his head, felt a bandage there, too. His skull ached. He tried to sit up, but that just compounded the pain. In addition, there was a great pressure on his lungs, as though someone had placed a heavy rock on his chest.

'Lie back, won't you?'

Alfred turned his head. It took a second for his eyes to focus, but when they did, he saw Harding, sitting on a chair opposite. He grinned at Alfred and then plucked a cigarette from behind his ear. 'Cannae smoke this in here,' he said, somewhat wistfully. 'The minister won't let me.'

It dawned on Alfred then that he was lying in the vicarage parlour. 'I . . . ' he began, again trying to sit up, and again giving up.

'There's some oxygen for ye, if ye need it,' Harding said and pointed at a gas cylinder standing next to the couch. 'Dr Cummings brought it. Reckons you'll nae need the hospital if you've some clean air.' He glanced longingly at his cigarette, but then stuck it back behind his ear.

'Isobel,' Alfred said, and immediately began coughing. The cough grated on his throat like sandpaper.

Harding rose from his chair. 'Here, son.' He took the mask that was attached to the cylinder by a thin tube and held it over Alfred's mouth. The air was pure and cold as it rushed into his lungs.

'Isobel is fine,' Harding said quietly. 'A wee bit shaken, but that's no surprise. She's asleep upstairs.'

Alfred widened his eyes, the mask still on his face, and Harding understood. 'The bairn is fine, too. Christ, Alfred, whatever devil rode ye back into that house, I'll ne'er know.' He sighed and shook his head. 'Mrs Fraser's in a bit of a bad way, though. They've taken her to Cumnock, to put her in one of those hyper – hypo . . . '

'Hyperbaric chamber.' It was Drummond, carrying a tray with tea and cake. He placed the tray down and came over to Alfred. 'She's in a special chamber to clear out her lungs. But the prognosis is positive.' He nodded gravely. 'We shall pray for her.'

'Quite the hero we have here,' Harding continued, picking up a folded newspaper from the table beside him.

Alfred took the mask off his face. The oxygen continued to hiss from the cylinder until Harding switched it off. 'Take a look,' he said and passed the paper to Alfred. It was the evening edition of the *Ayrshire Post*. Alfred folded it open and saw, on the bottom of the front page, a small article with the headline: LOCAL HERO ALFRED WARNER, 23, RISKS LIFE TO SAVE BABY.

'You seen this?' Harding asked Drummond.

Drummond nodded and passed Harding a cup of tea. 'Spelled his name wrong, though,' he said. Alfred glanced back down at the paper. It was true. Warner, it read.

Harding shrugged. 'Aye, but ye are a local lad now, ain't ye?' He laughed before adding more quietly, 'And it's nae a bad thing. To sound less German, I mean. And on the bright side, this should bump you right to the top of the housing list.'

The three men were silent for a while. Then Alfred asked, 'When can I see Isobel?'

'You'll see her soon enough. Let her sleep a while,' Drummond said. 'The house, I'm afraid, is beyond saving, but she doesn't need to know just yet.' He stirred sugar into his tea. 'But don't worry. Ye'll be staying here with me. Until September, that is. My replacement will need the vicarage then.'

Alfred managed to sit up. The oxygen had helped take the weight off his lungs. 'There were some men,' he said weakly.

'Aye,' Harding said. 'McKay heard them. Three of them, he reckons, shouting some filthy, filthy things.' He paused momentarily. Alfred could see Harding's teacup trembling on the saucer. 'It's shameful. If I ever – '

'Let's leave that to the police,' Drummond interrupted.

His voice was firm. 'I cannae imagine it were anyone from the village, but . . . ' he trailed off.

Alfred lay back down, overcome by a sudden weariness. His right hand was throbbing painfully and his lungs began to tighten again. He was leaning over for the oxygen mask, when he saw Isobel standing in the doorway. She was wearing a white nightgown and her hair was ruffled with sleep.

'Oh Alfie,' she cried, running over to him and burying her head in his chest.

'Easy now, Isobel,' Drummond said. 'Give the man a chance to recover.'

But Isobel clutched Alfred even tighter. 'I thought . . . I thought . . . when you ran back into that house – ' She started crying. 'Oh God, Alfie. You took so long, I didnae think . . . '

Alfred began to stroke her hair with his uninjured hand. 'Shhh, Isobel, it's all fine. I got out, didn't I?'

Isobel was still weeping loudly. 'Never,' she said, as the front of Alfred's shirt became wet with her tears. '*Never* do something so stupid again. I love you, you stupid, stupid man.' She continued to sob, and presently, Harding excused himself. He gave Alfred a parting wink and then slid the cigarette from behind his ear.

'I'll go and make a fresh pot,' Drummond said, and also left.

When Isobel had finally calmed down, she sat back on her heels and stroked Alfred's face. 'I mean it,' she said. 'You must promise me never to risk your life like that again. Promise me, Alfie.'

And Alfred, reluctantly and not quite sincerely, promised.

create a small concrete square. Several wooden troughs, which I knew contained flowering plants during the spring and summer, separated the square from the pavement.

'That's what?' I asked.

Alfred walked towards the square. 'The pharmacy,' he said, grinning, 'it's still here. And . . . ' he took a few more steps, 'the bakery. I used to come here almost every day, did I tell you that?' But he didn't give me an opportunity to answer. 'And this was a tailor . . . ' (now an electronics repair shop) 'and a stationer's,' (now an Internet café) 'and next to that a wig maker' (now a Thai massage parlour). He paused. 'Well, that was before. It became a women's hosiery shop when the war started. And there were a few more shops, but I suppose the café took up the space.' He looked as excited as a little boy who had just rediscovered a favourite toy he'd believed lost for good.

As for me, for the first time I got the uncomfortable feeling that something wasn't right. 'But Alfred, you do realise that this building is post-war?' I said carefully.

He turned slowly to look at me. 'I may be old,' he said, 'but I'm not stupid. This is, of course, not the original building. They must have decided to replace the shop front when they rebuilt after the war.' Then, without a word, he continued walking and I hurried to catch up with him. We walked side by side for a while. The streets were virtually empty. On Rosenheimer Straße, Alfred stopped and pointed at two little brass plaques inlaid among the cobblestones on the pavement.

'What's this?' he asked.

'*Stolpersteine*,' I answered. 'Stumbling stones. They're personalised memorials for the Jews who lived in this building, before they were deported.'

Alfred looked at them for a long time without speaking. Then, again without warning, as though he were out on a walk alone, he set off down the street.

'When was the last time you were here?' I asked when I had reached his side.

'Nineteen forty-four.' He spoke as though this were self-evident.

'Seriously? You haven't been back since?'

'No. We never visited. Isobel was afraid of flying.'

On the opposite side of the street, a man was engaged in an angry conversation on his mobile phone. We walked on a little, until the man's shouting had receded into the distance.

'She passed away last year,' he added.

'Oh. I'm sorry.'

After several minutes' walk, at the next junction, he stopped again.

'Berchtesgardener Straße is this way, is it not?'

'Yes, to the left.'

'May we?' he asked. 'I – I'd like to take a look.'

We took a left. Alfred had picked up his speed; it was as though he were in a rush to get somewhere.

'20, 22,' he said, looking up at the street numbers on the buildings. Then, 'Yes, number 24,' he said, stopping suddenly.

I realised at once what he had been looking for. Set into the pavement in front of us were four brass *stolpersteine*, rimed with frost:

Hier wohnte
Gustav Isaac Bronstein
JG. 1862
Deportiert 1943
Ermordet in Auschwitz

Hier wohnte
Margarete Bronstein
Geb. Jacobsohn
JG. 1864
Deportiert 1943
Ermordet in Auschwitz

Hier wohnte
Hans Rosenzweig
JG. 1905
Deportiert 1942
Riga
Ermordet

Hier wohnte
Klara Rosenzweig
Geb. Süsskind
JG. 1913
Deportiert 1942
Riga
Ermordet

I put my hand to my face. My fingers felt freezing against the warmth of my cheek. 'Oh Alfred,' I said. 'I'm so sorry.'

For a long while, we stood there wordlessly. When Alfred finally looked up, his eyes were wet. 'They invited some of the boys for *kaffee und kuchen* one afternoon,' he said. 'Did I mention that?'

I shook my head. Truth be told, I was feeling ashamed for having doubted him minutes earlier.

'Hmm, one forgets so much, doesn't one?' he continued quietly, ''36 that must have been, or '37. What a treat! Well, actually, we were scared stiff by Frau Bronstein. I remember us, five or six boys, dressed up to the nines, sitting in a row on an antique velvet-upholstered sofa, like so many birds perched on a wire. In front of us, on a low mahogany table, Frau Bronstein had set out the cake on an ivory-coloured lace tablecloth; each of us had a porcelain coffee cup and saucer filled with hot, black coffee. It was all far too sophisticated for children, of course – the cake too rich, the coffee too bitter – but I suppose the Bronsteins were more used to entertaining adults. None of us dared make a sound as we timidly ate Sachertorte and cream éclairs under the strict gaze of Herr and Frau Bronstein. And then – ' Alfred let out a chuckle, 'then one of us, David I think, took a sip of his coffee and sneezed, sending a fine spray of coffee right across the table, covering the cakes, the éclairs, the lace tablecloth. Oh, what a disaster! we all thought, and already, a few of us were on the brink of breaking into hysterical nervous laughter. But Frau Bronstein placed her cup carefully onto the saucer and said, "*Zay gezund*". I don't believe that woman ever lost her composure.'

He stopped and made a tiny bow.

On the way back to my flat, we walked in silence. Alfred seemed exhausted, so I let him hook his arm into mine. Without really meaning to, I began to count the *stolpersteine* on the short walk back. There were fifty-eight of them. When we arrived at my building, I took out the keys and held the door open for Alfred. He took a step forward and paused. 'Julia? I'm afraid I was a little untruthful with you earlier.'

'Oh?'

'Yes. I told you that I never brought Isobel here because she was afraid of flying.'

'She wasn't?'

'Oh yes, indeed, the thought of getting on an aeroplane terrified the life out of her. But – ' he made a waving gesture with his hand, 'but of course there are other means of transport. The truth is, for the longest time, I was never quite brave enough to return.'

1949

Alfred settled into his seat as the station whistle blew, his new identity tucked safely in his jacket pocket. With him in the compartment was a tired-looking woman in a worn jacket and skirt, a little girl beside her, and another man, dressed similarly to Alfred in a threadbare suit and scuffed shoes. The compartment smelled of stale smoke and sweat, but when Alfred went to open the window, the plump woman told him that it was stuck fast. So instead, he took out the book he had brought with him to read on the train, *Middleton's Gardening Guide*, and started reading, trying to ignore the incessant, excited chattering in his head.

Ooh, Mr Alfred Warner. Sounds awfully British.
What's Isobel going to say? Will she be pleased?
Who knows? He should have told her first.
Why, he doesn't need her permission!
And so on.

Just as the train was pulling out of the station, the compartment door was jerked open.

' . . . but this is bloody ludicrous! You can't expect my wife to travel like this. We've first class tickets!'

It was a young Englishman, a few years older than Alfred perhaps, talking to the train conductor in a tone of authority that belied his age. He wore a stiff grey homburg and a charcoal-grey gabardine suit beneath an expensive-looking wool overcoat, and was visibly annoyed. In the corridor on the other side of the door stood a woman, as elegantly dressed as the man, looking into the compartment.

'I shall be putting in an official complaint,' the man continued to the conductor. He glanced into the compartment and pulled a face. 'At least get us a compartment of our own.'

'Sorry, sir,' the conductor said, 'but as I've explained, I'm afraid the train's full. I apologise if this is inconvenient, but it cannae be helped.'

'Stop making such a fuss, Samuel,' the woman said. She pushed past him and sat down in the empty seat opposite Alfred, carefully smoothing down the back of her skirt beforehand. On her head, she wore a dark-green felt hat, the same colour as her coat, that swept up at a slant into an oversized bow.

Her husband stood for a moment at the door, but the conductor went to slide it shut and he quickly took a step back into the compartment. He eyed the padded bench seat with some suspicion, but then sat down next to his wife. The smell of his hair cream mingled unpleasantly with the smoke and sweat.

'Bloody ludicrous,' he said.

'Yes, you've already said that,' his wife answered. She looked around the compartment and gave her fellow passengers a tight-mouthed but polite smile. It looked rehearsed, the kind of smile one bestows on others below one's class. But her eyes, which were very dark, almost black, like her hair, suggested a flash of playfulness. Alfred smiled back.

'First-class bloody tickets,' her husband continued. 'This place truly is the backwater of Britain. Can't even get their trains to run properly.'

'Oh darling, stop being such a bore,' she snapped. 'It's only a couple of hours to Dumfries. It won't kill us.'

The man shut up and removed his hat, resting his head on the backrest, but appeared anything but relaxed. He tapped his fingers restlessly on his leg. After ten minutes or so, the train gave a sudden jolt and pulled to a standstill. Alfred looked up from his book and out of the window. The sun had broken through the low-lying band of cloud; the fields he was looking out at stretched in a sheet of mauve and purple towards the horizon and merged into the sky.

'Right, that's it,' the man said. He got to his feet. 'I'm going to find out what the hell is wrong with this train. No decent compartments, and now this.'

His wife gave a short sigh of impatience as he left. Alfred went back to his book. The little girl beside him had fallen asleep and her head was now resting against his upper arm. It was unexpectedly, but pleasantly, heavy and Alfred tried to turn the pages of his book as carefully as he could so as not to disturb her.

'Ah, Mr Middleton,' the woman opposite said presently.

Alfred looked up and saw that she was addressing him. 'Excuse me?' he asked, keeping his voice low.

She pointed at his book. 'Mr Middleton,' she said. 'I remember listening to him on the wireless during the war. "Dig for Victory" and all that.'

'Ah yes,' Alfred said. He knew about the gardening campaign, but had, of course, never heard any of Mr Middleton's broadcasts.

The woman smiled at him again. 'I'm sorry, I didn't mean to interrupt your reading. Do please carry on.'

Alfred gave her a small smile in return. She was undoubtedly a very attractive woman, more handsome than pretty, with pale, immaculately powdered skin and her lips painted ruby red – and the thought momentarily unsettled him. There were different types of attractiveness, he told himself, and Isobel had enough natural beauty not to need powder and lipstick. He lowered his head and continued reading. For some time now, ever since he and Isobel had put their name down on the council housing list, he had been planning their garden. The space would be tiny, naturally, but he had aspirations of a small vegetable and herb garden, set close to the house, and perhaps a climber or two, perhaps a *passiflora caerulea* or a hardy *clematis alpine*. And of course, his favourite, lavender.

Then: 'Are you a keen gardener?' It was the woman again.

'Aye,' Alfred answered. 'I know a little about it.' He could have added that he was a garden labourer, not quite a gardener, but didn't.

'Oh really? Then may I ask you a question? I don't mean to intrude, but perhaps I may have your opinion. You see, I have gardens – nothing too grand, but large enough – but I have an awfully conservative head gardener. These English gardens, they all seem to be just lawn and herbaceous borders – there's no . . . *architecture!*' She spoke with passion. 'And I do so believe in experimentation in the garden. Not that I'm an expert, more of a keen amateur.'

Amateur meets labourer, tee hee. What's your opinion then, Alfie dear?

Alfred ignored the voice and cleared his throat. 'You might consider adding dimension – horizontally, I mean – by growing climbers and roses up into the trees. If you have trees, that is. Depending on the budget, you could try *albertine*, or *mulliganii*, it all depends. And, well, I don't know your garden, but it can be quite effective to cram several varieties of shrubs in one space and echo them individually in other areas of the garden.' He began hesitantly, but soon found himself describing the kind of garden he longed to own, ignoring the calls of *Ooh, listen to him! Now he's showing off!* inside his head.

The woman listened carefully, nodding from time to time, and when Alfred realised he'd rattled on for too long, he finished by saying, 'Aye, well, that just an idea.'

'That was quite impressive!' she said. 'I shall bear it in mind. Thank you for your advice, Mr . . . '

'Warner,' Alfred said, 'Alfred Warner.' He tried, but failed, to suppress a grin at the ease with which this new name rolled off his tongue.

'Pleased to meet you, Mr Warner,' she replied and held out a gloved hand. 'Alice Singer-Cohen.'

With a small jerk, the train began to move again, picking up speed rapidly until the heather fields outside became a blur of purple once again. Alfred leaned forward and shook her hand. It was an unusually firm handshake for a woman, he thought.

A Jewess, now fancy that. Are you going to admit it? That you're German?

'No,' he answered firmly, in his head. 'Leave me alone.'

Mrs Singer-Cohen put her head to one side and looked at him, narrowing her eyes slightly. 'I don't suppose you're in need of a job?' she asked. 'Ever since we moved up from London to what Samuel so charmingly calls "the Potteries", I've been going spare trying to find a decent assistant to Mr Claxton, our head gardener. Someone who actually cares about the gardens. The chap we have now couldn't recognise a rhododendron, let alone spell the word.'

'Well,' Alfred said, shifting in his seat. He glanced around the compartment self-consciously. He felt a little uncomfortable at her openness, yet she seemed perfectly at ease, as though it were only the two of them sitting here and the most natural thing in the world for a woman to be offering a stranger a job.

'Actually – ' he hesitated, not knowing whether he should address her as 'Madam', 'actually, I'm, um, really quite settled here, thank you.'

She shrugged a shoulder. 'Well, there's no harm in asking,' she said lightly. Then she opened the clasp of her handbag and began rummaging through it. 'By the way, you have a most unusual accent, Mr Warner.' She gave him a peculiar look and Alfred's heart sank. Then she smiled, open-mouthed. 'But then again, I can't tell the Highlands from the Lowlands – or even the Midlands, come to think of it.' At this she laughed – an open, untidy laugh that was at odds with her polished appearance. She continued to rifle through her bag. 'Blast,' she said finally, 'he hasn't left me with a single cigarette.' She gave Alfred a questioning look.

It took him a second to catch on. 'Oh, I'm sorry,' he said, 'but I don't smoke.' For some odd reason, he felt himself blushing.

'Well bully for you,' she said, getting to her feet. Alfred looked for some trace of irony in her face, but she just gave the same unreadable smile she'd given him earlier and said, 'Very nice to meet you, Mr Warner.'

She and her husband didn't return by the time the train pulled into Mauchline; perhaps they had found a more preferable compartment. In any case, Alfred had almost completely forgotten about her when he arrived home with his new name, and it was quite some time before he had reason to recall their meeting.

The summer that year was dry and unseasonably hot. By the time July arrived, bringing nightly thunderstorms and much needed rain, Alfred and Isobel's marriage, though not as passionate as it had been, had regained the warmth he had so longed for after their daughter's death. Isobel was not yet ready to consider another pregnancy, but they shared a bed again, and for the moment, this was enough for Alfred. She had reacted with surprise and delight at the news of the name change; in fact, they decided to have a small celebration with Drummond and Harding and his wife. Harding, after a drink too many, inadvertently soured the evening by suggesting that they should try for a couple of boys: the 'Warner Bros.'.

The following Sunday, Drummond called Alfred into his study after the service, for 'a quick word'. Isobel was in the kitchen preparing lunch.

'Come in, Alfred, and please shut the door,' he said, gesturing for Alfred to sit down.

Noting the look of concern on Drummond's face, Alfred assumed it might be about the police enquiry into the arson attack.

'Any news?' he asked, but Drummond gave him an uncomprehending look. 'About the fire?'

Drummond shook his head. 'No. There's some talk about the new tenants, in the council estate, but that's idle gossip. Without a proper description of the men, there's precious little the police can do.' He sat down heavily behind his own desk and took some papers out of his jacket pocket. 'This is what I called you in for,' he said, and placed the papers on the desk.

Alfred could see immediately what they were.

'From the collection box,' Drummond continued. 'Enough clothing coupons for you and Isobel to replace what you lost in the fire.'

Alfred picked up the coupons. He didn't quite know what to say. 'This is – ' he began, but saw Drummond frowning heavily. Surely he should be pleased? 'What's wrong?' he asked.

Drummond sighed and reached into his other breast pocket. 'There was something else in the collection box,' he said slowly. 'I thought long and hard about whether or not to show you this, but I decided you must know. Here.'

He handed Alfred a folded scrap of paper. Alfred took it from him and unfolded it, feeling Drummond's eyes on him. The handwriting was crude, and the message was written in angular capital letters:

BITCH BRIDE OF ADOLF

Alfred looked up at Drummond, who just shook his head and said, 'Human good and human evil so close together.' He rose from his chair. 'I shall pass it on to the police, of course. I just cannae imagine who would do this . . . '

Alfred got up and left the study with Drummond. In the hall, Drummond lay his hand on Alfred's arm. 'I think it best if we keep this from Isobel. For now.'

Alfred nodded. 'Aye, of course.'

'And let's hope this is the last of it.'

Sadly, that wasn't the last of it. Although the hot sunny weather kept most villagers' spirits high, it became clear that the police were no closer to identifying the arsonists, or the author of the note. Isobel was also troubled about her father's impending departure, and although she hadn't spoken much about it, Alfred could tell it was causing her a great deal of anxiety. Thus, he wasn't surprised to return home one evening to find her in tears in the kitchen. She was at the sink, vigorously scraping the burnt bottom of a pan. 'I left the potatoes for all of five minutes, to fetch the washing in,' she said, sobbing loudly. 'And the kitchen was full of smoke.'

Alfred, still filthy from work, made her put down the pan and took her in his arms. She continued to cry. 'It's no bother,' he said gently. 'Potatoes are nothing to cry over.'

She sniffed loudly. 'No, Alfie. It's not that. It's – '

'Shhh, I know, I know,' he said, relieved that she was no longer keeping her unhappiness bottled up.

She looked up at him with tear-reddened eyes. 'So – so you've seen it, then? The door?'

'What door?'

'Oh Alfie, it's awful,' she said, putting a hand to her mouth and bursting into fresh tears.

'Isobel, for god's sake, what is it?'

'Here,' she said, taking his hand and leading him out through the kitchen door to the garden. She turned slowly, almost reluctantly, to face the cottage. There was no need to point out what had upset her. It was graffiti, scratched into the green paint of the kitchen door:

JERRY GO HOME !

And beneath it:

NAZI WHORE

Alfred glanced around the garden, but there was no one in sight. It was likely that this had been done during the night under the cover of darkness, but the thought that Isobel might have been on her own at home when it happened alarmed him. He tightened his grip on her hand. 'Go back inside,' he said.

She hurried back into the cottage, while he took a closer look. The scratches were fresh, as far as he could tell, and made perhaps with a key, or a screwdriver. There was no other clue as to who might be responsible. It unsettled him. He wasn't so much frightened for himself, but for

Isobel. Since the fire, it had been bad enough to witness her growing nervousness – flinching when she heard a door slamming or the telephone ringing – but if something were ever to happen to her . . .

That evening, he held Isobel until she fell asleep, then turned onto his back. He was too restless for sleep. If it were up to him, he thought, he would leave the village. As much as he'd been welcomed here over the past several years, as much as he now almost felt, in Harding's words, 'a local lad', it would not seem such a hardship to leave. But where would he go? He couldn't go back home, surely. Isobel would never cope, and neither, he thought, would he. He closed his eyes to try and stop the dizzying swirl of thoughts in his head.

A fresh start, Alfred. That's what you and Isobel need.

You're both young, you'll settle in wherever you go. As long as you have each other.

'But this is her home,' he argued. 'She was born here. She knows no other place. It would be like uprooting a flower.'

She's a hardier flower than you give her credit for. Nothing ventured, Alfred, nothing gained.

'It is not that easy,' he said, and must have mumbled it out loud because next to him, Isobel stirred.

'Alfie?'

'Shh, darling, go back to sleep,' he said softly.

'I wasn't sleeping. I cannae sleep. I've been lying here, thinking.'

'That won't do you any good.'

'But you cannae sleep either! Tossing and turning, it's like being on a ship. It's all I can do not to feel seasick.'

'I'm sorry.'

'Ach, don't be. Like I said, I was awake anyway. Alfie?'

Alfred turned onto his side to face her. Her hair was carefully put up in curls and fastened with hairgrips and her breath, which he could feel on his face, smelled minty. 'What were you thinking about?' he asked.

'I don't know. I mean, I *do* know, but –' she blinked a couple of times, 'Alfie, I'm frightened.'

He put out his hand and stroked her face. 'I know,' he said.

Isobel closed her eyes at his touch and they lay in silence for a while.

'Have you – have you ever thought about leaving?' he asked finally.

She opened her eyes. They were as round and vulnerable as ever.

'I'm serious, Isobel,' he continued. 'I'm afraid too. For your safety. The fire, the back door today. And there was something else . . . '

He told her about the note in the collection box. She continued to stare at him with a look he couldn't interpret. So he pressed on. 'With your father leaving, tell me Isobel, what is there here for you?'

'You want me to leave my home.' She spoke in a whisper. It wasn't a question, but a statement of fact. Almost an accusation.

'No – ' he began. He withdrew his hand and propped himself up on his elbow. 'I mean, yes. I think we should leave. Isobel, darling, don't you think we can make a home somewhere else?'

She dropped her gaze and remained silent for so long that he thought she might have fallen asleep again. But then she blinked again.

He pressed on. 'I had an offer of a job a while back. When I was on the train back from Kilmarnock. An Englishwoman – she said she's looking for a gardener.'

'And what did ye tell her?'

'What d'ye think? That I'm settled here, thank you very much.'

At that, they both fell into a brief silence.

Isobel teased a strand of hair from the hair grips and began twirling it around her finger. 'But now you want to leave.'

'I don't *want* to leave, Isobel. But – ' He paused, struggling for the right words. 'It might be a way to make a fresh start.'

'And this Englishwoman,' she said quietly, 'what was she like?'

'Friendly, very polite,' he responded, recalling the woman's pale skin and her untidy laugh. 'Alice Singer-Cohen, she said her name was.' He was surprised at how easily he'd remembered it.

'Sounds posh,' said Isobel, 'and a wee bit foreign.'

'No, it's Jewish.'

'Aye, but still – '

'It's Jewish, not foreign,' Alfred said, a little firmer than intended. He added in a softer tone, 'But you're right, that should make it easier to trace her.' The more he spoke, the more determined he became. The woman had seemed sincere, hadn't she? And he had surely learned from experience to trust his instincts – and his voices.

Isobel turned away from him. 'Aye. You do whatever you think is right, Alfie,' she said.

Alfred took her shoulder and pulled her back around.

He felt her muscles tense. 'No, Isobel,' he said grimly. 'I won't do anything you're not happy with. Not if that means . . .'

She breathed out heavily, and then relaxed under his grip. 'You're right, Alfie.' He put his hand to her face and felt her tears. 'I just want to be happy, and not so frightened.'

Sliding his arm beneath her shoulders, he pulled her tight. 'I'm sorry, Isobel, for everything. I love you so.'

He held her in this way until her breathing became slow and regular, and soon, he fell asleep too.

Contacting Mrs Singer-Cohen was more straightforward than he had expected. A young woman at directory enquires confirmed that she had a Mr Samuel Singer-Cohen listed as resident in Staffordshire, at March House. She could put a telephone call through, if he wished. Beside him, Isobel nodded, a brave smile fixed on her face. Alfred was making the telephone call from Drummond's study, and would rather have made it in private, as the determination he'd felt last night had now ebbed away completely. But he couldn't send Isobel out. He would just have to see it through.

Through a crackling line, amidst a jumble of faint-sounding voices on other lines, a woman's voice appeared, introducing herself as Miss Woolcroft, secretary to Mr Singer-Cohen. Alfred, stumbling over his words, said that he was an acquaintance of Mrs Alice Singer-Cohen and wished to speak to her. After a brief hesitation, Miss Woolcroft said, 'Very well, one moment please,' and there was a muffled silence as she connected him to Mrs Singer-Cohen's private line.

Alfred felt the heat rising to his face. The woman prob-ably didn't even remember him, and as he waited for the call to be put through, the foolishness of what he was about to do almost made him hang up. But when she finally answered, his uncertainty vanished at once.

'Mr Warner!' she said brightly. 'What a surprise!'

'Hello Mrs Singer-Cohen, I, um, well – '

'Are you also having such a hot summer? A bit of sunshine is all well and good, but we could certainly do with a few days of rain. The heat has been doing ghastly things to the lawn.'

'Aye, it's been hot here, too. Actually, Mrs Singer-Cohen, I was calling to enquire . . . Well, if you recall, on the train – ' He hesitated. Isobel took his free hand in hers and squeezed it. He continued quickly, just wanting to get it over with, now. 'On the train, you asked whether I might be in need of a job. It was a very kind offer, and – '

Her reaction was not what he'd hoped. 'Oh gosh, Mr Warner, this is terribly awkward. We just hired a new chap last week.' She sighed and clicked her tongue. 'He isn't much of an improvement as far as I'm concerned, but Mr Claxton seems quite taken by him. Oh dear, I do feel awful. But, you see, I did rather act on the spur of the moment on the train. I'm not really in the habit of offering jobs to men I hardly know.' She sighed again.

Alfred swallowed. His cheeks were burning. He freed his hand from Isobel's grip and turned away. 'That's fine, Mrs Singer-Cohen, I'm sorry to have troubled you.'

There was a long pause; the line crackled and fizzed and for a moment, Alfred thought she might have ended the call. But then her voice came back on.

'No, hang on,' she said. 'I'll tell you what. I'll have a word with my husband. This new boy, well, he's all thumbs, and none of them green.'

'But I dinnae want – '

'No, it's all right.' She paused again. When she spoke, her voice was low. 'This is all my stupid fault. Listen, Mr Warner. I can make you no promises, but I shall talk the matter over with my husband, and Mr Claxton, and get back to you as soon as I can. Leave your number with Miss Woolcroft. How does that sound?'

'That sounds very kind of you, Mrs Singer-Cohen,' Alfred answered, wishing for this conversation to finally end. 'Well, good-bye. And thank you.'

'Goodbye, Mr Warner.'

Two days later, Miss Woolcroft telephoned to invite Alfred for a formal interview.

Nineteen Ninety-Six (Part I)

The air is hot. The A/C has been off since this morning when the caretaker guy came to take the final meter reading. You wade slowly through the hot air in your room – no, the back bedroom, it isn't your room anymore – counting steps from door to window, wall to wall, trying to imprint the size, the shape, the feel of it onto your memory. The power has been switched off at the mains to stop the meter

Tick, tick, ticking –

so no lights, no cool air, even though outside, it's close to 100 degrees

Fahrenheit, but what's that in Celsius, huh? Huh? Come on, Brynja, work it out –

minus thirty divided by two, give or take, but even hotter in here

So, 100 degrees Fahrenheit minus thirty divided by two. Is what? I'm waiting…

seventy, divided by two – thirty-five! Thirty-five degrees

Celsius. Here used to be the bed, the shelf with your books, tiny pieces of scotch tape stuck fast to the walls, impervious to your mom's fingernails.

You've been biting them again, haven't you?

A circular rug made from Sabine's old nylons. White melamine nightstand left by the previous tenants.

Right down to the quick. I can see a hangnail . . . Go on, tear it off!

Bedside lamp with pink shade and white unicorns. You clench your fists. Suppress the urge to pick at the skin around your fingers. There stood your guitar stand *sans* guitar, left behind at summer camp two years ago. Here on the carpet a round burn mark, left by Sabine, despite the No Smoking Past This Point sign you stuck on the door a couple of years ago.

Bryn! BRYNJA!! Get moving! Where are you? your mom shouts.

You stand in the center of the room, surrounded by the heat. Time to go. You leave the room, slowly, and walk down the short dark hallway. Sabine – surrounded by boxes, picture frames, potted plants that will never survive the move, garbage bags, more boxes – stands leaning against the kitchen wall, smoking. Nervous, you can tell, from the way she sucks on her cigarette and blows out short puffs of smoke. You hate the smell, the way it clings to your clothes, your hair. Some of your friends at school smoke, but there's no way you will. Ever.

Yeah, she's disgusting. You need to keep an eye on that one.

She's my mom! you answer in your head. Accept and Acknowledge, is what the last therapist advised you to do: **I ACKNOWLEDGE YOUR PRESENCE BUT I AM FREE FROM YOUR INFLUENCE.**

Sabine turns, spots you. Pushes herself away from the wall. What have you been doing in there? I need you out here. They'll be here any minute. She draws on her cigarette, winces as the glowing tip almost reaches her fingers and looks around, helpless, for somewhere to put it out. Shit, she says. I knew I should have kept one ashtray unpacked. Walks to the window, opens it, flicks out the butt and gives you an apologetic shrug. Oops.

Selfish bitch.

It scares the crap out of you, talking back to the voice. You've tried, but you're scared of her and she knows it. How could she not know? She lives in your head.

Sabine glances around, looks puzzled, as though she suddenly has no idea what's going on. Then, Grab that box, Bryn. She points to a cardboard box on the floor. You look inside. It's full of books and is hopelessly heavy.

There are too many books in here, you say. The bottom will fall out.

Your mom says, Nah. We'll put *See? Stupid* a couple of *and selfish. Like* blankets in. *mother like* We have to, anyway, *daughter, huh, Brynja?* I got no *Huh?* boxes left.

Your mom and the voice-woman speak at the same time. What?

A couple of blankets, your mom says. Any more stuff in your room? Come on, Bryn, focus. I can't do all this by myself.

You stand there, undecided. Sabine comes and stands in front of you. Looks into your face and pushes a strand of hair behind your ear. Smiles softly. We'll be good, *liebling*.

The doorbell rings. That's the movers! Excited. They're here!!

1949 – 1950

Alfred and Isobel rented a small, semi-detached furnished cottage, in a row of houses all owned by Mr Singer-Cohen. It was located in the small village of Checkley, just a mile from March House. It had green-painted window frames, a gable roof with gutters in need of repair, a sturdy-looking chimney and faux timber beams on the greyish brickwork. To Alfred's delight, a lilac wisteria plant covered most of the brickwork, clinging to the front of the house and dripping with tiny purple flowers. The rent was higher than at their previous house, but the wages Alfred had been promised were double that of his old position, so Isobel quickly began to plan adding some personal touches – net curtains for the windows, matching floral bedspreads, a few small porcelain ornaments for the mantelpiece – and Alfred was pleased that she looked to their new life with such optimism.

On the morning of their third day, the day Alfred was to begin work at March House, there was a knock at the front door. Alfred was upstairs in the bathroom, shaving, so he cracked open the small window and looked out. A grey Bentley was parked outside – the only car on the street. He quickly washed the shaving soap off his face and pulled a shirt on. By the time he got downstairs, Isobel had already opened the door to Mrs Singer-Cohen. She wore a close-fitting jacket and skirt, showing off her very narrow waist. Her black hair was pinned up and arranged in artful curls around her head.

'You must be Mrs Warner,' she said, flashing a broad smile at Isobel and extending a white-gloved hand. 'I'm Alice Singer-Cohen.'

Isobel hesitated for a moment, and then wiped her own hand on her print cotton dress and held it out. The skin was slightly reddened; Alfred presumed it must have been the hot water from the washing-up. 'Pleased to meet you,' she responded and, noticing Alfred, turned to give him a quizzical look.

Alfred combed his hair quickly with his fingers. 'Won't you come in?' he asked.

Mrs Singer-Cohen gave a quick shake of her head. 'No, I wouldn't dream of imposing. I just wanted to come by and say hello and welcome. I can't tell you how pleased I am that you took the job.'

For a moment, the three of them stood there in silence – Alfred and Isobel in the gloom of their small hallway, and Mrs Singer-Cohen on the other side of the doorstep in the bright summer light. Then Alfred and Isobel spoke simultaneously: 'That's very kind of you,' Alfred said, while Isobel said, 'Are you sure you won't stay for a cup of tea?'

'You're most welcome, and no, unfortunately I can't stay,' Mrs Singer-Cohen answered. Then, as if changing her mind, she took a step forward into the house. She brought with her the honeyed scent of the wisteria that grew at the front of the house. 'I'm on my way into Hanley for a nine o'clock appointment.'

She didn't explain further, but instead glanced around the small hallway and through the door that led into the living room. Alfred saw her take in the worn stair-carpet, the cheap reproduction oil painting that hung above a scuffed sideboard, the faded fabric of curtains and sofa – and although these things had all been in the house when he and Isobel moved in, he knew Mrs Singer-Cohen was associating their tawdriness with him, and it made him slightly uncomfortable. But her face betrayed no judgement. Instead, she just said, 'You know, my husband owns all these houses, and I don't think I've ever set foot in one of them.' She fixed a smile on Isobel. 'What a pretty dress you have on,' she added.

Isobel's face reddened and she rubbed the fabric of the cotton dress – small blue flowers on a pale yellow background – between her fingers, nervously, Alfred thought.

'Well, I shan't keep you any longer,' Mrs Singer-Cohen said finally. She said her goodbyes, and that she looked forward to discussing all things gardening with Alfred in due course. When that would be, she didn't say. She was almost at the car when she turned. 'Oh, Mr Warner. Would you like a lift up to the house?' she asked. 'We pass by it on my way into town.'

Isobel spoke quickly. 'Oh no, thank you, Mrs Singer-Cohen. Alfred's nae had his breakfast yet.'

Mrs Singer-Cohen rolled her eyes. 'Of course. Silly

me. Well – ' she waited for the driver to open the car door. 'I'll see you later, then. Good-day, Mrs Warner.'

As soon as they heard the car pull away, Isobel shot a glance at Alfred. 'You told me she was an old lady,' she said sourly.

'No I didn't,' Alfred answered, surprised at her comment as well as her tone.

'Well, you made her sound like one.'

Alfred frowned. 'I don't think – '

But Isobel interrupted him. '"*What a pretty dress you have on*",' she mimicked.

He put his hand on her arm. 'Isobel. What's the matter?'

She shrugged him off. 'With her posh frock and silk stockings, knowing full well pigs'd fly before I could afford something that fancy. And did ye see the way she looked around the house?'

Alfred shrugged. For some reason, he didn't want to tell her he'd found it awkward, too. 'I thought she was quite charming,' he said.

'Exactly,' Isobel replied and walked into the house and through to the kitchen, letting the door swing shut behind her.

Alfred stood for a moment in the dark hallway. He knew that Isobel was house-proud; he guessed – although he didn't know for sure – that she felt embarrassed about the faded curtains and the unswept floor. That perhaps . . .

Goodness me, Alfred. Wake up! She's jealous!

'Jealous?'

A second voice. *Oh, he's such an imbecile at times. Kssss, of course she's jealous!*

'But why is she jealous?'

You know perfectly well. We know what you're thinking, Alfred. Always.

The third voice-woman joined them: *Let's not be too hard on Isobel. She just feels a bit lost, that's all. So far away from home. And you have to admit that Mrs Singer-Cohen was just a touch condescending.*

Kssss, I admit no such thing! She was being nice.

You saw the look she gave Isobel. I don't call that being nice.

It was.

It wasn't.

Yes, it was . . .

Alfred tuned out their squabbling and went into the kitchen. Isobel was at the kitchen table with their ration books laid out in front of her. The kitchen was as dark as the hallway, north-facing with only a small window set in the back door that led out to the garden. Alfred switched the light on, but the low-watt bulb did little to brighten the room.

'I'll have to take these to the Food Office,' Isobel said without looking up. 'Get the address changed.'

Alfred went and sat beside her and put his large, warm hands on her small ones. Looking down at her from this angle, he could see the bluish shadows under her eyes – she hadn't slept well since they'd arrived here. Her fair hair, cut into a short bob just before they'd left Mauchline, was frizzy from the humidity of the hot water in the sink, and he suddenly understood how unfavourably she must feel she compared to the elegance of Alice Singer-Cohen.

'I'm sorry, Isobel,' he said.

She retrieved her hands from his and placed the ration

books atop each other. She said, in a controlled whisper, 'Whatever for?'

Alfred was at a loss for words. He reached out and stroked her hair, feeling the softness of it beneath his fingers, like the down of a small bird.

'I'm sorry that you're so unhappy,' he said finally.

Isobel sniffed and gave a pinched smile. 'I'm nae unhappy, Alfie. Ach, I don't know. I'm just . . . I suppose I'm missing home, is all.' She looked up at him. Her summer freckles, which appeared on her face and across her shoulders after only the briefest exposure to the sun, were pale in the dull light of the kitchen, and she looked to Alfred as pure and delicate as she had the day they met. His heart lurched at the thought that he'd been the cause of her unhappiness.

He got to his feet and pulled her out of her chair, holding her small, slender body in his arms. Her shoulders, which only reached up to his chest, felt frail in his grip, and he was again reminded of a young bird. 'You're homesick, my love,' he said. 'And I know how wretched that can feel. But I also know that it'll pass. Just give it time.' He kissed the top of her head, where her hair smelled of almond soap.

With a somewhat heavy heart, he set off for his first day at work. It was only a short distance – fifteen minutes at a brisk walk, with his voices chattering away incessantly, though quietly, at the rim of his hearing – that led him out of the village along a country lane bordered by hedges. The hedges were high and well-kept, but a closer look revealed brown, paper-dry leaves on the insides, a consequence of the too-hot summer. Once, a car sped past him, churning up clouds of dust and making him wary of walking on the road, so he kept as close to the hedges as he could. Then the hedgerow dropped away, opening up to large meadows with scatterings of sheep grazing sleepily beneath a fat, hot sun. Finally, sweating already in his heavy jacket, he reached a large gate, which he recognised as the one he'd been driven through on his first visit. It was a double wrought-iron gate, with a fancifully scrolled decoration that was reminiscent of a peacock fanning its tail. He stood before it, looking around for a bell-pull, but not finding anything, stepped forward and pushed against one side of the gate. It opened easily, and so he started walking up the gravel path, March House white and clean – a very modern building with angular geometry and a total absence of decorative fancy – sitting up ahead at the top of the drive.

When he got to the front door, he rang the bell noticing the small silver cylinder attached to the doorframe on his right. It was the first he'd seen in over ten years, and as he lifted his hand to touch it – an instinctive gesture – something tugged painfully at his memory. But before the feeling turned into a stronger sense of nostalgia, he heard footsteps approaching from inside. The door was opened by a young dark-haired housemaid, dressed in a black skirt and blouse with a lace cap and apron.

'That's a mezuzah,' she said, nodding at the cylinder. Her tone was slightly bored, as though she were called on to explain it often.

'I know,' Alfred replied, lowering his arm. 'My name is Alfred Warner. I'm to report to Mr Claxton.'

'This way,' the maid said, but instead of letting him in the house, led him around the side along a paved terrace that ran the length of the house. 'I'm Emma, by the way.'

'Nice to meet you,' Alfred said.

When they got to the back of the house, Emma pointed towards a small outbuilding – a type of flat-roofed hut – some fifty yards ahead. 'Mr Claxton's just up here,' she said.

Alfred looked around and couldn't help but let out a low whistle. Now he understood why Mrs Singer-Cohen had referred to her gardens in the plural, rather than the singular. Before him lay a huge verdant expanse, more a park than a garden, with several circular patches of perennials, which, though pretty, gave the garden a flat look. To his left was a line of conifers, marking the edge of the property, and to his right, what looked to be a long stone wall. He took a deep breath. It would require an incredible amount of work to turn this into the sort of garden he'd described to Mrs Singer-Cohen on the train, but rather than discourage him, the space in front of him gave him a thrill of anticipation, like an artist in front of a blank canvas.

'You coming or what?' Emma asked impatiently. She was several yards ahead of him now.

'Yes, of course,' Alfred responded, and hurried to catch up with her.

'And don't worry,' she said when he'd drawn level, 'they have some local lads come in for the mowing in spring.'

Claxton emerged from the hut, carrying a spade in one hand and a small shrub in the other, its roots neatly parcelled inside a hessian ball. He gave Alfred a brief nod and mumbled a hello. Over the next two hours, he exchanged barely a word with Alfred, pointing out only where the lawn needed watering, handing him a pair of pruning scissors with curt instructions to deadhead the roses, and getting him to sweep the terrace path. It was hot and thirsty work, and despite the cheerful stream of singing his voice-women kept up in his ears, Alfred found himself becoming increasingly miserable. But just as he began wondering whether the move from Mauchline to Checkley had, indeed, been such a good idea, he spotted Alice Singer-Cohen emerging through the French windows at the back of the house.

'Ah, Mr Warner, already in the thick of it, I see,' she called out, smiling.

He gave her a strained smile in return. Claxton appeared from the shed.

'I'm still showing him the ropes,' Claxton said, 'he's a lot to learn.'

'Good, good. Well, if you've a moment to spare, do come and join me on the patio and we can discuss my plans.' She led the way across the lawn towards the patio at the back of the house, where she had laid out a bird's-eye sketch of the gardens on a table and weighed it down with stones on each corner.

'It's not to scale, I'm afraid,' she said, 'but it should give you some idea of the possibilities.'

Alfred had already begun tracing a mental image of the gardens in his mind from the moment he arrived, and he was delighted to be standing here, now, with the entire garden laid out in front of him. 'What's this?' he asked, tracing a line on the south side of the gardens, which was oddly straight given the curves on the other three sides.

'That's a brick wall, the boundary to Tean Estate,' she said. 'All of this,' she passed her hand across the sketch, 'used to be part of that estate.' She explained that the

Worthingtons, owners of Tean Estate for centuries, had sold off parcels of their enormous property after the war. 'They just couldn't afford to run it all any more, I suppose,' she continued. 'So when my husband saw it on the market, we jumped right in. The house was only finished last year, and as for the gardens, well . . . ' She sighed, and then caught Alfred's eye and smiled. 'I see them as a blank canvas.'

Claxton was breathing noisily through his nose and frowning, occasionally folding and then unfolding his arms across his chest.

Alice Singer-Cohen looked up at him. 'Why so glum, Mr Claxton?'

He let out a heavy breath. 'A lot of work to be done there, though, if you don't mind me saying.'

'Indeed, Mr Claxton,' she said, and then looked at Alfred and smiled. 'So it's a good thing you have such a fine help now, wouldn't you say? Oh, and Mr Warner, please feel free to use the library.' She nodded towards the house. 'You'll find I have quite an expansive gardening section.'

And with that, she rolled up the paper, gave them a little nod and retreated inside.

Alfred and Claxton walked back to the shed in silence. When they got there, Claxton turned back towards the house, where Alice Singer-Cohen had reappeared and was now reclining on a wooden lounger, her face turned towards the sun.

'I suppose a perfect English lawn in't good enough for them lot,' he said, flicking his head in the direction of the house.

Alfred wasn't sure whether he meant 'them lot' as

referring to the upper class, or Jews, or city-dwellers, or just *nouveaux riches* who had taken advantage of an increasingly impoverished landed gentry – but he didn't ask. He decided he'd rather not know.

Despite Alfred's hopes, Isobel's homesickness didn't pass; instead, it manifested itself in a clumsiness he had never seen before in his wife. She frequently bumped into furniture, hitting her hip against the kitchen table, banging her shoulder against doors, and even on one occasion tumbled down several stairs. Apart from some bruising, she was never seriously hurt, but she complained regularly about differences in English houses, that the dimensions of the furniture were all wrong, the dresser too high, the staircase too steep; that the doors opened at queer angles, and even that the gas cooker, on which she once burned her arm, produced flames that were too hot. Alfred tried to humour her as best he could, although he knew her complaints to be unreasonable, if not physically impossible, and hoped that it would only be a matter of time before she settled in.

But when the winter was over and spring arrived, and the gardens at March House began to yield the results of the autumn and winter labour, Isobel's clumsiness turned into restlessness. Often, Alfred found her waiting at the doorstep when he returned from work, the house meticulously cleaned and dinner on the table.

'Alfie, I'm bored,' she said one evening after supper. They were sitting in the living room, a coal fire burning in the hearth, because despite the warm days, the evenings still brought with them a damp cold. Isobel was darning a pair of Alfred's socks and he was reading a book from Singer-Cohen's library, a leather-bound, crisp-paged copy of *Physica* by Hildegard of Bingen. He had picked out the book purely by chance, and had become intrigued by Bingen's descriptions of the different plants' healing powers. Alice Singer-Cohen had recently suggested expanding the kitchen garden to include more herbs, and Alfred's mind was already wrapping itself around a range of possibilities, which seemed to please his voice-women.

Yarrow – distinguished and subtle powers for wounds

Parsley – generates seriousness in a person's mind and attenuates a fever

Dill – of a hot, dry nature that extinguishes the lust of the flesh . . .

Isobel's voice broke into his thoughts. 'Alfie!'

'Sorry?' he said distractedly.

'I'm bored, Alfie,' Isobel repeated, without looking up from her sewing. 'And I've been thinking. Maybe I could get a job.'

Alfred lowered the book onto his lap. 'A job? What sort of job?'

She shrugged, pushing the needle into the cotton and guiding it past the wooden egg that she had placed inside the sock. 'I don't know. Any job. Something to get me out of the house. Maybe . . . ' she paused and looked across at him. 'Maybe in Mr Singer-Cohen's factory. Belle worked there, before she had the twins.'

Belle was a local woman, a coal miner's wife Isobel had made friends with.

'I don't know, Isobel,' Alfred said slowly, feeling a little puzzled at this suggestion. She had never mentioned wanting to get a job before, and in all honesty, he wasn't sure what to make of it. 'A factory job, I don't know. It's hard work, on your feet all day, you don't – '

'But Belle worked as a painter,' Isobel interrupted. 'She painted designs on china teacups. That's not such hard work. I can do that. I'm good at painting.'

'Well, I don't know if you can just get a job like that without any training. Else all the girls would be wanting to do it.'

'But can you ask him? Mr Singer-Cohen, I mean. Can you ask him, at least?'

Alfred sighed. He leaned forward and reached out for her hand. After a brief hesitation, she laid her sewing to one side and put her hand in his.

'We're comfortable, aren't we?' he said softly, catching her eye and holding it. 'I'm not earning a fortune, but it's enough to keep us comfortable. There's nothing you're lacking, is there?'

At this, Isobel lowered her eyes. There was, of course, something lacking, although neither of them would talk about it. They hadn't been using any protection against pregnancy for some time, and yet Isobel's bleeding came on every month like clockwork. Alfred squeezed her hand. 'It's probably just the time of year,' he said gently. 'Everyone feels restless in the spring, eh?'

She swallowed and returned his squeeze. 'Aye, I suppose so.' Then she slipped her hand out of his and picked up the sewing.

But in May, any notion of Isobel working in a factory became irrelevant. She informed Alfred one morning, somewhat shyly, that her periods were late, and a visit to the doctor in Stoke-on-Trent confirmed the pregnancy.

Hearing of what happened in her previous pregnancy, the doctor prescribed as much rest as she could afford, plenty of orange juice, and told her that a caesarean section would be unavoidable.

Isobel's morning sickness was mild in comparison to the previous pregnancy, leading her to predict that it would be a boy. She was still in close contact with Amy Fraser – they wrote to each other almost weekly – and Amy claimed that only girls make their mothers sick. This, however, was the only reference she and Alfred made to Isobel's pregnancy with Brynja. Indeed, it proved to be a tense time. Even when the first trimester passed – and with it, Isobel's sheer endless exhaustion – and her hair grew thick and glossy, her skin became tinged with a rosy glow, and her belly developed into a round, perfect bump, she was anything but carefree. Alfred's attempts to lure her out of the house with tickets to the cinema, or leisurely walks in the lush autumnal countryside were declined with a tired smile.

'I really don't think I should, Alfie,' she would say, her hands never straying far from her stomach.

As for Alfred, he hardly dared think about the birth. All the anticipatory joy and hopes he'd felt during Isobel's last pregnancy he kept firmly bottled up; any notion of fatherhood, that miraculous sense of creating another human being from something as simple, as primitive, as intercourse, he ignored as best he could. Even the voice-women, who had lately taken to invading his dreams with strange, alien songs and chants, he disregarded. The fear over what might happen – to the baby, to Isobel – subdued him; even his sexual appetite, which for a healthy twenty-four-year-old should be rampant, only arose sporadically, when he woke in the mornings to the sight of Isobel's now-swollen, white-skinned breasts peeking out from the top of her nightgown, or – more shamefully – at the neat curve of Alice Singer-Cohen's buttocks beneath her tight-fitting pencil skirt.

DAY FIVE

———

At lunch, I noticed a stain on Alfred's sweater.

'You're welcome to use the washing machine,' I told him. 'Or just put whatever you want washed in the laundry basket.'

His face fell, and his forkful of leftover fricassee hovered midway between plate and mouth. 'Goodness, do I smell?' he asked quietly. His hand began to tremble slightly.

I watched a kernel of rice fall from his fork. 'No. Not at all. I just thought . . . well, you've only brought a small suitcase, and you'll need clean clothes sooner or later.'

At this, he let out a long sigh, but didn't respond.

'I mean, Christmas is over tomorrow,' I continued softly. Now seemed as good a time as ever to bring it up. 'Things'll be more or less back to normal. And, well. I . . . you're welcome to stay for a little while longer. Until you sort things out. Or until Brynja . . . ' I didn't finish my sentence.

Alfred put down his knife and fork. 'You haven't been paying attention,' he said grimly.

'What?' I was taken aback by the sharpness of his tone.

'I trusted you, Julia,' he said, raising his voice now. 'I trusted you. All I asked for was for you to pay attention and listen to my story. And you haven't understood a thing!' He got to his feet. 'I am going to die tomorrow, and Brynja . . . Brynja . . . ' His head was shaking very badly. 'You've let me down, Julia.'

'What?'

'You've let me down,' he repeated. 'And worse than that, you're letting Brynja down.' His words seemed to hover in the air.

Before I could control it, a sudden anger swept over me. 'I've let you down?' I said, rising from my chair. 'How can you say that? After all I've done for you! I cook your meals and wash your clothes and clean up your mess and go out of my mind with worry while you disappear for hours on end. And you still treat me like a child. I've put my life on hold for you! I should be out with friends, going to concerts, and films, and parties. But oh no – nothing I ever do is good enough for you!' I clamped my hand over my mouth, and, realising I was on the verge of tears, slumped down onto my chair.

Outside, the snow had turned into sleet, drumming against the window pane as we sat there in silence. Finally, I spoke. 'I'm sorry Alfred. That was out of order. I – '

'No Julia. I'm the one who should apologise.' He got up and went into the living room. When he returned, he was holding a large manila envelope. 'Here,' he said, pushing it into my hands.

'What's this?' I asked.

'Everything you need to know for when I'm – well, afterwards.'

I took the envelope.

'It's all there – my bank details, name of my solicitor, where I'd like to be buried. You know, the formalities.'

I cleared my throat. 'Right.'

He reached over and brushed my cheek lightly with his fingers. 'You'll see, Julia.'

1951 – 1955

On 15th January 1951, John Karl Warner was delivered by caesarean section, plump and rosy, weighing eight pounds, two ounces. Isobel recovered remarkably quickly from the operation. So quickly, in fact, that several hours after she'd woken from the anaesthetic, Alfred found her sitting up in bed, looking a little pale but fresh, the baby chewing hungrily at her nipple. When the nurse saw Alfred coming down the ward, she quickly covered the baby's head with a muslin cloth, but Isobel scarcely seemed to notice.

'How are you?' Alfred asked her, leaning down to kiss her forehead. Her damp hair had fallen forward across her face, and he could smell the iodine from the surgery. Then he drew back the cloth and looked at his son. The baby had a thatch of dark hair; his skin was very pink, almost reddish, and he was working furiously, breathing loudly through his nose, to extract the milk from Isobel's ripe breast.

'Is he nae the most beautiful thing ye ever saw?' she whispered, not taking her eyes off the baby for a minute.

'Aye, Isobel.' He stroked a strand of hair back behind her ear. 'Just . . . beautiful.'

They watched the baby in silence for a long while, until he had exhausted himself and fallen asleep, his lips open and a thin trail of saliva running down the corner of his mouth. A trolley rattled by noisily and he twitched.

'May I hold him?' Alfred asked quietly, reaching out his arms. But Isobel tucked the blanket around him more tightly and shook her head.

'He's sleeping so soundly,' she said, continuing to gaze down at the baby. 'And I want to hold him until they take him back to the nursery.'

Alfred withdrew his arms, slightly disappointed, for his chest was bursting with joy and love and tenderness for his child, but he understood that anything he was feeling, Isobel was feeling a thousand times over. He remained at their side until a nurse called out that visiting hours were over, and kissed his wife and child goodbye.

On his way out, the ward sister rose from her desk. 'Mr Warner,' she said, 'I wonder if you might speak to your wife about the nursing.'

'The nursing?' he asked.

She glanced down the ward and lowered her voice. 'Giving the child her breast. Under normal circumstances, I would let her get on with it – hygiene issues aside – but taking into account the operation and all, well, it's just not very sensible. We've tried talking to her, but I fear she's being a little unreasonable. It's not as if the war was still on!' She gave a little shake of her head. 'Perhaps you might have a word.'

But when he mentioned it on his visit the following day, Isobel wouldn't hear of it. 'I'm perfectly capable of feeding my own child,' she said. 'I'm all he needs.' And Alfred had to admit that she was probably right.

By summer, the gardens at March House had begun to take shape and baby John was able to sit up on his own. In late autumn, what remained of the lawns was covered in yellowed leaves and John was crawling, and on Christmas Day 1951, when the world outside was covered with a thin veil of unromantic snow, the boy took his first tentative, wobbly steps.

'Isn't he clever, Alfie?!' Isobel cried. 'Aren't you the cleverest little lad, Johnnie?!' She held out her index fingers and John curled his fat, pink hands around them, and they took a walk around the Christmas tree. 'Walking before his first birthday, that's special.' She picked him up and kissed his plump cheek. 'Now,' she said, putting him down, 'let's see if you can walk all the way to your dad.'

But John let himself fall onto his bottom and began to grizzle.

'He's tired, love,' Alfred said. 'Why not put him to bed.'

Isobel kneeled in front of John and held her fingers out again. 'Come on, Johnnie, walk to Daddy.'

John screwed up his face and began to cry more urgently.

'No, he's not tired,' Isobel said, picking the child up once more. She put a finger to his mouth and parted his lips. 'He's teething. Look, the gum's all red and swollen. Oh poor, poor laddie,' she murmured. 'Alfie, would you fetch the gin?'

Alfred took a bottle of gin out of the walnut side table

and passed it to Isobel. She soaked a handkerchief and began rubbing John's gum with it. Soon, the boy stopped crying and finally fell asleep in her arms. The window rattled in its frame with a sudden gust of wind and Isobel shivered. Alfred got up to add some coal to the fire. It was early afternoon, but the December sky offered little light, and so they had switched on the floor lamp in the corner and the Christmas tree lights. The smell of the turkey dinner they'd eaten earlier still lingered in the room. Alfred sat down in an armchair opposite Isobel and watched her watch the baby. She had lost all the weight she'd gained in pregnancy – her light blue dress, fashionably nipped at the waist with a tapering skirt, was one of the few dresses she owned that wasn't soiled by John's sticky hands and mouth, or the contents of his stomach.

Looking at her now, as she stroked the boy's head with her small, soft hands, her neatly plucked eyebrows rising and falling in synchrony with the child's slow breathing, Alfred couldn't help but marvel at her devotion to the child. Early on, John had been a fussy baby, crying for hours on end for no apparent reason, with such unfailing gusto as to drive him, Alfred, almost to despair. But Isobel seemed to possess a sheer infinite source of patience and tenderness for the child. During the first few months, she had survived on as little as three hours of sleep a night, usually waking even before the boy began to cry for a feed – and yet she retained a brightness that was almost unnatural. It was clear that the baby had triggered a profound change in her, and at times, Alfred felt as though he were struggling to keep up.

But he wasn't dissatisfied; he had a good wife who was

a good mother to his son. So what was he aching for? He felt suddenly drowsy and closed his eyes. The voices were murmuring among themselves just outside his range of hearing, though he couldn't so much hear them as feel them. Suddenly, for the first time in several years, he found himself missing the daughter that had never lived with an acuteness that was almost painful. Then sleep snatched him away before he even realised it.

In the summer of '54, rationing was finally lifted completely.

'And to celebrate,' Isobel told Alfred, 'we're going to have a picnic in the park. With Sue and Mick.'

'Remind me?'

Isobel gave him a playful slap. She was evidently in a good mood. 'Sue Cartwright. From church. Anyway, we've arranged it for next Sunday, three o'clock. They've got two children, just a wee bit older than Johnnie. It'll be fun!'

The following Sunday, they gathered on a section of grass behind the school, locally known as the park. It was a cool, dull day, but spirits were up, perhaps in anticipation of the promises implied by new consumerist liberties. Isobel had baked enough scones and jam tarts to feed two full-sized football teams; Sue, a rather unremarkable woman with a semi-permanent smile attached to her face, provided a surprisingly delicious cold lamb meatloaf and some oatcakes. Alfred recognised Mick from the local pub, and gave him a broad smile in greeting. Apart from three-year-old John, the two other children were Sally, eight, and William, four. Mick had brought beer and pop, and handed out the drinks.

'Here's to the end of austerity,' he called, holding up his bottle.

'And to the beginning of gluttony,' Alfred echoed.

Fat chance of that.

He ignored the voice. His voice-women were particularly unsettled today, the youngest bristling with mischief, almost (he contemplated that evening) as if they were invoking some sort of trouble. Instead, he clinked his bottle of beer against Isobel's lemonade and gave her a smile. Presently, the children began to whine that they were hungry, and Sue declared the picnic officially open. The two Cartwright children were allowed to help themselves to whatever took their fancy – jam tarts and scones, mainly – but Isobel insisted that John eat something sensible first, a sandwich, or perhaps a slice of meatloaf.

'Come and sit here,' she said, patting her lap. 'Now, which do you want, sweetie? The meatloaf? Or a sandwich? Look, I could scrape off the yucky pickles for you.'

Grudgingly, John sat down onto her lap and took two bites of meatloaf, which she fed him. Then she produced a handkerchief, licked a corner and wiped John's mouth with it. A look passed between Sue and Mick, and Alfred caught it, and felt momentarily embarrassed for his son. A moment later, before his mother could stop him, John grabbed a couple of jam tarts and headed off to where the other two children were playing across the field.

The adults then also helped themselves to the picnic and soon they sat in satiated silence among the empty hampers and baskets. Mick lay down on the blanket, propping himself up on his elbow. He lit a cigarette and looked up at the low grey sky. 'The summer's nowt to write home about.'

'No,' Sue agreed. She turned to Isobel. 'Or do you prefer the heat, Isobel?'

'Mmm.' Isobel, who now gave this non-committal response, had for the past twenty minutes been casting nervous glances to where the children were playing at the edge of the field. She stood up.

'John!' she called. 'Johnnie! Stay away from the stream! Be a good boy now!'

Sue looked over at the children. 'Oh, don't worry. They'll be fine. It's only a yard wide. William and Sally love to jump over it. The worst that can happen is wet socks.'

Isobel waited until John had moved away from the water and sat down again. 'Children have been known to drown in a couple of inches of water,' she said in an unnecessarily cool tone that surprised Alfred.

'Well,' Mick said, 'Sally's a strong swimmer. She'll save him, if need be.'

Alfred checked Mick's face for a trace of sarcasm, but found nothing. Soon, the two boys had each picked up a long branch and were whacking the heads off dandelion clocks. Isobel shot them a worried glance.

'He's fine,' Alfred told her quietly, sensing her tenseness.

'I don't think he should be playing with sticks,' she said.

'Boys and sticks,' Mick said jovially, 'the most natural union in the world. You know, when I was a young lad – hey! Watch it!'

John had come flying across the group to Isobel, pursued by Sally, upsetting Mick's beer and squashing a half-eaten sandwich into the blanket with his foot.

'Steady on,' Mick said, righting his bottle.

'She pinched me,' John said to his mother in a voice close to tears. He held out his arm. 'Look.' There was a reddish mark on his skin.

'He was trying to look up my skirt,' Sally said indignantly. 'With his stick.'

Behind her, William let out a snort of laughter.

'Now, Sally,' Mick said, but Isobel was already on her feet.

'Did you pinch him?' she asked Sally, a small tremor in her voice.

Sally folded her arms across her chest. 'He was trying to look up my skirt,' she repeated.

'But did you pinch him?' Isobel asked sharply. Her face was flushed.

Sally pressed her lips together.

Alfred took John's arm and rubbed it. 'No harm done, love,' he said to his wife. 'They were just playing.'

'Yeah, boys will be boys,' Mick added.

Isobel suddenly reached out to grab Sally's wrist. 'He's just a little boy,' she hissed.

Sue stood up. 'It's all right, Isobel,' she said, her smile now vanished. 'I'll scold my own children, if you don't mind.' She put out a hand for Sally and Isobel dropped the girl's wrist. 'And you can scold yours,' she added.

'Now, now,' Mick said. 'Let's all calm down. Here – ' he retrieved a tumbler from one of the hampers and filled half of it with beer. 'I'll make you ladies a nice shandy, what d'you think?'

Isobel shook her head, and then sat down and took John onto her lap.

They sat in silence for some time, until presently, the

children got up and ran off again laughing, their quarrel now seemingly forgotten. Isobel stared after them for a long while. Alfred and the others began to reminisce about all the meals they'd missed during rationing, when a deep rumble of thunder came through from some black clouds to the west.

'Let's hope that rain brings a bit of cool air with it,' Sue said. 'This weather must be awful for the lawns at March House, eh, Alfred?'

'We could certainly do with some – ' Alfred began, but he was interrupted by a scream, followed by a howl. The adults' heads turned like one to where the children were now racing, John in front, towards them. The boy was pale, a look of terror on his face.

'Mummy!' he shouted. 'She's going to hit me!'

And indeed, Sally was almost on him, a stick in her raised hand. When she got closer, they could see tears streaming down her face.

'What the – ' Mick began, getting to his feet.

'John, sweetie,' Isobel said, also standing up and holding her arms open. John reached her and she took him in a tight hug, casting an angry look at Sally.

'He hit me,' Sally wailed, 'he hit me with the stick.' She half turned and put her leg out to show them. On her calf she had a nasty red welt, its edges already beginning to swell.

'She pinched me again, Mummy,' John said. 'She pinched me really hard so I hit her.'

All the adults were on their feet now. Sue and Mick were standing either side of Sally. Sue put her hand to Sally's leg, but she pulled away, wincing. 'Don't touch it!'

Alfred spoke to John. 'Why did you hit her?'

'She pinched him again,' Isobel said. 'She pinched a boy less than half her age.'

'Look at her leg!' Sue cried. 'He might be little, but he's old enough to know not to whack people with sticks.'

'He was looking up my skirt again, Mum,' Sally said in a flat voice.

Isobel pressed John closer to her. 'He doesn't know what he's doing. He's only a wee boy.'

'And that's all you're going to say, is it? He doesn't know what he's doing?' Sue kept her voice raised. 'He knew what he was doing when he attacked her with a stick!'

'Sally's a bully, that's what she is!' Isobel said shrilly. 'I've a right mind to – '

'To what?' Mick said, thrusting his chin out in her direction.

Alfred turned to him. 'Come on, now, Mick, let's all keep our tempers. They're just children.'

The air was heavy with the smell of rain. In the distance, in the neighbouring field, a herd of cows was moving towards the cover of the trees. Sue took a step forward to stand in front of Sally. 'No. I'd like to know what she has a mind to do.'

Isobel pulled back her shoulders. 'I've – I've a right mind to give her a good spanking.'

'Ha!' Sue let out a hard laugh. 'Spank *my* child? Well, beg my pardon for being frank, but I think you should start with your own. The little pervert.'

'Hey,' Alfred said, taking a step forward with his palm raised. 'Watch your tone.'

The children were just standing there now, subdued, fearful of what they might have unleashed.

'He's not a pervert!' Isobel cried. 'He's *three years old.*'

'He's a mummy's boy, is what he is,' Sue said, her voice low and dangerous. 'Ask anyone. A spoiled brat.' She looked to her husband for confirmation. He nodded gravely.

Fragments of sounds began to bounce around inside Alfred's head.

John – spoiled – pervert – brat.

'Is there something you'd like to say, Mick?' he asked before he could stop himself.

'I'm saying,' Mick said, taking a step forward, so that Alfred could smell beer and pickle on his breath, 'I'm saying that that son of yours obviously thinks it's okay to hit a girl. Now where could he've got such an idea from?'

A flash of anger whipped through Alfred. He felt his fists clenching

Now, don't let him provoke you, Alfred. Don't do something you might regret.

Fight! Fight! Fight! Ksss, show the bastard!

and his heart throbbing in his throat. The men stood facing one another wordlessly. It was Sue who finally spoke. 'Don't give him the satisfaction,' she said to Mick.

Mick lifted a finger and pointed it at Alfred's face. 'If it weren't for the women and children here, I'd have you.'

A hush fell over the group. Then Sue stooped to pick up her hamper.

'This could've been such a lovely day,' she said quietly. 'Come on, children. We're going home.'

Alfred opened his mouth to speak, but failed to think of anything to say that might salvage the situation. His heart was still beating hard. He waited until the Cartwrights were out of earshot, and then said to Isobel, 'I thought you were friends?'

271

To which she responded by taking John's hand. 'Apparently not.'

They got caught in the rain on the way home. Isobel didn't say a single word as they drudged back to the cottage, but Alfred was bristling with embarrassment, anger and sheer incredulity that the situation could have got out of hand so quickly. He hoped he wouldn't run into Mick Cartwright again soon.

For Isobel, by contrast, Alfred's actions at the picnic had elevated him to the status of hero. In the days, then weeks that followed, he would come home to find Isobel waiting at the living room window, John – always – in her arms. 'Here comes your brave daddy,' she would coo when he arrived through the door, planting a kiss on his cheek and lifting up John to do the same. 'Daddy's a big brave man,' she'd say, and 'The only one around here that's allowed to pinch you is me,' chasing a gleeful and whooping John around the room, pinch-tickling him until tears of laughter rolled down his face.

It disconcerted Alfred. It was one thing to stand up for your family, he thought, but another thing entirely to let the boy think that what had happened at the picnic – John's actions as well as his own – were somehow sanctionable. It had been wrong to let the matter get out of hand, and John should be made aware of that. Isobel evidently read the situation entirely differently; her son, that fountain of joy, that vessel of innocence, could do no wrong.

But Alfred now began to notice things. He noticed that Isobel, despite John's plump and sturdy legs, would carry the boy great distances rather than let him – make him – walk, hoisted on her hip as though he weighed only a few pounds. He noticed, for the first time (how could he have missed it so far?), when they took him to the playground where the other village children – some twenty of them between the ages of one and twelve – congregated, how quick and willing Isobel was to come to the boy's defence when he had kicked over another child's sandcastle or stood at the top of the slide, refusing to let others pass.

Alfred noticed all these things and didn't like it. At night, lying awake while Isobel slept beside him, waiting for the moment when John would inevitably come running – tap tap tap – into their room and slide into bed between them, he appealed to his voice-women.

You need to put your foot down, Alfred. You're the boy's father.

'I know,' he said silently, gloomily. 'But I don't think Isobel sees it the way I do.'

She's blind with love – she means no harm, but she's ruining the child.

'Don't you understand? She lost a child, remember?'

Of course, but then so did you. And your duty is now to this child.

Yes. Talk to her, Alfred.

But his attempts to discuss matters with Isobel were fruitless.

'He's just a wee lad,' she would say, when Alfred pointed out that the boy was perfectly capable of walking and didn't need to be carried all the time. Or, when John would snatch a toy from another child who came to visit, she'd say, 'He's a little impatient, I'll give you that, but just because he's curious.' His proneness to tears was due to his 'sensitivity', his temper tantrums were an expression of his 'high spirits'. John's transgressions towards other children, the kicking and hitting, she would pretend not to notice, or justify with, 'He didn't start it. He has a right to defend himself.'

And so it went on, until Alfred, coming home one evening shortly before John's fourth birthday, found that the boy had taken a knife to the wisteria roots at the front of the house, destroying, in one fell swoop, decades' worth of slow, delicate growth – and he realised, sickeningly and shamefully, that he actually disliked his own son. But the feeling, acute and fierce one moment, faded almost immediately, leaving behind, however, a vague sense of loss. And this might have marked the beginning of an entirely novel kind of heartache for Alfred, had he not one day witnessed something truly wondrous: he overheard John talking to himself.

NINETEEN NINETY-FIVE

The first thing the therapist says is Take your shoes off, please, because sometimes she asks people to lie down on the floor as part of therapy and it would be unhygienic to make them lie on a carpet that's covered in street dirt. You take off your shoes and cross the room and sit down on the chair the therapist points at. You look down at the carpet. It is the colour of mud. There are loads of grey fluffy bits sticking to it and probably billions of germs. You hope you won't have to lie down there.

The therapist is about the same age as your mom, maybe thirty-five or a bit older. She's not as pretty as your mom, though; her front teeth stick out over her bottom lip and when she speaks, a very white speck of saliva collects in the corner of her mouth. Every now and again, her tongue curls out and licks the saliva off. Her tongue is very red and shiny, like liver. She is wearing a blue wool dress and a long bead necklace that makes soft clicking sounds like dried bones whenever she moves.

To begin with, I like my clients to tell me a little bit about themselves, the therapist says, and you don't get it at first that she means you, because a client is someone who has a bank account or an insurance policy. The therapist crosses her legs and leans forward slightly. Her necklace clicks. So, she says, people are a little worried about you. Your mom especially.

You know your mom is worried about you going crazy. This makes you sad and guilty and ashamed. This makes you want to slice your thigh with a razor blade so you don't feel the sadness and guilt and shame as much.

And that's why your paediatrician sent you here, the therapist says, for a little chat. To see if I can help fix what's wrong. She picks up a pencil and notepad from the low table next to her. How do you feel about coming here today? she asks, holding the pencil over her notepad, hovering there, ready to start writing. On a scale of one to ten.

You say, I don't know.

The therapist writes something down. Do you have friends? You nod. And then you start making up names without knowing why you're making them up – Marlene and Hollie and Isobel and Heidi – but you can't stop yourself. You used to have real friends. Jessie and Aisha and Hannah. But you don't say this to the therapist. You don't know why you just lied to the therapist about your friends' names. You made a promise to yourself before you came here that you would do your best, tell the truth, pay attention and try and get better. You promised your mom, too. When your mom told you about the appointment, she looked away and you could tell she was trying not to cry, which was actually worse than if she had been crying.

And how about a boyfriend? the therapist says, her pencil twitching, and your face gets all hot and you shake your head and the therapist smiles and says, Nothing to be embarrassed about.

She leans back in her seat. For this to work, Brynja, you're going to have to talk to me, let me know what's wrong. Otherwise I won't be able to help you.

Part of you feels like telling the therapist all the stuff that's inside your head – like the first time you dragged the scissors up and down your arm and how amazing it felt! But that now the voice-woman makes you do it all the time. Or how you wake up in the morning already crying and just can't stop. Or that sometimes you can't get out of bed before you've counted all the leaves on the tree that grows outside your bedroom window because the little girl voice makes you. Or about the voices telling you how dumb you are, telling you to pinch the neighbour's baby really hard whenever no one's looking – but then the therapist will know how evil and crazy you are and you might get locked up. And that if you tell her anything, the voices will punish you.

Then you realise that you haven't been paying attention to what the therapist is saying, which happens a lot because you find it very difficult to concentrate sometimes, which is a problem especially in school and the teacher is explaining something, let's say, the effects of the Vietnam War on the global economy, and your mind drifts to the dandruff on Zoë Stewart's shoulders, who sits in the row in front of you, and to the fact that Zoë has really dark eyes, black almost, and the voice-woman comes and tells you to think about what it must be like to turn blind overnight, just wake up one morning and everything is dark. Everything. And then there are people who are blind *and* deaf –

– and then you get into trouble because you've been listening to the voice and thinking about dandruff and blindness and deafness rather than paying attention to the teacher, and in the last three months the principal has invited your mom for a talk at least five times. Saying, she's not a troublemaker, quite the opposite, what a good girl she's always been, I appreciate it's a difficult age, but she must really pay more attention in class, and by the way, she looks as though she's lost quite a bit of weight recently, or is that just the puppy fat coming off?

The therapist is telling you that it's okay to feel confused sometimes. You don't think it's okay, the therapist obviously doesn't know what it feels like to be confused. But you don't say that. You don't say anything. The therapist continues, I can see you bite your nails Brynja, and you feel a bit embarrassed but are glad that you stopped cutting your arms and switched to cutting your legs, because it's easier to hide the scars, even though the voice makes you cut your thighs so deep that it hurts for days, sometimes.

Are you being bullied? the therapist asks. At school, maybe?

The therapist says, You can tell me anything. I won't tell anyone what you say in here. Go on, give it a try.

But you can't just squeeze out words. That's like trying to go for a shit when you don't need one, and this thought makes you panic because now you are worried that if you say anything, the voice-woman will make you say shit and all words that rhyme with shit. That what's started to happen recently when you hear a curse word, then that's all she lets you think about. That word and all words that rhyme with it. Like fuck: muck, suck, duck, puck, buck, yuck, tuck, luck. That's why you don't dare squeeze out any words.

Okay, the therapist says, I'll be honest with you here Brynja. If you don't cooperate, there's no point in you being here, is there. Then you're wasting both our time.

At other times, the voice twists your mind to the opposite: makes it stick to one single thing like glue, and you can't think of anything else. Like now, all you can focus on is the saliva in the corner of the therapist's mouth, the way it starts out as a tiny speck and after a few minutes of the therapist talking, gradually becomes this huge glob, and then there's the red tongue, darting out like a frog's to lick it off. Talk, talk, saliva, tongue – talk, talk, saliva, tongue.

The therapist looks at her watch and says, Good grief! Look at the time. She smiles as though she's really pleased about something. We'll wrap it up there shall we? she says, and there is a soft knock on the door and your mom comes in. She asks if it's time and the therapist says, Yes, we've had a good chat haven't we? Brynja, would you mind waiting outside so I can have a word with your mom?

So you go and sit in the waiting room and stare at a picture on the wall opposite of a sun that's bleeding around the edges and wait for the voices to arrive.

1955 – 1958

Alfred, Isobel and John had taken a trip to the seaside – their first family holiday together – staying for three nights at a small B&B in Colwyn Bay. The room was cramped and not particularly clean, but it was cheap and they intended to stay outdoors at the beach for most of the day. It was on their second day there that it occurred. Isobel and Alfred had rented a deckchair each, and John played close to them in the sand. The weather was fair; now and again, a chill breeze blew in from the restless, pewter sea, but most of the time the air was still, and they felt the force of the white July sun on their skin. Isobel wore a pretty floral cotton dress and a wide-brimmed straw hat, and Alfred had rolled up his trouser legs, stripped down to his vest and fashioned a cap from a knotted handkerchief. He felt perfectly calm; it was good to be sitting here, doing nothing but read the newspaper and occasionally look out to the horizon. Isobel had a novel with her, its cover featuring a blonde woman and an Arab sheik entwined in a tight embrace, and every now and then, she would let out a sigh, or emit a sharp intake of breath. Presently, though, she rose from her deckchair. 'I'm off to get an ice cream,' she announced. 'You coming, Johnnie?'

But the boy shook his head. He was playing with the remnants of a sandcastle built yesterday by some other child. (In just under a day, John had succeeded in alienating all other children on the beach by destroying their sandcastles and throwing handfuls of sand at them.) He was trying to dig a trench from the sandcastle to the edge of the water, using his hands to scoop through the wet sand.

'I'll watch him,' Alfred said, and after a brief hesitation, Isobel walked off across the sand towards the promenade.

Alfred looked over at John; he was wearing only his shorts, and the skin on his shoulders was turning slightly pink. Alfred made a mental note to tell Isobel to get him to put on his shirt before he got sunburned. He went back to his newspaper, but was too drowsy to read. He folded the paper up and closed his eyes, resting his head against the back of the chair. Then he heard John speak. It was just two words – 'I know' – spoken quietly, but clear enough for Alfred to hear. Thinking the boy was addressing him, he opened his eyes and raised his head. But John was fully concentrated on his trench. Then,

'No! Not like that.' His voice was still quiet, inaudible to anyone five yards away.

Alfred sat up.

'I'm doing – '

A pause.

'All right then.'

A strangeness came over Alfred as he watched his son; he held his breath and tried to listen in. It couldn't be, the boy was only four-and-a-half years old. Alfred opened his hearing, but apart from the hiss and curl of the waves lapping the beach, and some excited shrieking coming from a group of children playing twenty yards away, he heard nothing.

'But if I dig here, then it'll – '

Alfred leaned forward. He didn't want to disturb the boy.

'Oh. Yes, I see.' John took his small spade and began to dig a second channel. 'Yes.' It seemed as though he were following instructions to keep the trench from collapsing into itself.

A sudden gust of wind made goose bumps appear on Alfred's arms.

'John,' he said quietly. John frowned and continued to dig. 'John,' Alfred repeated, more loudly.

John looked up at him. His eyes were grey, like Alfred's, but had the roundness of his mother's.

'Who are you talking to?' he asked, trying to keep his voice soft and inviting.

John held his gaze for a moment and then looked away. 'No one.'

Alfred got up from his deckchair and went to kneel beside John. 'Johnnie, who are you talking to?' He spoke calmly, although he could feel his heart beating strongly in his chest.

John pressed his lips together.

'Are you talking to someone in your head?'

For a moment, John seemed poised to speak. But then, 'No. No one.' Then he sighed. 'I'm building a trench,' he said. 'You see? So the sea can make a moat around the castle.'

'Yes. Very good,' Alfred said. He put out his hand and stroked John's hair. He didn't want to frighten him. For a while, they sat there in silence, as John continued to carve his trench out of the sand. But soon, Alfred couldn't stand it any longer.

Is that you? he asked silently. *Are you talking to John?*

A wave crashed noisily onto the sand, sending the group of nearby children into fits of squeals and giggles.

Is that you? he shouted in his head. But there was no response. He moved in closer to John. 'Johnnie? You know, son, some people can – '

'I'm back!' It was Isobel, carrying three cones of ice cream. 'Quick, they're melting,' she said, lifting her hand to her mouth and licking the creamy drips from her fingers.

John got to his feet and took a cone off her. 'Mummy?'

'Yes, Johnnie?'

'When I'm grown up and get married I'm going to marry you.'

Isobel bent down and kissed him on the nose. 'I think your dad might have something to say about that, eh Alfie?' She looked down at Alfred, who was still kneeling in the sand.

'Aye,' Alfred said, and added, 'I think he should put his shirt on before he gets sunburn.'

And so, over the following years, Alfred watched his son, this time in some amorphous anticipation of what he had witnessed on the beach to repeat itself. He asked the voice-women again and again if they'd spoken to John – this seemed the most obvious way of finding out – but they remained frustratingly silent about it. He lingered outside John's bedroom when he was playing there alone, in the hope of catching him talking to himself again, and invented bedtime stories that featured princes and talking faeries and wood-nymphs (inspired, in part, by his own experience of first hearing voices). But the incident didn't repeat itself, at least, not in Alfred's presence, and as time passed, he began to wonder if he might have imagined the whole thing, or prescribed some significance to it that wasn't really there. Then John started school and began to develop into a normal, physically healthy young boy. And although Alfred knew he should be grateful for this, in truth there was an aching space inside him that should have been filled with pride, but was instead filled – sickeningly – with disappointment.

On a wet, prematurely dark afternoon in July 1958, Alfred waited until Claxton had left for home, and then removed his muddy boots at the side entrance of March House. He was heading for the library; three of the plum trees in the orchard had become infected with some fungus he couldn't identify, and he was hoping to find some book on how to treat them. He stepped inside and almost bumped into Emma, who was polishing one of the many mirrors that adorned the entrance hall.

'Sorry,' he said, stepping aside. 'I'm going to the library,' he added.

'Suit yourself,' she replied with a shrug. 'But they've got some guests coming later. Friends from London or whatever. So don't be making a mess.'

'I won't be long.' He padded across the hall, self-conscious in his stockinged feet, hearing Emma mumbling 'Why they don't just have one big bloody mirror like normal people, I'll never know,' as he slipped through the oak door and into the library.

Because the room was dark, Alfred perceived the smells in here all the more keenly. He waited a few seconds before switching on a light, taking in – like some initiation ritual – the musty odour of old books and stale pipe smoke, undercut by the sharpness of beeswax and furniture polish. (Her brusque manner aside, Emma was a highly conscientious cleaner.) Not wanting to disturb the dark calm produced by these smells, Alfred decided against the shrill light of the huge chandelier and instead switched on only a small pearl-fringed Victorian table lamp closest to the shelf housing the gardening books. The lamp gave off a burnt-orange light, just enough to decipher the titles on the book spines. Alfred quickly found two books that looked promising – *Tree Fruit Growing* by Raymond Bush and *The Plum and Its Cultivation* by Edward Barker – and slipped them off the shelf. He then scanned the shelves of Alice Singer-Cohen's section superficially (he knew the collection well enough by now to spot any new additions straight away) and was turning to leave, gardening books in hand, when his eye was drawn to a book he didn't recognise. The spine was Egyptian blue with silver-embossed lettering, but impossible for Alfred to read at this angle. He pulled up a footstool to get a closer look. *A Comprehensive Introduction to Icelandic Mythology*, the title read. He slid his finger down the spine. The book was undoubtedly quite old, the blue fabric worn through to reveal a fluff of cardboard at the corners. It was curious he'd never seen it here before . . .

. . . *but then you've never looked properly.*

'Looked for what?'

Exactly.

'You're not making any sense.'

There was a pause, filled with the intermittent crackle of voices, like waiting for a caller to come through on a bad telephone line. Then –

You have to look more closely, Alfred.

Hush. You've said enough now.

He must have been standing there longer than he thought, because he suddenly became aware of voices – real, human voices – coming from the other side of the room. It was two women talking. Alfred hadn't heard them come in, and he froze, with his fingertips still touching the book. The women continued talking as though he wasn't there; they evidently hadn't noticed him.

'*Könnest Du Dir das vorstellen, hier auf dem Lande?*'

'*Auf keinen Fall. Natürlich ist es wunderschön, aber ich weiß nicht, wie sie's hier aushalten.*'

They were speaking German. They were wondering how the Singer-Cohens could stand to live in the countryside. Alfred held his breath. He hadn't heard any German being spoken in what seemed like a hundred years, and although he felt a little shameful about eavesdropping, he longed to hear more of this strange-familiar language. Very slowly, he turned around. Through the gloom, he could make out two elderly women, elegantly and expensively dressed.

'*Aber für Kinder wäre es herrlich,*' one of them said. It would be wonderful for children.

'*Aber nur solange sie noch klein sind,*' the other answered. Only while they are small. '*Und Alice wird ja auch nicht jünger.*' And Alice isn't getting any younger.

These must be the visitors that Emma had referred to. Alfred stepped off the stool as quietly as he could, wondering how he could make his presence known without letting them think he'd been eavesdropping. But the floorboard he stepped down on gave out a shuddering creak, making one of the women gasp aloud.

'*Ist da jemand?*' she called in a wavering kind of voice. Is somebody there?

'*Oh, ich wollte Sie nicht erschrecken.*' I didn't want to scare you. Alfred moved forward into the light. '*Entschuldigen Sie bitte vielmals,*' he added quickly, the German words of apology slipping fluidly and automatically from his mouth. One of the women – with deeply tanned, wrinkled skin – raised her eyebrows, but before she could question him further, Alfred folded his arms around the two gardening books and hurried out.

He dropped into bed heavily that night, taking a while to find a position that eased a nagging pain in his lower back he had been suffering for weeks now. Isobel lay with her back to him, snoring very slightly. He felt the voice-women bristling at the edge of his consciousness, trying to snag his attention, eager to chat with him about something or other, but before their voices took on shape, he'd fallen asleep.

DAY FIVE

'Ah, I've been meaning to speak with you!'

Alfred and I looked across at the cubicle door. A young, short, bearded man dressed in a white coat came in. He shook my hand and then Alfred's, vigorously, as if to compensate for his small stature.

'Is there any change?' Alfred asked. He sounded desperately hopeful. And indeed, Brynja looked much better than last time: the tube running from her open mouth to the ventilator had been removed and now she just looked like she was in a very deep sleep.

'Not much, I'm afraid,' the doctor said. 'Though her vital signs are as good as we can hope for. She's breathing on her own now, which is good, but she's still in a coma.' He sighed. 'But you never know – she might come out of it tomorrow, or next week, or perhaps . . . well, never.' He seemed to reflect on this for a moment. Then he said, 'Ah, but I do have something interesting I'd like to show you.' He plucked Brynja's patient chart from the end of her bed. 'We ran an fMRI this morning –

standard procedure for brain injuries – and discovered something strange.' He pulled out some colour images of what was, apparently, Brynja's brain. Alfred and I both took a close look. They were really rather striking, like butterflies flecked with indigo and purple, and small patches of bright yellow.

'What this suggests,' the doctor continued, pointing at the patches of yellow, 'is activity in the primary and secondary auditory cortexes. This is a bit unusual in coma patients – ' And he went on to deliver a speech containing terms such as 'morphosyntactic processing', 'superior temporal gyrus', 'arcuate fasciculus', ending with, 'akin to that observed during speech. Although no one was actually talking to her.'

I had understood very little of what he had just said, and looked over to Alfred, but he was staring at the top left corner of the room, apparently miles away.

'And what makes it even odder,' the doctor continued, 'is that certain parts of the medial forebrain bundle – I won't bore you with the details – appear to be active at the same time.'

I looked at him blankly.

'You know, the pleasure hotspot in the brain. But then again, the brain is very – how should I put it? – complex.'

'Is this a good sign?' I asked.

He shrugged. 'We'll just have to wait and see. Like I said, there's no way of knowing with coma patients. Now I'm sorry, but I have to be getting on.' He clipped the board back into place and turned to leave. As he strode towards the door, Alfred jerked back to life. 'Are you telling us that she is processing speech in a . . . in a good way?' he asked.

The doctor turned. 'I suppose that's one way of putting it. Stranger things have happened.' And he left.

On the drive home, neither of us spoke much. It was five p.m. on Boxing Day, and although traffic was light, the icy roads required my full concentration. Now and again, I looked over to Alfred, but he kept his gaze fixed forward during the entire journey. I hated to think what it must be like in there, inside his head, believing that he only had one day more to live.

1958 – 1960

Alfred's thirty-second birthday brought some completely unexpected trouble. It was a Sunday, and Isobel had promised him a day of idleness, during which she'd 'spoil him silly'. He got out of bed at around ten o'clock, putting aside the breakfast tray she'd brought him up, and got dressed at leisure, forgoing a shave. He passed by the window on the upstairs landing and looked out. It was raining silently outside, screening the meadow that stretched out from the back garden to the hills behind a sheer mist. He padded downstairs in the new slippers Isobel had bought him as a gift, made of burgundy leather and looking and feeling more expensive than anything he might have bought himself. He carried the tray into the kitchen, and received a mild scolding from Isobel for his troubles.

'Now you just go and make yourself comfortable on the sofa,' she said, taking the tray from him, 'and stop doing my work.'

She had flour dust in her hair; before her, on the

kitchen table, sat a round birthday cake decorated with white satin icing and, in blue letters, Happy Birthday Dad.

'Where's John?' he asked.

'I told him he could have a second slice of birthday cake if he went to Sunday school. So you can have some peace and quiet.'

Bribery was Isobel's preferred parenting technique, something Alfred found distasteful and counter-productive. But he didn't want to argue about it now, so instead, he leaned down to give her a kiss. Then the doorbell rang.

'That'll be Belle to fetch me for church,' Isobel said, untying her apron. She looked up at the clock that hung on the wall above the back door. It was quarter past ten. 'She's early,' Isobel said and smoothed down her hair with both hands, sending a small cloud of flour into the air. 'But she's probably come to wish you many happy returns.'

She left the kitchen to answer the door. Fancying another cup of tea, Alfred filled the kettle and put it on the stove. Then he heard a familiar voice in the hallway, but it wasn't Belle's. It was Alice Singer-Cohen's.

'Is your husband in?' he heard.

'Um, yes. He's through here, in the kitchen. I'll just go and fetch him. May I take your coat?' Isobel said.

'No thank you,' was the reply.

Alfred stroked the stubble on his chin and for a moment regretted not having shaved. Perhaps she'd come to wish him a happy birthday, he thought, although she'd never done so in the past. He opened the kitchen door and went into the hallway. When he saw Alice Singer-Cohen standing there, he knew immediately that something was wrong. She was impeccably dressed, as always, but she wore no makeup and her face held a look of severity he'd never seen on her before.

'It's Alfred's birthday,' Isobel said, apparently oblivious to the tension he felt was oozing from Alice Singer-Cohen. 'Won't you join us for a slice of cake?'

Alice Singer-Cohen didn't look at Isobel. She kept her eyes on Alfred, and in a barely controlled voice, said, 'I shan't keep you long, Mr Warner. I have come to inform you that you are fired. You have two weeks to vacate the cottage, but I do not want to see you up at March House. Ever again.'

She took a step back and bumped into Isobel, who looked quickly from the woman to Alfred, open-mouthed. 'What? Alfie? Mrs Singer-Cohen?'

'I – Mrs Singer-Cohen, what is . . . ?' he stumbled over his words. But she didn't stop to hear them. She turned and rushed down the path to the car, fumbled with the keys – she was driving herself – and pulled out before Alfred got to the front door.

'Alfie, what's going on?' Isobel said. She was white and trembling. 'Leave the cottage? What did she mean?'

'I don't know,' he answered, 'but I'm going to find out.' He put on his shoes, grabbed his jacket from the hook at the door and ran around the back of the house to fetch his bicycle.

He cycled hard. And the harder he cycled, the angrier he felt; in fact, he couldn't recall ever feeling this angry before, a white heat of rage starting in his gut that travelled up to just behind his eyes. The rain continued to fall, and he had to take care not to slip on the wet road. He thought of the look of distress on Isobel's face, the fear

Alice Singer-Cohen's words had induced in her. How dare the woman threaten to turn him and his family out of their home! He had no idea what he would say to her, but he wouldn't give all of this up without a fight.

When he reached the wrought-iron gate, he stopped to swing it open and rode up to the house, having to push down hard on the pedals against the friction of the gravel. The grey Bentley was parked outside. He came to a skidding halt at the front steps, let the bicycle tumble to the ground and tugged at the bell-pull. Emma opened the door.

'Is anyone expecting you?' she asked, with a look to suggest that he wasn't expected, and certainly not in his soaked-through jacket and muddy shoes.

'Where is she?' Alfred asked, taking a step forward.

'Mr Singer-Cohen's in London. Mrs Singer-Cohen is upstairs. She didn't say you was coming.'

'I need to see her,' he said, pushing past her.

'Be my guest,' Emma said, shrugging. 'But I'd appreciate it if you'd take your shoes off. It's not you who has to clean up the muck.'

Alfred hesitated, and then slipped out of his shoes. In his rush to get out of the house, he'd forgotten to put any socks on.

Emma glanced down at his bare feet. 'Mmm, lovely,' she said sardonically.

Alfred ran up the stairs, taking two steps at a time. He had never been upstairs before, and he came to a stop at the sight of a large spacious landing, as cluttered as the entrance hall downstairs, with five or six white doors leading off. He turned and leaned over the banister. Emma was dusting some ornaments very slowly with a large feather duster, presumably waiting for some trouble to kick off.

'Second door on the left,' she said, without looking up. 'But I'd knock, if I was you.'

'Thanks,' Alfred said, and strode across the landing to the door and knocked. As he waited for some response, he tried to gather his thoughts. There was no reason he could think of – *absolutely* no reason – why she should want to sack him. There were occasional disagreements over the garden; he'd sided – unusually – with Claxton a couple of weeks ago against her plans for an intricate water feature that would require too much maintenance to be worth the effect. But surely that was no reason to sack him! She was a highly intelligent woman, not one of those fickle rich who employed and dismissed their staff on a whim. Or had he misjudged her? He knocked again and waited for a 'Come in.' But instead, the door opened and he was suddenly confronted by a pale-faced Alice Singer-Cohen.

'I told you I didn't want to see you here again,' she said, but there was a trace of resignation in her voice, as though she hadn't expected any different. She wore a kind of housecoat – indigo satin with a cosmos of tiny silver stars embroidered on it – with matching slippers, and looked sad and tired. She rested the side of her head against the door and said, 'Please leave, Mr Warner.'

'I can't,' he said. He spoke softly. The sight of her like this, so tired and dejected, had cooled the heat of his anger. 'I need to know why.'

She closed her eyes for a moment. 'Leave, please.'

But Alfred pushed the door open gently, and after a brief hesitation she stepped aside to let him in. The room was smaller than he'd expected; a canopy bed with ivory-coloured raw silk drapes took up most of the space, and facing the window was a dresser, cluttered with small pots and brushes and perfume flacons, with a tri-fold mirror attached to the back. Here Alice Singer-Cohen went to sit down. Alfred, in his bare feet and damp jacket, remained standing near the door.

'I want to know why,' he said. 'I have worked for you for more than eight years. I've never taken sick leave. I've always done as was asked of me. My wife – ' he paused briefly to calm himself. 'That cottage is our home. We've always paid the rent on time.'

Alice Singer-Cohen straightened up and looked directly at him. 'Two of my husband's relatives, an aunt and a cousin, paid us a visit last week. They enquired about the handsome young German man they'd met in the library.'

Alfred felt a burning sensation rising up in him. She continued in a steady voice. 'I had no idea who they were talking about, so they described the man.'

Alfred opened his mouth to speak, but she cut him off with an angry look. 'I didn't quite understand, but she was adamant that you had spoken with a flawless accent. And I remembered something – do you recall, on the train? I wondered about the peculiar English you spoke?'

Alfred swallowed and nodded. 'I – '

She held up her hand. 'Let me finish. So I had Miss Woolcroft make some enquiries. It was surprisingly easy, actually, to find out. I didn't want to believe it. I have always liked you. And I'm not entirely sure what was worse, finding out that you are a former German prisoner of war, or that you have been lying to me all these years.' This last sentence came out louder than her previous words.

'Mrs Singer-Cohen.' Alfred took a step towards her. 'I didn't . . . I mean, I'm sorry if you think I was trying to deceive you. I was nae trying to be dishonest, it's just . . . it didnae seem to matter.' He stopped, aware at how hollow his words sounded. Of course it mattered.

Alice Singer-Cohen got to her feet. 'How dare you!' she shrieked, and all at once, the voices tumbled into his head, speaking in a chaotic medley that made it impossible for him to understand what they were saying. '"*It didnae seem to matter*"?' she said, mocking his accent. Her face had grown even whiter; she looked as though she were about to faint. 'I lost twelve members of my family!' Her voice was crumbling away at the edges, as though she were finding it hard to fight back tears. But she continued. 'Twelve people, including my three-year-old niece, boxed up and carted away like cattle, to be . . . to be . . . ' She didn't finish the sentence.

A barbed silence hung in the room. Alfred's voices had calmed to just a faint murmuring. Then he heard

Close the door. Then tell her. Tell her you were not one of them.

Almost mechanically, Alfred walked to the door. On the upstairs landing outside, Emma was making a fuss of straightening a lace cloth that was draped over a small side table. He caught her eye and she looked away, blushing. Then he closed the door. When he turned around, Alice Singer-Cohen had sat back down on her chair, no longer straight-backed, but looking very small and fragile.

'I was not one of them,' he said in a low, measured voice. 'I was a German citizen until several years ago, it's true, and I served in the Wehrmacht for a short time. I was eighteen years old. Before that – ' He stopped, assailed by a sudden, intense memory of teaching Salomon how to use a sling-shot, sitting in a shady corner of the yard, both of them with dirty scabby knees and ever-hungry bellies. 'I owe my life to the Jews,' he said quietly.

She looked up but didn't speak. Alfred continued. 'My parents died when I was young, and I was taken in by a Jewish orphanage in Berlin. They saved my life.'

Alice Singer-Cohen began to shake her head, very slowly, as though she were underwater. Then Alfred closed his eyes. He concentrated hard, and then the recollection rose up, like a fish on a hook, struggling to begin with, but then rose to the surface swiftly and inexorably. And in a soft, low voice, he began to sing the *Ma'oz Tzur*.

When he opened his eyes again, she had covered her face with both hands and was crying. She made no sound, but her slim shoulders were shaking beneath her satin robe. He went to her and crouched down, now oddly aware of the soft shag pile that lodged between his bare toes.

'I'm so sorry for causing you pain,' he said. He reached out his arm, touched by a strong urge to embrace and comfort her, but pulled back again.

Tell her, a voice whispered, and he knew that he must, that he owed her this leap of faith.

'I can hear voices,' he said, so softly he feared his words might have been absorbed by the sound of the rain against the window glass. 'I can hear voices,' he repeated more clearly, and her hands slid from her face onto her lap. 'Inside my head. Nobody knows about them. Not even my wife.' He thought, not for the first time, how Isobel – sweet, oblivious Isobel – might react if she knew. Another secret he should have shared a long time ago, he thought shamefully. 'I've heard them since I was a boy, and they're the reason why I was taken in by the Jews. I was going to be sent to the asylum, but the Jews took me in and saved my life. People like me were killed by the Nazis, too.'

When Alice Singer-Cohen spoke again, her voice was thin. 'Could you please fetch me a cigarette?' she said, pointing to a silver box on the bedside table. Alfred, feeling a cramp in his thighs from the crouching position, got up and did as she asked. When he'd given her a light, she inhaled deeply.

'I cannot pretend that this is anything less than incredible,' she said slowly. 'I just wish you had told me sooner.'

'So do I,' Alfred said, and meant it.

'And I really don't want to believe I misjudged you, Mr Warner, but you must understand that I will need some time to consider what you've told me.'

'Yes. I understand.'

She got to her feet and stubbed out the half-smoked cigarette. 'I shall call you later,' she said, and went to open the door.

Emma was nowhere to be seen. Alfred paused at the door and caught Alice Singer-Cohen's eye. He could see that he'd caused her great pain, and he was immeasurably sorry. They held the gaze for a moment, and Alfred knew she understood.

'It's a good thing I didn't tell my husband,' she said, before closing the door. 'He would have wanted to kill you.'

In the room at March House, alone with Alice Singer-Cohen, Alfred had had no sense of how much time had passed. When he arrived back at the cottage, to find a near-hysterical Isobel waiting for him, he was surprised to find out that he had been gone for two hours. There was a dull ache in his head and he felt a numb exhaustion, as though he hadn't slept for days.

'Oh God, Alfie, I thought you'd never be back!' Isobel cried, rushing at him and wrapping her arms around his waist. She hugged him tightly and then pulled back. 'Did you speak to her? What did she say?'

Alfred took off his sodden jacket. 'Where's the boy?' he asked.

'He ate half the cake,' she said. 'I – I couldn't stop him, because I was so worried and he just kept whingeing and whingeing. But then I took him round to Jane next door and told her I was feeling a wee bit under the weather. I didn't want Johnnie to know something was wrong.'

'She found out,' he said. 'She found out that I'd been a prisoner of war.'

Isobel let out a moan. 'So we have to leave? Where will we go?' She looked around, panicked. 'Oh God, Alfie, this is terrible!'

'No, I explained everything,' he said. 'She said she would need to think before coming to a decision.'

For several hours, Alfred and Isobel sat waiting for the telephone to ring. Isobel drank three glasses of gin to calm her nerves, while Alfred paced the small living room, already marking in his mind the furniture that had come with the house, and the pieces they had bought to make it into a home. When the call finally came that evening (Isobel hadn't had the energy to put John to bed, so he sat sleepily on the carpet as they watched – or rather merely looked at – *Armchair Theatre* on the television),

Alfred waited until the telephone had rung four times before he answered.

'Hello?'

'Mr Warner, you may, if you wish, come to work tomorrow morning.'

He waited to see if she would say anything more, half-expecting her to announce she would dock his wages, or that he would be put on a trial period, but she remained silent, so he said, 'Thank you.'

'Goodnight, Mr Warner.'

'Goodnight.'

DAY FIVE

That afternoon, while Alfred took a nap in my bedroom, I finally made a start on marking my pupils' exam papers. A joyless task, at the best of times, but I had to tackle it sooner or later. And I hoped that it might distract me a little. But I had barely got through two essays when I heard the sound of Alfred's voice coming from the bedroom. I couldn't make out the words, but he sounded agitated. I crossed the hall and tapped lightly on the door.

'Alfred?' There was no answer, so I went in. 'Alfred, is everything okay?'

He was standing by the window, his few strands of white hair sleep-ruffled. He was flailing his arms about and seemed quite distressed. 'But what about John?' he was saying. 'She needs to know. John. John.' Then he turned around and stared at me. 'What day is it?' he asked. There was panic in his voice. 'What day?'

I crossed the room to where he was standing and put my hand on his shoulder. 'It's Monday. The twenty-sixth.

What's the matter, Alfred? Come here, sit down.' I guided him to the bed. 'Now, calm down.'

He was breathing heavily through his nose. 'I'm running out of time,' he said. 'There's not much time . . . and they said . . . but what if? She needs to know about John!'

I crouched down in front of him. His hands were trembling so badly, I had to place mine on top of them to get them to stop. 'Everything's okay, Alfred. You probably had a bad dream. Take a few deep breaths. Yes, just like that. It's okay. And remember what the doctor said today? Brynja's doing much better. She's off the ventilator. She may wake up any day. Do you remember?'

Very gradually, he stopped shaking and looked at me. 'Yes. Yes, he did sound hopeful, didn't he?'

'Yes,' I lied. 'Very much so. And we'll go and visit her again tomorrow and perhaps things might have improved even more. Now, why don't you lie down for a bit? Here – ' I pulled back my duvet cover and helped him slide into bed. 'You just have a rest and I'll go and make us some lunch. How about I warm up what's left of that chicken fricassee? You liked that, didn't you?'

He put his head on the pillow and closed his eyes. 'And then I can continue with my story?' he asked.

'Of course. For as long as you like. Now – ' I patted the covers, 'I'll fetch you when it's time to eat, okay?'

1965 – 1967

John Drummond passed away in early October 1965, not entirely unexpectedly, as he had suffered several minor strokes over the two years leading up to his death. Isobel travelled to Scotland on her own for the funeral, leaving Alfred alone with John for the first time. He would have liked to go with her, but after Claxton's retirement two months earlier, he was now head gardener at March House. His new assistant, seventeen-year-old Daffyd Arthur, was enthusiastic and hard-working, but still very much reliant on Alfred's instruction.

'Make sure Johnnie does his homework,' Isobel said in parting, when Alfred dropped her off at the station. She looked frail and tired in her black coat.

'Don't worry about us,' he said. Even before they had received the news of Drummond's death, she hadn't been sleeping well. John had recently been in a spate of trouble at school – tardiness, failure to produce homework, talking back to teachers – with the threat of suspension if his misbehaviour continued. Isobel and

Alfred had doled out a series of punishments, which so far seemed to be having the desired effect.

'And he's nae to go out after dark,' Isobel continued, her voice gravelly with exhaustion and last night's tears. 'If that Mark Donohue calls for him, tell him John's grounded.'

Alfred pulled her forward gently and kissed her. 'Have a safe journey. I'll pick you up here on Sunday.'

She nodded vaguely and boarded the train.

The week with John was uneventful. He came home on time after school every day, went upstairs to do his homework, and dutifully washed the dishes every evening when they'd eaten the warmed-up casseroles Isobel had prepared for them. On their final evening alone together, Alfred offered to relax the no-television rule, but John declined on the grounds that he was tired, and went to bed early. Alfred didn't stay up late either, but – unused to sleeping alone – found it difficult to get to sleep. After what seemed like hours, he finally drifted off, but was woken with whispering in his ears.

Get up, get up.

He turned and groaned. It couldn't be morning already, he thought. The bedroom was coal black – even in October, the dawn was brighter than this. He lay on his back, waiting to hear more. But nothing came, and he wondered if he had been dreaming. He put on his slippers and crossed the hall to go to the bathroom, but stopped when he saw that John's bedroom door was ajar. John always slept with his door closed – he had become almost obsessive about his privacy lately. Alfred pushed the door open a little wider. In the orange glow of the streetlamp, which shone in through the cracks in the curtains, Alfred saw immediately that the bed was empty.

'John,' he whispered, then more loudly, 'John? Are you in here?'

No answer. All at once, a panic unfolded in his chest, a panic tinged with anger. He couldn't believe that John would dare to sneak out of his bedroom at night, but where else could he be? He hurried downstairs, trying to calm himself. Maybe the boy was getting a drink of milk. Maybe he would bump into him in the kitchen. Sleepwalking, even? He did that once or twice when he was little. But downstairs was as hushed as upstairs. Alfred checked the time. Twenty to three. What to do? Get in the car and drive around the village? Call Mark Donohue's house? But then he would undoubtedly wake Mark's parents and risk looking like a fool. A fool of a father who couldn't control his own son. His anger began to overshadow his panic. He paced the living room. He couldn't call Isobel; he didn't want to worry her unnecessarily. Should he just go back to bed and wait until morning? But what if John was lying in a ditch somewhere, needing help?

'What should I do?' he called finally. They were with him in an instant.

You're not looking in the right place.

'What?'

You're not looking properly.

'Well that's bloody obvious,' he snapped. He was in no mood for their riddles. 'So where is he, then?'

Ah, Alfred. It's up to you. You need to try much, much harder.

Kssss, you'd think we'd given him enough clues by now.

306

But before Alfred could respond, he heard something from outside. He hurried to the back of the house and opened the back door, half-expecting to see a fox or some other nocturnal animal roaming the garden, but it was empty. The meadow that bordered on the edge of the property stretched out in grey and green to merge with the range of hills that enclosed the village. Then the sound, again. A dull scrape followed by a moan, or a sob, coming from the garden shed. Alfred quickly headed outside, the soft lawn cushioning his steps, his earlier anger and worry quickly dissolving into relief. The moon had been swallowed by clouds, but he didn't need much light to navigate the flowerbeds and vegetable patches; he could have done so in his sleep. The door to the shed was cracked open an inch or two. Bracing himself, just in case some animal – or worse, an intruder – jumped out at him, he slowly opened the door. John was sitting in the corner of the shed, his back resting against the lawnmower. His hands were covering his face.

'John?' Alfred stepped forward. 'What are ye doing here? I've been worried out of my mind.' But he immediately softened his tone when he realised that John was crying. 'Hey son, what's the matter? Is this about yer grandad?'

He bent down. And then he smelt it, a sharp, fruity tang rising above the musty shed-smell. 'Have you been drinking?' he asked.

But John didn't answer. Instead, he began waving his hand around his face. 'They – ' he began, 'they – '

'Are you drunk, John?'

John continued flapping his arm about, mumbling

things Alfred couldn't make out. The boy was blind drunk, that much was obvious.

'Come on, up you get,' Alfred said. When John didn't move, he stepped forward and tried to pull him up. But John swatted his arms away.

'Get off of me,' he slurred, picking up a bottle next to him. 'Can't you all just fucking leave me alone?!!'

The expletive made Alfred suddenly angry. 'Stand up. You should be ashamed of yourself!' He had to control the volume of his voice. 'What the hell do you think you're doing? Get up. Now!'

He pulled John to his feet, knocking the bottle to the floor. John reeled, but regained his balance and stood in front of Alfred, swaying slightly.

'You're a disgrace, John Warner. It's a good thing your mother isn't here to see this. It'd break her heart.'

John's face went limp for a moment. But then he raised his head and stared at a point above Alfred's left shoulder. A nasty smile formed on his lips. 'I'd just tell the stupid bitch that I was sleepwalking,' he said.

Before he could stop himself, Alfred pulled his arm back and struck John across the face. It wasn't a hard slap, but hard enough to make John lose his balance and fall a few steps backwards, turning as he fell and crashing head first into the lawnmower. It was the first time Alfred had hit his son, and his palm stung. For a dazed moment, John remained slumped in his fallen position, but after a moment he heaved himself up, and Alfred could see a cut above his right eyebrow. Then, with a sudden roar, he charged at Alfred, head down, hitting him straight in the stomach. The two of them tumbled out of the shed onto the dark lawn. It had started raining softly, and the grass was slippery. But though winded, Alfred was sober and thus far more coordinated than his son, managing to pin him onto his back without much effort. He felt a fierce mixture of bewilderment and rage, heard his voice-women moaning and shrieking inside his head. He thought his head might shatter. He held John down for a long time, while the boy struggled and laughed and wept hysterically. Finally, John stopped struggling and lay perfectly still on the grass. His face was wet, and so pale that the red oozing gash above his eyebrow seemed to glow. He met Alfred's gaze.

'Don't tell Mum what I said,' he whispered. 'Please.'

At first, Alfred kept the incident to himself when Isobel returned. She appeared pale and subdued, and he didn't want to add to her troubles. But it wasn't long before they received another letter from school, informing them that John had been suspended for a two-week period for continued delinquent behaviour. That evening, while Isobel was washing up after dinner, Alfred told her how he'd found John drunk in the shed. He omitted John's comment about her and their subsequent fight.

'He's spoiled,' Alfred said. 'It cannae go on like this.'

Isobel wiped her hands on a tea towel. 'He's upset about his grandfather,' she said. She didn't turn to face him.

'Oh come on, Isobel. This started well before your father died. There's no good pretending otherwise.'

She didn't respond. Alfred got up and walked over to her. He put his hand on her shoulder. 'I don't want to upset you. I know this isn't a good time, but we need to do something about John before it's too late.'

Isobel let out a little snort. '*Do* something about him? Like he's a tomcat that needs neutering?'

She turned and went into the living room. Alfred followed her.

'You know what I mean,' he said, more calmly than he felt. Now he was finally addressing the problem, he intended to see it through.

'I know nothing of the sort,' she said. She switched on the television set and sat down. Alfred opened his mouth to speak, but she gave him a look that said, *keep your voice down.*

Her look irritated him. He turned the volume down on the television and stood in front of her, blocking her view. 'You've let him get away with bad behaviour for years. You've spoiled him. He always gets what he wants, and you're – '

'How can you say that? I've nae spoiled him! I've *loved* him, like a mother should! How can ye call your own son spoiled?'

'You're always too ready to jump to his defence when he's caused some sort of trouble.'

'It's my job to defend him,' she said. 'That's what mothers do.'

'Isobel, this isn't helping.'

'Oh, now just listen to you! Like you're such a perfect father.'

Alfred tried to ignore the bitterness in her voice. She wasn't thinking clearly, he told himself. She was tired. They should sleep on it and then have a rational, unemotional conversation. Once Isobel had rested, Alfred thought, she would see it as he did. But evidently, Isobel wasn't prepared to rest yet.

'You don't love him like I do,' she said sourly. The volume of her voice was inching up slightly. 'In fact, you *hate* him. I can see it in your eyes, in the way you look at him when you think no one's noticing.'

He felt the voices approaching, like a rush of air in his ears. But he blocked them out. This was his fight alone.

'That's not love you're talking about,' he replied. He was finding it hard to keep his voice steady. 'You're smothering him, Isobel, because you cannae bear it that you lost our wee girl.' He stopped. The words had slipped out of his mouth. But it was the truth, and after so many years of pretending it had never happened, that Brynja had never lived – even if it was only for a few, precious minutes – it felt strangely liberating, as though he had scrubbed himself painfully clean of years' worth of dirt.

Isobel, her face slack from tiredness, looked as though she'd been slapped. She shook her head, blinking slowly. She didn't speak for a long time. Finally, she said, 'You don't know what it was like,' so softly he barely heard her. 'You weren't there.'

Alfred stared at her uncomprehendingly. 'But of course I was there.' His voice was thick. 'I was with you when they told us she'd died. How could you have forgotten that?'

For a long time, Alfred and Isobel were too bruised to discuss the matter again. Several weeks after Isobel's return, they were informed that Drummond had left her an unexpected inheritance of £ 5,000. Without the need for much discussion, they quickly decided to use the money to buy a house, and so, three months after Drummond's passing, they moved into a new semi-detached house only one street away from their previous house. At first, it seemed as though the move – and their new, proud status as homeowners – had given them the chance for a fresh start, and the thought of trying for another baby – surely they were still just young enough? – came more frequently to Alfred. He imagined a little girl, with blonde curly hair and Isobel's cherubic face, a little girl who would laugh girlishly when he swung her onto his shoulders, whom he would teach how to make perfume out of rose petals or lavender buds, a little girl who may just turn out to be the special one.

Indeed, Alfred's longing for another child was compounded by the further deterioration in his relationship with John. Although John's problems at school seemed to subside, his behaviour at home became more erratic. His appetite vanished overnight. Isobel was, of course, the first to notice, but all of her attempts to get him to eat more, often slaving for hours in the kitchen to dish up one of John's favourite meals, were to no avail.

'Your mother's spent hours on that,' Alfred once said quietly to John, as the boy poked listlessly about in the steak and kidney pie on his plate.

Isobel shook her head. 'I don't mind that. But Johnnie, please do eat something. You're turning into skin and bones.'

John pushed his chair away from the table. 'Why can't everyone just leave me alone?' he cried and left the kitchen. They heard him climbing the stairs, and then the scrape and clunk of the key as he locked himself in his bedroom.

And that was another thing. He began to develop a

furtive, shifty manner, locking himself in as soon as he'd returned from school, and on the rare occasions he left his bedroom, he appeared agitated, scanning his surroundings with hasty, twitching eyes, occasionally flinching without any apparent cause. Alfred didn't like it. His son was acting as though he were up to no good. Yet it was difficult to put his finger on any specific misbehaviour, and the last thing he wanted was to initiate another series of rows with Isobel. But one evening, several months after they'd moved into their new house, and despite Alfred's attempts to keep the peace, another argument erupted.

Isobel had managed to coax John out of his bedroom for supper. He took a seat at the kitchen table opposite Alfred, casting a nervous glance around him. His once plump face was now gaunt and pale, making the blotches of acne on his chin and forehead appear all the more livid. A large bowl of rabbit stew sat on the table, its dark, rich aroma making Alfred's stomach growl in anticipation.

'Smells delicious,' he said to Isobel. She smiled absentmindedly; she hadn't taken her eyes off John since he'd sat down.

'C'mon Johnnie,' she said now, taking the ladle and heaping a generous portion onto the boy's plate. 'Ye'll like this.'

'Not so much,' John said, but she ignored him and dipped the ladle into the bowl for another spoonful. Then, as if stung, John shot out his arm and blocked her hand.

'I said – ' he began fiercely, but Isobel had let the ladle drop back into the bowl and grabbed his wrist. She let out a small gasp.

'What's this?' She pulled John's arm across the table towards Alfred. Peeping out from the end of the cuff were two or three ugly red welts on his skin.

John pulled his arm back and held it across his chest. 'It's nothing,' he said dully.

But Isobel wasn't satisfied. 'Show me, John. Now.'

Very hesitantly, John unfolded his arm. Isobel unbuttoned the cuff and he winced. Alfred leaned forward. Three long parallel gashes were visible beneath John's rolled-up sleeve.

'Christ, son,' he said. 'You're hurt. What happened?'

John swallowed and shook his head. 'Nothing. I mean, I got scratched. By a cat.' He was tripping over his words.

'A cat? Oh my goodness. When did this happen? It looks infected,' Isobel said. 'Oh you poor, poor lad.'

'Yeah,' John continued, suddenly eloquent. 'It was a cat. On my way home from school. It was playing just outside the pub, and I went to stroke it and it just scratched me.'

Isobel let go of his arm and instead pulled him closer so his head was pressed against her waist. 'You poor thing. I think we should mebbe get a doctor to have a look. What do you think, Alfie?'

But Alfred was certain the boy was lying. It was something about his tone, the strange smirk he had on his face right at that moment. He said, 'You must mean Harry's new cat. The ginger one.'

John nodded. 'Yeah, that's the one.'

'Got a little bell around its collar?'

John nodded again. Alfred took a deep breath. 'Why are you lying to us, John?'

Isobel snapped her head around in surprise. 'What?'

'Harry has a new cat, but it's black and white. There's nae a ginger cat in the whole village. So,' he continued to look at John, 'why are you lying?'

'I'm never lying!' John shouted. He looked up at Isobel. 'Mum?'

Isobel sat down slowly. The look she gave Alfred was cold and hard, but when she spoke, her voice was unsteady. 'Why are you doing this, Alfie?'

'What do you mean?' he asked, astonished and angry that she was turning on him like this. 'Doing what?'

'Twisting everything he says. Everything he does. Making everything . . . wicked and toxic. Why on earth would he make something like this up, hmm? What possible reason could he have?'

Alfred shook his head. 'I . . . I don't know. He's probably been in a fight or something, and doesn't want to get into trouble.'

'Aye, think the worst. That's all you ever do.' She turned to John, who was now sitting silently, his eyes darting around in that preoccupied, agitated way Alfred had come to loathe. 'Johnnie. Let's get ye upstairs and I'll dress that cut.'

Alfred was left on his own in the kitchen. He took several deep breaths, but that did nothing to alleviate his exasperation. Finally, he grabbed his jacket from the hook and headed outside. He began walking westwards, with no direction in mind. It was raining hard, but he barely noticed. The longer he walked, the greater his frustration became, until he felt it was suffocating him. He stopped in the middle of a meadow and roared: 'What's happening? What am I doing wrong? He's lying! I know it!'

He felt the voice-women's presence, thought he felt one of them about to speak, but in the end, they remained silent. He had been walking – randomly, zigzagging the village and fields and meadows surrounding it – for what seemed like hours. Then, a sudden weariness surged through him, and he knew he had to return home.

He was about a mile outside the village when he heard a car coming towards him, so he stepped off the road, pressing his body against the hedgerow. The car passed him by, its headlights sweeping the hedges and turning them from black to green momentarily. Then he heard it stop several yards behind him. He turned to see the back door open and a woman poking her head out.

'Mr Warner?' It was Alice Singer-Cohen. Alfred walked up to the car and leant down.

'Hello,' he said.

'I thought I recognised you,' she said. 'You're out and about quite late.'

'I'm taking a walk.'

'In the rain?'

He shrugged.

'Well then, can we give you a lift home?'

'Oh. Thanks for the offer, but I'm heading in the other direction.'

She shuffled to the other side of the car. Her silk dress slid invitingly across the seat as she moved. 'That's not a problem. Come on,' she patted the seat next to her, 'get in.'

Alfred hesitated for a moment, but then climbed in beside her. The car was full of the smell of her spicy perfume. 'Thank you,' he said. 'I don't mean to – '

'Nonsense,' she said, cutting him off. 'It's no bother,

316

really.' She leaned forward to give instructions to the driver, but then turned back to Alfred. She looked at him quizzically. 'In fact, if you're not too tired, may I invite you back to the house? I've just escaped from a dinner party at Tean Hall – the company was tedious and the food plain awful. So I told them I felt a migraine coming on and left.' She gave him a mischievous smile. 'And now I'm positively starving, but I do so hate eating on my own. Please say you'll join me.'

Alfred took a moment to consider, but then his stomach growled, as though it had been invited to join the conversation. The rabbit stew would be cold by the time he got home, and a part of him – a childish, malevolent part of him – wished that Isobel could see him now, invited to have supper with another woman. He nodded. 'Yes, that would be nice.'

When they got to March House, Alice Singer-Cohen led him straight to the kitchen.

'I have no idea what we'll find,' she said, opening the fridge. 'Ah, lovely! Cook's left some meat pie. Shall I heat it up, or are you all right eating it cold? Delicious, both ways, I assure you. And do sit down.'

Alfred took a seat at the large rectangular table. 'Cold is fine, Mrs Singer-Cohen,' he said.

She took the pie out of the fridge and placed it on the table. 'Oh, please.' She pulled a face. 'Let's stuff the formalities, Alfred. It's about time you started calling me Alice.' She smiled at him, and then frowned. 'Now, where's the cutlery?'

When they had finished eating, Alice sat back in her chair and lit a cigarette. 'Samuel wanted to hire a Jewish cook when we first moved here. But the first three that I interviewed had such peculiar ideas about food that I decided we'd hire on merit alone. Even if it does make me a bad Jew.' She gave an odd laugh and stubbed out her cigarette.

Alfred was just about to thank her for the meal and take his leave when she said, 'Let's get some fresh air.'

She crossed the kitchen and threw open the double doors that led to the garden. Alfred followed her. The rain had receded, and a fine drizzle now veiled the grounds, so that they could barely see past the vegetable and herb garden. Alice lit another cigarette.

'I do so love the garden,' she said.

'Yes. So do I.'

Alice drew on her cigarette and suddenly grimaced. Her hand flew to her forehead. 'Damn,' she said.

'Everything all right?'

'I think I've a headache coming on.' She gave a dry laugh. 'I suppose it's my punishment for pretending to be sick.'

'I'd recommend a chamomile tea,' he said. 'Except it's not in bloom yet. But hang on – ' he stepped outside and circled the herb garden, stooping to pick a fresh green stem of parsley. 'Here, try this,' he said, handing it to her. 'Try chewing on it. It's supposed to bring instant relief.'

Alice bit into the parsley. She chewed on it, and then pulled a face. 'Bitter.'

Alfred laughed. 'Did your mother never tell you that medicine isn't supposed to taste nice? If it tastes bad, that means it's good for you.'

Alice tossed what was left of the parsley back into the garden. 'You would have been burned as a witch, you know,' she teased. She looked out into the darkness. 'Hildegard of Bingen, ever heard of her?'

'Of course.'

'Hmm. Fascinating woman.' She turned her head to look at him. 'She heard voices too, didn't she?'

'She did indeed.'

'May I ask – can you hear them now?'

'No,' he said. 'But they're never far away.' In fact, he could feel them right now, just beyond the edge of his hearing. Even when he couldn't register them aurally, he most often had some subconscious awareness of their presence.

They were silent for a while. Alice leaned against the doorframe. 'You know, when I first moved here, I hated the place.' She lifted a shoulder in a shrug. Her shawl slid off, revealing her very pale skin. 'To be honest, there's a lot I still hate.' She paused to smoke her cigarette. Alfred stared out into the blackness of the garden, wondering if Isobel had noticed he wasn't in bed beside her.

Then Alice said, 'At dinner, tonight, Samuel was talking about moving to Israel, for the business opportunities. Israel, I ask you!' She let out a short laugh.

'He wants to leave?'

She sighed and waved her hand across her face. 'I don't know. Perhaps he thinks the climate is conducive to fertility. He has strange ideas sometimes. But you never know.' She pinched out her cigarette on the doorframe. 'I would turn into a beetroot in that climate.'

'I – ' Alfred began, but stopped. It had never occurred to him that the Singer-Cohens might one day leave.

She shivered slightly. He lifted her shawl, which had slipped almost to her waist, and draped it over her shoulders, feeling the coarseness of his fingers against her soft skin. She gave him a shy smile. 'Thank you,' she said.

319

'Israel, that's very far away,' he said, speaking his thoughts out loud.

'It is. But perhaps . . . ' she trailed off and stepped back into the kitchen. 'Well, let's be honest. Nobody else really wants us.'

Alfred closed the doors. He went and stood behind Alice, wanting to say, '*I* want you', but was stopped by a rustling in his ears – *sssss, iiisssss, Isssobelll.*

Alice turned and looked up at him. He held her gaze, and saw her slowly blushing pink. She raised her hand, as though to place it on his cheek, but dropped her arm again and looked away.

She said, 'Listen, Alfred. I really should be in bed when Samuel gets home, or he'll know I was fibbing. Thank you so much for keeping me company.'

Alfred nodded, said goodnight and left. The journey back home seemed longer than ever before. This route, so familiar – he must have travelled it a thousand times, and yet with every step he took, moving through the darkness like some deep-sea diver at the bottom of the ocean, he became more and more lost.

In the bedroom, Isobel lay huddled, foetus-like, beneath the covers. He slipped his clothes off and lay down beside her.

NINETEEN NINETY-FOUR

Four weeks. That's all it takes to turn you into a crazy person.

Week one: Your mom has gone out and said she won't be back till late, Be a good girl Bryn. And don't wait up! She forgot to fix dinner, so you make a peanut butter and jelly sandwich and eat it in front of the TV. You flick through the channels and settle on MTV. The sound goes fuzzy for a moment, like there's some static interference, then –
Brynja! Brynja!
Whispering, coming from the kitchen. You turn MTV to mute. You call out, Mom?, even though it's not her voice. You wait, hold your breath. There's a tight feeling in your gut. The light from the silent TV twitches and sputters.
Brynja, can you hear me?
She's not listening.
Who's there? you call. Your voice is shaky. You slide

off the sofa, slowly, and tiptoe into the kitchen. It's empty.
A sudden rush of air on your left.

Mom? you call again. Who is it? Who's there?

Now the sound is coming from the den. A humming,
hissing, whining. You hear your name being called. Over
and over. Different voices.

You run back into the den in a flutter of panic, SHUT
UP! LEAVE ME ALONE!, and turn up the volume on
the TV, until the Beastie Boys are flooding the space of
the room and you curl up in a ball and cry, dark, damp
sounds coming out of your throat, until the *thump thump
thump* on the wall is telling you to turn it the hell down.

Week two: Geometry class. Construct a line perpendicular to the given line using a compass and straight edge.

You read it three times.

Baa, baa, black sheep have you any wool?

It's a little girl's voice. You look up. The other students
sit quietly, heads down.

Yes sir, yes sir

Her voice is honey-sweet. It makes you sick. You pick
up the compass. You start sweating. Perpendicular. Put
the spike on the paper and adjust the hinge.

three bags full

You draw a circle. Good. Now you have to draw
another one, right? Or do you use the straight edge? You
can't concen–

Mary, Mary, quite contrary

You hiss, Shut up!

Brynja! Mrs Robson stares at you from the front of the
class. Quiet please.

How does your garden grow?

You didn't tell your mom about the voices last week. She'll know you're crazy. Perpendicular. Where two lines meet at a right angle. You feel the muscles in your face twitching, getting ready to cry. Your hands drop onto your lap. One is still holding the compass.

With silver bells and cockle shells

You lift the compass and place the spike on your jeans. Perpendicularly. You push down. There's a small *pop* as the denim gives way to the pressure. Then a sharp pain.

And pretty maids all ...

The singing is fading. You push harder. Your eyes start watering. And the singing is gone. You rub your leg and go back to your geometry task. Your heart is pumping in your mouth.

Week three: You say, Don't go out Mom. Please.

Why? She checks her hair in the mirror. You feeling sick?

No, I'm – you bite the skin around your nails.

Don't do that, *liebling*. Your mom pulls your hand away from your mouth. Look, I'll only be an hour. Maybe two. I gotta go now. I'm late.

She hugs you tight. Smells of smoke and musk and coconut dread wax.

Mom?

She pulls back, holds you at arm's length and smiles. Hey, I've been thinking. Maybe we can go on vacation together this summer. SeaWorld, what do you think? There's a flyer came today, with a discount coupon. Hmm, *liebling*? Now – she opens the front door – I really gotta go. Be good. And don't wait up.

You wait up. They come in the dark.

Brynja

Shut up! you whisper. If you ignore them, they'll go away.

If you send us away, the others will come
You're the one

I hate you! you scream. Go away! I hate you!

Week four: *You're a rude, rude girl. A pitiful excuse for a human being.*

A new voice. You've got Bruce Springsteen on your Walkman but it doesn't help. You squirm on the bed, take your hand out of the bag of Doritos, wipe your fingers on the bedspread.

You eat too much, you know that? You're a fat, revolting pig. You stink.

The voice is inside your head. Deep inside you. You turn up the music but it hurts your ears.

Take those headphones off! Now!!! Don't you dare ignore me.

You remove the headphones. Then you remember something and sit up. You get off the bed and go to your desk. They're here somewhere, you open a drawer and – yes – take out a pair of scissors. Go back to the bed.

What are you up to, Brynja?

You sit, look down at the inside of your left arm. The pale, soft skin. You're frightened, but kind of fizzing with energy. Then you drag the scissors across the inside of your arm. You gasp. The pain is shocking. Amazing. You close your eyes –

Aaargh! Stop it! Please!

Her voice is clear and desperate. You sit up straighter,

can almost taste the blood in your mouth. You make another parallel cut, deeper, increase the pressure.

Aaargh! No Brynja. Stop! Aaargh! Don't –

She shuts up, suddenly. You lay down the scissors beside you on the bed. Your heart is pumping fast. The pain makes you feel sick. The edges around the wound are throbbing, but it's quiet now. Peaceful. You sit and wait, feel the blood leaking from the cut, don't move. For a long time. You take deep breaths. Your heart has stopped racing, and –

HA HAHAHA! Oh Brynja, that's funny! That's so – hahaha, wheeeeee! You thought, you actually though you were – hahaha – hurting me!

You whisper, No.

Oh, that was a good one. Hey, listen. I've just thought of a good little game to play. Just you and me. Okay?

You start shaking.

OKAY?

You nod. Okay.

Good girl. Now, in this game, I give you a riddle. You know what a riddle is? And if you solve it, you win. But if you don't, hmm, let me think – I know! If you don't solve the riddle, you have to cut your other arm, nice and deep. Okay? We want things to be symmetric, don't we? Right, here it comes . . .

1968 – 1969

On a cold, clammy October morning in 1968, Alfred collapsed at work. Perhaps it was due to working outdoors in the increasingly chilly temperatures or the fact that he rarely slept more than five hours a night or his concerns over his son – or most likely, a combination of all of these. Whatever the reason, Alfred was standing atop a six-foot ladder trimming the hedge with a large pair of shears, when he was overwhelmed by a sudden, raw exhaustion. It began at his feet, and then surged rapidly up through his body, draining him of all energy. He was finding it hard to breathe, and every thin, shallow breath he managed to take caused him acute pain, like so many knives stabbing his lungs. With great effort, he held his arm out to the side and let the shears drop to the ground. Then he climbed down the ladder, slowly, carefully. He placed one foot on the damp lawn, heard a long, drawn-out moan – *oooooooooooohhh* – and passed out.

He woke briefly to white, painful light and the sharp stench of disinfectant. He was in hospital. His eyelids were almost too heavy to lift, but he could make out Isobel leaning over him. He opened his mouth.

'Hush, Alfie. Don't speak. You're in hospital. They think you've got pneumonia.'

He began shivering violently, yet the blood rushing through his body felt like lava. He closed his eyes and fell asleep again. When he next surfaced, he was feeling calmer, although he still couldn't take a deep breath. He could no longer smell any disinfectant, and even with his eyes closed he could tell that the light was much dimmer now, which seemed odd, but perhaps they'd moved him off the ward to a single room. He opened his eyes slowly. He was lying in some kind of cubicle, around six by eight feet, windowless, and a white curtain instead of a door. He was soaked through with sweat. A woman, standing with her back to him, turned around. Alfred gasped, painfully.

'Johanna!'

Johanna sat down gently on the bed next to him. She wore a dark blue blazer with a flower broach in its lapel. Her hair was shot through with grey, but her hands were smooth and white, like a young girl's. He reached out and touched her arm.

'You're here,' he said, stroking the fabric of her jacket. 'I thought you were dead. I thought – ' He found himself blubbing.

'Shh, *mein Täubchen,*' she said, picking up a damp cloth and dabbing his forehead with it. Her touch made him shiver. 'Don't strain yourself.'

'Why didn't you answer my letters?' he asked. His tongue felt thick inside his mouth. He was fiercely thirsty.

'But I did. I answered every one. Look.' She pulled

a thick pile of letters from her bag, tied together with a white ribbon.

He gave her a puzzled look. A throbbing pain flashed through his head. 'But –' Then he passed out again.

He woke again minutes later with a surge of panic, afraid he might have just imagined her. But there she was, sitting in a chair beside his bed. She was reading a book, but he couldn't see the cover. Somewhere close by, a clock was ticking loudly.

'Johanna,' he said. 'You found me again. You're here.'

'Yes, I'm here.'

'You look lovely. Older.'

She smiled. 'Well, you haven't exactly fallen into the fountain of youth, either.'

He tried to laugh, but fell into a painful, wheezing cough. Then he grabbed her wrist. 'Johanna,' he said urgently, his chest on fire, 'I must tell you something.'

'What is it?'

'I should have told you years ago. I – ' He looked from left to right, but they were alone. He whispered, 'I can hear voices.'

A warm smile crossed her face. She reached out and stroked his cheek. 'Yes, *mein Schatz*. We all hear them. All of us.'

Alfred frowned. 'All of us?'

'Yes.' She pointed to a corner of the cubicle. Three small blond children, whom he hadn't noticed before, were playing quietly with some dolls. 'Don't we, children?'

They looked up, a boy and two girls, and nodded. 'Yes, Mama,' one of them said, and they went back to playing.

Alfred sank back onto his pillow, a smile on his face. 'How wonderful,' he said. 'What are their names?'

'But you know their names,' Johanna said, sounding a little annoyed. 'Emil, Marie and Brynja.'

Alfred coughed again painfully.

'I managed to get out,' Johanna whispered urgently. 'Before they put up the wall.'

'The wall?'

'Yes. Didn't you hear? They built a wall. Right across the city.' She sliced the air with her hand.

He tried to sit up, but couldn't. 'I don't understand,' he said weakly.

'You're just very tired,' she said. 'And ill. You must rest.'

With all his strength, he raised himself into a sitting position. Waves of ice and heat washed through him. He was trembling. 'Who are these children?' he demanded.

Johanna got to her feet and leaned over him, pushing his arms back onto the bed without much effort and pinning them down. She smelled of apples. 'You need to rest, Alfred. Now be sensible.'

He tried briefly to free himself from her grip, but it was in vain. His muscles were too weak. 'I don't understand,' he managed to say, and was suddenly engulfed in exhaustion and was gone again.

He was woken by the sound of footsteps and the rustle of stiff fabric. He could still feel Johanna holding his arms down, but when he opened his eyes, he saw that there was now a white-clad doctor holding his left arm, and a nurse holding his right. They were speaking in urgent whispers, but he couldn't make out what they were saying.

'Johanna?' he asked, a fresh panic overcoming him. There was a high ringing sound in his left ear. 'Where's Johanna?'

'I'm here,' she called, and it took him a moment to discover where her voice was coming from – she was standing near the white curtain, and was being held from the back by a man who looked, to Alfred, vaguely familiar.

He struggled to free himself, 'Johanna!' he called, but the arms holding him down were too strong. He writhed and fought, managing to free his right arm, while Johanna was shouting, 'Let me go! Kssss, Alfred, Alfred! Help me!' He lashed out at the doctor on his left, but the doctor caught his free arm and held it down firmly across his chest, making it almost impossible to breathe. He strained to look across the room, but Johanna was gone, and then, feeling the sharp prick of a needle in his shoulder, he slid into unconsciousness.

Three days later, his fever broke, and he was transferred to the main ward. Isobel came to visit him every day, looking tired and concerned, telling him over and over how worried she had been. Once, she brought John, but he just sat on a chair, looking nervously around the ward.

When he had first woken to find that his body temperature had dropped back to normal, his head clear, his breathing painless, Alfred assumed that Johanna had been nothing but a figment of his imagination, a cruel hallucination created by the fever. But as the days went by, and his mind and lungs became clear again, he began to suspect that his voices had brought her. They had brought her – for reasons he could not understand – and then snatched her away again. They couldn't just leave well enough alone. He felt betrayed. And now, they wouldn't respond to his calls. He wanted Johanna back, just for an hour. He longed to talk to her, if only to say goodbye. For the first time in his life, he began to hate his voices. His grief consumed him. For days, he passively absorbed the hospital routine of waking, eating, doctor's rounds, medication, Isobel's visits, during which he hardly seemed to hear what she said.

Finally, ten days later, he was discharged. He would no longer need hospital care, but was told that a full recovery would take several weeks, perhaps even months. The doctor told him he had also had a severe infection in his left ear, but that any discomfort or mild hearing loss should pass with time. Isobel came to accompany him home. He packed his few belongings into the small bag she had brought, together with a copy of his discharge summary. On their way out, the ward nurse stopped him. 'Dr Barnes wants a word before you leave,' she said.

'Oh?'

'Yes. He . . . he's a specialist. On the first floor, room fourteen. He's expecting you.'

Dr Barnes was a tall man with a mat of black hair and long, slim fingers with disproportionately large knuckles, which he repeatedly flexed and cracked. Beneath his white coat, he wore an open-collared shirt and blue jeans.

'How are you feeling?' Barnes asked Alfred, once he and Isobel had taken a seat opposite him in his office. Isobel was worrying a button on her jacket, and when she looked up, Alfred gave her a reassuring smile.

'Much better, thank you,' he replied.

'I gather you suffered smoke poisoning some years ago. What with the pneumonia, it might take a while before your lungs have fully recovered.'

'Yes,' Alfred said, a little impatiently. He had heard

all this from the doctor who had signed his release note. 'Yes, I understand. But – ' he reached over to Isobel and gave her hand a gentle squeeze, 'I'm already feeling much better.'

'Good, good,' Barnes said, leaning back. His chair made a small squeaking sound. 'Now, Mr Warner – or may I call you Alfred?'

'Please.'

'Great. Alfred. Now, you were pretty sick when you were brought here. Do you remember that? Anything about the first couple of days here?'

Alfred turned to look at Isobel, but she kept her head bowed and wouldn't meet his gaze. And it slowly dawned on him what kind of specialist Barnes was.

Barnes' chair squeaked again as he leaned forward. 'We were all pretty worried about you. Your temperature was at 105 degrees for several days.'

Alfred cleared his throat. 'Yes, I know. Dr Watkins explained this all to me just half an hour ago. He has prescribed four weeks' convalescence, and after that, I'm certain I'll be fine again. So, what exactly can we do for you, Dr Barnes? I'd like to get home.'

Barnes nodded. 'Right, right. I'm sure you do. Very well, Alfred, I'll get right to the point. Have you ever experienced, hmm, episodes of severe confusion, or disorientation?' He pulled at his long fingers, producing a soft, nauseating popping sound. He continued. 'Or perhaps even hallucinations, hearing or seeing things out of the ordinary? Hmm?'

Alfred's hands started trembling in his lap, and he faked a cough to cover it up. Finally, he said, 'I'm not sure what you mean.' His voice rang dull inside his head.

'You see, many patients experience this sort of thing when the body temperature exceeds a certain level. But in your case, it was so extreme, so beyond anything I or my colleagues have ever witnessed, that I'm concerned it may have been a – ' he paused. 'I'll be frank with you, Alfred. It appeared very much like a psychotic episode. And given its severity, I would have to guess that this wasn't the first time it's happened.'

'I see,' Alfred said slowly, trying to ignore the scratching inside his chest brought on by his coughing fit. Beside him, he could hear Isobel picking at her nails.

Barnes continued. 'Alfred, if I am right, then you need treatment. In my experience, these things only get worse. They don't just go away by ignoring them. And there have been some real breakthroughs recently, in terms of medicating this sort of problem.'

Alfred took a deep breath. So this was it. All he had to do was confirm Barnes' suspicions, and he would be free. Free. It was almost a revelation. He had never asked for the voice-women – they had come to him when he was six years old, so very young, too young to defend himself. He had never been given any choice. At this very moment, he could hear one of them crying softly, and it angered him. They had betrayed him. He felt so very, very tired. Barnes was looking at him expectantly, invitingly, his look a bridge Alfred could cross. With the shortest of words, the smallest of gestures . . . Suddenly, his lungs tightened so that he could hardly breathe.

And then Isobel spoke up. 'I don't think there's anything wrong with my husband, Dr Barnes,' she said, her voice small but steady, breaking the thick silence. 'I understand why you might be concerned, but I can assure you that this sort of thing has never happened before. Not since we've been married, anyway. I – I don't want him to be taking any medication unnecessarily.' She held out her hand for Alfred, and he took it.

Barnes let out a loud sigh. 'Very well, Alfred. I don't want to talk you into anything. But if you ever . . . ' He took a small prescription pad from a desk drawer and quickly wrote something down. 'This is the name of a colleague of mine. Very fine chap.' He passed the note to Alfred, and then rose from his chair and walked them to the door. 'Thank you for coming. I hope you recover quickly.'

He and Alfred shook hands. When the door had closed behind him, Alfred tore the note into little pieces and stuffed them into his pocket.

When they arrived home, John was watching television. At first, Alfred feared he had been suspended from school again, but then remembered it was a Saturday. John jumped up when they came in.

'Hi Dad,' he said. 'How are you feeling?' He went to take Alfred's bag, and their hands touched briefly. John's face had the soft, spongy look of a much younger boy; for a moment, he wasn't the hard-edged sixteen-year-old Alfred knew.

'I'm much better,' Alfred said. 'Thank you.'

John stood awkwardly in the middle of the room with the bag in one hand, and then shrugged his shoulders, as though shrugging off his boyishness and reapplying his armour of adolescent indifference.

'I'll be upstairs,' he said, leaving the living room with the bag. 'I did myself beans on toast for tea.'

Isobel closed the door behind him. 'He's been very worried about you,' she said.

That night Alfred slept fitfully. His dreams were vivid and wild, but always vanished the moment he broke the surface of sleep. In the early hours of the morning – a pale dawn was stealing into the room – he woke once more, startled. His heart was racing.

Isobel's voice came into the semi-darkness. 'Alfie? Is everything all right?'

'Yes,' he said. 'Sorry, did I wake you?'

'No.'

There was a long silence. Alfred's heartbeat gradually returned to normal. He closed his eyes, thinking Isobel must have fallen asleep again.

'Alfie?' Her voice was soft, but not sleepy.

'Yes?'

'That doctor, the psychiatrist – '

'Yes?'

He heard her turn onto her side. 'Alfie, I know you talk to yourself.' She spoke very quietly.

He kept his eyes shut. 'It was the fever,' he said. 'I had some very . . . disturbing dreams.'

'No, Alfie. I don't mean when you were in hospital. I mean – ' He heard her take a deep breath. 'You have conversations. I've heard you. Many times. Usually when you're in the garden, when you think you're alone. The first time, back home – ' She was talking about Mauchline. 'After the fire, my dad was out and I'd gone for a nap upstairs, but I couldn't sleep. I heard you talking to someone, and I went out onto the landing and saw you, sitting on the couch, talking to yourself.'

He didn't speak.

'But it wasn't just yourself you were talking to. You were having a real conversation. I sat there and listened for a while.'

'You never said anything.'

'What was I to say?' She sounded tired – not sleep-tired, but weary. 'I thought it was just something . . . some reaction to what had happened. You know, the shock of the fire, or something. But then I caught you doing it again. And I was going to ask you about it, but – '

'But what?' He was slightly breathless; he felt a jagged tickling sensation at the bottom of his lungs.

She whispered, 'Why did you never tell me?'

'Was this why Dr Barnes wanted to see me?' he asked. His heart was beating fast again. 'You told him?'

'Of course not! I cannae believe you would think that.' She sat up. Her silhouette was blurred in the dim light, and he couldn't make out the expression on her face. 'Twenty years, Alfred. For twenty years I've said nothing, wondering if I should be worried, concerned that I may have married a man who has some . . . some mental imbalance. And I've waited, waited for you to speak to me – at times I thought it was *me* who was going mad. And I've been so bloody lonely.' She covered her face with her hands and started crying.

Alfred sat up and put his arm around her shoulders, drawing her in to him. 'I'm so sorry.'

'When you were sick, and you started ranting, it was . . . it was *terrifying*. Then they told me they'd like you to see a psychiatrist, and I thought: This is it! They've found out and they're going to take you away.'

There was panic in her voice. 'And what would I do then? Without you?'

It took Alfred six weeks to recover fully after his release from hospital. During that time, Isobel fussed around him constantly, serving him breakfast in bed, ensuring the fireplace was always lit, insisting he wrap himself in blankets at all times, making him endless cups of tea. On occasion, he would catch her staring at him, and then she would give him a conspiratorial smile and a nod, as though to say, 'It's all right. Your secret's safe. You're free to talk to them now.'

But she never said as much out loud, and besides, Alfred wouldn't have done so. Not only because communicating with his voice-women had hitherto been intensely, almost painfully private, and that asking him to talk openly with them in Isobel's presence felt tantamount to being told it was all right to defecate in front of her. But also, more importantly, he didn't *want* to talk to them. He hadn't yet forgiven them for bringing Johanna and then snatching her away so violently. So when they came – calling his name

Alfred! Alfred!

commenting on his improving state of health when he managed a two-mile walk without feeling exhausted

Well done! You're doing so much better, aren't you?

offering helpful advice in the kitchen

Look out, Alfred! The milk's about to boil over

reminding him of appointments

Don't forget the doctor's at two o'clock

– he ignored them. For several days, they called and shouted and yelled his name, but he blocked them out. He needed time without them. And after a while, they gave up, leaving behind a silence so unfamiliar, so profound, Alfred didn't know whether to feel exhilarated or terrified.

The silence wasn't to last for long.

They came one night, as Alfred lay in bed beside Isobel. He and Isobel hadn't made love since before his illness, but now he felt healthy and strong again, and the sight of her slightly parted lips, the curve of her hip beneath the blanket, the pale swell of her breast, aroused him. He slipped his hand under the sheet and placed it on her warm upper thigh, and

Eeeeeeeeeeeeeeeeeeeeeeeeeeeeeee!!!

an ear-splitting, dizzying screech, causing him to snatch his hand back from Isobel's thigh. Isobel stirred. Alfred lay back down slowly; his eardrums felt as though they were on fire. For a few minutes, all was quiet. The ringing in his ears died down and he wondered whether the sound might have been nothing but a particularly loud night owl. Slowly, he reached out and stroked Isobel's face. She stirred again, and smiled, her eyes still closed. Taking a deep breath, as though she were breathing him in, she shuffled closer and moved her hand onto his groin.

Filthy disgusting whore! You like that, don't you Alfred? That your wife is a whore.

It was a voice Alfred didn't recognise. It wasn't one of the voice-women, he was sure of that. But it was inside his head. He grabbed Isobel's wrist.

But he'd rather be stuffing Alice, wouldn't you, Alfred? Right up her tight Jewish arse.

'What is it, Alfie?' Isobel whispered. 'I'm sorry, I thought – ' She pulled her hand away.

Alfred couldn't speak. His pulse was racing. He tightened his hands into fists and pushed his knuckles into his temples. What was happening? Who was talking to him? He increased the pressure with his knuckles until the pain seared through his skull.

Finally, Isobel turned away. Alfred lay awake for many hours, drifting off only when the first dull light of dawn stole into the room.

They reappeared the next morning while Alfred was shaving.

HEY!

His hand slipped and he nicked his skin with the razor.

You stupid good-for-nothing pathetic excuse for a man.

The blood dribbled down his cheek and into the sink.

'What do you want?' he whispered.

But there was no answer.

Over the next three days, they assailed him remorselessly. Loud, crude, taunting him, mocking him. In hindsight, three days out of a man's life seemed like nothing, the blink of an eye, and yet these three days brought Alfred to a point of desperation he'd never experienced before. They didn't let him sleep; they didn't let him eat. Conversations with Isobel were interrupted by comments so vulgar – *you want to suck those ripe tits, you can smell her cunt, you want to stick it in there* – they shamed him.

'Are you all right, Alfie? Is it your chest?' Isobel asked him once at the breakfast table. It was the morning of the third day since the new voices had arrived. 'You look very pale.'

He'd be all right if you wrapped those soft lips around his cock, he would!

'I – I'm . . . ' He couldn't finish his sentence.

Isobel frowned and put her hand on his. 'Go and lie down, Alfie. I'll bring you a cup of tea in bed.'

Oooh, she wants you in bed, the randy whore.

Alfred bit his tongue so hard he drew blood. He stood up. 'No. I . . . I think I'll go outside. Some fresh air.'

And before Isobel could object, he rushed out through the back door. He crossed the sodden lawn – trying, failing, to block out the laughs and shouts – and locked himself in the shed. He stood there motionless, taking uneven shallow breaths, and waited. His eyes slowly adjusted to the gloom, and his glance fell on the gardening shears he'd sharpened and cleaned the previous week. A week ago, before they had come. Before he had renounced his voice-women. He took a step forward and picked up the shears, running his finger across the cold blade.

Go on, Alfred. Do it. Or are you not man enough?

The blade was sufficiently sharp. He would only need to apply a bit of pressure to slice through his carotid artery. He would haemorrhage within a few minutes. He trembled as the cold touched his skin.

Do it. Do it. Do it. Do it. Do it. Do it. Do it. Do it. Do it. Do it. Do it. Do it.

He held the blade at an angle across his throat. But a sudden brush of air to his left and a soft moan in his ear made him stop. He could feel a familiar presence there in the shed. His heart lurched and he dropped the shears.

'Where are you?' he whispered. 'Are you there? I'm sorry. I'm sorry I ignored you. I'm sorry I wanted you

340

to go away.' He fell onto his knees and found himself weeping. 'I'm so sorry.'

A fizzing, then a crackling.

Goodness me, Alfred! You can be so silly at times.

Don't be too hard on him. It can't have been nice.

He got to his feet on shaking legs. 'Where have you been? I'm . . . I don't – ' Again, his voice failed him.

Shhh, Alfred. No need to cry. We couldn't possibly leave you to the Others. We've been through too much together, haven't we?

Yes. Now wipe that face of yours and go eat your breakfast. Isobel's waiting.

He nodded and wiped his face on his sleeve. They were back. They had given him a second chance. And he couldn't have been more grateful.

Nineteen Eighty-Eight

It's freezing cold today so your mom is wearing a woollen cap. And a long coat with a fluffy collar. You look around, but there are no other kids here. Opposite, on the other side of the big hole – the grave – some people are crying. Two men are holding hands. It's cold. You shiver. Your mom reaches down and clasps your gloved hand. She's crying really hard now. Her nose is red and puffy. You think you should feel sad, too, but even though you try, you don't. Not really.

Afterwards, when the men have lowered the coffin into the hole, people gather around you and your mom. A woman you've never met comes over.

He was a great guy.

I'm sorry for your loss, kid, someone else says and pats your head.

You need to pee. When are we going home, Mom? you ask. You tug at her hand but your mom is talking to the people.

Yeah, your mom is saying, I only found out on

Thursday. Josh called. She lets go of your hand and covers her face. Starts crying. He just left, you know. Left us sitting in California, without a word. And since we came here, Brynja and me, I've been looking for him everywhere. If I'd known Josh knew where he was, I would've – She stops to blow her nose – Now I'm going to have to, you know, *get tested.* Her voice is nearly a whisper, but she's stopped crying. And Brynja too. His own child!

You turn away. Some people are leaving already. You see a tree, almost black, the branches like arms, the twigs like fingers reaching up into the sky, the kind of tree that's fun to climb. You study it for a while, trying to memorise its shape and energy, so you can draw it when you get home. Is it an ash tree? Or a beech? In the fall, you went on a school trip to Prospect Park to learn how to tell the type of tree from its leaves. But it's January now, all the leaves are gone. Most of the trees here in Brooklyn are different anyhow. A lot of things are different. You hated it at first. Hated the cold. You still hate the cold. You still need to pee.

Your mom is talking to the people. Their breaths form white smoky clouds on the air. You pick up a small twig from the ground and pretend it's a cigarette. You pretend to suck and puff. Your breath is white and smoky too. Then you hear someone crying, close by. A kid. There are a couple of gravestones huddled together near where you're standing. It's where the crying is coming from. You step closer, a bit spooked, then the crying stops. You take another step forward and realise you're standing on one of the graves. Beneath your feet, some dead person. You jump quickly to the side. The crying starts again.

Oh, oh, oh.

A little girl. You creep forward. The sound is coming from behind one of the gravestones.

It's not fair. It's not. Oh, oh.

Hello? You speak softly. You don't want to frighten the girl. You touch the stone, pull your hand back quickly. The mossy, spongy feel grosses you out. Your wipe your hand on your coat and look around the back of the stone.

Nothing.

Hello?

The crying stops. There is no little girl behind the stone. Your mouth is dry and your heart is bouncing wildly inside your chest. You shiver, and hiss-whisper Go away, even if there's no one there. You suddenly feel very, very scared and so you run back across to your mom.

There you are, *liebling*! Your mom hugs you. Come here, it's time to say goodbye to your papa. She kneels down. You do too. Your heart has stopped bouncing; now you can just feel it skipping. The coffin with your papa is in the hole. Here. Your mom gives you a white flower. Throw it down, *liebling*. You let the flower drop onto the other flowers lying on top of the coffin.

You can't remember what your papa looked like. You try to remember but you see Dave's face instead. Dave lives with you and your mom now on Himrod Street. Your mom met Dave when he came to the house to fix the front of the roof, where the rain was coming through. You like Dave, because he takes you for hotdogs even though your mom says that it's wrong to eat meat. And sometimes, when your mom doesn't wake you on time and you miss the school bus, Dave drives you to school in his pickup truck and you listen to country music on the radio.

You like going to school. All days start at the same time, Monday through Friday; all class periods are the same length, except double periods. The teachers say nice things to you when you try hard. And you try hard most of the time. You are already reading third-grade books – *Charlotte's Web* and *Pippi Longstocking* – even though you are only in first grade. You would like to read the books you bring home from school, but your mom says you're too clever for them, because she didn't teach you to read and write before you even started first grade for nothing. Instead, she reads to you from her favourite book by a man called Hermann Hesse. You don't understand the story, and Dave says, Are you reading her that book by Hermann the German? You both laugh – you and Dave. But your mom doesn't laugh and says it's not *Her*mann. It's pronounced '*Hair*mann', so it doesn't rhyme with 'German'. But then Dave puts his hands through his hair to make it stand up and says Hair-man, watch out Brynja, Hair-man's comin' to gctcha, and chases you around the room and you have to laugh so hard you think you'll pee your pants and your mom gets mad and shouts a word you don't understand and leaves the room and slams the door, hard.

In spring, you come home from school and Dave isn't there. Your mom says I don't want to talk about it and you don't see Dave again after that.

1969 – 1972

Alfred's life was back to normal. He returned to work, still a little weak from his illness, but strong enough to concentrate on the herb garden, which was taking on ever larger proportions. Daffyd took over the heavy physical work, while Alfred experimented with various herbs, planting a knot-shaped kitchen garden with a soft, scented chamomile lawn in the centre, surrounded by rosemary, parsley, sage, thyme. Beside this, he also created a psychic garden inspired by his reading, experimenting with the curative properties of various herbs against headaches, stomach upsets, skin abrasions – testing them on himself first, and then with increasing confidence, preparing different teas to drink and dried roots to chew.

All the while, his voice-women treated him with particular kindness and affection, as though they were as relieved as he was that their brief separation was over. Despite this, the 'Others', as Alfred came to call them, had bruised him badly, and it was many months before his fear that they might return abated completely.

Then, in May 1969, Alfred came home one afternoon to the sound of Isobel laughing. His first – hopeful – thought was that John had emerged from one of his black moods and was chatting with his mother in the kitchen. But when he entered, he saw a woman sitting beside Isobel at the table. She had very short hair, and wore a chocolate brown shirt and mustard yellow flared trousers. She had a look – a kind of defiant stylishness – that was quite unusual, certainly for the women that lived in the village. She turned in her chair as Alfred came in.

'You must be Alfred,' she said cheerfully. Then, giving Isobel a wink and a smile, added, 'I've heard all about you. And it's all terribly wicked.'

Isobel let out a giggle. 'I told her nothing of the sort,' she said.

'I'm Amelia, by the way,' the woman said to Alfred. 'At number twenty-two.'

Alfred wiped his hands on his trousers. 'Alfred,' he said, changing his mind about offering his hand. 'Alfred Warner.'

'Well, Alfred Warner, nice to meet you too. Now, I must be off. The movers will be here any moment.'

'Well, it was lovely to meet you,' Isobel said. 'And are you sure you're free for dinner on Thursday?'

'Sounds lovely, Isobel.' She nodded at Alfred. 'I'll let myself out. See you on Thursday.'

'She's just moved in,' Isobel explained when Amelia had left. 'And I thought it would be nice, you know, to cook for someone new for a change.'

Amelia arrived on Thursday evening with wine and some LPs, which they played while they were eating.

'We don't normally listen to music at dinner,' Isobel said, while Joan Baez' honeyed voice sounded in the background, 'but it's nice. We should do it more often.'

John, who had showered and shaved in time for dinner (by threat or bribe, Alfred suspected), agreed. 'Yeah. We normally eat in front of the telly.'

'We do no such thing!' Isobel said, glaring at him.

'Silly me,' John said in a flat voice. 'Of course. We do no such thing, Miss Fairclough.'

Isobel lowered her fork. 'It's Mrs Fairclough, John.'

Amelia shook her head. 'Actually, it's neither, really,' she said, and then added by way of explanation, 'I'm divorced. And anyway, please call me Amelia.' She put a hand on John's arm and he turned bright red.

'So,' Alfred said, changing the subject. He didn't want Isobel's evening spoiled by John. 'What brings you to Checkley, Amelia?'

She waved her hand vaguely. 'Oh, I thought it would be nice to live in the country for once. After the divorce and all that. I'm just renting the place though, until I find something more permanent in Uttoxeter. I've got a part-time job there. Receptionist at the vet's.'

'My mum's never had a job, have you Mum?' John said.

Isobel smiled selfconsciously. 'Well, you know . . . ' she trailed off.

Amelia said, 'Raising a child and cooking and cleaning for a family may well be considered a job, John. Even if she doesn't get paid for it.'

John blushed again and said nothing. Alfred was pleased she had set him straight.

When they had finished eating, Amelia leaned back in

her chair and lit a cigarette. 'That was delicious, Isobel,' she said, tilting her head back to blow the smoke towards the ceiling. 'Thank you so much.'

'It was a pleasure having you,' Isobel replied, and then got to her feet and began clearing away the plates. Amelia got up to help, but Isobel shook her head. 'Please sit down. You're the guest.'

'Nonsense,' Amelia said. 'It's much quicker if I help. But I'm not staying to do the washing up.' She laughed.

Alfred turned to John. 'Come on, lazy bones, help the girls clear up.'

Amelia put down the plate she was holding. 'We're not girls, Alfred. We're women.' Her tone had an edge to it, but when Alfred looked across at her, she was smiling.

Alfred failed to warm to Amelia in the same way Isobel evidently had.

She's rude, that what she is.

Nonsense. She's very self-assured, that's all. And it's good for Isobel to have a friend. Don't you agree, Alfred?

'Mmm.' Alfred was pinching out the side shoots on his tomato plants. The voice answered in sing-song –

Alfred doesn't like her, Alfred doesn't like her . . .

'You're wrong. It's not that I don't like her, it's just – '

It's just what?

He straightened up and felt a pulling in his lower back. He stretched to loosen it. 'It doesn't matter whether I like her or not. Isobel likes her. And you're right, it's nice that she has a friend.'

But?

'But what? That's enough about Amelia.' He didn't want to talk about the sharp, fizzling edges Isobel brought

349

home with her every time she'd met with Amelia. Best to just ignore it, he thought. He went back into the house. The smell of roasted meat unfurled into kitchen. Isobel turned from the stove and gave him a smile.

'I've made a roast,' she said, bending over to baste the meat. Her hair was tied back and covered with a blue scarf. Small beads of sweat formed on the back of her neck. She shrugged. 'I didn't think it was going to be so hot today.'

'Smells delicious,' Alfred said, stepping out of his boots. He grabbed a teaspoon from the draining board and began to scrape the mud from the bottom of his boots.

'Alfie?' Isobel said.

'Yes?'

'I just wanted to say that from now on, you're going to have to make your own tea every Tuesday. Amelia and I are taking an evening course,' she said. 'At the college in Stoke.'

'Really?' A pebble was lodged tight in one of the grooves. He worried it until it came loose and the spoon went flying. Isobel went to pick it up.

'Are you listening to me?' Her voice was suddenly edgy, challenging.

Alfred put his boot down. 'Sorry, love. You were saying – '

'Political philosophy. Every Tuesday from seven till nine.'

'Political philosophy?'

Isobel went to the sink and began washing the teaspoon under the tap. 'Yes. Don't sound so surprised. Do you think I'm too stupid, or something?'

'No,' he replied. 'You've just never shown an interest in that sort of thing before.'

'Perhaps that's because you've never asked me. Perhaps that's because you never ask me my opinion on *any*thing.'

Alfred shook his head. He didn't want to argue. 'If you're looking for a fight,' he said, heading into the living room, 'pick someone else.'

That summer, John surprised his parents – and presumably himself – by passing his A Levels with half-decent grades and receiving an offer to study geology at Manchester University. Isobel took the news tearfully but bravely. The day after John left, in late September 1969, she went up to the bedroom that had been his for the last few years, and Alfred stood and watched her packing up the remainders of their son's childhood – story books, a Captain Scarlet figure that had been disfigured with a lighter, stuffed toys, a collection of rocks and fossils, discarded LPs. She packed the things into cardboard boxes, carefully, like a museum curator, as though these were items of priceless value that would one day be reclaimed by their owner. At one point, she held a stuffed pale blue bunny to her nose and sniffed, smiling – a very private reminiscence. Alfred was suddenly overwhelmed by how quickly his infant boy had become a man.

You can't turn the clock back, Alfred.

'I know,' he answered silently, dejectedly.

He's gone.

'I don't know what's more remarkable,' Alfred said out loud to Isobel, to stop the feeling blossoming, 'a man walking on the moon or our son getting into university.'

'Well, people can change,' she said in a flat voice.

One Tuesday evening, Alfred was in the kitchen, whisking a couple of eggs in a bowl. Isobel came in and looked over his shoulder.

'Eggy bread?' she asked. 'Make some for me, will you?'

Alfred looked up. 'No Foucault or Sartre tonight, then?' he asked. He hadn't read either, but had seen the books on Isobel's bedside table.

'Amelia's in London for the week,' she said flatly. 'She's gone to an anti-war demonstration.'

He clicked the gas stove on and put a knob of butter into the pan. 'Isn't she a little old for that kind of thing?'

'What, taking a stand against an immoral war?'

'Christ, Isobel. You know what I mean. Here, pass me the bread, will you?'

She took four slices of bread out of the wrapper and handed them to him. He soaked each slice in the egg mixture and placed them in the pan. It smelled good. Isobel came and stood close to him. 'You've become quite a dab hand in the kitchen, haven't you?' she said, smiling.

'Left to my own devices,' he replied. Then he said, 'How about we eat and then I give you a lift to Stoke in the car? Maybe I'll even join you.'

Isobel was silent for a moment. The bread sizzled in the pan and she nudged him to turn the slices over. 'No thanks, Alfie,' she said finally. 'This is something I want to do on my own. I'm doing it for me.' She placed her hand on her chest for emphasis.

'Except for when Amelia's not here to do it with you,'

he said without thinking. When he looked at her, she had turned bright red.

The next morning, he apologised.

'Save it, Alfred,' she said, buttering a slice of toast. A night's sleep evidently hadn't thawed her.

He put the kettle on and waited for it to boil.

Apologise again. Go on. Tell her what a good wife and mother she is.

'Stay out of it,' he murmured.

Don't take your bad mood out on us.

'Enough!' He flicked his hand past his ear as though waving away some annoying gnats.

Isobel glanced up from her toast and raised an eyebrow. 'I gather you're holding your own private little conversation there,' she said coldly.

'Isobel, I'm . . . ' The sound of the kettle boiling drowned out his words. He filled the teapot and went to sit beside her at the kitchen table. 'Isobel. Please. Let's not start the day this way.'

But she shrugged and stood up. 'I've got things to do. I don't just sit around here all day enjoying myself, you know.'

'But I've never suggested – '

She left the kitchen before he could finish his sentence.

Things hadn't improved the following evening. Alfred was at pains to avoid any confrontation, but it seemed as though Isobel was itching for an argument. Even as she put down his dinner plate in front of him, he could sense her bristling. He decided to say as little as possible. He waited for her to sit down and then began to eat. She had made liver with mashed potato, something he generally enjoyed, but his first mouthful was tough and gristly, and as he chewed at the meat, he felt her eyes on him.

'Anything wrong?'

'No,' he said, swallowing the half-chewed piece of liver. 'Not at all.'

They continued to eat in silence. When they had finished, Isobel said, 'An occasional thank you would be nice.'

'Sorry?'

'For serving you food every day.' Her voice was dangerously low.

He sighed. 'Thank you, Isobel, for cooking for me every day.'

It wasn't enough – or perhaps it was too little, too late. Isobel continued. 'You don't respect me, Alfred.'

'Of course I do!'

'No. You don't.' She made it sound like a statement of fact. 'Christ, you don't even let me read the newspaper!'

'That's nonsense!'

'Oh really?' Her face was pinkening. 'How many times have you sat there reading the paper, and read me things you thought might be "of interest"? Hmm? Instead of letting me make up my own mind?'

Alfred shook his head. 'Bloody hell, Isobel. That's just ridiculous.'

But she's not wrong, really, is she?

'And you refused to let me get a job? D'you remember? Before John?' She stood up and began clearing the plates from the table, noisily. She spoke in a rush. 'You dragged me down here, and expected me to be your little *hausfrau*, nice and quiet and obedient and dependent. Escaping to the pub when things got difficult. Leaving me to mop up the mess. Well, I've had enough!'

'That's Amelia talking.'

Touché.

Isobel banged the plates onto the draining board. 'Oh, of course, because I'm not capable of thinking my own thoughts.'

'Well, are you? Because right now, it doesn't seem like it.'

'You know what, Alfred? Just . . . fuck off.' She stormed out.

'Where are you going?' he called after her. 'It's the middle of the night!'

'To Amelia's. She left me a spare key.' And she walked out of the house, leaving the door wide open.

Ten days before Christmas, the postman delivered a letter and a postcard, both relaying the same information, albeit in different ways. The letter was from the University of Manchester, informing Alfred and Isobel that John had been absent for four consecutive weeks, and advising them that failure to produce documentary evidence justifying the absence would result in his suspension from his degree course. The postcard was from John himself. It showed a sunset over the Golden Gate Bridge, with the words *Greetings from San Francisco, Calif.* across the front. On the back, John had written:

Hi Mum, hi Dad,
This'll come as a surprise, I know. Can't explain right now why, but had to leave. Looking for a life that's bigger.
Love, John

Alfred came home to the news. Isobel was sitting on the couch, red-eyed, in her dressing gown. Amelia was sitting beside her. Isobel jumped up as Alfred came in, but Amelia broke the news.

'John's dropped out of university and gone to America,' she said bluntly. She gave Isobel a sympathetic nod of the head.

Alfred looked at Isobel. 'What?'

'It's true,' Isobel said, her voice hoarse and cracked from hours of crying. 'Look.' She picked up the postcard and the letter and handed them to him.

Alfred quickly read both. 'Why didn't you call me at work?' he asked. He was stunned. He'd expected many things of John, but nothing like this. He couldn't understand why his voices had stayed silent, hadn't given him some kind of warning. He repeated, 'Why didn't you call me?'

Amelia stood up. 'Don't bully her, Alfred. She's had quite enough blows already. She's been so upset, haven't you, Izzy?' She put a hand on Isobel's arm.

Alfred cleared his throat. It grated on him, the way she abbreviated his wife's name. 'Well, thank you, Amelia. For looking after her. I think it's probably best if we discuss this in private.'

'He's young,' Amelia said. 'Like I said to Izzy, he probably just wants some adventure, see the world, experience what's out there. God knows I did when I was his age.'

Isobel started weeping again.

'I think – ' Alfred began, but couldn't quite arrange his thoughts. He looked at the postcard again, at the tacky, kitschy sunset. What was John thinking? How could he be so selfish? Alfred had a sudden image of himself when he was John's age – the beginnings of that glorious final summer in Berlin stretching out before him, when despite all the misery and wretchedness of war surrounding him he had felt carefree and happy, only to be plucked out of his youth and sent off to kill. The memory weighed on him, and with a trembling hand he tossed the postcard down. What did John know about a 'bigger life'?

'I think,' he said to Amelia, 'that you should leave now.' He put a proprietary arm around Isobel.

Amelia ran her hand through her short hair. 'Perhaps I should be off,' she said finally. 'Will you be all right, Izzy?'

'She'll be fine,' Alfred said.

Amelia ignored him. She gave Isobel a peck on the cheek and said, 'You know where to find me.'

Alfred's enquiries went nowhere. The university hadn't seen him since late October, and he was told politely but firmly by the police that they could not file a missing persons report. Not only did his parents have an indication of his whereabouts ('He sent you a postcard, didn't he?'), but he was now of legal age, the age of majority only recently having been lowered from twenty-one to eighteen ('Can't say I agree with that myself,' was the policeman's opinion, 'but there you have it.').

Two more postcards followed during the next six months. Both were from California. The one from Los Angeles read: *Life is great! Love, John.* The one from Monterey read: *I'm sorry. I wish you were here. John*

Over the next few months, Alfred and Isobel's arguments continued, culminating one evening in a row over Alfred's apparent over-generous use of Fairy Liquid.

'There's bubbles everywhere!' Isobel cried when she came into the kitchen. 'What the hell are you doing?'

'I'm washing the dishes,' Alfred responded, and added, 'I thought that's what you wanted. A little help around the house.'

'A little help. Around the house,' she repeated slowly.

'Yes,' Alfred said. He continued to rub the dishcloth around an already clean plate. 'I thought that's what you want. Isn't that what you want?'

Isobel's voice dropped to a growl. 'Don't you dare put this back on me, Alfred Warner.'

Alfred let the plate slide back into the soapy water. He turned to face her. 'Isobel. I don't know what you're talking about.'

She gave him a stare. 'No, you don't, do you?' She left the room.

Damned if you do, damned if you don't!

These were Alfred's thoughts exactly. A short while later, Isobel complained about his snoring, so he ended up sleeping on a camp bed in John's old room. After more than twenty years, Isobel said, she was entitled to a good night's sleep.

The marriage had become wretched and exhausting, and so when Alfred returned home after work one day in April 1970 to find a letter from Isobel waiting for him, the first thing he felt was a perverse relief.

Dear Alfie,
Everything is falling apart. I have been a wife and mother for most of my life and at times I feel - no, I know - that I have failed miserably. I understand now that my failure was the result of trying to be someone

I'm not, and now I have to take control of my life and be who I am meant to be. This is not an impulsive decision; I have thought about this for a long time. Please don't be worried. I am going to live with a group of women who understand me and who will be there for me, as I will be there for them.

And please, Alfred, do not try and contact me.

Isobel

Alfred let the letter fall back onto the table. His absurd relief quickly turned into panic. He ran upstairs to the bedroom. She'd taken only a few clothes as far as he could tell, but her suitcase was missing from the top of the wardrobe, and on her bedside table, lying forlornly beside the small rose-coloured lamp, was her wedding ring. He ran out of the house and went to Amelia's. He rang the doorbell, pounded the door with his fists, but there was no response.

'Amelia!' he shouted. 'Isobel!'

He ran around to the back of the house, cupped his hands to the window and looked in, but there was no sign of life. A mad charge of anger rushed through his body and he smashed his fist against the glass, cracking it but not breaking it, which left him feeling strangely impotent.

'Where is she?!!' he called into the dark, but there was no answer. He went back around to the front, and noticed curtains twitching on the other side of the street. A neighbour's dog began to bark furiously. Alfred stood in the night air for a while, breathing heavily, and then went back home.

Upstairs, he grabbed as many of Isobel's clothes as he could hold and took them downstairs, then stuffed them into bin bags. He picked up the letter and tore it into tiny pieces. Afterwards, sick with rage and shock and wretchedness, he got himself a bottle of gin and went to sit in the middle of the back lawn, under a waxing moon, to get drunk.

'I don't deserve this,' he said, into the darkness.

What do you deserve, Alfred?

'I don't know. Not . . . not this.' He waved his arm around.

Don't forget, you lied to her for many years.

'I know, but not to *hurt* her. How could she just leave like this?'

Well, it's hard, I know. But –

'But what? What did I do wrong?'

Some questions have no answers.

And with that, they left him again. When the bottle was empty, he staggered back into the house, removed Isobel's clothes from the bags and returned them, neatly folded, to their rightful place. Again, he noticed how little she had taken with her – did this mean she was coming home soon, or was she leaving her old life behind her? For a moment, he couldn't breathe. He leaned forward and put his hands on his thighs, gasping for air, as his whole world folded up on him. When his breathing became regular again, he got to his hands and knees and slowly, with shaking hands, pieced together Isobel's letter with Sellotape.

The next morning, feeling dazed and still a little drunk, he drove to Uttoxeter. He knew from Isobel that the veterinary practice where Amelia worked was just off the

High Street. When he entered, a bell above the door tinkled, setting off a cacophony of squawking, barking and growling. Five or six pet owners sat around, shushing and stroking their sick animals. Amelia was sitting at a high-topped counter, wearing a white coat over a chunky knit sweater, talking on the telephone. She looked up and a pained expression crossed her face when she saw him, but she quickly gathered herself. She looked as though she had been expecting him. He crossed the waiting room.

'Where's Isobel?' he demanded in a loud voice. 'Where's my wife?'

She held up a forefinger and mouthed, *Please*, before speaking into the telephone. 'Well, bring him in at eleven, but you'll probably be in for a bit of a wait. Good-bye.' She put down the receiver.

'Hello Alfred,' she said guardedly.

'Where's Isobel?'

'Look, I can understand that you're upset, but – '

'Upset?!! I'm more than bloody upset.'

Amelia got to her feet. She was a tall woman and stood at his eye-level. 'Please, Alfred. Not here. I'm on a break at – ' she checked her watch, 'in twenty minutes. There's a café around the corner. I'll meet you there.'

'I haven't got long,' she said when she arrived.

'Where is she?' Alfred asked. The coffee he'd ordered had gone cold, and the smell of old cooking grease was making him queasy.

Amelia cleared her throat. 'She didn't leave because of me.'

'No, I suppose it was because of me.'

'I didn't say that.' She waved the waitress over and ordered a coffee, and then lit a cigarette. 'In fact, I tried to talk her out of it. But, Alfred – ' she looked directly at him, 'she was in a bad place.'

'What's that supposed to mean?' he said, more loudly than he intended. Amelia flinched.

Hush, Alfred. Get a grip of yourself. Or she'll walk out of here and you'll never find Isobel.

'I'm sorry,' he said. 'Please, Amelia, tell me where she is.'

Amelia shifted in her seat. She stubbed out her half-smoked cigarette and lit another. 'I promised not to say.'

Alfred rested his elbows on the table and rubbed his face. He felt the toxic remnants of the gin in his bloodstream and the inside of his mouth tasted fetid. The waitress brought Amelia's coffee, setting it down carelessly, so that the brown liquid sloshed over the sides of the cup onto the table.

'She said she needed to get away and think. You have to understand how overwhelmed she was by John leaving, by the fact that she thinks she's done everything wrong up to this point in her life. And she's done nothing wrong.' Her eyes were suddenly fierce. 'She's cared for others for all her life, and now she just needs a rest.'

'Where is she?'

Amelia waited a long time before answering. When she did, her voice was low. 'Okay. But you must swear not to try to bring her home. Not only because I promised I'd keep quiet, but honestly, I think if you try to bring her home before she's ready, you might lose her for good.'

Alfred swallowed and nodded. His voice-women were whispering assent.

'She's staying with some women in Birmingham. It's a co-operative. For women who need to be with other women.'

'You mean a commune? With some sort of hippies?'

'Call it what you will, Alfred. Like I said, I tried to talk her out of it.' She got to her feet. 'I'd give you the exact address.' She paused. 'But like I said, I don't think she's ready . . . ' She shrugged. 'All the best, Alfred.'

For several weeks, he pretended it hadn't happened, that she hadn't left, or that she had just gone for a few days to clear her head and would be back any day. He woke every morning, ignoring the fact that her toothbrush and face-cream were missing from the bathroom shelf, and went downstairs for breakfast, half-expecting her to have come home during the night. He would cycle to work, forcing a hum or whistle, blanking out the voice-women who moaned and whined inside his head. He avoided the pub, knowing how quickly rumours spread through the village, not wanting to hear whispered talk and lewd jokes about his wife.

Soon, though, his denial gave way to raging self-pity, and then to a sadness that numbed his spirit. He was aching to reach the lowest point possible, in the hope that from there, things could only get better. His voice-women were more vociferous than ever; he could feel them plucking and pinching at him with their words of consolation, encouragement, reproach:

Better to have loved and lost
She might be back tomorrow, you never know!
Pull yourself together
You're still a young man . . .

But more often than not, he blocked them out, wanting instead to let the numbness creep over him and eradicate the memories of Isobel's smell, her laugh, her small, soft, familiar body, the mother-of-pearl scar across her belly, her dark nipples, the freckles on her shoulders. He couldn't do it. He couldn't forget. He couldn't imagine his life without her. He still loved her, urgently. Surely she had once loved him, hadn't she?

And as urgently as he missed Isobel, he began to ache with memories of his son. Or rather, the lack of memories. It struck him how little attention he had paid to the small things that made up John's childhood, things that may have seemed trivial at the time, but taken together, made up his son's essence. He couldn't recall John's first words, the names of his school friends, how it felt to hug him. The memories he did have were smudged and unclear, and this shamed him. He was adrift in a huge space of sadness.

One day, on his way to work, he spotted a removal van outside Amelia's house, with several burly men heaving boxes and furniture into the van – and his mood took a new turn. Despite the fact that he and Amelia lived in such close proximity, their paths had rarely crossed recently. Alfred would spend almost all his waking hours in the gardens at March House, the only place he could quash the sense that he was crumbling away on the inside. Amelia, it seemed, spent most of her evenings out. Alfred hadn't been back to Uttoxeter to speak with her. For one thing, he had believed her when she told him she had tried to talk Isobel out of going away. For another, she had represented the only tie to Isobel that remained, and he had been fearful of antagonising her. He had secretly hoped that she would, in time, supply him with details of Isobel's whereabouts.

Now she was leaving, and that meant that Isobel was gone for good. A fresh panic overcame him. He barely got through the day. His mouth was dry and his head throbbed viciously. Thankfully, Daffyd ignored his frequent visits to the garden shed, where he locked himself in and found himself hyperventilating and in crazed conversation with his voice-women. He remained bent over with his head between his legs until he felt his breathing calm down. By the end of the day, he was dizzy with exhaustion. But then, just as he was swinging his leg over his bicycle to head home, Alice approached him. The sun was just setting, and her face was cast in a pink-grey light.

'Can I have a quick word?' she said.

'Of course.' Alfred leant his bicycle against the wall, went up the steps and removed his shoes. He followed her into the house. She led him through to the morning room and switched on a small Tiffany table lamp that gave off a pleasant, multicoloured light.

'Would you like a drink? Something to eat?' she asked, and without waiting for an answer, went over to a large mahogany liquor cabinet and took out a bottle of cognac. 'I'm having one,' she said. 'Do please join me.'

'All right,' Alfred said. 'Thank you.'

Alice handed him his drink and sat down. 'You've been working very hard, lately. The garden is looking quite marvellous.'

Alfred gave her a strained smile. He knew she knew about Isobel – everyone did. 'Keeps me busy,' he said. 'And there's nowhere I'd rather spend my time.'

At this, she let out a small sigh, almost a mewing sound. 'Oh dear, Alfred. I'm afraid I have some bad news. I've been meaning to tell you for a couple of weeks, but I wasn't sure how.'

'Is everything all right?' he asked, knowing that anything she had to tell him couldn't possibly make him feel any worse. He was wrong.

'Yes. No.' She threw her hands up. The cognac sloshed around in her glass but, by some careful design on the part of the glassblower, didn't spill over the sides. 'We're leaving England.'

'Oh.' Alfred took a sip of cognac and felt its heat immediately. His stomach was practically empty.

'Oh?' Alice echoed. 'Is that all you've got to say?' Then she put her glass down and placed her hands in her lap. 'I'm sorry, Alfred. I didn't mean to snap. It's just . . . well, Samuel has just gone ahead and done it. Sold the factory, sold the house, just decided he's some kind of Zionist all of a sudden, for God's sake.' She sniffed. 'So he's left me here to pack up, and I'll be joining him in Tel Aviv in September.'

Alfred said nothing. What was there to say?

'The Worthingtons are buying the house. God knows, some relation died and left them the necessary funds. They want to turn Tean Hall into some kind of hotel and move in here.' She looked around the room. '*C'est la vie*, eh? Anyway, Tean Hall estate will be pulled back together. That'll make a lot of people around here happy, I'm sure.'

'Not me, Alice.'

She put her head to one side. 'I know. And I'm sorry, Alfred. I talked to Elizabeth Worthington, and she says they won't be needing you. I told her what an asset you are, how she'd be lucky to find anyone to match your skills, but she was . . . stubborn.' She sounded unhappy, and tired. 'You'll get a good severance, though. Samuel is generous, if nothing else.'

Alfred drained his glass. He didn't care about any severance pay. He was losing his garden, he was losing Alice. He almost didn't hear the voice-women.

Severance? She thinks it's that easy just to pay you off?

It's the least she can do. It's not as though she really wants to go, is it?

Oh, leave him alone. Alfred's heart is breaking as we speak.

He ignored them. The cognac left him feeling dazed and slightly sick. He felt the numbness that had protected him for so many months being scraped away, leaving him raw and exposed. Alice was staring at him, her dark eyes asking him a question he couldn't read. She was close to fifty now. Her black hair was shot through with streaks of silver, and the skin in the hollows beneath her high cheek bones had begun to sag. But her eyes still held that fierce spiritedness he'd seen when they first met. She was even now extremely beautiful.

'I'm sorry,' he said again.

Alice shook her head. 'So am I,' she said despond-ently.

For a while, they sat in silence as the darkness unfurled outside, throwing the corners of the room into shadow. Alice got up and walked over to the window. Alfred could see her face mirrored in the black glass. She opened the window and the fragrant, woody smell of a recent bonfire drifted in. 'What the hell am I going to do in Israel?' she said, sounding close to tears. 'I'm not observant, I only go to the synagogue on High Holy Days. What do I know about kosher, or mitzvah? There are over six hundred of them, for crying out loud!' She gave a strange, strangled laugh.

Alfred got to his feet. She looked so fragile, so unhappy – she was a reflection of his own misery. He went over to her and turned her gently around, and then placed two fingers on her mouth. He could feel the softness of her lips and the sticky lipstick that covered them. 'It's all right,' he said, and pulled his hand away.

'I'm frightened, Alfred,' she said, tilting her head back to look up at him. Two fine creases curved from either side of her nose to the outside of her mouth. Smile lines. Her throat was smooth and white. He couldn't imagine it tanned by the Mediterranean sun. She raised herself onto her tiptoes and kissed him. Her mouth had the sharp, aromatic taste of cognac. Alfred closed his eyes and held the kiss, indecisive for a moment, but then finding himself increasing the pressure until her lips had parted. He put his arms around her back. Her back was pleasantly toned, and he rubbed his hands up and down, feeling the slight movements of muscle beneath her dress.

Then there was the sound of footsteps outside the room. Alice pulled away and wiped her mouth with the back of her hand.

'It's Emma,' she whispered.

Alfred took a step back. 'I'm sorry,' he said. 'I'm sorry,' and he fled the room.

When he got home, he sat in the dark for a long time. He still felt aroused, but also ashamed for failing to control himself. A whole concoction of emotions rose and fell inside him, as though they were being pulled back and forth by the moon, making him seasick. He didn't know how long he sat like this, but after a long while, there was a knock on the front door. He rose from his armchair, becoming aware only now of the patter of rain outside.

'May I come in?' It was Alice, strands of wet hair clinging to the sides of her face. 'I'm soaked. I borrowed Cook's bicycle.'

Alfred took her hand and led her into the house, and immediately, the tidal wave inside him subsided and was replaced by pure, vibrant longing. They began to make love on the living room floor, in front of the cold, empty fireplace, and when Alice started shivering, Alfred picked her up and carried her upstairs. She was as light as he had imagined.

They undressed each other, unhurried, wordlessly. The skin on Alice's belly was still amazingly taut, the skin white and flawless. He pushed the image of Isobel's caesarean scar out of his mind. He slid his hand up between her legs and she let out a soft purr – he couldn't imagine any sound more sensual, more sexual. They spent a long time exploring each other; Alice ran her hands across his stomach, his shoulders and upper arms, making small appreciative noises that told him she was enjoying his body.

She fell asleep first, and Alfred watched her, trying not to think beyond the moment.

After this first night together, Alice came to his house most evenings. She waited until he had left March House after work, and joined him less than half an hour later. Here, they acted out a kind of mock marriage; she would cook something simple, they would eat together, watch television or listen to music, play Scrabble – as though they needed some kind of domestic facade to justify the passion with which they made love every night.

'Stay here with me, Alice,' he said one night, when she was getting dressed to go home, pulling her stockings up slowly, reluctantly, and fixing them to the suspender belt.

'Not tonight. Perhaps on Saturday. Emma's staying at her sister's overnight.'

'I don't mean for the night,' he said. 'I mean – stay. Here, in England. With me.'

'You know that's not possible,' she said.

'But why?'

She leaned over and kissed him. 'Don't spoil things, Alfred. Please.'

The affair lasted six weeks. When it was time for Alice to leave, Alfred offered to drive her to the airport. She declined.

'I'm no good at that sort of thing,' she said. Her voice was liquid. 'You know – tearful goodbyes and all that.'

Ten months later, he was watching the news distractedly when there was a knock at the door. He got up, wiped some toast crumbs off his shirt and went to answer. It was Isobel, a small red suitcase in her hand. Her hair had grown down to below her shoulders; she wore dark blue jeans and a beige kaftan he didn't recognise. She didn't smile, or cry; in fact, her face held very little expression. She looked familiar and alien at the same time.

'I'm back,' she said quietly. 'If you still want me.'

Alfred opened the door wider and stepped aside to let her in.

1972 – 1987

Isobel had changed, of course, during her ten-month absence, but in a way Alfred found difficult to put his finger on. She seemed to have shed all her remaining girlishness and acquired instead a toughness that took him some time to become accustomed to.

'I don't want you to think I'm shutting you out,' she said that first night, her hands gripping the cup of hot chocolate Alfred had made her, 'but there's a lot I discovered about myself while I was gone, and I need to do some sorting out.'

Alfred was silent for a moment. When he had opened the door to find her standing there, in the dark, like some forlorn fairytale princess, all the anger and despair he'd felt over the past several months flashed through him, and he didn't know whether he wanted to strike her or take her in his arms. He did neither. Instead, he went into the kitchen and busied himself with making a hot drink. She took it gratefully, and they sat wordlessly in their living room, the quiet buzz of the television still on in the background.

Give her some time.

You are angry and hurt, but you must let her know you still love her.

They were right. He did still love her. So he asked the only question he really cared about. 'Are you staying?'

Isobel blew on her hot chocolate, took a sip and said, 'I'd like to Alfie, I really would. But we'll have to wait and see.'

She went to bed – in John's old room – shortly afterwards. The next morning, Alfred came downstairs to find her making porridge in the kitchen.

'So,' she said. Her hair was wet from the shower and she had tied her old apron around her waist. The scene was so familiar to Alfred that for a moment, he wondered if he had just imagined her absence. 'How are things at March House?'

He laughed. He had most definitely not imagined her absence – he hadn't been back to March House for eight months.

She eyed him quizzically. 'What's so funny?'

So he told her: True to her word, Alice had arranged for him to receive a severance payment large enough to live off for an entire year. But several weeks after her departure, when one day sludged into the next, and Alfred began waking and sleeping to an increasingly irregular rhythm, rarely bothering to shave or, on some days, even bothering to change out of his pyjamas, the voice-women decided it was time for him to start looking for a new job. They woke him with screeches at seven in the morning, chided him relentlessly until he had bathed, shaved and dressed properly, and instructed him to get in the car and drive southwards, towards the small town of Stone. Alfred obeyed without objection. He was too empty to fight them.

Ooh, wait until you see what we've found!

Just the thing for you, Alfred.

'Shut up! I can't drive with this racket,' he mumbled angrily, as he drove the car along the narrow country road, slowing at corners in anticipation of on-coming traffic. When he approached the black, wrought-iron gate of March House, he turned his head away until he had driven past. It had rained heavily during the night, but now the sun was bright and hot, and he cursed his voice-women for making him wear his thick corduroy jacket.

A left at the next junction, if you please.

Alfred flicked his indicator on and turned at the junction. Then –

A sharp right, now. Now!

Alfred yanked the steering wheel to the right and found himself driving down a tree-lined dirt track, wet and muddy from the night's rain. After a few hundred yards, he arrived at a building, a large barn or farm outbuilding, with a long corrugated plastic extension at the side. Above the barn door, there was a hand-painted sign, *Herbaceuticals Ltd.*, in kaleidoscopically swirling patterns. It clicked into place – Alfred had read about this place recently in the local paper. A couple of Oxford graduates had started up some manufacturing company in the area. A short paragraph, nothing more.

A young man in a faded t-shirt, jeans and wellingtons was standing at the door, smoking. Alfred stopped the car and switched off the engine. He smiled at the man as he got out.

'Can I help you?' the man asked, a little suspiciously. He had a cut-glass accent.

'Hello,' Alfred said, wondering where to start. His voices had brought him here to ask for a job, he presumed, but the young man didn't appear too welcoming. He took a few steps in his direction,

Mind the – !

but it was too late. He'd stepped into a puddle and his right foot was soaking. The man grinned and pinched out his cigarette.

'Are you here for the job?' he asked, now more friendly.

'Yes,' Alfred answered quickly.

The man took a few steps towards him and held out his hand. 'Nice to meet you. Alistair Marcus.'

Alfred shook his hand.

'Hang on,' Alistair continued. 'I'll go and fetch Hugo. He's the business side of things.' He walked back and opened the door to the barn. 'Hugo! There's a man here for the job.'

A moment later, another man appeared. It was immediately obvious that the two men were brothers, if not twins. The second man, Hugo, had the same dark hair, albeit covered partially by a blue bandana, the same square jaw and straight narrow nose. The only difference was that Alistair held himself with less self-assurance, as though not quite knowing what to do with his long arms and legs.

'You're here for the job?' Hugo said to Alfred.

Alfred repeated his 'yes', although less hastily this

time. He still had no idea what job he was here for, and his voice-women were keeping quiet.

'Hugo Marcus, how do you do?' He also shook Alfred's hand, though more forcefully than his brother. They had the same impeccable manners, which contrasted oddly with their informal, somewhat dirty clothes. They would look more at home in suits, Alfred suspected.

'Please, come into the office,' Hugo continued and led the way inside.

The office was a space in a corner of the barn, separated from the rest of the building by a makeshift wall made of wooden planks. The window, which was missing a pane of glass, had been covered with transparent plastic sheeting. The light that came in was speckled. A large table was covered in neat piles of papers and folders, and a stack of books.

'Please, take a seat,' Hugo said, dropping onto a chair behind the table. He frowned. 'I'm sorry, I don't believe I caught your name,' he said.

'Alfred Warner,' Alfred said, sitting down opposite him. 'And this might sound a bit odd, but – '

Hugo waved his hand across his face. 'It's all odd around here.' He let out a low, melodious laugh. 'Alistair and I – we're brothers, as you might have gathered – have been going spare trying to find someone to fill the position. You wouldn't believe how many oddballs there are out there who claim to know all about chemistry.' He leaned forward. 'You're not one of those, are you?'

'I – ' Alfred began, uncomfortably aware of the wetness of his right sock. 'I'm here for the gardening job.'

Hugo straightened up, pulling his eyebrows together. 'The gardening job?'

'Yes,' Alfred continued. 'I'm recently out of work, and I thought – '

Hugo interrupted him gently. 'God, I'm sorry. I think there's been a misunderstanding. We're looking for a chemist. For the processing. Distillation, fractionation, fermentation, that sort of thing. For the herbal products.' He gave Alfred an apologetic look. 'And you have no idea what I'm talking about, do you?'

Alfred shook his head slowly. As he was wondering how to best extract himself from this awkward situation and ask his voice-women what exactly they had thought they were up to, he heard a knock behind him. Hugo moved his head to look at a spot behind Alfred's shoulder.

'Not now, please. I'll be with you in . . . in a couple of minutes.' He looked back at Alfred. 'I'm very sorry. Like I said, there's been a misunderstanding.'

Then Alfred heard a voice. 'Mr Warner? Is that you?'

He turned to see a ginger-haired man standing at the door. It was Daffyd.

'Mr Warner!' he said, his face breaking into a broad smile. He had never quite got used to calling Alfred by his first name. 'So nice to see you!'

'You two know each other?' Hugo asked.

Alfred nodded, about to explain, but Daffyd was evidently excited to see him there, and got in first. 'Yes, Mr Marcus, I mean Hugo. Mr Warner was my boss, at March House. Is he going to be working here? Are you going to be working here, Mr Warner?'

Hugo got up. 'Actually, Daffyd, I was just telling Mr Warner that we're looking for a chemist, not another gardener.'

Daffyd's shoulders slumped, then rose again. 'But he's

an expert. Tell him, Mr Warner.' He took a small step forward. 'He knows everything about herbs. About – ' he grimaced, 'what's her name again, Mr Warner? That lady with the herbs?'

His exuberance made Alfred smile. 'Hildegard of Bingen,' he said. Then he turned to Hugo. 'I'm sorry if I've wasted your time,' he said. 'There was, as you say, a misunderstanding.'

Hugo crossed his arms. 'You've read Hildegard of Bingen?' he asked.

Daffyd opened his mouth to speak, but Alfred silenced him with a look and said, 'Yes. I'm very familiar with her work.'

'She's not too specific about her recipes, unfortunately.'

'I like to think of her work as inspirational more than instructional,' Alfred answered.

Hugo had the beginnings of a smile on his lips. 'We're having a little trouble with the aloe vera. Any ideas?'

'Perhaps the soil is a little too moist?' Alfred offered. He knew that Daffyd was over-generous with the watering.

Hugo nodded slowly. Alfred glanced over at Daffyd and saw the tips of his ears glowing red. Daffyd was thirty years old now, but still reminded Alfred of the gangly teenager he'd first met.

'And how long have you been a gardener?' Hugo asked Alfred.

Alfred let out a rush of air. 'Over twenty-five years, now.' Had it really been that long?

'Hmm.' Hugo put a finger to his mouth and tapped his lips. Finally, he said, 'Would you mind waiting here for a moment? I'll just go and have a word with Alistair.'

He left Alfred and Daffyd in the office. Daffyd's grin

was still fixed on his face. 'Would be great, wouldn't it? You and me working together again.'

'How long have you been here?' Alfred asked.

'Only three weeks. I was gutted when the job finished at March House, what with Janice pregnant again and all. But then I saw a job advert in the paper and they took me on right away. Mrs Singer-Cohen wrote me a great reference.' He looked down at his boots. 'Were a shame she had to leave. I really liked her.'

'Yes, so did I.'

They stood in silence for a moment. From beyond the wooden wall they could hear the two brothers in quiet conversation.

'So this place,' Alfred said. 'It's herbal products?'

'Yes. Medicinal products, they want to make, you know, from nature. But also beauty products. Stuff for ladies. Janice says it's a craze, it'll never last, but you never know, do you?' He shoved his hands in his pockets. 'And it's a job.'

They both turned as Hugo came back in, Alistair trailing behind.

'Well,' Hugo said firmly, 'we've had a little chat, and would like to suggest something to you. As you can see, we're just starting out,' he spread out his arms for emphasis, 'and we, well, we hadn't planned on hiring more staff than absolutely necessary. Two gardeners might be stretching it.' He glanced at Daffyd, who shot a nervous look at Alfred. 'But don't worry, Daffyd, we hired you first, so we're keeping you on.'

Daffyd gave out a small 'oh' sound. The red on his ears had spread across his face, but he looked extremely relieved.

'So to get to the point,' Hugo continued, 'your kind of expertise sounds incredibly valuable, Mr Warner, so we'd like to suggest a week's trial. If that works out, then – '

'That sounds perfect,' Alfred said.

'We can't afford to pay much,' Alistair piped up. He gave Alfred a bashful smile, and Alfred realised that what he had earlier taken to be unfriendliness was actually shyness.

'That's fine,' Alfred said, and it was.

'Well then,' Hugo said, 'let me give you the grand tour.'

By the end of that first week, Alfred had been offered a permanent job. At March House, the herbs had been his territory and responsibility, so he spent a fair amount of time instructing Daffyd in the art of cutting and comminuting, and on how to distinguish an edible plant from its toxic *doppelgänger*. Daffyd displayed a nimbleness and intelligence Alfred had never noticed before, and he felt a shade of shame that he hadn't encouraged the man's skills when they both worked at March House.

Hugo and Alistair eventually managed to recruit a chemist – Gillian, a recent chemistry graduate who, despite holding a first-class degree, was finding it difficult to find a job on the grounds of her gender. At forty-six, Alfred was the oldest by far, and was treated by the others with a respect and admiration he was unaccustomed to. Alistair though, who had a fair knowledge of traditional medicine himself, was always eager for Alfred's advice. He bowed to Alfred's authority and experience, and read the books Alfred recommended with insight and enthusiasm.

In all, it was hard yet immensely gratifying work, and over the years, the company – in contrast to Janice's early prediction – flourished and grew. By the time Alfred retired eighteen years later, the company employed thirty full-time staff.

Over the days that followed Isobel's return, Alfred waited for her to tell him of where she'd been, what she'd done during her absence, but she remained frustratingly silent. It took an incredible effort for Alfred not to lose his temper and tell her to leave again, if she weren't prepared to talk to him. But he waited.

That's the spirit, Alfred! Time heals all wounds.

Ksss, unless you keep picking at the scab, ha ha.

It was two months before she finally broke her silence, and not quite in the manner he had expected.

'I ran into Janice today,' she said one evening, as an episode of *Coronation Street* was drawing to a close. (Alfred never watched the programme, and was surprised that Isobel was so *au fait* with the intricacies of the plot – and then it occurred to him that she hadn't been living on another planet during her absence, but rather a mere fifty miles away.)

'Daffyd's wife?' he asked.

'Aye. Out for a walk with the bairns.' She gave him a wistful smile. 'Have you seen the twins? They're just the sweetest things.'

Janice and Daffyd now had four children – the most recent pregnancy had produced a couple of red-headed boys, much to Daffyd's delight.

'And so,' Isobel continued, 'I thought it'd be nice to have them round for dinner. What do you think?'

'I think that's a great idea,' Alfred said. He got up and turned the sound down on the television. 'In fact,' he added, 'if you're up to it, why not invite Hugo and Alistair as well? I know they're keen to meet you.' He felt that now she had opened the door a chink, he needed to make the most of it.

Isobel shrugged. 'Sure. Why not? And, of course, Gillian. She sounds like a most interesting young woman. How about two weeks on Saturday?'

'Beats me why Alfred kept you a secret,' Hugo said, letting his spoon fall onto his plate. 'That is the best Baked Alaska I've ever tasted.'

There was a consenting murmur from the other dinner guests. Isobel smiled graciously. She sat very straight, these days, Alfred thought. It must be those exercises she did every day, the ones in which she seemed to tie herself – effortlessly – in knots.

'Yes, it was lovely,' Janice said, placing her hands on her stomach. 'It's a slimming week coming up for me, I think. But – ' she pushed back her chair to stand up, 'I'm afraid we'll have to be off. Babysitters are horrendously expensive these days.'

'Thanks for having us,' Daffyd said, following suit and getting to his feet. 'It was splendid.'

Janice and Daffyd left behind the suspended air of anticipation of whether the other dinner guests – Hugo and his girlfriend Kate, Alistair and Gillian – should also take their leave, but Isobel waved them down. 'It's nae even ten o'clock,' she said, beginning to clear up the dinner plates.

Alfred got to his feet. 'Let me do that,' he said, and she

381

smiled at him and sat down. From the kitchen, he heard the conversation resume. They talked briefly about Janice and Daffyd, the fact that the couple seemed intent on covering the entire county of Staffordshire with their red-haired Welsh offspring. Then, just as Alfred was carrying some coffee cups into the dining room, he heard Kate ask Isobel, 'Do you and Alfred have children?' He stopped at the doorway and looked over at Isobel. Several fine creases appeared in the corners of her eyes – only Alfred knew this to be a shadow of her earlier pain. 'No,' she said quietly, 'no children.'

'Right,' Alfred said in an attempt to sound jovial. 'Let's move into the living room.'

Here, Hugo and Kate searched through the record collection and finally settled on the Beatles' *Revolver*. There wasn't enough room for everyone on the sofa and armchair, so Isobel hastily threw some scatter cushions on the floor. Alfred took a seat on one of the cushions, resting his back against the sofa.

'So,' Hugo said, picking up where he'd left off earlier, 'where have you been hiding her, Alfred?'

'He hasn't been hiding me anywhere, Hugo,' Isobel said. 'I went to live in Birmingham for a while. I needed some time away.'

Alistair and Hugo exchanged a look, and Kate seemed to cringe slightly, but Isobel continued. Perhaps she needed the safety of an audience to tell her story, Alfred thought. 'I went to live with a group of women. A lot of them were there because of violence, abusive husbands, you know? Cigarette burns, bloodied lips, traumatised children, that sort of thing. It was pretty awful.' She breathed in and out, deeply. 'I suppose I needed to . . . to *see* that.'

'What for?' Gillian asked, the only one apparently not embarrassed by Isobel's unselfconscious disclosure.

'To realise how privileged I am,' she said, and squeezed Alfred's arm. 'To realise how very special my husband is.' It was the first time she had touched him like that since coming home.

Gillian leaned forward. 'There's a place in Stoke,' she said. 'A women's refuge. They're looking for volunteers, if you're interested.'

'Oh, leave it, Gill,' Hugo said, in a bored voice. 'For once, let's not talk about women's lib, or Bloody Sunday, or Nixon. Let's just chill.'

Gillian scowled at him, but Isobel said, 'No, that sounds very interesting. Thanks, Gillian.'

Alfred suddenly remembered the coffee he'd started making earlier, and was about to suggest a cup for everyone, if only to ease the tension, when Hugo jumped up and fetched his jacket.

'I think we all need to chill,' he said, producing a couple of joints from his jacket pocket. 'You don't mind?' he asked in the direction of Isobel and Alfred. (Alfred knew that they grew marijuana plants in the company green-house – which was fine by him, as long as they didn't expect him to tend to them.)

'Go right ahead,' Isobel said, in a tone that surprised Alfred. When John was still living at home, she had been vociferously anti-drugs.

Alistair lit the joint and inhaled. Then he passed it to Isobel. Without hesitating, she put her lips to the end and took a long draw. Then she nodded and handed it to Gillian.

When the joint had almost come full circle, and Hugo

offered it to Alfred, he shook his head with a smile. 'I'm all right, thank you.'

'Come on, old man,' Hugo said. 'It won't kill you. And it's herbal.' He let out a laugh that sounded like a bark.

The room was already filled with sweet, earthy-smelling smoke. Alfred looked over at Isobel, who had her eyes closed, her head resting against the side of the armchair. She appeared totally at peace.

'Why not?' Alfred said, before he could change his mind. He wasn't an old man, no matter how much his bones ached sometimes. He was not yet forty-eight. He drew quickly on the joint and blew the smoke out in a thin stream. It tasted better than a cigarette, at least. But Hugo gestured for him to hand him the joint back.

'You have to keep it in for a bit,' he said, and demonstrated by inhaling deeply, holding his breath, and then letting the smoke out through his o-shaped mouth. 'See, like that,' he said, in a thin, nasal voice.

Alfred took the joint again and sucked on it deeply. Then he held his breath.

Oh, goodness, do we think this is a good idea?

I think not...

Kssss, come on! Let's have some fuuuuuuunnnn!

It burned and scraped his throat, but he managed to suppress a cough. A moment later, his heart began pounding, but it wasn't unpleasant – quite the contrary, it was . . .

Your turn again, Alfred.

Already? He took the joint from Hugo's hand and inhaled. He had never thought about what it might be like to get high. Nothing special, really, his mind was perfectly clear. Just that . . .

Melting sensation, right?

'Yes, exactly,' he answered in his head.

Then, after his third puff, he heard Kate shushing everyone as the staccato strings of 'Eleanor Rigby' filled the room. 'Shhh, I love this song,' she was saying. 'It's so . . . '

This is goooood! Ksss – you should do this more often, Alfred

'It's weird,' he replied. 'It's making me . . . '

Can't think of the word? Doesn't matter

'This is a very sad song,' he said to the voice.

I know. That's the shift from C-major to E-minor

'But the lyrics too. So sad. A very sad song indeed.'

And then – he woke to a gentle, persistent tapping on his shoulder. 'Alfie. Alfie.' It was Isobel. 'They've all gone home. You fell asleep.'

He tried to sit up, but his limbs felt too heavy. 'I'm sorry, I – '

She laughed gently and lay down beside him, nestling her body into his. 'You were talking to your voices,' she whispered. 'But don't worry – everyone was too stoned to notice.' She paused. 'It was funny though. A running commentary on "Eleanor Rigby".' She started to giggle, and before he knew it, he was giggling alongside her, until the two of them were laughing so hard it was difficult to breathe. Then they kissed – softly, chastely – and a moment later, Isobel had fallen asleep next to him on the floor.

Two months later, Isobel got a job as a volunteer at the women's refuge in Stoke; a year after that, she was offered a full-time job. Gone was her girlishness, but with it, also her mood swings, her snappishness, and although Alfred sometimes missed the Isobel he had first kissed in Mauchline, the girl with the bright laugh and uneven temperament, he knew he would marry her again if he had his time back – and that, surely, was the measure of a happy marriage.

Then, almost fifteen years after Alfred and Isobel had received the last postcard from John, he returned unannounced.

NINETEEN EIGHTY-SIX

You don't get the first one right. You try again – circle
for the head, then the legs. No, there's something goes
between the head and the legs, you remember. The belly!
You draw another bigger circle under the head, then the
arms attached to that and the legs.

Hey, Brynja, what'ya doing?

Papa crouches down on the floor beside you.

I'm drawing, you say.

Cool. Want some juice? It sure is hot today.

Mmm, yes please.

Papa goes to the kitchen.

The fingers – one, two, three, four, five – you count
out loud. Soon, you have lots of people.

Here's your juice. He sets the glass down on the floor
beside you and goes to sit on the couch. The curtains
are drawn but it's a sunny day and the light in the den is
buttercup yellow. You sip your juice. It's sweet and cold.

Hey Brynja. When Mom gets home from work, we

can all go to the beach. What d'you say? You wanna go to the beach?

You wipe the juice moustache from your mouth with the back of your hand. Yes. You nod. You live close to the beach but you've only been a few times. Do I get ice cream?

Sure. Papa laughs and lights his pipe. The smoke smells spicy and sweet and makes you dizzy.

But I gotta finish my picture first, you say.

What's your picture of? Come and show your Papa. Smoke comes out of his mouth with the words.

You pick it up and take it over to him. These are the princesses. And these are the princes.

And that one?

That's Mom. She's the queen.

And that's me, huh?

You nod.

I'm the king, right?

No. You're a prince.

Not the king?

You shake your head. You're a prince.

Just a prince? His voice is sleepy.

Uh-huh. But you're the best one.

Papa smiles. The best of princes. I like that. He strokes your hair and closes his eyes.

You climb onto his lap. Yes, Papa. That's what the ladies told me. You're the best of princes. His eyelids are yellowish and quivering, with spidery blue veins. You reach out your finger to touch one, but then his eyelids open.

The ladies? he says. He blinks very slowly.

Uh-huh. They said.

You smile at him but he grabs your shoulders, squeezes them hard, and then he's yelling at you – You're making that up, Brynja, there are no fucking ladies – and he's shaking you by the shoulders so your teeth clack together and you start crying.

In the evening: Did you have a baby today, Mom?

You're in the bathtub. Mom is rubbing your legs with a flannel. Millions of soap bubbles covering your body. Some of them have rainbows in them.

I did, sweetie. A little girl. Pink and rosy.

Can you bring one home?

Mom laughs. She picks up a plastic cup. Put your head back, sweetie.

The warm water flows from the cup through your hair, into your ears. You jerk your head forward. Now you have soapy water in your eyes. Mom!

You have to keep your head back, Brynja. Sorry.

A towel! A towel!

Mom hands you a towel – you rub your face.

But I can't bring one home, sweetie, Mom says. The babies aren't mine. They belong to the women who give birth to them. I just help them do that.

You want a baby. A little sister. To play with.

Mom squeezes shampoo onto her hand and rubs it into your hair. You like the way Mom rubs your head. But then she stops.

What's this, *liebling*? She touches your shoulder where Papa grabbed you earlier. Is that a bruise? She pulls your hair back and looks at the other shoulder. Brynja?

You pull your knees up to your chin.

Brynja, talk to me. How d'you get these bruises?

Very quietly, you say: Papa got mad with me because of the ladies.

Papa did this?

Uh-huh.

Mom rinses her shampoo fingers in the water. Hang on, sweetie, I'll be right back. She gets up and leaves the bathroom.

You turn onto your front, pretend you're swimming. You push yourself backwards and forwards – your soapy body slips and slides along the bottom of the tub. It's fun. The water sloshes up and over the sides. You hear Mom shouting.

You hit our *baby*, you son of a bitch?

It's not what you think, Sabine. I didn't hit her. She was acting crazy. I just tried to –

Crazy, huh? *She's* the crazy one?

You turn onto your back and lower your head into the water. Just your face above the surface, now. Your ears are underwater. You can't hear what they're saying. Just shapeless watery sounds, without the sharp edges. You lie there for a while. The water's getting cold and the bubbles have nearly all gone. You sit up. The door flies open, crashing into the side of the tub. It's Papa. You shiver.

What the fuck? You can't leave a four-year-old in the bathtub unsupervised!

He lifts you out and wraps you in a towel.

My hair, you say. It still has shampoo in it.

But Papa just carries you through to the den and sits you on the couch. Mom's standing at the door. The lights are off. The TV is flickering, but the sound isn't on. Tom and Jerry.

Like what? Like *I'm* the bad parent now? Mom's voice is low, but you can tell she's very mad. You shouldn't have told her. She comes and picks you up and sits you on her lap. She rubs your head with the towel. Too hard.

Ow, Mom, you're hurting me!

Sorry, *liebling*. I'm sorry. Mom hugs you close. It's warm inside the towel. You hitch it up over your head, like a hood.

Papa is walking up and down, like he needs to walk but doesn't know where to go. To the window, turn, back towards the door, turn, to the window. He stops to pick up his small metal pipe.

Not now, Mom says to him. Her voice is very quiet and tired. You put a finger to your mouth, chew your nail.

Don't tell me what to do, Papa says, but doesn't light the pipe. Then he shakes his head and heads quickly towards the door. I'm sorry, Sabine. This isn't working.

1987 – 1988

John sat on the living room sofa, holding a cup of tea between his hands, as though to warm himself. It was mid-afternoon on a hot summer's day; the windows stood open, but the breeze, when it came, provided no relief from the heat and only served to tease the net curtains.

'Please eat something,' Isobel said, pushing a plate of sandwiches across the coffee table closer to him. Although she avoided the sun, she was developing light brown spots on her hands, shaped like jigsaw pieces. 'I made some sandwiches.'

John shook his head. 'I ate on the plane.'

'But – '

'It's okay, Mum, really.' He made it sound like 'Mom'.

Isobel looked to Alfred for support, but Alfred didn't want to add to the awkwardness that hung in the room. So instead, he said, 'I bet John's saving his appetite for a proper home-cooked meal, aren't you?'

John smiled and let out a tired, relieved sigh. 'Yes, Dad.'

Alfred helped himself to a cheese and ham sandwich, noting that Isobel had cut off the crusts, just as she had done for John when he was a child. Truth be told, he also wished that John would eat something. When he had answered the door an hour earlier, he hadn't at first recognised his son. Before him stood a man with dusty blond hair, tall and painfully thin, the skin stretched across his face so as to accentuate the squareness of his jaw and the almost unnatural roundness of his eyes. The image of an Auschwitz survivor flickered briefly across Alfred's mind. Then the man stepped forward and said, 'Hi Dad', and Alfred was momentarily unable to speak.

'Can I come in?' John said, and when Alfred nodded and opened the door wider, John turned back to where a taxi was waiting and gave the driver a sign that he could drive on.

Now, an hour later, John – thirty-five years old, no longer their surly, adolescent son – was in their living room, declining the offer of his mother's sandwiches. The air was still and heavy with questions and reproaches, but neither Alfred nor Isobel seemed to want to take the initiative. Perhaps they were both afraid of where it would lead them.

Finally, Isobel got to her feet and broke the silence. 'Well then, I'll pop upstairs and make up a bed for you. I'm afraid there's only a fold-out mattress. Your room, well . . . ' She trailed off and hurriedly left the room.

Then Alfred and John spoke at the same time.

'How was your flight?'

'You look well.'

They exchanged the pleasantries simultaneously, making them both laugh nervously. Alfred leaned forward.

'Are you sure you won't eat any of your mother's sandwiches?' he asked.

John shook his head.

'Then another cup of tea?'

'To be honest, I'm feeling a little nauseous,' John said.

Alfred smiled. 'Then I've got just the thing. Come with me.' He stood up and went into the kitchen. John followed him. Alfred took two large glass jars from a wall cabinet and then went to fill the kettle.

John opened one of the jars and sniffed. 'What's this?'

'That one's dried yarrow, the other is balm,' Alfred replied. 'We'll make you a tea from that. Works well against nausea.'

They waited for the kettle to boil. The muted thump and whoosh of the dishwasher filled the silence.

John said, 'You know what, Dad, you don't sound that Scottish anymore. The Midlands have got to you.'

'And you sound like a Yank,' Alfred responded. They both laughed, less nervously this time.

Alfred poured the boiling water over the tea. 'Let that infuse for five or six minutes. Works wonders on an upset tummy.'

'Thanks Dad.' He grinned, causing the skin to stretch even tighter across his face and making him look ten years older. 'You've become quite the Hildegard of Bingen.'

Alfred smiled. 'Actually, you're not the first to say that.'

They heard Isobel coming down the stairs. She popped

her head around the kitchen door, avoiding John's eye. 'If I'm going to cook tonight, I'd better go shopping,' she said. 'I'll be an hour or so.'

When they heard the front door fall shut, Alfred said, 'Give her a bit of time. She'll come round.'

'She's still very pretty.'

'Aye, she is.' Alfred stirred the herbs around with a teaspoon and then removed them. 'She left me for a while, years ago,' he blurted out. 'Not long after you'd gone.'

'Really? Why, what happened?' He sounded genuinely surprised. 'Were you having an affair?' He tried to make this sound jokey.

Alfred shook his head. 'No. I don't really know why she left.' He looked at John. 'Maybe she was looking for a life that's bigger.'

John frowned.

'You wrote that on the first postcard you sent us,' Alfred said.

John screwed up his face. 'God, I was such an asshole back then.' Asshole, not arsehole, Alfred noted. John pulled a pouch of tobacco out of his jeans pocket. 'Do you mind?' he asked.

'Of course I mind. You're my son and it's bad for your health.'

John looked pained for a moment, but didn't speak.

'Outside, then, if you must,' Alfred said. He took the mug of tea and they went out into the garden to sit on a wooden bench that stood at the back of the house. The sky was a spectacular blue, and the sun blazed down on them. Alfred broke into a slight sweat.

'Not too hot for you?' he asked.

'Oh no,' John said. 'I love the heat. When I moved to

New York last year, I thought that first winter was gonna kill me.'

'So that's where you live now?'

John nodded. He took out some papers and began rolling a cigarette. His fingers were thin and his knuckles disproportionately large, his nails ridged and yellowish. He noticed Alfred staring.

'So, don't you want to ask me anything?' He sounded anxious and challenging at once.

Alfred was silent for a while. Where to start? Should he ask him why he left? Why he broke his parents' hearts? What he had been doing all these years, with no letter, no telephone call, no sign of life, other than a few shabby postcards? Should he tell him that they had been grieving for their son? Finally he said, trying to keep any sign of reprimand out of his voice, 'I suppose what I'd really like to know is, have you been happy?'

John let out a long sigh, a kind of *pshhhh* sound. 'I guess I've had my moments.' He took a sip of tea. 'Nice.'

'How long are you staying?' Alfred asked, realising then that he wanted John to say, 'For good'.

John lit his cigarette. 'A week, if you'll have me.'

'Of course.'

'I came over with a friend of mine, Jackie. She's visiting a cousin in Manchester. I'll need to give her a call and let her know.'

Alfred looked out across the garden. Several butterflies were dipping and rising around the summer lilac. The neighbouring honeysuckle looked thirsty; its dark green leaves were drooping slightly among the brilliant magenta flowers. He'd have to make sure to water it generously that evening.

'Jackie. Is she . . . ? Are you two . . . ?'

John smiled. 'No. She's a good friend from New York. My best friend's wife, actually.'

'And you? Do you have a – '

John was overcome by a sudden, lengthy coughing fit. It was a rasping, grating sound, and confirmed to Alfred that his son's state of health was anything but good. Finally, he stopped coughing and spat a lump of greenish mucus onto the ground. 'Sorry,' he said.

'Are you all right?' Alfred asked.

John didn't answer this. Instead, he said, 'No, I never got married. I – I had something going for a while. But . . . ' he trailed off.

Alfred gestured towards the mug. 'Helping any?'

John took another sip and nodded. 'Dad?'

'Yes?'

'Well, the woman, the one I was with for a while.' He looked across at Alfred. His eyes were dull, his pupils over-large. 'She – we had a baby.'

Alfred felt a little bubble of air rise up his throat. 'You mean I have a grandchild?'

John shrugged. The bones of his shoulders were clearly visible through his t-shirt. 'Yeah,' he said, very quietly. 'A little girl. But . . . '

'But what? Can we meet her? How old is she?'

John rested his elbows on his thighs and put his head in his hands. The cigarette he held between his fingers was trembling visibly. 'Shit, Dad. I – I did a lot of crazy stuff.' He ran his hands through his hair and sat up. 'Nothing I'm too proud of. Drugs . . . and stuff.'

'But your daughter?'

He shook his head. 'It just didn't work out. Sabine and

397

I – that's her mother – we, well, we decided to split when the kid was three.'

'So she's living with her mother?'

'Yeah. At least, I guess so. I haven't seen Brynja for over two years.'

Alfred's heart churned. 'Brynja – is that her name?'

John gave him a warm smile. 'Yeah. I remembered you telling me once when I was a kid that you would have called me that if I'd been born a girl. You said it was my grandmother's middle name.'

Pearls of sweat broke out on Alfred's forehead. The heat was making him feel slightly faint.

John looked momentarily panicked. 'Did I get it wrong?'

Alfred shook his head. 'No. You got it absolutely right.' He thought he might cry.

'I've been trying to find her since I – ' He stopped and seemed to sink into himself. 'We split when I was still living in San Francisco. I was kinda . . . out of my head at the time. The drugs, you know, you think they're gonna give you answers, but they just mess you up. God – ' he shook his head. 'I'll spare you the details, but it was pretty ugly. And not good for a kid.'

Everything seemed to have come to a standstill. The air was hot and brooding, even the butterflies were no longer flying about and had settled tiredly on the shrubs. All that could be heard was the faint gurgle of water flowing through a pipe that fed the dishwasher on the other side of the wall.

'And now?'

John took a deep breath. Alfred could hear his son's lungs whistling. 'Now I guess I'm paying the price.'

Then, not at all suddenly – in fact, Alfred felt that

everything had been leading up to this moment – John leaned into his father and rested his head on his shoulder. He began to cry. 'I'm dying, Dad.'

'He's got AIDS,' Alfred said to Isobel in the dark.

When there was no response from her side of the bed, he turned and found her lying on her back, her face twisted into a grimace of pain and grief. She was sobbing silently, deep down in her throat. He slid his arm under her neck and pulled her around, so that he was holding her tight in his arms.

Alfred hadn't known what to expect from Isobel. He had feared that she might smother John with the love she had stored up over all the lost years, and that John might run away again. But she didn't. She was soft and calm, asking him in a measured tone to explain the medication he was taking, the side effects, the doctor's prognosis, any complications he might expect. She made him tea, offered blankets when he shivered, and never once insisted that he eat when he complained of a lack of appetite.

Alfred hadn't had the heart to tell her about their grand-daughter that first night, and as each day passed, there never seemed to be the right moment – the moment when he would give her a grandchild and snatch her away at the same time. He approached John again on the subject when Isobel was at the hairdresser's. She had wanted to cancel the appointment, she didn't want to miss a moment spent with her son, but John had insisted, promising they would all go out for a meal afterwards and that he would eat everything on his plate. She smiled at this and left reluctantly.

'Is there no way of contacting her?' Alfred asked John.

They were taking a walk through one of the fields at the back of the village. The corn stalks were over six feet high, and Alfred could remember a time when John would delight in playing hide-and-seek here, much to the farmer's annoyance.

'I tried, Dad,' he said. He was wearing one of Alfred's thick woollen jumpers, despite the heat. 'Sabine never wanted alimony. I think she was pretty mad when I left, and then it was just her and Brynja. But ever since . . . since I got the diagnosis, I've called everyone who we both knew, Sabine and me, but it's – ' His chin was trembling. He took a deep breath and swallowed, his over-large Adam's apple rising and falling in his throat. 'It's pretty hopeless.'

Alfred put his arm around John's shoulder. He was an inch or two shorter than his son, but he felt immeasurably larger. They began the short walk home.

'You remember that fight we had?' John said.

Alfred didn't respond. It was something he would rather not remember.

'You know, when you found me drunk in the shed,' John continued. He shivered slightly. 'Dad.'

'I don't want – ' Alfred began, but John interrupted.

'Dad.' He stopped walking. His long arms hung at his sides. 'I need you to know that I don't blame you for anything. For what happened. For all the shit. It's just . . . I don't think I'm like regular people. I mean normal people. Like you and Mom.'

Alfred turned to face him, and his heart broke at the sight of his dying son.

When it came time for John to leave, he asked to call a taxi, but they insisted on driving him to the airport. John's friend, Jackie, was waiting for him there. She embraced him, and then gave Isobel and Alfred a brief, surprising hug. Jackie had already checked in, so she waited with Isobel and Alfred as John went to the counter.

'Are you guys okay with each other now?' she asked.

'Yes,' Isobel said softly.

Jackie nodded, moving her shoulders back and forth, as if in emphasis.

'Jackie dear,' Isobel said, in a thick voice. 'You will call us, won't you, when . . . ?'

'Sure,' she whispered.

Jackie called eight months later.

Day Five

It was Alfred's idea to visit the orphanage. The night was wet and cold, but I'd brought two thick blankets to wrap ourselves in. I'd also filled a thermos flask with *glühwein* before we left the flat.

We sat on a little wall on the opposite side of Berliner Straße, just staring across at the building. It looked exactly as I'd imagined it from Alfred's story: a neo-baroque white facade, red-painted window frames, Juliet balconies (*sans* geraniums at this time of year), the inscription on the gable – it was all there. I sat there, sipping my hot wine, while Alfred pointed out his dormitory window, the classrooms, the wall that ran around the property to the yard at the back.

'The prayer room is on the other side, on the third floor. It's a shame I can't show you. It's beautiful.'

We had tried the front gate as soon as we had arrived, but it was, of course, locked. An information board hanging on the right of the gate told us that the building had been extensively renovated and reopened in 2001, and that it now housed a public library, a private school and a prayer room. I made a mental note to bring my pupils here on a day trip when the term started again in January.

'And up there – ' he now pointed to a window on the second floor, 'that was the boys' common room. You know, sometimes when the *Jungvolk* marched by, boys the same age as us, we would stand at the window and admire their smart black uniforms.' He shook his head. 'Can you imagine?'

'Perhaps you just wanted to belong.'

He shivered. 'Yes. Yes, I suppose we did.'

'Come on Alfred,' I said, yawning. 'It's freezing. Maybe we should go home now.'

He tucked the blanket more tightly around his legs. 'Just a little while longer, Julia. Please.'

We sat there for some time. I finished the rest of the *glühwein*, while Alfred began a hushed conversation with himself – or his voices. I yawned again, and was about to suggest heading home, when in the building behind us, someone opened a window and the sound of swing music drifted out. I've always liked the lilting, offbeat rhythm of swing, and before long, I found my feet tapping along to the music. I felt Alfred's eyes on me, and turned to find him smiling at me.

'How about it?' he asked.

'How about what?'

'You know.' He winked at me. 'May I have this dance?'

'Oh. I don't think – '

'Come on, Julia. Do it for me. It may well be my last.'

And before I knew it, he had slipped his arm around my waist, taken my right hand in his left, and guided me onto the pavement as though it were a dance floor. He held the rhythm in his body; I felt it in the squeeze of his hand on mine and the slight pressure he applied to my lower back. I began moving freely, stepping back, then forwards, amazed at how my feet seemed to be moving of their own accord, despite my tiredness. Alfred whirled me around to the music, with the energy and stamina of a much younger man, until I was crying with laughter. And then – just crying. Presently, he slowed down and took my hands in his.

'I'm sorry,' he said. 'I didn't mean to upset you.'

He pulled out a handkerchief and offered it to me. It turned out to be perfectly clean after all, smelling only very vaguely of violets.

1990 – 2005

Their final years together, between Alfred's retirement and the onset of Isobel's illness, slid by unremarkably. A stillness had entered their relationship, as though something, some *thing*, that had fluttered around between them for the past forty odd years had finally come to rest after a long, dusty journey, filling an otherwise empty space. Indeed, when Alfred had cause to look back, the time ran together in his mind; Christmases, birthdays, weekend trips to Cornwall and the Lake District, once or twice to Scotland – in their repetitions, these events became increasingly indistinct from each other. Few new memories were formed; instead, old memories were snatched up and held close like lifebuoys. Family photographs took on a grand importance, imbued with a sense of perfection of the moments captured – John in his first pair of swimming trunks, snapshots of Alfred decorating the Christmas tree, Isobel as a little girl on her father's arm outside the vicarage.

Indeed, the inability to form new memories was the first sign of Isobel's gradual, cruel decline. Of course, they both began to suffer the eccentricities of age – mislaying their reading glasses, keys, library books – but soon, Isobel's memory loss became more disturbing and frightened them both. Once on the way to the supermarket, she sat beside him in the car, nervously, tensely, and when he asked what the matter was, she said, 'We're on our way to the doctor's, aren't we?', in a voice so full of fear that Alfred answered, 'Yes', and drove past Tesco and into town, where, by the time he'd parked the car, she had forgotten all about the doctor's.

When some roof tiles needed replacing, she paid the contractor twice, costing them five hundred pounds, which Alfred only managed to reclaim by threatening to involve the police. And although he knew that it wasn't her fault, he couldn't help but get angry and frustrated at times.

'Don't cook potatoes if you can't remember to turn off the cooker,' he shouted at her once, when she had left the potatoes to boil dry and started a small fire in the kitchen.

Isobel stood in the corner miserably, as he doused the fire and wrenched open the windows to clear the black smoke. 'We're old, Alfie,' she said, her voice shaking. 'Old people are entitled to forget things now and again.' And he regretted having raised his voice.

Shortly after this incident, he had the gas cooker replaced by an electric one, after coming home to the smell of gas. The young man who came to install the new cooker spent over an hour with Isobel, explaining how to use it, kindly and patiently. On his way out, he said to

Alfred, 'Give her a day or two, mate. There's nowt much can go wrong, but change can be difficult to handle.'

Alfred woke that night to find Isobel's side of the bed empty. He discovered her standing in the kitchen in her nightdress, staring at the new cooker. Her small, frail figure was illuminated by a smear of moonlight, making her appear almost ghost-like.

'Alfie,' she said, her voice quivering. 'Someone's been in the house. They've taken our cooker.'

Alfred moved forward and put his hands on her shoulders, wanting to reassure her, but then he noticed a sudden awareness in her eyes, as though she had briefly surfaced from great depths of confusion. For a moment, she understood, and it terrified her. Although, thankfully, she remained physically capable of washing, dressing and eating (when prompted) until she died, the disease ate through her brain at a brutal, merciless rate. By the time she turned seventy-seven, she didn't recognise herself in the mirror. She had no memory of ever having children. She didn't know her own name, the day of the week, the year. But she knew Alfred to the end; even when she was no longer capable of coherent speech, he saw it deep down; beyond the milky surface of her eyes, he saw that she knew and loved him.

In 2004, Isobel died of a stroke beside him in bed.

For almost a year, Alfred lived alone. He cooked and cleaned for himself, unwilling to hire domestic help. He noticed, but ignored, the fact that the house was falling into increasing disrepair. When the layer of grease on the cooker refused to yield, even with the fiercest scouring and dousing in bleach, he reckoned that the heat from the hob would kill any dangerous bacteria, and left it. When he could no longer bend over to clean the bathtub without severe back pain, he reckoned that it would clean itself with the soap in the bathwater.

But one evening, as he got into bed, he was hit by the stench of sweat and urine and something not quite definable, but certainly not pleasant, and he realised that he hadn't changed his sheets since Isobel died, months earlier. He muttered some sarcastic thanks to his voice-women – why couldn't they remind him to do these things? Or were they, like him, subject to senility? So he decided to set a date, changing his bedding on the first Sunday of every month, and adding a small spray of Isobel's perfume to his pillowcase – he had chosen the brand for her, a subtle, violet-scented fragrance, as a tenth wedding anniversary gift and she had remained loyal to it for the rest of her life.

He had never been a fussy eater, and was thus quite satisfied with the contents of the different tins of food he'd pick up in the supermarket – ravioli, beans, goulash. A check-up at the doctor's several months ago had revealed high blood sugar levels, and Alfred was instructed to watch his intake of sweets and do thirty minutes' worth of brisk walking a day. The walking was no problem, but he found it difficult to forgo his daily biscuits – something, he ultimately decided on balance, life was too short to do. On occasion, when he felt the need for company other than his voice-women, he went to the pub. Overall, he managed.

Then one day, he slipped trying to get out of the bath. He simply lost his balance. He grabbed hold of the shower curtain with his right leg already out of the bath, knowing even as he did that it wouldn't hold his weight, and watched as the plastic rings holding the curtain in place popped off the bar, one by one, as if in slow motion.

Oh crikey! he heard, falling awkwardly, trying to retrieve his right leg back into the tub, and then felt the pain slice through his hip as he hit the edge of the bath. He must have passed out for a while, because presently, the water was tepid and he was shivering. There was a fierce, hot throbbing in his right hip, and when he tried to sit up, it was agony. He lay back gingerly, trying to find the position that was least painful.

Christ! How are you going to get out of this one, Alfred?

'I don't know,' he said, and began to cry.

After a while, his tears subsided and he began shaking again, each spasm sending a jolt of pain from his hip across his pelvis and down his thigh.

You have to remain calm, Alfred. Now, first things first. You need to let the water out of the bath, or you'll die of hypothermia. Can you reach the plug with your foot?

Holding his breath against the pain, Alfred managed to clasp the chain of the bath plug between the toes of his left foot.

Yes, good, now give it a quick tug.

Alfred tugged and cried out as the pain shot through his other leg, but the plug had slipped out and the water slowly drained out, leaving him lying wet and cold in the tub.

'What now?'

Towel. Can you grab the towel?

Alfred reached his arm out and pulled a large thick towel from the rack on the wall. Then, moving as little as possible, he covered himself up.

It's late. I'm afraid you will probably be here all night, my dear. Won't be terribly comfortable, but shouldn't kill you, either.

No. It's going to be a balmy night.

'How are you going to get me out?' he said, almost in tears again.

Kssss, what are we – your fairy godmothers?

Shhh, Alfred. Don't cry. You've no choice but to stay where you are. In the morning, we'll see what we can do. Now sleep, if you can.

Alfred closed his eyes. For what seemed like hours, he just lay there, his thoughts going around in circles, but eventually, shock and exhaustion overcame him and he fell into a shallow, pained sleep. He woke to the sound of birdsong. The light coming in through the open window was bright, bouncing off the white tiles and almost blinding him. And then

Rise and shine! Let's go go go!

It took him a few seconds to remember where he was, and almost instantaneously, he felt a sharp pain in his hip.

Okay. By my reckoning, the postman will be here between eight and eight-fifteen. It's now seven fifty-two. So let's stay on our toes!

'But he won't know I'm here,' Alfred said, and started to panic.

Calm down, Alfred. Let's think about this.

Alfred lay very quiet, trying to focus on the birdsong outside and away from his dread of dying of cold, or thirst, or pain – alone and naked in his bathtub. Then, he heard the most joyous sound of the garden gate squealing open, the crunch of footsteps on the gravel, and –

Quickly, Alfred. No time to spare!

'Help!' he called, his voice strangled and pathetically low. 'Help! Help me!'

The muffled clunk of the letterbox, footsteps retreating back down the path.

Right. Shouting's not going to do it. Throw something out of the window. Quickly!

Alfred looked around, desperate and in terror.

The shower gel! Now, Alfred, now!

He took the bottle of shower gel from the ledge of the bath and raised his arm to throw it.

You have to sit up, get some traction. It's going to hurt, very much, but it's your only chance.

He didn't stop to think. If he had, for a moment, imagined the excruciating pain that was to follow, he might well have chosen to die here in the bath. But he sat up, heard the scrape of bone on bone inside his hip, felt a dizzying rush of agony, and with a strength he didn't think he possessed any longer, tossed the bottle towards the open window. He watched it fly through the window, a perfect aim, and lay back again, hoping unconsciousness would take the pain from him. For a moment, there was silence; even the thrush had suspended its song. Alfred hardly dared to breathe.

'Oi!' It was the postman. 'Oi! Watch it!' A pause. Then: 'Hey, Mr Warner, that you? Everything all right?'

'Help,' Alfred whispered. It was all he could manage.

The postman's voice, loud and clear: 'If that's a burglar, I'm calling the police. I've got my phone with me.'

With his eyes closed and his stomach queasy, Alfred heard the postman speaking on his phone. 'Yeah. 24 Barton Road, Checkley . . . Something's going on . . .

Yeah, quick as you can, please . . . Best send an ambulance too, just in case.'

Fifteen minutes later, Alfred was on his way to Stoke-
on-Trent City General Hospital, and through the fuzzy
haze of morphine, he realised that at the age of seventy-
eight, he was riding in a blue-light-flashing ambulance for
the very first time.

When he woke from the surgery, a youngish woman was
sitting on a chair next to his bed.

'Good morning,' she said, chirpily.

Alfred frowned. 'What's the time?' he asked. His
voice was raspy.

The woman smiled and rolled her eyes. 'Not literally.
I meant, because you've just woken up . . . oh, never
mind.' She looked a little annoyed, as though he had
spoiled her favourite joke. Then she put a smile back
on her face. 'I'm Mandy,' she announced, 'the Geriatric
Care Officer.'

Alfred let his eyes slide shut. He was intensely thirsty.
He swallowed with difficulty. 'Can I – some water please?'

'Oh, right. Sure.' Mandy got up and filled a paper cup
with water from a water-cooler in the corner of the room.
'Here.'

Alfred drank it in one draught, although it was icy-cold.

'Right, Alfred,' Mandy continued. Her voice was thin
and high, and she smelled very strongly of hairspray.
'As I said, I'm the Geriatric Care Officer, and I'm here
to discuss a couple of things with you. I'm sorry to do
this right now, but I have to pick up my daughter from
nursery school at three, and my co-worker, Jill, is down
with the flu. Do you think you can manage a little chat?'

Alfred nodded weakly.

'Now – ' Mandy looked at a chart she was holding. 'We had quite a fall there, didn't we?'

Alfred touched the back of his right hand, where the drip needle was held in place by a plaster. It was extremely itchy underneath. He wasn't, as far as he could tell, in pain, but he felt fuzzy and tired.

'Ooh, don't pick at that,' Mandy said, reaching over and pulling his arm back. He didn't have the strength to fight her. 'Now. You've been given a new hip, the old one was well past its sell-by-date. I suppose you can consider yourself lucky – some people have to wait months for a hip replacement. But then, I'm a glass-half-full kind of girl.' She gave him an oddly laboured wink, like something she'd practised in the mirror.

'When can I go home?' Alfred asked.

'Ah. Now that's what I'm here to discuss with you. You see, you'll need someone at home with you for the first week or so. Have you a daughter, perhaps, who can take some time off work? Or a nice neighbour? If all goes well, and you don't develop any infection or other postoperative complications, you should be discharged within six or seven days. Then you'll have a spell of physical therapy, and before long, you'll be good as new.'

Alfred blinked. Oddly, his eyes were watery while his throat felt parched, as though the fluids had taken a wrong turn somewhere inside his body. 'No,' he said. 'There's no one.'

Mandy sighed. 'Oh dear. That's a shame. Well, Alfred, then we're going to have to think about residential care.' Alfred blinked again and felt a tear running down his face. Mandy held up a hand. 'Now, there's no need to cry. I know it can come as a shock to realise we are no longer able to look after ourselves. But there are some nice homes. Some very nice homes.' Her tone held the implication that there were also some very horrible homes.

Alfred turned his head to the side.

So this is it.

Day Five/Six

I woke with a start. I must have had a bad dream, but try as I might, I couldn't remember the content. It was one of those awful dreams that bleed out into consciousness and leaves one with an indeterminate feeling of dread. It took a moment to shake off the anxiety it caused.

The room was pitch-black, but I got out of bed quietly and put on my dressing gown. I opened the bedroom door and crept through to the living room to check on Alfred. He was lying on his back, perfectly still, and for a moment I was overwhelmed by a sudden fear that he might have died in his sleep. I tiptoed over to him, but saw his chest rise and fall in slow, even movements. A momentary, urgent desire washed over me for the day to pass by quickly, so that tomorrow morning I could wake him with a cup of tea and say, 'You see? You're still here. You and your silly premonitions!'

2005

The worst thing about Gladstone Court Care Home was the smell. But it was also the best thing, because it was only a matter of days before Alfred's nose no longer detected the eye-watering stench of stale urine, disinfectant and boiled vegetables. When any visitors came to the home, the assault on their senses was immediately visible, by the flared nostrils and the way they switched to breathing through their mouths. Soon, Alfred realised that he might well smell bad himself, although he couldn't tell, which was comforting and discomforting at the same time. But because he had no visitors, it didn't much matter to him. And the olfactory system, it turned out, was highly adaptive. Unfortunately, the same couldn't be said about the permanent semi-darkness; for reasons unknown, the nurses insisted on keeping the curtains drawn all day, and the low-watt light bulbs hardly gave off enough light to mimic daylight. It was something he never got used to.

*If this is a nice home, I wouldn't like to see the alternative.
The food's all right, though.
That's because Alfred'll eat anything, won't you, Alfred?*

It was true. Although his appetite seemed to decrease steadily with each week that passed, he enjoyed the soft, gummy food that was easily masticated and allowed no sores to develop beneath his false teeth.

'I'm not a fussy eater,' he replied. 'I make no excuses for that.'

Yes, the food was fine. But the perpetual twilight – it sucked any sense of time passing out of him

That is, of course, the whole point . . .

and often he would fall asleep in an armchair and wake up, not knowing if it was morning, afternoon or night, or whether, indeed, he had really woken up at all. Such was his loss of temporal orientation, that he was astonished, one day, to find two of the nurses draping silver tinsel over the reproduction oil paintings in the common room.

'Christmas already?' he asked.

'Well, not quite,' one of them said, a young Irish woman with a mess of ginger hair and a pierced eyebrow. She winked at him and clicked her tongue. 'It's only November, but it's nice to have a bit of cheer around the place, isn't it?'

Alfred gave her a smile. She was one of the nice ones, although he could never quite remember if her name was Mary or Michelle. The other residents liked her too. The nurse helping Mary/Michelle was another of the residents' favourites. Her name was Magdalena, from Poland, and she looked as though she had just walked out of some women's high fashion catalogue, with a tall, slender body, pronounced cheekbones and a round pout of a mouth. Her only flaw was a gap between her top front teeth that showed when she smiled, which she did often. She knew each resident's preferred brand of biscuits – in Alfred's case, these were ginger snaps, which he would dunk into his tea until soft enough to munch without too much chewing.

When she had finished putting up the tinsel, Magdalena wheeled the tea trolley into the middle of the room and began serving tea and biscuits.

'Chocolate digestives, today, I'm afraid, Alfred,' she said, rolling the 'r' in his name. Her accent was strong. She placed a mug of tea on a table beside him and put one biscuit beside it. 'And only one. Otherwise Jocelyn will – how do you say? – get my goat?'

'You mean, it will get *her* goat if she sees you giving me two biscuits,' Alfred replied. Since they found out about his diabetes, his sugar consumption had, unfortunately, been reduced to almost nil. And Jocelyn, the head administrator at the care home, seemed to take sadistic pleasure in monitoring his diet.

Magdalena waved a hand across her face. 'Her goat, my goat. Well, it's a silly language, with all the goats and such.' She laughed, and he could see a moist sliver of pink tongue between the gap in her teeth.

Steady on there, Alfred.

Ah, if you were ten years younger, eh?

'Make it twenty,' he said out loud.

'Twenty what, Alfred?' Magdalena asked.

Alfred smiled and shook his head slowly. (Over the past few months, his head had taken to shaking involuntarily, so he took care to make slow, deliberate movements whenever he was negating something.) 'Just talking to myself, dear,' he said.

At this point, he no longer cared who heard him, or what they thought of his conversations with his voice-women. Half of the other residents were dotty, anyway, and it was only Jocelyn who ever seemed bothered by his conversations. In addition to scrutinising the residents' diets, she was always on the lookout for signs of dementia. It seemed to terrify her, as though it might be contagious.

It was Mary/Michelle who brought Alfred a letter on the last day in November.

'Rosemary, another two for you,' she said, handing a couple of envelopes to a very old woman with a spectacularly bent spine. 'You'll be winning our Christmas card competition, at this rate,' Mary/Michelle continued with a wink. Then she looked down at the letters still in her hand. 'But, oh, not so fast. Here's one for Roger, and – ' she peered at the last letter closely, as if she were finding it difficult to read the handwriting on the envelope. 'Fancy that. One for Alfred.' She handed it to him. 'Now. Who's for a cup of tea?' Several trembling hands went up. 'Right you are. And if any of youse needs a hand with reading, give me a shout.'

Alfred looked at the letter and let out a quiet gasp. It was, in fact, not addressed to him at all, but to Isobel. The letter was postmarked Berlin, Germany, and it had been sent originally to the house in Checkley, with a Post Office sticker on the front informing him that it had been forwarded to Alfred's new address. He didn't stop to wonder who from Berlin might be writing to Isobel and carefully tore it open. The letter was written on lined paper and less than a page long.

Dear Isobel*,
I hope this finds you well. My name is Brynja, and I am your granddaughter. My father was John Warner, but he died a long time ago. I was very young at the time and can't remember much about him. Sadly, my mother also passed away two years ago. This upset me terribly, and it took me a long time to gather the courage to go through her stuff. When I did, I found a letter addressed to my father (I don't know why my mother kept it; but then, she was always a bit of a hoarder!), written to him by you in 1987. I thought it was a very sad letter, but also very loving. I'd be happy to let you have it back. Anyway, the letter had a return address, and this is the one I'm sending this letter to. I have no idea if it will reach its destination, but it would be nice to think you are reading this now. It would be lovely to hear from you. I have no other family.
Love,
Brynja x
*Should I call you that? I'd rather call you Granny or Grandma, but then again, we've never met so perhaps I should stick with Isobel.

Alfred didn't hesitate. He asked Mary/Michelle for sheet of writing paper and a pen.

A week later, Brynja had responded. She expressed her condolences over the death of Isobel ('How I would have loved to meet her!'), but had been 'overjoyed' to receive

Alfred's response. This letter was much longer than the first, the handwriting more erratic, and it took Alfred a while to decipher. In it, she wrote briefly of her early childhood in America, her move to Berlin, the death of both her parents. She also wrote that she would love to meet him, but that

it's hard to explain, I'm not I get what you might call anxiety attacks sometimes. You know what that is? It's when Doesn't matter really. What I want to say is I can't handle flying because do you think there's any way you could come here and visit me? For Christmas? Plane tickets are fairly cheap, and I can organise everything from this side. I really need Oh please say you'll come, Grandad!
All my love,
Your granddaughter Brynja xxxxx

Alfred folded the letter and placed it neatly back into the envelope.

'Oh dear, Alfred, bad news is it?' It was Magdalena.

He raised his head, although it felt impossibly heavy, and looked up at her.

'Here, wait, I'll get you a tissue.' She pronounced it 'tissue' rather than 'tishue'.

'I'm fine,' Alfred said, but gratefully accepted the tissue from her and wiped his eyes. When he next spoke, his voice was thick and heavy. 'My granddaughter wants me to come for Christmas. But I'm just too old. I'm just too – ' He stopped when he noticed that Magdalena had walked over to Frank Martins and was now wiping Ribena off the man's chin.

You're not too old, Alfred.

'Far too old. Too tired.'

Ah, come on now. Besides, you don't really have a choice.

'My hip.'

Oh nonsense. Your hip's right as rain now. Titanium. Unbreakable.

At the far end of the room, Magdalena was handing over the shift to Jocelyn. The cheap plastic clock that hung above the door read six o'clock. A dark gravy smell unfurled from the direction of the kitchen, but it did little for Alfred's appetite. He didn't feel hungry in the slightest.

You have to tell her.

'Tell her what?'

There was no response.

'Tell her what?!' he repeated, in a louder voice.

'Alfred Warner!' It was Jocelyn. She was standing right next to him. 'I have told you before. Just . . . *stop it!*'

She glared at him briefly and walked off.

Stupid cow. Kssss.

Alfred let his head fall forward again and closed his eyes. His chin was almost touching his chest. His Brynja. His little Brynja. After all this time, she was finally . . . real. But out of reach.

Oh stop feeling sorry for yourself, old man.

'I'm not, I'm – '

Shall we tell him? Do we tell him now?

He opened his eyes. 'Tell me what?'

Never a good time. But he has to know. They all have to know sooner or later.

He was about to say 'Know what?', but changed his mind. He didn't really care. There was a stain on his trousers, something hard and crusty.

*All right, I'll do it. Here goes . . . oh no. I can't. You do it.
No. You do it. I did it last time.*

*For crying out loud! He's seventy-nine! He knows it's coming.
Right, Alfred. Listen up. You have exactly – blast, what's the
date?*

Tuesday the thirteenth.

*Right. Okay Alfred. You have exactly two weeks left. Not
our decision. Just the way it is.*

Alfred tried to scrape off the stain, but bits of whatever-
it-was were stuck in between the ribs of the corduroy.

Are you listening to me, Alfred?

*Of course he's listening. It's a lot to take in. Goodness me, you
are rubbish at this, if I may say so. I'll do it next time.*

'I am listening,' Alfred said.

*Good. I thought so. Now, the thing is, with only two weeks
left, I'm afraid you have no choice. You have to go and see
Brynja. You have to tell her.*

'But why? Tell her what? I'm too old. Leave me alone!
Let me just die in peace!'

But before he'd finished his sentence, Jocelyn was
upon him again, hands on hips. 'Okay. You've left me no
choice. I am issuing a second warning, Alfred Warner.'
Then she turned and stomped out of the room.

That evening, Alfred wrote back to Brynja, telling her he
would love to come for Christmas.

Brynja's next and final letter contained a photograph of
herself. He stared at this for a long time, over and over,
studying it for features she might have inherited from
him, from Isobel, from John. She had Isobel's slight
build, and his mother's blonde hair, and – yes – there

was John's smile, the hint of a dimple on her left cheek. But the longer he stared at picture, the more blurred it became. Eventually, she became a stranger again.

The letter also contained a sheet of paper with lots of things printed on it, and Alfred had to ask Magdalena to explain to him what it was. She laughed and told him it was his boarding pass for flight EJ 6341 to Berlin-Schönefeld.

A week later, Alfred went to see Jocelyn. The door to the office was open, so he walked in without knocking. Jocelyn was typing something into the computer, her mouth set in a straight line as she concentrated on placing her fingers on the correct keys. Alfred cleared his throat to announce his presence.

'Have you never heard of knocking?' Jocelyn asked with a sigh.

'The door was open,' Alfred said, 'so I – '

'That doesn't mean you don't have to knock.'

Alfred took a step back and rapped the open door with his knuckles. 'Knock, knock,' he said.

She didn't find it funny. 'So, Alfred. What do you want?'

'I'd like to speak to my solicitor,' he said.

Her eyebrows shot up. 'Oh? And this would be with regard to what? You agreed to our Terms and Conditions when you signed the contract, you know.'

'I know,' Alfred replied slowly. 'I wish to speak to my solicitor regarding my will.'

The effect of these words was almost cartoonish. Jocelyn's facial features relaxed immediately, an unfamiliar smile crept onto her face and her voice softened. 'Oh, of course, Alfred. Shall I call him now? We have the details in your file, don't we?'

He nodded.

'Well, why don't you pop to the common room and I'll call him right away.'

Not five minutes later, she came to the common room, where Alfred was setting up a game of backgammon with a fellow resident.

'Alfred, I've just spoken to Mr Wilson, and he can come in on Tuesday. I hope that's okay. I told him three o'clock, so you've plenty of time for lunch and a nap.' She smiled – it was a touch grotesque. 'Now, how about a cup of tea?'

'Thank you, Jocelyn, that would be lovely.'

She leaned over him, and he could smell her deodorant. 'And shall I bring a couple of chocolate digestives with that?' she asked.

'I've already had a slice of cake,' Alfred replied truthfully, upon which Jocelyn gave him a playful nudge and said, 'Well, I won't tell anyone.'

On Tuesday, in the presence of his solicitor Mr Wilson, Alfred wrote a will, naming Brynja Warner as his sole heir and benefactor. Mr Wilson seemed pleased – it was not an unsubstantial amount of money, and he said he had hated the thought of it going to waste (by which he meant the Crown).

'Alfred! Phone call for you!' It was Mary/Michelle.

Alfred made his way to the reception desk in the main hall and took the receiver from her.

'Hello?'

'Grandad! It's Brynja!' She sounded bright and excited.

'It's so nice to hear you, your voice, I mean. In person. I hope this is a good time to call?'

Alfred didn't quite know what to say.

Brynja continued. 'So you got the ticket? You're really coming?'

'Yes, yes, day after tomorrow.'

'God, that's so – ' she paused. 'That's so cool. I really can't wait to meet you.'

'I'm looking forward to it, too.'

'I think I mentioned in my letter – did I mention it? – that, well, I can't really handle a plane journey right now. I get kinda . . . I mean . . . you know, a bit anxious. I did mention that, didn't I? Otherwise, I'd be coming to see *you.*'

Alfred didn't like to tell her that he had never flown in an aeroplane before and that the thought of it terrified the wits out of him. But his voice-women had given him little choice. 'Yes, you mentioned it.'

There was a short pause.

'So anyway, Grandad,' she continued. 'God, that sounds so weird. I never called anyone that before. I mean, my mom's parents died before I was born, so I never got to call her dad Grandad. And he was German, anyway, so I guess I'd have called him Opa or something. But then,' she paused, 'but then you're German too, so . . . '

She was rambling. Alfred couldn't tell if this was nerves, or excitement, or just the way her mind worked. 'You called me about something, Brynja,' he said gently.

'Oh, of course. Actually, I just wanted to say I'm so sorry, but I won't be able to pick you up from the airport. I have an appointment I just can't miss.'

'Oh.'

'I'm really sorry,' she repeated. 'But there's a train that takes you from the airport right to Hauptbahnhof. Takes about half an hour. I'll be there on the platform to meet you. Two o'clock. Promise.'

Alfred's heart began thumping in his chest. *Don't be stupid*, he told himself. *You've taken trains before, there's nothing to be nervous about.* 'All right,' he said finally, easing as much confidence into his voice as he could. 'Hauptbahnhof.'

'It's easy to find, Grandad,' she said. 'Just take the regional train all the way from the airport. You can't get lost. Wow, I'm really excited about it!' She laughed. It was an unusual laugh – sweet, childlike and it made him smile. He was looking forward to meeting her.

DAY SIX

It was very quiet in the room, apart from the hissing and beeping of the machines – but I'd got used to them by now. It was early evening by my watch, although it was impossible to tell the time of day in the dull light of the cubicle. Alfred was sitting in his usual spot, on a plastic-covered armchair at Brynja's bedside, while I sat on the chair opposite. He had finished telling his story an hour before we left for the hospital. Then, after lunch, I helped him pack his suitcase. He insisted on taking it to the hospital with him, and now the small brown case was sitting on the floor at the foot of Brynja's bed.

For a long time, I watched Alfred watch Brynja. He believed – he *truly* believed – he was close to death. How could he possibly be so composed? It was almost unbearable. My dad died kicking and screaming, fighting all the way. He died with an expression of surprise and outrage on his face. He took it personally.

Alfred caught me looking at him and smiled. 'I'm fine,' he said, reading my thoughts. 'And you'll be fine too.'

'Alfred – ' I said quietly.

He raised his hand to stop me. His tremor had vanished. 'I think it was when I was lying in the bathtub, frightened and in pain, that I finally understood. I couldn't believe it had taken me so long. All those years, I thought it had been Brynja, *my* Brynja – and I never really gave John a proper chance. I spent my life listening to voices, yet I didn't think to listen to him. Not really. But by then it was too late to tell him that he was the special one.'

He blinked a few times and I could see that he was crying. He pulled a handkerchief from his sleeve and blew his nose. 'I've had a better life than I deserve. But perhaps, at least, I can save Brynja.'

He closed his eyes, and after a while, began emitting soft, low snores. It was a soothing sound, and before long I drifted off myself.

It was a short nap. Some disruption to the monotony of the machines must have roused me. I checked my watch and saw that I'd dozed for twenty minutes. Then I turned to Brynja and nearly exclaimed out loud. She had her eyes open and was looking directly at me.

'Hello Julia,' she whispered.

I felt a sudden sinking sensation in my gut, like when an aeroplane loses altitude rapidly, and I immediately turned to look at Alfred. He was still sitting in the armchair, his head leaning against the backrest, his mouth slightly open. But he was no longer snoring. I remember thinking I should have felt panicked, but instead, I felt remarkably calm. When I turned back to Brynja, her eyes were shut again, and I wasn't sure if I'd just imagined her looking at me, whispering to me. Oddly, I didn't stop to wonder how she would know my name.

I got up slowly and walked over to Alfred. His skin was warm to the touch as I smoothed down a few unruly wisps of his hair, but he was completely, utterly still. Then I went to fetch the nurse.

Day Three Hundred and Seventy

It is exactly one year since Alfred passed away. The official verdict was heart failure, but I dislike that term. His heart didn't actually fail; it had merely come to the end of close to eighty years of service, and I rather like to think of it bowing out gracefully and compassionately (causing, as it did, no apparent pain to its owner when it ceased pumping). But this could hardly be entered as the cause of death on the attending physician's certificate.

As per his wishes, Alfred was buried at the cemetery on Stubenrauchstraße, with only myself and the funeral director in attendance. I chose the garden section of the cemetery – which means there is no gravestone – because I thought Alfred would have liked the idea of his remains providing fertile soil for the ancient trees and wildflowers that grow there. In summer, the site where he's buried becomes a meadow, sporting poppies and cornflowers and garden phlox – plants that attract an abundance of bees and butterflies. The cemetery is a twenty-minute walk from my flat, and takes me through the Volkspark. I like to think this is why Alfred chose it.

It took me several weeks to write down Alfred's story, and when I had, I took it to the hospital. Brynja's condition was still stable, although her doctors warned me that with each day she remained in the coma, the chances of a full recovery were diminishing. But I chose to believe differently. She had woken once. She had whispered my name. I was quite sure of that now. And that is why, for many evenings, I sat at her bedside and read Alfred's story to her until my throat grew unpleasantly dry and I was speaking in little more than a hoarse whisper. When I came to the end of the story, I sat watching her for a long time. I had come to the end and didn't know what next to do. The machines continued to bleep and hiss. At one point the nurse popped her head around the door.

'Everything all right in here?'

'Yes,' I answered. 'No change.'

She gave me a reassuring smile and left.

I felt like crying. What had I been expecting? Sleeping Beauty wakes from a kiss and they all live happily ever after? The pages of the manuscript I'd spent hours and hours typing, and then reading aloud, slid off my lap.

'I'm sorry, Brynja,' I said quietly. 'Alfred didn't tell me what to do from here. I suppose I hoped . . . I don't know. It would've been incredible, anyway. I mean, it was a nice story. But – ' I stood up and reached out to stroke her face. 'I'm sorry,' I said again in a thick voice. 'I tried.'

And then it happened. Her face twitched slightly, her eyes opened, and again I found her staring at me.

'That's all right, Julia,' she whispered. 'I – ' Her eyes left my face and darted suddenly to the left. For a moment, she looked terrified, but her features softened almost immediately as she smiled and let out a long, soft, 'Ohhh.' And then her very pale lips began to move, and although I couldn't make out what she was saying, it was clear that she was in conversation.

I waited for a minute or two to make sure she was safe, and then gathered the papers off the floor and left.

She moved back to New York recently, eight months after the accident, following a long, hard rehabilitation process. Although she recalls her accident only vaguely, she told me that she no longer felt comfortable living in her flat. Contrary to the doctors' prognosis, she made a full recovery with no damage to her brain functions, and other than a very slight droop to her left eye, nobody would guess how close she came to dying.

We spent many hours talking over the period it took her to recover, during which she picked my brain for details about Alfred that I may have omitted from the story I'd written down, and also told me about her life.

'And now?' I asked one afternoon, as we sat in the hospital gardens, enjoying the first fresh days of spring.

She was silent for a long time, her eyes closed and her face tilted up towards the sun. 'It's difficult to explain,' she said finally. 'They're always there, like before. Even when they're not speaking. But – ' She paused. 'These ones are nice, and funny. Kinda familiar. Like I've heard them before, in a dream or something. I don't know how to explain it.' Then her hand shot up to her head as if she were in pain.

'Are you all right?' I asked. Her bandage had long since been removed, and I could see a glimpse of the dark red scar tissue beneath her fair hair.

She nodded slowly. 'Yeah, I'm fine. It just, I don't like to think too hard about . . . before. I never want to go back there. Even though the voice-women tell me not to be scared that the others might come back.' She turned to look at me. 'Which is easier said than done, sometimes. But then I try to think about Alfred, how he just accepted them, without questioning who they are or where they're from. I just wish . . . '

'What?'

'I just wish my dad had known. It might have saved his life, too.'

Behind us, a nurse rolled out a trolley with tea and cake.

'And you're sure you want to go back to New York?' I asked, as we got up to join the other patients and visitors who began crowding around the trolley.

She nodded. 'It's home, you know?'

'But if you ever feel you want to come back – ' I began.

Brynja put her hand on my arm and smiled. 'I'll be fine,' she said. 'It turns out I'm not crazy after all.'

Before she turned away, her expression changed and – for the briefest moment – her eyes flashed with the life force of the generations that had gone before her. And I knew she was going to be fine.

Two Thousand and Fifteen

The pain rips through your body. Stealing your breath, your thoughts, your ability to move. It intensifies, reaches its crescendo, and then recedes into a raw lazy throbbing. Your legs shake uncontrollably. You throw up into the cardboard pulp kidney dish.

The woman – Aubrey – kneads the small of your back. Strong fingers. Experienced. She says, You should have arranged for a birthing partner. She sounds disappointed. It's not easy to do on your own, she says.

But you're not on your own, are you, Brynja?
We're right here.

Aubrey wipes your mouth with a wet cloth, feeds you some ice chips. She moves to the end of the bed. If you want an epidural, just say the word.

You nod, grunt, then shake your head. You don't want to smother this pain. You don't even want to take the edges off. No, I . . .

You feel her hand right up inside you. Probing. Eight

centimetres! She peers up at you between your knees. Smiles. But it's now or never with the epidural. You're getting close. Peels off her latex glove.

The pain returns, sooner than expected. Oooohhhh.

Focus, Brynja. Keep your eyes on the machine. The waves, see? Up up up

Aaaaaaaaghhh!

Here, see?

You turn your head. You try to concentrate on the paper coming out of the machine in small jerks. Two needles scratching quickly, furiously.

It's reached its peak. Now it's going down again.

The left needle scratches out your contractions, your pain. On the right, the scribbles of his heartbeat.

Beating strong and steady. Now try to relax before the next one. Breathe.

Aubrey says, I'd like you to take a few deep breaths, Brynja. Can you do that for me?

The pauses between the waves of pain are delicious. You breathe in as far as your squashed lungs will allow. But now, another contraction, a flare of crimson. It makes you want to vomit again. You wait for it to subside; you need a moment to recover. But this one doesn't stop.

I can't wait to see him! Kssss, I'm so excited!

You're doing really well, Brynja. Nearly there. Oh!

A sudden gush of liquid escapes your body. Honey scented.

The midwife smiles. Here. She takes your hand, guides it down between your legs. Feel that?

You touch. Feel something warm, pulsing. Hair. Is that hair?

Black as a raven!

Just like you, Brynja. When you were born. Oh, isn't this wonderful?!

Okay, Aubrey says. You're gonna feel like you have to push, but I need you to pant. Quickly, like this: huh huh huh huh.

You try – huh huh huh – but it's impossible not to push. Your muscles contract wildly, you have no control over them. You feel your bowels opening. Can't prevent it. You let out a sob.

Hush, Brynja. That's quite normal.

Brynja! Aubrey's tone is urgent now. Impatient. You need to pant! Or I won't be able to stop you from tearing.

Listen to us. Listen and keep your breaths quick and shallow.

They start to sing.

Sofðu unga ástin mín,
Úti regnið grætur.
Mamma geymir gullin þín . . .

Their song fills your head, fills the room. Floats above and around you, sweet and beautiful. You manage a few thin breaths.

You're doing great, Brynja, says Aubrey. Now, when the next one comes, push as hard as you can. Okay?

A tidal wave. It rises and roars and crashes. It howls. A dark, primitive animal sound escapes your throat. Your voice-women are wailing, ululating. Then a different pain – stinging, burning, searing. He opens you wide. He slithers out.

He is here.

AUTHOR'S NOTE

I do not hear voices; I never have. But when a friend of mine once admitted to having heard voices during adolescence, I was instantly intrigued: both by the fact that he had framed it in terms of an admission, thus implying it was somehow 'wrong', and also by the very notion of hearing voices that no one else can hear.

Voice-hearing, or auditory hallucination, is an ancient phenomenon that has been reported and described in almost all known cultures. Famous voice-hearers include Socrates, Sigmund Freud, Mahatma Gandhi, Joan of Arc and Hildegard of Bingen. It is a universal phenomenon, by any standards. But with the emergence of modern psychiatry in the late nineteenth century, voice-hearing became a mental illness, something 'wrong' inside the brain, a symptom of insanity. Before that, and in other cultures across the world, the phenomenon is and has been constructed in entirely different ways: saints have been canonised *because* they heard (divine) voices; in Africa and India, many voice-hearers associate *positive* experiences with their voices, as guides or like elders advising the young. Socrates relied on an inner voice that warned him when he was about to make a mistake. Many artists have stated that their voices are an integral part of the creative process.

Tragically, some instances of voice-hearing (especially threatening and abusive voices) can be the result of traumatic experience, such as sexualised violence in childhood, and may well require clinical and/or pharmaceutical therapy. Certainly, modern psychiatry can help to save lives. But not all voice-hearers can be lumped into this category. In recent years, voice-hearers in Western cultures have begun to challenge the assumption of psychiatric illness. The Hearing Voices Movement, for example, attempts to raise awareness of the diversity of experience among voice-hearers, putting forward the notion that voice-hearing is a multifaceted, meaningful experience to be explored beyond pathology.

In *The Uncommon Life of Alfred Warner in Six Days*, I chose to contrast the experience of the same phenomenon – hearing voices – in two very different ways: Alfred, for whom voice-hearing is a gift, and who could not possibly imagine life without his voice-women; and Brynja, who experiences voice-hearing as highly distressing and humiliating, driving her to the brink of insanity. And while these characters are entirely fictitious, I wanted to question the dominance of any single interpretation of this phenomenon. My aim was to defend the validity of complex human experiences that do not fit into a very narrow understanding of what it is to be 'normal'.

The sources I consulted for research purposes are too numerous to mention in full and include interviews and first-hand experiences of voice-hearers as well as academic papers. Among the books I found particularly useful are: Daniel B. Smith's *Muses, Madmen, and Prophets: Hearing*

Voices and the Borders of Sanity (Penguin, 2007); John Watkin's *Hearing Voices: A Common Human Experience* (Hill of Content, 1998); and Julian Jaynes' *The Origin of Consciousness in the Breakdown of the Bicameral Mind* (First Mariner Books, 2000 ed.). Finally, for anyone who has concerns or questions, there are many resources available for more information, including online resources from the Hearing Voices Movement, such as *hearing-voices.org* and *intervoiceonline.org*.

Writing a novel is a highly collaborative process, and I would like to thank everyone who supported me, directly and indirectly, in particular: David Conlin; Lilo Conlin; Jake and Fay Walsh; Michael Walsh; Super-Agent Jenny Brown; Simon Burke, Chris Kydd and the entire team at Black & White; Henry Steadman; the lovely people of Mauchline village; my Stammtisch-Tanten Gela, Barbara, Marion, Anita and Karin; the Verein der Förderer und Freunde des ehemaligen Jüdischen Waisenhauses in Pankow e.V.; and, of course, my love Chrissi (ohne e).